Sisters & Friends

PRAISE FOR *SISTERS & FRIENDS*

"*Sisters & Friends* is a joyful celebration of faith, family, romance, and God's delight in all the little details."
~ LAURA FRANTZ,
Christy Award-winning author of *The Lacemaker*

"With highest praise for *Sisters & Friends*, this book will knock you over almost as quickly as a very large dog. So be ready for anything. Susan Marlene brings together all the right answers in some of the most unexpected places. This story is a journey of the heart, discovering what can be accomplished when you keep your chin up and find faith from within."
~ KATE JUNGWIRTH,
co-author of the *Mystery at Point Beach* series

"Moving back home with a critical, over-controlling mother, fostering a massive out-of-control puppy (when you hate dogs), doing a face plant in front of a man with molten green-brown eyes… In *Sisters & Friends*, Susan Marlene masterfully employs a technique used by all great writers—put your character in a bad place, then make it worse, and worse—to keep us turning pages. Susan's debut novel will have you hurting, rooting for, and rejoicing with heroine Courtney MacDuff."
~ BECKY MELBY,
author of more than 20 Christian fiction titles

"In *Sisters and Friends*, Susan Marlene skillfully weaves together the threads of lives and hearts to give us a tapestry of faith and family I did not want to let go. Beautifully written!"
~ REGINA SCOTT,
award-winning author of *Nothing Short of Wondrous*

"*Sisters* love and fuss, embrace and argue, support and question. But above all they love!"
~ DIANN MILLS,
author of *Long Walk Home* ebook, Christy Award Winner,
Director - Blue Ridge Mountains
Christian Writers Conference

"Susan Marlene's debut novel, *Sisters & Friends*, is a story about relationships. Daughters, mothers, sisters, and friends harbor tender feelings, intricate, yet at the same time volatile. Susan Marlene's characters are true to life and grow dear to the heart. Unexpected twists and turns keep the pages turning. The heroine's love-hate relationship with her Leonberger dog kept me smiling—and wondering what would happen next. Even the hero's intentions kept me guessing. I hoped for future possibilities, but was unsure until the story's conclusion. Susan Marlene's ability to weave beautiful description coupled with emotion has me yearning for her next book."
~ REBECCA MCLAFFERTY,
author of the debut novel, *Intentional Heirs*

HEARTS FOREVER FAITHFUL

Sisters & Friends

SUSAN MARLENE

TIMELESS
SIGNIFICANCE

I gratefully dedicate this book to three.
Calvin, my husband.
Provider—you always find the right technology and programs. Inspiration—you have this uncanny way of finding the perfect books and internet sites that spark ideas with what you call 'useless information'. Protector—you make me settle down when I want to run, but it is best to rest. Thank you for being all of these to me so that I can chase my muse and write stories for my King.

Pat Vincenti
My God-given sister and forever faithful friend.

Rebecca McLafferty
My God-given friend and ever-faithful sister in spirit.

SISTERS & FRIENDS
Copyright © 2020 *Timeless Significance LLC*
P.O. Box 103, Two Rivers, WI 54241
www.susanmarlene.com

Typeset and cover design by Roseanna Designs,
https://roseannawhitedesigns.com/
Printed in the United States of America, 2020—First Edition

ISBN: 978-0-578-70979-6 (trade paper)
ISBN: 978-0-578-70980-2 (eBook)

Library of Congress Control Number: 2020941414

Keep your heart with all diligence,
for out of it spring the issues of life.
~ Proverbs 4:23

One

COURTNEY

Beaver Falls, Pennsylvania, July

Courtney Rosemarie MacDuff invaded her tenant's living room with a sigh that could rival a twister. She really should've finished the walls first, but there was just something about glossy wood floors that kept her motivated. The first renters planned to arrive from New York in one week. This 1890s home that Courtney and her business partner were turning into apartments required so much work. Why oh why had she promised almost instant availability? How dare she believe in her "seamless" renovation plan? Reality proved that a lot more needed accomplished—starting tonight. Glancing around the room to find some encouragement, she reached for the paintbrush, but her grip wrapped around bristles. Paint coated her fingers and palm. She tossed the paintbrush on the drop cloth.

Her phone vibrated, demanding attention. One glance at the caller's name stirred emotions she found more difficult to untangle lately.

Why did Mother trigger the need to escape? She grabbed the rag off the cardboard box posing as a table, accidentally tipping a small paint can, and knocking her cell phone to the floor. Clattering sounded on the polished wood planks, and white goo splattered over the plastic drop cloth, dangerously close to the hardwood floor. Should she pick up the practically empty can, or take the call?

Snatching the cell phone away from the spilled paint with careful fingers, Courtney pressed the speaker button. Every touch left white fingerprints despite the quick, vigorous rub she'd given them. "Mother, could I call you tomorrow?"

"We need to talk about our trip to Williamsburg, unless you plan to avoid your sister's graduation party. I thought you would at least *pretend* to be glad for her success."

Dangling the phone to survey the mess, Courtney frowned at the smudges covering the screen as well as the tone she'd had great difficulty in dodging. "That's not—"

"Well, enough said about that. I have your plane ticket. It cost quite a fortune to have us sit together. I've secured rooms at Magnolia Inn; you can share a bed with—"

"Sorry, Mother, I've already *secured a room* at the Market Square Tavern." She gritted her teeth. No need to send negative vibes and prolong this conversation.

"I can't believe that you would…" Mother's voice hiked-up several notches, signaling another time-wasting argument.

Courtney lowered the volume and slid the phone, now encased in a paper towel, onto the floor. The slap of the cell case hitting a hard surface drew her head lower to listen. *Had Mother noticed?*

"Also, I'm expecting you to…"

The sandpaper-sharp demand yanked Courtney's temper into high gear. She backed away and stood. That way, she couldn't hear every word. Her glance darted to the finished wall to reward her efforts. Nicely done. Except the bottom corner needed a touch-up. Sigh.

She righted the near-empty can of white semi-gloss, thankful that so little spilled. Grabbing paper towels, she mopped up the puddle of paint and tossed the soiled sheets into a nearby garbage can.

Stretching her cramped legs and neck taut with tension, she also moved her arms and shoulders. Viewing the living room as she turned full circle revealed how little she'd accomplished. Invisible pressure made its presence known in the stabbing pain pulsating down the length of her back. She—well, they—had one slim week to get this all done. Where did Tanya Gaston hide today? So much for her business partner's promises, such a partner who seemed more interested in keeping her nails in perfect condition than making the apartments ready to rent. She snatched a putty knife and smoothed a glob of lumpy plaster drying on a prominent wall. Her mother continued the one-sided conversation.

She should at least share her decision about driving herself to Colonial Williamsburg. That way, her parents could save the cost of those *horrendously expensive plane tickets*. And she'd not have to spend time...

Pain wrapped her heart. This was her mother, the only one she'd ever have. Why couldn't they laugh together and agree—on anything? Her phone chimed, reminding Courtney she needed to arrive at Natalie's in forty minutes. Best friends didn't grow on trees after all. Turning off the alarm, Courtney breathed in putty-scented air and coughed. Exasperation took hold of her. A mixture of wet and dried plaster covered her hands. She rubbed them on her already spoiled shorts. Lifting the phone with two fingers, she said, "Mother, I want you to know that I'm driving to Williamsburg. Return those plane tickets. Save some money." Silence for several long seconds stilled her heart. "Mother?"

"You've never appreciated anything I do for you."

Courtney's hands shook in time with her insides. "Mother. Mother, I have to go." She hated the way her voice cracked. Had Mother heard her? Courtney hung up. That seemed the only response left. Seeking peace seemed as elusive as sunshine today. She slipped the ringer off. Cleanup was required and not only for herself. Remodeling supplies scattered about her feet in an all too familiar disorder.

⁕ ⸻ ⚜ ⸺ ⁕

COURTNEY

Fifty-five minutes later, the road dropped away beneath Courtney's tires, launching her stomach into a somersault that paralleled her emotional state of mind. Her fingers floundered before tightening their grip on the wheel. It seemed like her pulse sped up to match the numbers on the dash. In a lengthy half-second, the car landed hard on wet blacktop, shuddered and bounced in and out of a pothole, jarring her teeth. Courtney slammed on the brakes until her PT Cruiser slid on gravel and came to a jerky stop. She knew better than to let a tiff with Mother push her gas pedal like that, in weather like this. But she'd reacted anyhow.

Even though she was the queen of not-reacting, as far as her friends were concerned.

Raindrops pummeled the windshield, blurring the countryside beyond the swipe of her wiper blades. The noisy storm vied for attention, striving against the sweet lyrics that pulled at something deep in her spirit. Jenah Ross Shank's song, *New Road,* seemed appropriate. A moment later, an annoying screech from a too-old wiper blade twisted her nerves into a knot. Something else she'd have to fix.

Cranking the volume higher, she anticipated Jenah's tunes would calm her jittery insides one more time. She flicked the rose-scented car freshener dangling from the rearview mirror and drew in a breath of fragrance before pulling away from the side of the road. A little slower this time. The beam from her headlight shimmered off wet asphalt, only to be swallowed up by an unforgiving black night. Darkness, shadows, and the deluge made everything appear different. Though she'd helped her best friend move last week, she still couldn't find Cardinal Street. That's where Natalie Lawton's Victorian Bed and Breakfast hid, tucked into a tree-lined corner. The lack of streetlights on this Pennsylvania country road made it seem impossible to find.

Her Bluetooth earbud announced Natalie's call. She said, "Accept."

"Hey, Natalie." Lightning flashed and thunder boomed, sending a chilling shudder through her body. She lurched sideways, and the right-hand tires of the PT crunched on gravel. She jerked the wheel, pulling the car back onto pavement. *Way too close for comfort.*

"Oh, this storm! I knew you'd be late. So much for living only a few minutes away." Natalie's voice slid from irritation into concern. "You're not in a ditch, are you?"

Just about. "I'm nearly there." She shifted into gear and tapped the gas. A street sign reflected the headlights, and she couldn't catch the name, but it had to be the road. When she turned right, she could just make out the last part of the sign. "Oh, wrong street."

"But you were here just last week."

Lightning continued to pulsate as she pulled into the first driveway to the left. A place she recognized. "I'm on Landing Avenue. Remember Orlando's cottage? My dream home?" She leaned toward her driver's side window. Her gaze traced the miniature antique cottage, stone by stone. Light escaped the partially shuttered windows. Flashes of lightning lit the sky again. *So perfect.* Her heart warmed to see its silhouette. Yet, why did it appear—different? She squinted. Something lacy reached over the stone fence toward her.

"Go south on Riverside Lane. I'm the next right turn and the first house you'll see."

Courtney turned her car off, grabbed the flashlight on her keychain, and clicked it. A dark red rose, buffeted by the storm, bounced next to the driver's window. Roses, her favorite. She resisted an urge to dig scissors out of the console and take a souvenir. Would her business partner ease up on the landscaping budget so that she could tuck a couple flower gardens around the apartments? Maybe not, yet there was still a significant amount of funds left in the bank account the last time she'd looked.

This place had never appeared so beautiful. Lamps glowing inside and porch furniture out front adorned the small house with classy flair. There'd not been a bush to be found when she'd called in an offer. The yard and home looked wan and run-down at the time. The obvious tender loving care to her gorgeous dream-cottage made it somehow easier on her heart that someone else's bid had been accepted.

Easing back against her seat, she closed her eyes to file away the ideas that this wrong turn inspired for her next manuscript. Though anything written would be for her eyes only. Her imagination could play nice with a secluded stone cottage and the fragrance of ros—

"I'm watching for you," Natalie's voice urged over the car phone.

Banging her knee, she yelled. "Ouch." The porch spotlight shot through the night, causing her to gasp. The front door opened, and a middle-aged lady, hair haloed by the soft inside glow, stared in her direction. Rain diminished as quickly as it had arrived.

Time to go! Courtney's shaky hand inserted the key, cranking the engine before shifting into reverse. Gripping the wheel tight, it was only a few minutes before she found her way onto

Cardinal Street. She parked on the road in front of the bed and breakfast.

The new sign her friend had painted to drum up business glimmered under an outside light and hung fairly visible to the road; in spite of the trees she'd suggested Natalie remove. Who would find this artistic masterpiece tucked away in such an isolated wooded area? A person had to search for the home on purpose. She couldn't imagine how this business could thrive. And she could imagine a lot. Once she'd unfolded herself from the car, she slammed the door and moved toward the sidewalk.

"Well, aren't you a sight?" Natalie's voice broke the damp earthy silence blanketing the grounds.

Courtney jumped. She'd not noticed her friend sprawled on generous front porch steps.

Maybe, just maybe she was a sight. Hadn't her car mirror revealed evidence that would support her friend's observation, such as indigo-tinted smudges that Courtney forgot to cover with an undereye stick? Her fingers made a self-conscious swipe that accomplished nothing. She followed the sidewalk curving alongside the Victorian home. Dipping her head beneath rain-weighted branches, she said, "Did you have to do that?" Her tone of voice seemed tethered to the earlier conversation with Mother.

"You startle so well." Natalie's voice chipped away the edge in her own.

"Sitting under your vintage sign, I see." She moved toward her friend.

Nat nodded. "Yep, in all its glory." She dragged a container holding baked goods closer, which scraped against the porch's wood planks. Nudging her head to the right, she said, "Grab the plates from the table."

"Paper plates? Eating outside? How come?" What a non-Victorianish way to eat. Natalie usually dove into her dream and stayed there for at least two months.

"Change. I believe things are about to change."

Why did Nat have to say something so *uncomfortable?* Courtney hugged herself. Such bulky, weighty thoughts weren't safe. Especially now when Courtney's sense of self-control seemed a departed dream. "Well, sure, I'll have renters. You'll have vacationers and dining room customers." *If they can find you out here in the near-wilderness.*

She nabbed the paper items, then scooted next to her friend. The porch rubbed dry from all traces of the storm became their tabletop, minus a linen cloth and finery. A casual meeting instead of the specialness she'd hoped would distract. Fancy may have eased the less-than-ordinary commonness of her existence. And may have helped shake the uneasy buzz inside her stomach from that *things are about to change* comment.

Her friend peeled the foil off the top of the container and handed her a warm scone. "Rose-flavored icing. You'll love this." Excitement vibrated off of Natalie.

How did she do that? Know what Courtney needed and when she needed it?

Natalie grabbed the carafe and began to pour. They leaned over the cups to inhale the chai tea aroma permeating the air. "I mean change concerning something bigger than renters and dining room customers."

Backing away from Nat—who seemed intent on pursuing uncomfortable tonight—her friend, so obsessed with this new place, took her attention—where? She bit the scone. They both had more than enough to take care of with their new business-es. What could be more important than that? Her stomach quivered at the thought. New topic time. "I love these rose flavored scones, so melt in your mouth delicious. Will they be offered for your Victorian breakfasts?" She licked her lips.

"Probably." Nat took a sip and smiled an impish grin. "What's bothering you? Or did you find *Mr. Right?* Did instinct tell him that you want a romantic voyage on the Gateway

Clipper? Or are you upset because you didn't find him? Or…"
She turned toward Courtney and seemed to study her. "Something else is troubling you."

The scone balled in Courtney's throat as she tried to swallow. She took a drink and pushed it down. The steamy chai burned a pathway to her stomach. "The usual. *She* irritates me." Why did hoping for a better relationship with Mother make her nauseous? The apartment complex she'd bought with Tanya was supposed to show how responsible and skilled she'd become and reap some respect. So far, this purchase had increased arguments with Mother, shattering their fragile relationship further. Was trying to win her favor even worth the effort?

Her friend nodded. "You like to pray, don't you?"

"God is too busy for something insignificant like this." Inside she cringed over the whine in her voice. What was going on with her? She needed more distance from these emotions.

"Lillian is still on you about the apartments being a bad investment, right? And she'd said her previous business experience taught her to not trust people like Tanya, which doesn't help." She waited for Courtney's nod. "Makes me kinda wonder about Tanya. Still, I'm glad she's your mother, not mine. Prove yourself with these apartments. That'll earn her respect, and she'll come around."

Sage advice from a friend who didn't have a mother—whose mother had deserted her when she was two. She tempered the anger that wanted to spew. It tasted like acid, ruining the scone. "Just because Mother was a wiz in the corporate world doesn't mean she understands small-business setup."

"She understands finance and businesses. Maybe you should listen."

A breeze pushed damp-chilled air across the trees, dipping large droplets of water, and invading the porch to rattle the ancient door and porch windows. Courtney shivered and drew her arms close to her body before shifting away. She bit down another mouthful. Swallowed hard.

"I've not lived with them for six years now. That should show Mother I'm not …"

Her throat closed over the next words. *Worthless, cowardly. Just because she ran when the going got tough.* She would stick with this. She would.

Two

COURTNEY

Ringtone jarred Courtney awake from a fretful night's sleep. Eyes half-open, she squinted at the silvery rays fingering their way through the crack in her brocade draperies. She yawned and rolled over crinkling manuscript pages as she snatched her cell. With her free hand, she transferred the pages to the nightstand beside her bed before dropping her lids over gritty eyes.

"Good morning, Butterfingers."

"Dad," a smile graced her lips. She curled her body around the phone. "What a nice surprise." She didn't want one of his words to escape.

Something heavy depressed the other side of the bed. She peered at the large hairy-black face approaching fast. One obnoxious sniff before a long tongue slobbered on her cell phone. "Ah, oh. Get awa—"

An enormous golden-red body of fur crushed her chest as it flopped on top of her. One massive paw knocked the phone out of her hand. Courtney shoved with all her might but barely budged the shaggy beast. She pulled two long hairs out of her mouth. The taste of unwashed dog made her gag.

"Tanya, come get Puddles." Why had she chosen a room-mate with a dog? The indecently huge puppy licked at her face. She ducked her head and spied the destruction. "Puddles *ate* my new shoes!"

Adrenalin pumped away the last of her sleepiness as she wiggled free from the Leonberger. Avoiding paws and teeth, she grabbed her slimy phone off a muddy footprint. "My new sheets." Martha Stewart would shudder. A glance at the mirror showed a dirty smudge and something shiny on her face—puppy drool. She pulled her sleeve over her face. *Aaargh!*

"Dad, wait." She pushed the speaker button on before grabbing some less-shredded tissues littering her new carpet to wipe it down.

Puddles shrill bark speared her ears. Several times the canine hopped on her bed.

"Hey, Tanya!" She yelled louder this time. The kitchen door banged, and she heard voices outside, her absentee business partner and a deep baritone.

Courtney ran to the window and shoved the heavy curtain aside. "Hold on, Dad." She undid the latch and pushed the window open. She leaned out of air conditioning into the rain-touched, sticky air. "Tanya, get back here!"

Car doors slammed, and the bumping of base-loaded music sounded from Tanya's hatchback as it revved to life, before pulling away from the curb outside her window. Tanya sped down the road kicking up mud in her direction like a rude farewell.

"Rotten girl."

"The dog or Tanya?"

"Humor will get you nowhere." She was sure he could hear her poor attempt at levity. "Dad, I have to stuff Monster Dog into her crate. Tanya ran off, so bizarre." *Where's that leash?* Courtney grabbed her manuscript and bolted from the room as one-hundred twenty-five pounds of two-year-old puppy jumped off the bed with a thud and chased her down the carpeted hallway.

A dog crate dominated what used to be her favorite side of the dining room. Right next to her antique American Empire hutch. She avoided looking at the chew marks at the corner of the base and spied the leash wrapped around a note and manila envelope. Puddles bounced into the room behind her.

Snapping her fingers, Courtney turned and pointed, "Get in there."

The canine looked toward the oversized dog cage harboring treats before fleeing down the hall.

Taking her manuscript pages, Courtney ripped them in half and tossed them in the waste can by the door. "I get to destroy these this time, not you." Her yell chased after the dog.

A muffled male voice reminded her that her dad still waited on the phone. She cringed and pulled the cell from her pocket. "Sorry, dad. Tanya's going to get a piece of my mind."

"Your mother is calling for help. I'll get back to you."

"Later Dad," So like Mother. She picked up the note secured with the leash. *Take care of Puddles.* Ha! Take care of Puddles. Open the door and throw a steak outside—call Puddles—lock the door...

Courtney picked up the large envelope and looked inside. She found vet records as well as a letter from Stover, Handley, and Garston.

Why were their business lawyers contacting them? A headache arrived, burdening her gray matter.

The kitchen door slammed.

"Tanya?" Courtney placed one fist on her hip and fingered the envelopes with her other hand. She glared in the direction of the doorway, waiting to aim questions like tungsten tipped darts.

"Nope, it's me. I came to claim your skills." Her sister's voice rolled around the corner.

Bethany's sunglasses, positioned on top of her head, pinned long strands of auburn hair away from her face. She strolled into the room, eyes sparkling with mischief, as a smile the size of Texas overtook her face. She smelled of coffee and vanilla lotion.

"Wipe that goofy grin off your face. What's happened?" Courtney's smile slid into a comfortable angle. Her sister could always grab joy from deep inside her. Even on desperate days. Courtney placed the envelope and note on the table.

Her sister tilted her head. Her grin twisted crooked as it always did when she was about to share a secret. She moved toward the table and produced two cappuccinos she'd held behind her back.

Something extraordinary was up. Courtney's heart warmed as she squinted at her sister. "You're the best." Claiming her drink, she took a sip. "Mmmm. Delicious. Hold on, I need to check Monster Dog."

They tiptoed toward the hallway and peeked around the corner. "Tanya left me with those envelopes and a wild, loose-in-the-house, puppy," Courtney whispered. Puddles lay sleeping in the hall with a protective paw cradling her gigantic bone. They ducked out of sight.

"I love Puddles. Isn't that the type of bone Tanya told us not to give her?"

"It should provide a few minutes of peace for us after she wakes up." Courtney grinned.

"I'm not saying a word. But what if that bone hurts her?"

"That's a God-approved bone."

"How so?" Bethany squinted at her.

"It saved Puddle's life on more than one occasion—from me." She sipped her cappuccino and breathed in caramel-vanilla fragrance with pleasure. "She's one of God's creations, but I don't like her."

"Gotcha, but don't joke about God."

"God has a sense of humor. I'm sure of that." She took in Bethany's dubious expression. "Pastor Dean said so." She placed her cappuccino on the table. "I was just going to—"

"Bethany pointed at the envelopes. Did you look at those?" Glancing down, she spied the waste can. "What's this?" Bethany leaned over and picked up the discarded papers from the trash. Her eyes scanned Courtney's chapter, and her smile slid into overdrive. "You ought to see about publishing this." She chuckled. "Is this the only story you've completed so far?"

"Yeah." Courtney's hand twitched. How she itched to grab the sheets out of her sister's hand and toss them back into the can. Why did Bethany pay such close attention to her writing?

"Well, I know someone—"

"That's okay. I write for me—not to share. Besides, I'm too busy remodeling these apartments so we can rent them." Putting her writing into a stranger's hands was like exposing her underbelly to a hungry lion. She picked up the letters. The correspondence from the lawyer puzzled her. Addressed to Tanya and her, with a note scribbled in purple pen. *Courtney read this first.* She opened it. As her eyes skimmed the pages, heat filled her face, and her heartbeat kicked into overdrive. She slapped the table, and her eyes filled with tears. "This is the final letter of foreclosure. Tanya never mentioned this to me. I have to be out by…" She glanced over the letter. "July 24—two weeks!"

"Where will you go?" No one squeaked panic like Bethany.

Dropping into the chair, Courtney stared hard at the table. Her limbs began to tingle. Everything that mattered was tied up in the apartment complex. Now, *poof,* it would be gone with nothing to show for it. "How could Tanya betray me like this? Not even one word—"

"Um-hum. We can have you moved before Williamsburg."

The family trip and continuing conflict between Mother and herself was Bethany's reward for graduating college with honors. At least one of the MacDuff daughters had accomplished something noteworthy. Courtney groaned.

Puddles trotted into the room and tilted her head onto the table, sniffing their drinks before her sleepy eyes slanted toward Courtney.

"Is Tanya coming back for her?"

Grabbing Tanya's note, "Who knows?" She tossed the dog a look. "Who cares? All my money went into the joint business account for these apartments. I wonder how much is left. If anything."

"All your money?" Bethany turned white. "What will Mom say?"

"We both know that answer. I'll find a job before she finds out." She looked around at her antiques. "It took too long to collect these pieces. I can't get rid of them now." She scanned the note. "She's not coming back." Her voice sharpened, pitching higher. "This awful woman dared to ask me to keep Puddles. What nerve. Oh, by the way, we're evicted, and can you watch my destructive dog? She," nodding to the puppy— "is going to the pound." Puddles yawned and flopped on the carpeted floor between them with a deep groan.

"Bathroom." Bethany stood and pointed down the hall. Her cell phone rang as she retreated. Several minutes later, her sister re-entered the room. "I'll tell her, Dad. Love you."

"What?"

Bethany dropped a USB port and her cell phone inside her purse before zipping it up. Lifting a tear-laden gaze, she said, "Mom fell and broke her leg. They're at the hospital now."

"What happened?" Courtney dropped the papers she held and leaned forward.

"Mom's been having dizzy spells. This time she hurt herself. She's asked for you to stay with her. Especially when Dad goes to Afghanistan for that construction job."

"Dad can't leave, just for a job. No, no. I don't make her happy—ever—but you—"

"He'll only be gone a year this time. I've already told them about your situation." She nodded to the paperwork. "I'll be in and out of town."

Courtney's hand flew to her forehead. "Why did you tell them? I didn't want Mother—"

"She requested you, Courtney. Don't desert her," Bethany snapped.

How could she blame her sister? Bethany had never stirred their mother's ire and negativity. Courtney alone owned the talent to inspire Mother's critical, nettling nature, and she responded in kind. Their only resemblance—and one she'd worked hard to obliterate.

Mother's "I told you so" would be her first words. Their recent argument churned her insides. Every attempt at job and apartment seeking would meet disapproval. How could she move forward with negativity nipping at her heels? Approval? Well, that never happened. Puddles's long wet tongue licked her bare feet. "Yuck. What's the number for the pound?"

"I suppose it's better to get rid of the puppy. Mom could never tolerate her. Look how messy she is." Bethany frowned as she gazed at the mop of hair and slobber between them.

"Doesn't Tanya ever groom her?"

"She brushes Monster Dog." Courtney grabbed her sister's arm. "Mother would hate a toe licking, overly rambunctious, muddy-footed puppy. Wouldn't she?" A smile stretched wide over her face. "I'm obligated to keep her for Tanya after all." She let go of Bethany's arm and clapped.

Her sister's eyes narrowed to slivers. "You'd not put Mom in jeopardy—would you?" Disbelief threw her alto into soprano. "Mom might have crutches."

"You're right. I can't live with Mother. Her safety has to

come first. Sigh. I'd have to run back to my own apartment to take care of Puddles, of course."

Bethany smiled. "Hmmm, getting a break from one another." She nodded. "Pure genius. You should keep the puppy." Bethany didn't sound all that upset anymore.

Courtney slumped in the chair and pulled her feet out of tongue reach. "I'd be running from one stressful situation to another. Have you seen Puddles when she has been left alone all day? Ridiculous."

"Do you know Zander Hayward?"

She wrinkled her brow. "He sold me that American Empire hutch." Her eyes caressed the piece. When her view dropped to the chew marks at the base of the antique, she frowned.

"He's a dog trainer too. If she were trained, she'd be a great companion."

"Companion. Sure. I could probably talk him into offering me free lessons. He practically gave me that hutch." Courtney smiled at the memory. She loved the challenge of making a deal that bent the advantage in her favor. "Puddles is almost two. How hard could it be?" She took a satisfying sip, which reminded her of Bethany's secret. "So, what's your news?"

Bright blue-gray eyes smiled at Courtney. Her sister lifted her hand. The diamond ring winked in the sunlight sliding through the window.

Courtney gulped. "Wow! I didn't think Brandon would ever ask."

Her sister snorted as she turned her hand from side to side.

"This is a Pinterest moment." Courtney positioned the ring finger just-so on top of a bowl of fresh-cut flowers from a vase on the table. Grabbing her phone, she took the shot. "To be preserved online forever." She uploaded the photo and a short announcement.

"Help me. Be my maid of honor." Her sister's smile had lost the glimmer that shone at the beginning of their conversation. The uncharacteristic plea stilled Courtney's heart.

"You know, plan the wedding and reception, and accomplish all the other duties you're not going to have time for."

Pulling up the smile that always worked, she said, "Let's think this through." Pressure from the foreclosure and Mother's request triggered a headache behind her eye. Ignoring the pain, she tried to focus. There certainly wasn't time to plan a wedding. Besides, how could Bethany trust her after she'd skipped town before her sister's last engagement party? Though everyone was grateful that her sister hadn't married Ken—they still remembered. "What's the date?"

"August twenty-forth. Six weeks away." Bethany selected a flower from the vase.

A laugh escaped Courtney's lips, "The big questions are: do you think Mother will think I can pull this off? And do you want to put up with her disdain if I fail?"

Again, hung in the air between them like a black cloud. She hungered for an answer that wouldn't slap her down.

"I've always believed in you, baby sister, the past is past. I trust you with my impossibly too soon-to-be wedding." She twirled the flower between two fingers, blurring the pink petals in the air, while she slathered healing balm over Courtney's aching heart.

Courtney gasped. Could she possibly not disappoint her sister this time? When had she ever finished anything? Her mother was right. So far, she'd never measured up. Maybe she never would.

Watching the glow of her sister's joy ratcheted anxiety to a full simmer in her belly. Bethany, the perfect sister, daughter, and friend, deserved better than what Courtney had to offer. If she botched this wedding planning—no matter that no possible way existed to accomplish the task—she'd never forget it or forgive herself.

And neither would anyone else.

Three

COURTNEY

Sitting on the back of Natalie's father's pickup truck in front of her dream-not-come-true, flat out hurt. She kept telling herself these were just rental apartments. But the disappointment of her should-have-been-renters echoed in her mind. Gnawing at her conscience. The sun beat down from its highest pinnacle as its conspirator—humidity—hovered in the ninetieth percentile. If Courtney were in an oven, she couldn't feel more dehydrated.

"She took *everything*? All your money? Courtney how could you be so—"

"Don't be cruel. She took *just about* all of my money. Tanya was so, organized—"

"Manipulative—"

"So, connected with the community."

Natalie slapped her leg. "Gangsters and criminals." She jumped off the truck bed and motioned for Courtney to do the same. "Let's finish this." Once Courtney dropped to the pavement, Natalie slammed the tailgate closed. She moved around the vehicle, checking the ropes that the movers had tied.

"Maybe I was a tad too trusting." Courtney lifted her gaze

to survey the apartment complex she'd remodeled for the last few months. The windows shone, mirroring oak leaves and blue denim sky with just a hint of promise. Shadowed with broken dreams.

Another failure.

She'd tried not to get too involved with the business end of apartment ownership so that it would succeed. But her jinx prevailed. She grabbed onto the wrought iron fence lacing the edge of the property. Burning hot metal seared her hand. "Ouch." She pulled away.

Metal clanged metal as it wedged itself against the sturdier fencing.

"You okay?" Natalie's grin wobbled on her face as though she at least tried to hide her amusement.

"Um-hmm." Courtney inspected her hand for burns. Red blotches splayed over her fingers and palm. She grabbed a clean rag lying on the truck bed to use as a makeshift potholder before unjamming and repositioning the fencing into place.

It almost appeared unbroken.

"I'll say too trusting. For once even I thought you might—"

Courtney's hand shot up, "I get enough of that from my mother, thank you very much." The gate stayed put, and she glanced at her friend. The moan of a distant train whistle matched her mood.

Natalie narrowed her eyes to slits, and her expression pulled tight as it always did when she wore concern like a second skin. She walked toward the front of the truck and opened the door before she dug into the cooler behind the driver's seat, crunching ice until she pulled two drinks into view. "You should stay as far from her as you can when you're on vacation. Are you driving or flying?" Her voice had softened to a gentle purr. She handed over a half-frozen raspberry ice tea.

Mentally she forgave Natalie for her tactlessness since she'd eased-up. Courtney's dry lips spread into a painful grin.

"Thanks." Taking a large sip spiked brain freeze. She winced. "Mother bought a plane ticket for me, but I've opted to drive. It'll save them money and give me some time to think." But did she really want to be alone? It was becoming increasingly more difficult to divert her thoughts. "Your dad will have his hands full with Puddles. Tell him thanks for dog-sitting for me." She rubbed the cold bottle across her burning fingers to subdue the burning sensation.

"You told him thanks around ten thousand times already. Don't worry, he loves dogs more than people."

Courtney's heart tightened. Natalie's father spoke gruffly to everyone and barely spent time with his daughter.

"I'm sure Puddles will be tired when you return from Williamsburg. Same destination for all this?" Natalie pointed at the precariously tied antiques. "Your parent's place?"

"Nope, they're going to be used as props in a Victorian house, which is up for sale in Sewickley." Courtney fingered the double-wrapped blankets cushioning her pieces against scrapes and dings and smiled over the shock registering on Natalie's face. She could imagine the thoughts coursing through her friend's mind. *Did you sell this stuff? What price? Who was dumb enough to pay that much for worn-out furniture?*

"So, Courtney, where did you find a sucker to buy this broken-down stuff you call, 'a touch of history'"?

"You'd be smart to invest in a few authentic pieces for your business. They'd bring ambiance to your bed and breakfast. Besides, my precious furnishings are *not* for sale. If they were, they would catch a pretty price. This agreement is for renting—earning me a little cash in the meantime." She opened the passenger door and climbed inside.

"Are you sure about this?"

A weak nod equaled her reply.

"No, really, did you check these people out?" Natalie

climbed into the driver's seat and turned the key. "You seem to be really easy to deceive lately."

Wincing, Courtney said, "It's fine. Bethany knows Zander Hayward. He stages homes for a living." He was a dog trainer on the side, and she planned to take advantage of those skills too, not that she'd tell Nat. "I've got a contract signed and filed away in a safe place."

She hoped she could find it if any need presented itself. "This is the only way I could store my valuables and make some money until I can make some money." She wasn't even going to mention that she'd bought some of her pieces from him last year. They'd also researched the value of her two tables together. Suppressing a smile, oh, yep, she knew him too.

"Why do I get the feeling that you are not telling me everything? But hey, I suppose if you're going to get ripped off, it may as well be by someone with a cool name."

⁘ ⸎ ⁘

ZANDER

Be punctual.

Zander Hayward tread the reddish paving stones lining Duke of Gloucester Street in Colonial Williamsburg with that family motto reverberated inside his head—against his will. Old brick and sided buildings housed the shops he'd visit. A glance at his watch showed nine o'clock this morning, still time to take in the sights around this revolutionary city until his two o'clock appointment with Elegant Furniture Company.

The sun had chased over the horizon and streamed through his hotel window way too soon after he dropped into bed last night. He'd hardly slept, especially when history crept into his dreams and ran away with his imagination.

He squinted against the piercing sunshine and steered toward the generous shade offered by one of the trees lining the walkway. A warm, fragrant breeze stirred the leaves hanging low above his head and slowly teased the tiredness from his mind and body. He needed inspiration. Here it was. Every brick, shingle, and iron-bound barrel he passed captured his attention and dragged his desires further in the direction he had no resources to follow.

If only he'd been born in the eighteenth century. How he'd have loved carving out a living during such radical times.

A colonial dressed peasant hurried past him. "Morning, sir."

Holding in a snort, Zander grinned in reply. Wealth wasn't even a dream for the Hayward's until his father's blood, sweat, and ingenuity created Hayward & Son's Furnishing & Manufacturing Company. In the 1700s, he'd have been a peasant, barely scraping out an existence. Picturing himself loaded down with the responsibility of a wife and a house full of kids gave him a start that didn't draw him closer to his dream. Would he have had the courage and discernment needed to accomplish what his father did? His chest tightened.

The importance of turning additional attention to his real estate with house staging, as well as his dog training businesses, dug new depth into his consciousness. Launching these businesses fueled his day and kept his mind engaged. He'd make the most of his time here and explore purchasing pieces his clients needed. Renting Courtney MacDuff's furnishings proved timely and actually opened an important opportunity for a business connection, but he needed more.

His dad offered him the predictable path, co-ownership in a thriving business, which didn't inspire or fulfill that ache for conquering fresh challenges. They viewed life differently.

Where was the Prentis Store? Pausing a moment to catch his bearings, he pulled the Colonial Williamsburg map out of his pocket. Directly west on Gloucester. Turning, he retraced his steps and collided with a man walking three Standard Schnauzers.

"Mr. Mancel!" This man's influence was phenomenal. He could offer financing and substantial connections. Or ruin the best of dreams.

The middle-aged man almost dropped his cell. Irritation that was hard to miss landed his lips into a frown. Zander stood his ground, resisted crossing his arms, and hoped to flip this offense.

"Oh…" Mancel groped for a reply.

"Zander Hayward. I've contacted you recently about some business ideas."

"Yes, Mike Bevy told me about your dog training idea. I like it. I like it a lot." Three of those reasons barked and strained at the leash in his hand. "Down Sampson, Thor, Trend." He chuckled. "Take a treat, boys."

So, Mike finally came through. As Zander watched the interaction between the man and his dogs, his expectation changed from impending disaster to a sure deal. The warm tone of voice confirmed Mancel's, *I'm on board with this project.* Too bad he didn't mention needing a real estate agent with the sideline of staging furniture. Expensive antiques and Mancel-type connections would jump-start Zander's more substantial business interest and cause it to thrive.

"I would make one suggestion. A minimal detail really, but necessary for me to become invested financially."

"What would that be?"

Sunshine splashed across the clean simplicity of the town laid out before him. The high pitch whine of a young boy teased one of the colonial workers as they made their way towards South Botetourt Street. "What's that car called? I forget." The youth waved a large photo of a red convertible at the man dressed as a tradesman. The volunteer's deep laugh was followed by a purely refined colonial speech. "I knoweth not what thou asketh young sir."

Grinning, Zander decided that maybe this first visit wouldn't be his last.

"Find someone terrible at handling dogs. Teachable though. Bring that one individual through all the lessons, so the viewer will see firsthand that this method works."

Zander's smile plummeted into a straight line, and he turned toward a shop window, trying to reign in his expression. "My original idea was to show numerous dog breeds. I believe that would draw more people to the lessons."

"Trust me on this Zander, and I'm in." The note of finality for either in with him or out with him couldn't be missed.

Rubbing the back of his neck, Zander swallowed hard. Temporary, only temporary played ping-pong inside his head. This conversation could make or break his business dreams. Fulfilling this goal, which otherwise waited out of reach, was what mattered. Future movie series for his dog training techniques and advertisements for his specialty real estate business and book contracts strutted across his imagination. After a bit of success, he'd be free to call the shots.

"Hayward, are you with me here?"

One of Mancel's Schnauzer's jumped on Zander's leg, and he resisted the urge to correct the dog.

"Thor, down." Mancel pulled the leash, forcing the dog away.

"I see the wisdom of your idea. I agree." His few words, the only ones he could muster, had dipped deeper in tone than he'd intended. His heart tensed, had he been convincing?

"Find the perfect dog, and inexperienced trainee and I'm in. Make the customer feel superior right off the bat by allowing them to think that even they're not that bad. This will unique-up this series—make it work."

"Sounds good." He heard the hollow echo of his words.

Had he persuaded Mancel? Should he go with a highly recognizable or unique breed? He'd probably have to take whatever untrained dog showed up on his doorstep. Hopefully, not a mutt.

Who would humiliate themselves to this degree, for the minimal pay he could afford? That was the real challenge. The Red Barn Theater back home might have a starving actor dying for exposure. It could work—if they owned an untrained dog. He shuddered; this wouldn't be so easy after all.

COURTNEY

"We're here." Bethany gracefully danced off the horse-drawn carriage parked in front of the Governor's Palace in Colonial Williamsburg, Virginia, with the aid of the coachman.

The imposing Baroque styled building even took Courtney's breath away. She'd expected something less impressive. Her sister's joy was practically tangible, resulting from either the ambiance of the town or the fact that Brandon Strege, her sister's fiancé, stood waiting next to the sturdy brick and iron fence. The beautiful metal door opened to the pathway leading toward her sister's favorite spot on earth. Okay, both Brandon and Williamsburg were at fault here.

Everyone filed in behind the engaged couple, and all seemed right with the world. Birdsong graced the slight breeze.

"Court, take your mother's arm while I run back to the carriage." Her dad slipped her mother's arm safely into the bend of her own.

Lillian's stiff posture reminded Courtney how this trip had taxed her mother's strength. She'd become surly and difficult when not provoked, even with her dad. He'd not revealed what the doctor's findings were after the fall, which heightened Courtney's concern.

Bethany laughed with pleasure when entering the exquisite white double-doors leading into the walnut-paneled room. Their shoes clicked against black and white tiles.

Her mother tugged her arm to slow their pace as they stepped over the threshold. "If you'd graduated from college, we could have taken you on a trip like this." Her voice dipped low and grating. "As it is, you hardly graduated high school. Good thing I make excellent triple fudge brownies or Ms. Russo would have made you repeat your senior year."

Biting her lip so that she wouldn't reply, Courtney looked upward at the displays. Though sharp comparisons and criticisms from her mother were not unusual, this unexpected comment reached a new level. The barb hurt.

Across the room, Bethany spun around admiring the woodwork and weaponry adorning the walls until their eyes locked. Liquid joy spilled uncontained.

Courtney pushed her best—I'm so glad we're here smile—hoping it reached her eyes. Refusing to ruin this graduation vacation for her sister, she pulled her attention toward the muskets and hangers adorning the walls and forced admiration in her tone. Courtney awed and oohed to keep up this imperative facade. She stayed perfectly aware of her mother's pace but discouraged further discussion. Footsteps sounded behind them. Good, dad had returned.

Turning to meet him, Lillian reached for his support, but he stood too far away.

"I forgot the camera at the hotel. I'll return soon." Dad nodded to Lillian, and fled before Courtney could offer to go instead.

They moved farther inside. Pine floors and beautiful walnut paneling blurred together, perfectly complementing each other, but Mother's glib remarks and commands dulled their impressiveness. Her sister was dizzy with laughter and took too many photos.

Beautiful ornate doors, showcased at the end of the hallway, were visible through the open middle of all three rooms, teased her with freedom—too far from reach. Mother's need fastened to her arm, while her unyielding negativity shriveled Courtney's spirit.

Elbows pressed tight into her sides, while Mother pulled to loosen her arm, just like when she'd been a child. Courtney had gained independence, so how could she possibly live with Mother now? Acid burned in her belly. Stepping into the ballroom splattered her senses with color like being sprayed with a paint gun. Bright blue walls and loud carpeting resembling styles from the 1970s muffled their footsteps. Though the carpeting was accurate for the period, it just felt wrong.

"Are you coming already?" Lillian's tone grew testier since Dad left.

Heaviness sunk like a rock on her chest. Why did Dad have to take that job in Afghanistan and complicate her life?

*　—　✦　—　*

COURTNEY

Evening announced itself with a wash of orange, purple, and green hues splashed over the far edge of the skyline. Humidity hung its hat over the area, moistening foreheads and making their walk sticky and slow as they moved down Duke of Gloucester Street for their authentic colonial meal.

"We need to talk." Courtney folded her arm around Bethany's. "This way." She aimed for the walkway across the street to dodge conversations with family, friends, or Brandon. The wedding sped toward them headlong, and her sister, though smart and efficient in many ways, was not a planner of events.

There lies the problem, for neither was she. "I've thought of some ideas you may like for your wedding, and I wanted to talk them over with you."

Tipping her head to acknowledging the need, Bethany's anxious expression suggested that the timing wasn't the best.

A sideways glance at her cell reassured her that they would have ten or fifteen minutes before they needed to arrive at King's Arms Tavern to meet everyone. Courtney's attention riveted on her sister and held. "I need to know if your wedding is to be traditional, modern, or hippie style."

Bethany burst out laughing, "I'm sure Mom prefers hippie."

"Good, I was picturing you with the traditional white dress loaded with Chantilly lace. Your feet sticking out from under the gown adorned with beach sandals. No pedicure for you. You'll keep those calluses." Courtney's attention dropped to Bethany's feet.

Her sister stumbled on a pavement stone. "What, how dare you suggest I bare my calluses?"

"I take that back. They'll be eliminated already because we'll have Zoë, Zete, or whatever her name is, come to Natalie's house to perform an excellent pedicure on all of your bridesmaids, and yours truly."

"Zeta is her name. So, my bachelorette party will consist of callus removal?" She strung an uneven grin across her face.

"Complaining?" Courtney tilted her head. "We can turn this event over to Mother." Their grins competed for size. "Pink flowers or blue? I know you're super picky about types of flowers. What's your choice there?" She slipped a small spiral notebook out of her pocket and clicked her pen.

"Bethany, is that you?" A masculine voice smooth as a cream latte drew their attention from behind. They stopped walking and turned.

Zander Hayward strode toward them. His curly, dark

brown hair and his tan emphasized his dressed-to-kill white polo shirt and khaki shorts.

ZANDER

"Courtney." The MacDuff sisters? Here? This trip was definitely looking up. Her eyes lit, and a gentle smile met him. He could stand to see that welcome more often.

He nodded his head a couple of times, to buy time. "Nice surprise to see you here." He focused on Courtney. "Matt and Tim told me they had no problem moving your furniture into the Draper's house. Your pieces stage nicely since they are from that period."

"Thanks, they are my pride and joy. Take care of them and make sure the buyers know they're not part of the seller's price." Her blond hair slipped backward across her shoulders as she tilted her face toward his.

"I'd like to wheel and deal with you to buy that hutch back. What do you say?"

She winced. "I have a puppy. Actually, I'm holding onto Puddles for—someone. Anyway, she chewed the bottom corner of the hutch." Courtney pressed her eyes shut.

Inwardly, he winced also. That American Empire hutch had been in perfect condition. He'd check it when he got home to make sure it would still work in the Draper's home and not distract from the ambiance he desired to create. "So that's why you could temporarily part with the furniture. You want to keep the puppy's teeth away from your pieces." He slipped her a smile to de-edge his words. "What breed?"

"Monster—"

"What Courtney means to say is Leonberger. Too bad she

isn't trained, because she has a sweet temperament." Bethany's brows hiked up on her forehead as though she hinted—what?

The wheels in his head started turning. Could this be happening? Leonberger—a unique, new to AKC breed, which could become popular—would definitely work. Mancel would approve. He dropped his gaze toward the bricked sidewalk, took a breath to compose himself. "I've not met the breed—only heard about them. I train dogs in my spare time. I'd love to work with her." *And you.* He glanced up to gage Courtney's reaction.

Her smile melted into a frown. "Bethany mentioned that you train dogs. I'm interested if the price is right." She flipped that frown into a smile again as natural as the sun peeking out from behind a cloud.

Bingo, this was the girl for the dog video. Now to convince her to allow him to film the lessons. They'd work out as long as her dislike for the puppy didn't show. Firsthand experience showed him she could attract customers. Courtney could be rich on commission, if she were in sales, because of her natural charm. Oh, the money that could have been made from that antique hutch he'd sold her six months ago. His hand absently patted his pocket until he realized what he was doing. Watching her turn on pleasant to animated excitement confirmed how effortlessly she coaxed people's hard-earned cash out of their pockets. Mainly his. She could make him a mint. He caught himself tapping his wallet again and pulled his hand away. On all accounts, she kind of owed him for taking him to the cleaners on that hutch deal.

He'd have to be on guard against those dark baby blues and spontaneous smile and take the lead on this business opportunity. "I'm sure we could work out a deal." He flashed what he hoped was a winning grin.

Bethany pulled her phone out of her pocket. "We're late. Zander, have you eaten dinner?"

"No, where would you suggest?"

"The King's Arms Tavern. Want to come? My treat unless you're busy."

COURTNEY

After climbing porch steps and being admitted inside the King's Arms Tavern, Courtney stepped past a waiter dressed in white and blue 1700s clothing. Daylight streamed in through a window, while anxiety tightened her throat. This dinner was no big deal. Nothing to worry about. So why was she? All she had to do was slip her thoughts into historical musings. Her glance around the rooms was rewarded. Appreciation for red flocked wallpaper embraced by white trim got her thoughts rolling in the right direction. She worked a less rigid smile on her face.

Family and friends had gathered across the room around a couple of dark wood tables. Mother's smile for Barney Whippier, a longtime family friend, hinted that maybe she'd not noticed they were late. Courtney's shoulders relaxed.

Mr. Whippier turned toward them as they approached. He narrowed his eyes while tipping his balding head toward Mother and speaking. She faced them, her glance dipping toward her watch before bouncing to Courtney with a sharp-edged question.

Bethany stepped halfway in front of Courtney breaking the

uncomfortable stare. Reaching her hand toward Zander, she pulled him close and said, "Look who I found on Gloucester."

"I don't think I know you." Mother's voice purred.

"Zander's dad owns Hayward & Son's Furnishings." Conversations ceased. Everyone's focus trained on Zander. He switched his stance and turned his feet toward the exit.

Courtney took advantage of the distraction and moved to a nearby table, slipping into a chair next to her Great-Aunt Helen.

"Let's get a photo with Bethany." Mother struggled to stand, and Dad took her arm. They scrunched together, laughing and smiling through several shots. The perfect family.

Twisting a tissue with her fingers, Courtney watched from the sidelines. She thrilled in the pride and joy her parents showered on Bethany, but something clicked inside—a longing to be included. Heaviness pressed against her heart and made it hard to breathe. Did Courtney even belong? Bethany deserved every complement and display of affection, and though Courtney celebrated her success, she wished their parents would be proud of her too. Pressing a desperate wish-it-was-real smile, and forcing her attention away, Courtney looked at her aunt. "I've not seen you for a while. How are you, Aunt Helen?"

Her great-aunt beamed a smile. Quiet as always.

Mr. Whippier approached until he stood over Courtney. "I hear you're looking for work." One hairy eyebrow lifted dangerously out of proportion to its mate. His long fingers wrapped around his coffee cup as though he were strangling it.

Opening her lips to speak, Courtney—

"She'll be taking care of me from now on, Barney. Once Dan goes overseas, I'll depend on her completely." Her mother emphasized her statement by lifting one of her crutches.

Now or never. "What type of job?" Heat rushed into Courtney's face.

"You own that apartment complex on Summer Hill Street,

don't you?" Zander leaned in her direction as he'd found a seat across the table. He watched her intently.

Deliberately lowering her gaze. Her fingers still twisted a napkin. Separating her hands, she pressed the wrinkled napkin flat. "Tanya and I have had a change of plans." She rubbed her neck. Tension loved creating hard-muscled pain along her spine when inspired by questions like that lately. She glanced at Mr. Whippier.

He smiled and stood straighter though his form never left the table's edge. "I'm practically a manager at Leman's Fine Furnishings, and I know we'll need a salesperson very soon. I'll put in a good word for you." His smile spread but never found his eyes.

"Thank you, Mr. Whippier." She turned her attention to her water. Took a sip.

"You'd have to earn most of your money by commission." Mother said. "Isn't that right?" Before she received an answer, she added, "You'd starve."

Courtney choked on the water and struggled to compose herself.

"Yes, Lillian, much of the income is commission." He aimed a regretful smirk toward Courtney.

Zander shifted in his seat, "I'd put money down that sales would go up if Courtney worked there." He pinned his challenge on the formidable Mrs. MacDuff.

Lillian lifted her head. Fingers trembled when she carefully placed a three-prong fork on the table. Giving him the once over, she asked, "How long have you known her?"

"Longer than six months. Maybe a year."

"That explains it. If Courtney gets the job, you're on, only I don't want money for payment. I take it you're handy around the house?"

COURTNEY

Morning's orange glory disappeared behind the two-story tan-sided home at 4995 Steffin Hill Road. Courtney picked up her cell and punched her parent's number. When had the hill planted beneath her parent's house grown so large?

"Yes," Mother answered.

"I'm here, is Dad around?"

"He's here. The door is unlocked. Of course, I couldn't open it if it were locked."

Mother's so-called dependence grew significantly since their trip. Slipping her cell inside a pants pocket, she stared into the back seat by using the rearview mirror. "This is why I kept you, you're going to secure my independence, right Puddles? Only don't hurt her. Just scare her, okay?"

What if Puddles knocked her mother down? Dark whispers from her conscience singed her heart and almost made her drive to the pound. *Dad come near. Mother, please stay in your chair.* She glanced at the back seat. Dog hair floated on the wispy breeze threading its way through the Cruiser's open windows. Breath released in a puff when she noticed what the canine was doing.

Puddles slobbered on the half-open window, slurping and licking the glass.

Disgusting.

A shudder ran through her shoulders, visions of scrubbing car windows tormented her. She hated washing windows. Hated the goop dribbling between the windows and doors. Would a case of window cleaner even get rid of this mess?

Mother would definitely agree that they could live elsewhere, but she'd still have to live with Puddles. Getting rid of the puppy meant she'd have to move-in with Mother. Which was worse? Mother. Definitely, Mother, though the canine was a close second. Even with the specialized training collar, she'd purchased at Pet Supplies Plus, this dog asserted her strong will. Canine-muscle-power pulled her until she flew like a human kite following a tornado.

Courtney sized up the hill and cement steps again. How they'd get up there was a complete mystery. Getting down—impossible. Puddles refused to tread down to the basement at home. Why hadn't she thought of this before?

Attaching the pinch collar and pulling Puddles tight against her side hadn't stopped the metallic tang on her tongue. A vision of them falling—with leg-breaking results—caused her to question her decision of not fleeing the country. She definitely needed a cola, but maybe caffeine would make her heart pound stronger and that she didn't need. Firefighters helped people and animals out of houses, right? She'd place the call—after this convincing introduction. Oh, how she hated dogs, especially large and unruly ones.

The canine's hesitation and confusion disappeared when her muscled legs took the grass with surprising ease. Courtney followed two steps at a time, trying to keep up. At the door, the puppy licked the glass leaving several smears a couple of inches wide. Courtney stuffed her laughter. So far, so good, Mother hated smudges. Nothing to worry about, so why did her heart beat irregularly?

She opened the sliding glass door, and Puddles pulled her along. Courtney yanked her into a stop several feet later and moved back to close the door.

"I'm in here," Mother yelled.

Puddles lunged toward the voice before trotting gracefully to the living room with her tail curled high.

Lifting her head like always, when Mother met a challenge. "What is *that*?"

Courtney grinned. Thank goodness mother was sitting. "A

dog." Whom Courtney struggled to hold at her side. "Where's Dad?"

Hindered by a broken leg and sitting in a chair didn't defuse her aura of power. She narrowed her eyes at Puddles and remained silent.

Anticipating Mother's predictable response almost made her giddy.

Mother leaned forward in her chair. "What kind of dog?" Her eyes never leaving the struggle as Puddles stretched her neck and sniffed the legs resting on the recliner.

"Where's Dad?" *Why isn't she screaming for me to remove the dog right now?*

"Answer the question." She held her out fingers, offering what? Welcome?

Courtney pushed down on the dog's rump. "Leonberger." She didn't sit.

"AKC?"

"Yes, I'm pretty sure." Tanya had said as much if you could trust her.

"Your dad is in his quiet room."

That was it? *No get the beast out of here and by the way, you're not welcome either.* The *quiet room.* Dad's escape from noise and commotion where he could dream and plan for his next getaway—adventure. Once he returned from a trip, he'd tack up evidence of his latest accomplishments on the corkboard. She needed to convince him that she and Puddles couldn't stay—for Mother's sake.

"Tanya left her in my care until who knows when." Puddles slowly dragged Courtney forward and cautiously sniffed the crutches before laying her head in Lillian's lap. *No, no. She couldn't move here.*

Lillian hesitated, touched Puddle's ears, and laughed. "So soft. We're going to be good friends, aren't we?" She glared up at Courtney. "She's beautiful. You may keep her."

Did Mother suspect—? Her jaw dropped before snapping closed. How could she know that Puddles was her escape plan? And why did she always feel dismissed after a statement like that? Mother needed a little help to understand. "Actually, I wanted you to see her, so you'd realize how impossible it would be to have her here. I'll get an apartment where I can keep her from messing up your house or knocking you over. Puddles doesn't know her own strength I'm afraid—"

"It would be boring around here without her, now that I've laid eyes on her. She will sleep in your bedroom—"

"Mother, she would have to go to the bathroom. The steep hill...." Courtney thrust her arm toward the front yard beyond the bay window, "I really can't—"

Puddles turned toward Courtney and hopped several times.

Laughing out loud, Lillian paused to say. "You'll have to make do. She's too entertaining. You just brought her in from the backyard, which isn't as bad as the front. Just scoop her... leftovers. You'll need your own garbage can for that." Mother's voice had slipped into that accusatory tone that reinforced Courtney's need for an apartment.

"I want to see Dad." Yes, if she explained, he'd help. Courtney marched out of the room and down the hall until she found the brass nameplate, "Quiet Room, Enter at Your Own Risk." She gave the oak door three quick knocks, even paused a moment before entering. Her father stood with a sword in hand, swiping at imaginary foes.

"Hey, Dad."

"Courtney, who's that?" His eyes dropped to the panting mass of hair beside her. He lowered his sword and slipped it inside its sheath.

"Puddles. She's the reason I need my own place. She's too much puppy for me to have to take care of here, along with Mother. You agree, right?"

"You're leading the question for a designated answer. What does your mother say?"

Wheels squeaked as the walker approached. "Mother says the dog can stay," Lillian stated. "The backyard is fenced in, and she can run and play out there. She will sleep with Courtney at night. Besides, she will protect us while you're gone."

Dad's eyebrows shot up, shortening his forehead. Mother had never allowed a dog or cat into her *Better Homes and Gardens* domain before. Courtney could tell by his pleased expression that he'd overlooked Mother's tone. The one that put Courtney on edge.

"What about her slobbers and how she chews *everything*?" Courtney lowered her voice. "What if she knocks you down?"

Lillian leaned on the walker. Puddles stretched around Courtney's leg, sniffed at it, and backed up a step, before sitting down.

That little maneuver won her dad. "She's doing fine. We'll give it a try." He'd always wanted a dog, a large one. Something else she'd forgotten. "Let me show you and the puppy to your room." Lillian nodded. He nodded in return. Dad's pleasant baritone almost made her forgive him. "Isn't this great?"

No. No, it was not.

COURTNEY

"Garage sale isn't in my vocabulary." Courtney sighed.

Bethany tugged the oversized metal door open. It rumbled its resistance.

Their parent's overloaded tables formed a daunting U-shape in the shadowy garage, but when they flicked on the light, they both stood dumbfounded. Crates filled with cushions, furniture, collector tins, and a thousand other items blurred into one big pile and threatened to tumble into further confusion.

"I can see why they want help to purge their stuff. I told them Brandon and I didn't want anything and that you probably wouldn't agree to take it off their hands either. That's when they decided to let it go."

"Turn off the light."

"Don't go there." Bethany's temper edged her response.

"Katie Durum has a pool party going on today. Wanna go?" Courtney swatted at a fly.

"Courtney."

"Just saying—"

"You wouldn't leave."

"Oh, yes, I would." She tasted the dust, but she wanted pancakes with syrup and some tea.

"Maybe you would, but not this time. How could our parents collect so much stuff?" The overcast sky blunted anything cheerful, which contributed to their murky moods.

Turning around, Courtney spied three groups of people heading down the driveway. Her stomach rumbled, but there was no time to eat now. Once the morning crowd left, which shouldn't take long, she would catch a bite. Who came to garage sales anyway?

※ — ❀ — ※

ZANDER

Eight o'clock in the morning, Zander parked his SUV across the avenue from Courtney and Bethany's garage sale tables. Four vehicles hugged the side of the narrow partially paved lane at the back of the MacDuff home. A small crowd of people mulled around. He stepped out of his vehicle and jogged toward them. Catching Courtney's eye, he winked before allowing his focus to zigzag around the garage. Looked like there could be profit lingering in this mess.

A lady covered in blue denim headed toward an amusing antique grandfather clock in the far right-hand corner against the wall. He sputtered, "I want the grandfather clock, that lamp with the yellow shade, and the inlaid box." The denim woman tossed him a nasty look.

"Sold to the man in the periwinkle shirt." Courtney laughed.

"I saw it first." Denim lady's face flushed a light purple, while her finger pointed at the grandfather clock.

Redirecting her to a smaller clock, Courtney purred, "This one is better if you ask me. Why don't you give it a look?" She acted as though they conspired together. Her smile warmed the frost right off Ms. Denim's face.

"Blue, Courtney, just blue. Men don't do periwinkle."

Bethany shook her head. "Here Court, the cashbox. I've got stuff to take care of."

Courtney snorted. "Leaving me responsible?" Her hand swept the span of the garage. She leaned toward her sister. "That's ridiculous. No one does that." Her tone was hushed. She shifted her gaze toward him with an expression he couldn't identify before she took the cashbox. Well now, the bride to be owed him something for her sister's cooperation.

Bethany's cell phone rang, and she left the crowd, encompassing five older women and four teenage boys, who continued to dig through dusty cardboard boxes and piles, leaving messes in their wake.

"Where is your Leo?" Zander moved some books aside to inspect a box of possibilities.

"Chasing some poor rabbit or squirrel in the backyard, I imagine. You want to see her?"

"What about your customers?"

"They'll miss me, but they'll wait." She stuffed the cashbox under a pile of magazines and motioned for him to follow. "Let's avoid the crowd and take the inside route." They climbed the steps leading to the kitchen. What a feast for the eyes, French provincial style, and so large. This kitchen showed impeccable taste. Outside in the backyard, a large-boned reddish-blond dog with a black face chased a rabbit to the far borders. Magnificent. Perfect for the DVD project. He turned to Courtney. Her straight, shoulder-length blond hair gleamed; her attitude and beautiful personality equated into his new movie star. She did say the price was right. Free, and he agreed.

She tossed a quick, embarrassed smile his way then turned to watch the dog. Pulling the sliding glass door open grabbed the dog's attention. "Puddles, you have company."

The puppy's hair rippled with each reach of her legs as she dashed toward them at full lumbering speed.

"Step out of the way, before she knocks you down. She's done it to me."

Why did Courtney seem to not like the dog? How could that be with such a beautiful animal? Zander enjoyed her approach. She jumped at him as soon as she shot through the door. He raised his knee, preventing her from making contact with his chest. She repeated the jump, and he blocked her again. He allowed her to sniff his closed fist, and she wiggled under his caress.

Courtney nodded approval. "Have fun with Monster Puppy. I had no idea we'd have so many customers." Her stomach rumbled, and she flushed red before she turned to the fridge. Grabbing some taquitos out of the freezer, she said. "Would you like some?" She popped them into the microwave.

"No thanks." *Wonder if she can cook?*

Snatching her food, she turned to him. "Come find me when you're done playing, and please put her back outside." She turned with natural-born grace and was gone too soon.

Puddles took advantage of his distraction and jumped

again, making contact. He laughed. What personality this dog had. He found a ball to throw in the backyard. She didn't disappoint as she ran down the ball with all she was worth. He was more convinced than ever that this Leonberger would be the perfect dog. Would Courtney be able to handle a bit of humiliation? That was the question. The thrill of a challenge and pleasure at the thought of time spent with both of them stepped up his heart rate. A question cornered him. Was it the dog or her owner that intrigued him more? He didn't mind taking some time to find out.

COURTNEY

Eating her taquitos as she headed down to the garage, she noticed there were fewer people. Just as she suspected, the crowd had diminished to a smaller handful. Tennis shoes slapped against blacktop as the teens ran toward the alley.

Her sister walked down the driveway toward her with offerings in her hands.

"Coffee?" Courtney inhaled the aroma. "Oh, cappuccinos."

Big sister nodded. "Vanilla flavored. I have an extra for Zander."

"He's playing with Puddles." Grateful that many customers were gone, for now, she looked around. Not much stuff, it seemed, had left the premises, though they had filled the cashbox with money.

"Before anyone else comes, I need to talk to you."

Her serious tone. "Sure, what's up?" Curiosity settled a burden of dread in the pit of her stomach. Bethany's know-it-all grin rankled. Courtney resisted the urge to bite her bottom lip.

"Brandon called. He found some jobs in the paper for me

to investigate. There are several opportunities that I'm qualified for, located near his work."

"That's wonderful." *Why didn't it feel that way?* "I suppose we'd better step up the wedding planning. Once you send your resume, you'll get calls for interviews." She shoved a smile onto her rebellious face.

Bethany cringed a bit. "Brandon actually sent in my resume and cover letters for me. I've got appointments set up for this week. I'm flying to Indianapolis."

"But what about...the wedding?"

"We still want the same date. It's the only date that will work since I'm hoping to have a job soon, actually immediately after the wedding." Bethany looked like she could burst with joy.

Courtney's hope of skirting Bethany's wedding plan decisions crashed and burned in front of her eyes. Her chest felt like a rope twisted into a strangle-knot that didn't ease for several painfully-long seconds.

ZANDER

Zander made more noise than he wanted to as he walked down the steps into the garage. Courtney appeared upset when she turned to look at him, and Bethany seemed ready to explode with happiness. He wasn't going to get in the middle of that. He hoped this was the right time to make his intentions clear. "Courtney, what is your plan to have Puddles trained?"

She seemed taken by surprise. "I'm so sorry. What did she do now?" She checked him over, and her eyes stopped on the spot where Puddles muddy paw left its mark. She frowned.

"I'm impressed with her, and I think training will make the biggest difference for you. Are you free in the evenings for lessons—"

"Where's the cashbox?" Bethany dropped a box filled with tin cans as she was looking around the table. An impatient customer waited at the table.

"Under the magazines." Courtney turned back toward him. "For now, I'm free at night." Courtney handed him a coffee. "Want some?"

"Sure. Are you going for that job Mr. Whippier told you about?" He had to ask.

"I hadn't planned on it."

Zander took a couple of steps toward her and accepted the drink, "Why not? You'd be perfect. They've expanded the business to include antiques, and they need a buyer with some knowledge and expertise to travel and make purchases for them."

Interest softened her eyes a bit. "I've not heard of them doing that." Her tone sounded wistful though she still seemed— overwhelmed? Maybe distracted?

"Seriously, you would be excellent in that position, Courtney. Now about the dog, I really want to work with Puddles. If you allow me to film the training sessions, I'll train her for free."

"Well, the price is right. Okay, name the day."

"Oh no! The cashbox is gone!" Bethany's strained tones gripped their attention.

COURTNEY

Mother remained unforgiving about the cashbox for several days. "Courtney, how could you?" She said at every opportunity. Who could have watched her hide the box under those magazines? That should've been a perfect hiding place, in her opinion. She needed a break from family, so when Zander called about training Puddles, she jumped at the opportunity.

First, she took care of Mother's needs. Next, she called Bethany and told her they'd be talking wedding plans tonight after her nails were done with the perfect classy design. Next, it was time to drop off monster doggie for training, so she could enjoy some free time with Bethany. The need to know more details about what her sister and Brandon wanted for this wedding overwhelmed her at times.

Driving to Zander's didn't help. Courtney blew unsuccessfully at the dog hair dangling from her recent manicure. This humid heat had obviously softened the polish enough to capture the stray hair floating off the stiff breeze. With careful movements, she stepped out of the Cruiser and off the leather seats that burned her legs. The car sweltered like a furnace. A glance at her pedicure confirmed that she hadn't bumped her toes.

Air stirred dust from the graveled drive. She cringed. Would her manicure and pedicure survive handing Puddles to Zander? She glanced at the dark stained siding and stone edged ranch spread out before her, paying particular attention to the windows. No sign of Zander. She wouldn't have figured him to be—a ranch-style homeowner, tucked away in the country— kinda' guy. Nice.

Bending into the car, she carefully lifted her phone off the passenger seat. Puddles leaned forward to sniff her hair. Courtney tucked her shoulder up toward her ear to fend off the mass of hair and slobber, threatening to ruin her day. The phone vibrated in her hand.

"Bethany. I'm dropping off the monster dog, and I'll be right there. Taking lessons was your most brilliant idea yet. I can't thank you enough."

"Are you sure he is training Puddles alone?"

"Well, yes. Of course." Birdsong tweeted, drawing her gaze. No close homes. Bunnies and squirrels dashed around the trees several feet away. Maybe she should leave the dog in the car until Zander could take over.

A paw pounded the window and door, followed by a bark that rattled her eardrums. "I need to call Zander, so he can come here and fetch her out of the car."

SISTERS & FRIENDS

"You can't leave her in there in this heat." Bethany's voice climbed, grating her nerves.

"I can hardly hold her back from running away and dragging me with her into the deep dark woods. This place—"

Zander rounded the corner, decked out in denim, brown leather boots, and a t-shirt showing off muscled arms. Somehow, he appeared to belong to the rustic out-of-doors as much as his slicked-up suit coat. She'd made the right decision. He could hold back one-hundred twenty-five pounds of excited-determined-puppy with no problem.

"Puddles's dog trainer is here."

"But—" Bethany began.

Courtney ended the call. She'd be there soon enough. She pushed a smile past the deep bark Puddles used to disturb the peace.

He nodded at her and frowned when he looked at the dog.

Courtney sighed. Puddles must already be annoying him. It wouldn't do to upset the trainer before the first lesson.

"She shouldn't be left in the car. Why don't you show me how you take her out?"

Mouth dropping open, Courtney's glance bounced from her nails to him. He'd crossed his arms; his frown took over the pleasant expression that evaporated once he had seen the dog. She yanked the hair bobbing at the end of her nail with two fingers and tossed it aside.

"Very well." She pushed the trunk button and retrieved the leash already attached to the pinch collar, all the while protecting her nails. Then she shoved the trunk closed.

At the door, she paused and worked up her best smile. "Could you? I've just gotten a manicure to show Bethany. For the wedding." She lifted the collar and leash positioning her nails just right. Then she watched with disgusted fascination as dog drool slid down between the confines of the window and door. How awful.

"I'd like to see how *you* handle her. And soon, before she cooks inside there." Zander slid a grimace at her.

It struck a nerve that he seemed more irritated with her than with the canine. Puddles, who was making a scene inside her car and losing hair all over the seats.

She wanted to square her shoulders but needing to bend toward the car to hook up the dog. She heaved a sigh. "Puddles, here, Puddles. Stop. No… settle."

Zander's laughter pulled her attention toward his approach. Okay, maybe he'd seen the need to take over—if he was a thoughtful man. He moved close to her and reached for the pinch collar. Slipping it around Puddles's neck, he then allowed her to jump out of the car.

That's more like it. Courtney allowed an approving glance to meet his eyes.

"This way." He motioned to the side of the house and then handed her the leash.

"But I'm meeting—"

"For the contract." He turned to follow the gravel path that crunched under his feet.

Contract? Courtney stepped back. She pressed her lips together to prevent herself from sputtering. Maybe that would be a good idea after all she'd been through. Signatures would protect both of their interests. But what interests were there to protect? Well, who knew? She blew out a breath. Okay, sign this contract and then leave for Bethany's. It could only be that simple.

Puddles pulled on the leash to follow Zander. So much for thinking he was a gentleman. She'd liked him better when she didn't have a dog. Sometimes this was the only way to really know someone. Keeping up wasn't so easy when they reached tall grass. Foliage splayed itself across the path and seemed to lay in wait to destroy her pedicure.

Once they arrived at the fenced-in area, she bent to pull a long strand of grass from between her toes.

"I'll take Puddles, so that you can sign… ," his finger pointed, "right here."

Peppermint breath invaded her space. She had always liked mint. Then he reached for her leash, before handing over those dreadful legal papers.

She bent her head to read them but glanced up a couple times to find Zander watching. So much for being able to concentrate. Everything seemed in order though the words blurred together on the page as she tried to pick out details. She took the pen he offered and signed. A nervous swirling sensation moved inside her stomach. If anything were wrong with that contract, she'd regret it. Hopefully, this agreement wouldn't turn out like the apartment fiasco.

He handed the leash back to her.

"You're going to train Puddles tonight, right?"

"Training both of you will be a lot of fun."

"Both of us? Fun?" She took a humungous extended breath and pushed it out of her lungs. Fear's fingers wrapped themselves around her heart with a chokehold. She gripped the leash tight. Her legs began to shake. It took all her strength to steady her voice. "I told Bethany—"

"You have to train her while I'm filming you." He waved the contract at her.

"I—"

"Contract." He smiled as he lifted the camera into position.

"I didn't see that in there." She crossed her arms across her chest.

Glancing over the contract, he pointed at the spot where she'd unknowingly agreed to train the dog and being filmed.

Swallowing her anger, she said, "What about Bethany—I'll need to call her to postpone our meeting. An important wedding meeting."

"Go ahead. I did mention that filming you training your dog waives the fee." He seemed preoccupied with the camera and not at all moved with sympathy over her circumstances.

"Oh, right." At least she didn't need to pay for this *opportunity* too. She called her sister. "Bethany looks like I have to train Puddles. I'll get to your house later tonight."

"I told you so—" Courtney ended the call.

Yanking the gate open to a large fenced in dirt field—just as the dust swirled a foot off the ground—added to the mind-numbing shock. It muffled his short explanation about the lesson until he finally took her shoulders in hand and pointed her in the right direction. Her legs hesitated to move, and she resisted the urge to check her nails and pedicure until he turned to pick up his movie camera. Several nicks already, she'd better be careful, or her nails would be destroyed.

His smile looked forced once he turned around. Courtney knew all about that. Wasn't her own just as deliberate and joyless? What in the world did he have to worry about? He didn't have Puddles on the end of the leash or nails to protect. Zander carried a look she classified as no-patience determination.

"It's not necessary to hold on with a death grip." He reached over and loosened her fingers. "This will be like a walk in the park. I'll guide you." He shifted his camera, keeping it away from Puddles. "Concentrate on what I say. That way, you won't get stressed or anxious."

Too late.

He took her shoulders with his warm hands and pointed them toward the other end of the pen. "Remember, Puddles will sense negative feelings. Relax."

A breeze gusted, and she enjoyed the scent of his aftershave and soap until she thought about how dirty her feet became as they moved under his direction. If she could only be miles away from here.

"Sit Puddles beside you. Tug up on her collar and push down on her backside."

There it was, that look she deciphered as...*expectant*. Courtney gazed at him, hoping her anxiety didn't show. "Sit." Her voice sounded fragile, transparent. Nothing happened. She repeated the command a few more times, and the dog looked around the pen.

"Remember to pull her leash up and press down on her backside."

She complied, and Puddles obeyed. Thrill surged through her veins. Maybe she could learn this, after all. Trial and error and a few successes later stirred hope and a touch of pleasure she'd not expected to experience with Puddles.

"Command her to walk. Then step forward at a reasonable pace. Tug her leash when she gets more than a foot ahead of you. Say, 'Back.' As soon as she succeeds with any command, compliment her. Say, 'Good dog.'"

Again, and again, Courtney moved around the pen, following his direction. Her shoulders began to loosen.

Once they were finished for the day, Zander came alongside them and patted Courtney on the shoulder. "Great job. I don't know when I've seen more improvement." Did his face hold a touch of wonder, or had she imagined it?

"My improvement or Puddles?"

"Of course, Puddles." Though his expression seemed to vie with the truth.

She laughed aloud.

Puddles lunged past Zander toward a rabbit running at the other end of the pen. Courtney moved to the left, trying to avoid slamming into their trainer, while the leash pulled her forward. She tripped over the puppy's back foot and ended up face-first in the dust. A cloud lifted around her—not hiding the embarrassment filling her now. She rolled over and sat up.

Her legs were covered with brownish-grey powder. Dirt embedded her toenail polish.

Zander bent in half laughing, causing her to erupt with emotion too. Frustration fueled her anger when she couldn't stop laughing—how dare he make her react this way when she was so mad! Puddles ran after the rabbit, right next to the camera on the tripod. Reminding her that the camera might still be filming this escapade.

Was there anything she'd do that didn't end up in disaster?

SIX

COURTNEY

Ringing Bethany's doorbell and calling her cell didn't arouse her sister's attention. Once Courtney carefully picked her way to the window, soft snores met her ears. She knew it. Must be nice to sleep like the dead. It was only 7:30 p.m. when she pulled into the driveway. Charcoal clouds smudged the sky, throwing the house in shadow. She shoved the prickly bush aside and crept closer to the glass to see if Bethany locked her windows.

To make up for laughing at her, Zander offered to keep Puddles so she could meet with her sister. She'd jumped on that offer as fast as the last syllable left his lips. He'd drive Puddles over to her parent's house around 9:30 that night. Courtney drove to Natalie's house and took a quick shower and dressed in fresh clothes since half of her belongings were still there. She almost felt like herself. Except for the pedicure. If she'd only taken a photo and not hesitated when Zander turned his attention on her. Unfortunately, the nail polish hadn't set, and both large toenails were ruined beyond repair.

She turned as a police car stopped in front of Bethany's house. The officer's face aimed toward her. Of course, she appeared suspicious, all tangled in scratchy bushes, positioned in front of the window. Courtney tapped on the glass. Then knocked harder. "Oh, please, Bethany, get up."

A stick snapped behind her. The officer approached. "Excuse me, ma'am?" His voice originated from only about five feet away.

Trying again, harder Courtney heard Bethany's snores stop. She wanted to watch the window, but his shoes crunched the gravel surrounding the bushes.

"Why don't you step away from there, and explain what you're doing?"

Courtney lifted her eyes to his face. How did a man ever grow so large? "She might be waking. I need to… we were… meeting, but I'm late. She fell asleep, and I'm trying to…" Rambling—she was rambling.

He didn't appear amused.

Once more, she banged on the window, "Bethany, if you love me, wake up *now*."

"Step away from there."

The severity of his tone bit her resolve. Would he draw a gun if she chanced one more knock? Her hand flew to the window, and she knocked just as Bethany's sleepy face appeared. Bethany fell away from the window for a second before she reappeared and flipped the lock open. Courtney picked her way out of the bushes as they tore at her skin and clothing.

"About time you're here." Bethany's husky voice said. She turned on an inside light.

The officer flipped his frown into a smile. "Are you the owner of this house?" He directed his attention toward Bethany's face in the window.

Courtney felt he'd kept aware of her movements also.

"Yes, I rent here." She held her hand over her mouth, probably to stifle a yawn.

"Your name is?"

"Bethany MacDuff, until I'm married in a month."

He turned toward Courtney, "Okay, looks like your alibi worked out. In the future, don't hang out under someone's window. Try a phone call." He directed his glance toward her sister, "Congratulations." Then he turned and walked toward the squad car.

"Don't you tell anyone about this, Bethany." She frowned at the back of the officer's head.

"Or what?"

Or what? How would she know? She tossed her sister a purposeful grimace before she turned to approach her car. She grabbed the tote with almost everything her sister wanted to borrow.

Minutes later, Bethany's modern kitchen table supported her elbows. Fragrant cinnamon apple tea slipped down her throat, chasing forkfuls of warmed homemade apple pie a' la mode. "Awe mmm, so good. Did you make it?"

"Of course, no store-bought apple pie will cross my kitchen door. Mr. Whippier gave this to me to give to you." Bethany slid the Leman's Fine Furnishings application over the glass table in her direction.

Scrunching up her face, "I'm not sure I want to work... there."

"It wouldn't hurt to have a job, some money coming in, and a good excuse to get out of the house since the dog idea didn't work."

Courtney picked up the application and glanced over it. "I suppose I can try it out." Maybe she could ask for a shift other than what Mr. Whippier worked. Zander did mention antiques. What could it hurt?

"How did dog training go tonight?"

Shifted her gaze toward the wedding notebook, Courtney replied, "You're tired, I'm tired. Let's work on some ideas. We'll catch up on that later." *Or never.*

They began their *definitely do* and *not do* lists. Victorian and busy were out. Bethany wanted a modern flair mixed with traditional. Some variation of color was allowed, with the main focus being medium or dark blue. No pastels, red, pink, or orange, and the accents had to be gold, not silver.

"You have to find my dress and the bridesmaid's dresses since I'm leaving tomorrow. I've got an interview the next day. Here are my measurements."

Eyes rapidly blinking, Courtney stood up. "I can't do all that. How do you expect me to pick out your dress? And, Mother, how am I to get away from her to shop like I'd need to?" She paced the kitchen as she wrapped her arms as far around herself as she could reach.

Bethany slid a freshly-inked note across the table to her. "Cassie and Nicole are my bridesmaids. They'll help you. Just calm down. Help me, little sister." Something like worry, dependence, and I need you, passed behind her sister's eyes.

Courtney's muscles melted into weakness, and she slipped into the chair. How could she resist the impossible? Cassie and Nicole helping and not fighting? That would take a miracle. One worth seeing. Bethany knew that, but she was… desperate. She could identify with desperation. She was feeling it now too. "Who did Brandon pick for the best man and grooms?" She leaned toward her sister.

"Best man is Bruce Cooper. The grooms are Zander Hayward and Gary Thornton."

"Zander Hayward. Did you have anything to do with Brandon's choices?"

A wicked grin developed on her sister's face. "Nope. Remember, Brandon is the reason I met Zander, and then you met him because of that furniture you prize so much."

"That's true." She leaned against the back of the chair. At least he wasn't the best man. "Do I need to talk to you or…"

Courtney leaned over the green cursive note, "Gary Thornton, to coordinate matching tuxes?"

"Just me. I'll wrangle with colors with your future brother-in-law."

"Do you have any other surprises?"

"Brandon wants me to start looking at houses immediately. He has a list of half a dozen homes to visit already."

Courtney cringed inside, "Sounds time-consuming." By the silky sound of her sister's voice, she could tell that not only the groom wanted to find a house right away.

"I know I'm leaving a lot up to you."

"Everyone is leaving period. Tanya, then Dad, and now you…"

"Please don't put me in her category."

"Sorry, but I depend on you guys. You've all flipped things on me." The whine in her voice was unbecoming, but this wedding and Mother were impossible to deal with.

"You depend on too many people, Court. Maybe it's time to show what you're really made of." She could feel Bethany watch her as she stared through the glass table toward the ruined pedicure. "You see this face?" She added a little bounce to her words.

Courtney lifted her gaze to see an exaggerated smile and bugged-out eyes that made her laugh. "Wow, do I see that face." She picked up the pen and hugged the pad of paper with the list next to her chest.

"Well, this is a contented face. You know my style that I'm a daisy and gardenias person, not a calla lily or orchids person. No one else respects that."

"Except, Natalie."

"Well, Natalie is unique, but she's not my sister. You'll do just fine at picking out my wedding dress and the bridesmaid's dresses—"

"And everything else." Her shoulders sagged under the

weight of responsibility. She had to hang in there for Bethany, but she'd rather run. "Do you think Mother would—"

"Mom would, but I want you. I don't want old fashioned style dominating my wedding decorations. Plus, you know how extravagant she is, and I have to pay for half of this wedding. She actually suggested that I cover suckers with silver foil with a bit of lace. Then tie on a silver wedding ring with ribbon for the shower favors. She *knows* I hate silver. I trust you to look for what I want."

They both shared a laugh. "Maybe Mother wanted to suggest that you and Brandon make a sweet couple."

"You know her well. I'm thinking that too many jokes about us being suckers for marrying would make me mad. I'm not chancing the comments."

"Okay. What if I choose something just as irritating or wrong for your wedding? Planning this way… you'll not have input on your own wedding."

"It will feel like Christmas."

"Surprises all around for sure. You'd better hope they don't turn out like a box-of-coal-in-your-stocking type of surprise."

Bethany yawned again. "It'll be fine."

"Where do you want the rehearsal dinner? The Gateway Clipper dinner cruise?"

"Wouldn't that be your dream date? Mr. Perfect is supposed to take you there and dance the night away. Yes, I remember. But don't forget, I get seasick just thinking about a boat. Windsor Room at Olde Stonewall Golf Course will do nicely if you can reserve the room. Let's get motoring on this list before I fall asleep." The next hour and a half flew by too quickly. Some progress and some loose ends, but Bethany would be leaving around 9:00 a.m., and she needed enough sleep before the long trip.

"Time for me to go." They hugged before turning to move down the hallway toward the door. Panic hit just when she thought her mind could relax, "The invitations? They will need to be sent, and you don't even have any. And the addresses!"

"Yes, pick something elegant—yet plain with gold letters. Bethany scribbled several figures on a sheet of paper and handed it over to her. "This is how many to order, and this is the cost to stay below." Bethany pulled a spare house key out of her pocket. "I almost forgot to give my spare key to you. Could you water the plants?"

She reached for the key. Had plants ever survived her attention? She glanced at the beautiful specimens happily potted around the room. "How long are you staying away?"

Courtney's heart actually fluttered.

"Undecided as of right now. Go home and get your puppy settled. How do you like it at Mom and Dad's?"

Courtney nodded. "I feel like I'm ten years old."

"I'm thinking that could be good for your skin."

"Okay, thanks for the sympathy." Courtney grinned and pulled the door shut as she stepped into the darkness. The haven of Bethany's house wouldn't stem the tide of muscle tightening, heart fluttering confrontations waiting to dominate and paralyze her every move. The click of the door triggered unwelcome images in her mind. She jumped as though some presence were hiding in the bushes poised to grab her ankles or become an exasperating back seat driver.

Seven

COURTNEY

Wedding ideas, decisions to be made—Courtney's mind spun as she traveled down Hwy. 18 onto 7th Ave. She heaved a heavy sigh. Her fingers cramped from grasping the steering wheel too tight. If she'd known that Bethany would be away so much, she'd have declined. Told her to elope. Yes, even faced her sister's disappointment rather than set herself up for a failure not of her own making.

She pressed the breaks, but not soon enough, and flew past 25th St., which lead to her parent's house. She didn't want to go *home* anyway. Nothing turned out the way she'd wanted it to lately. In two minutes, she turned right onto 24th St. Almost fifteen minutes after nine. Zander would arrive soon.

As she made her way down Steffin Hill Road, she saw him waiting. Beeping the horn, she waved, "Follow me." After a couple of turns, they traveled down narrow Alabaster Avenue leading to her parent's backyard. She pulled off the road, and Zander pulled in behind her. Dust rose and blanketed their cars. The need for rain grew. Borderline drought seemed to be the weatherman's favorite topic. That and fear-filled reports about thieves who set fire to homes they robbed.

Puddles bounced with uncontained joy on the passenger side of his SUV.

Courtney's heart leapt at Puddles unexpected greeting. She thought the puppy would've changed her allegiance when she stayed with Zander. Who wouldn't? The man embodied warmth and wasn't hard on the eyes either. If he'd only deal with that laughing problem of his.

She swung the fence door open to allow them inside. "Thanks for taking care of her." A backpack drew her curiosity. *Dog treats, books, or what?*

His eyes shined with their own appreciation. With slow, calculated steps, Zander walked Puddles at his pace though Puddles tried to lead. He made her sit each time or go back to where they started until they reached the inside of the fenced area under his authority. Then he released her.

Courtney locked the gate and turned as Puddles ran toward her, jumped up, and almost knocked her down. By gripping the metal chain link fence, she prevented her second fall of the day.

"Off." Zander's command came quick and firm. "Lift your knee to block her, but not kick her when she does it again. Now!"

She lifted her leg waist high, and Puddles made contact with her knee and then bounced off the ground with an exuberance that made Courtney want to laugh and run at the same time. Lifting her knee-high again, Puddles backed down, looking innocent and amazed all at the same time. The canine sat and waited in a way she'd never done before.

"When does your dad leave?"

Swatting at mosquitoes that feasted on her arm and neck, she glanced into his eyes with a plea, "He leaves this weekend. Saturday. Want to come inside?"

"For a cool drink—I'd follow you anywhere."

"Come on then. We have a few of those." She turned toward the house. The yard seemed larger than she realized. This will be another chore she'd have to accomplish if they didn't hire a teenager soon.

"Is that what I think it is in your hand?"

Tilting her hand, she glanced at the application. "Mr. Whippier got it to me."

"You could sell sand in a desert. You'll do well there if you take the position."

"I think your thirst is talking?" They laughed while Puddles trotted on behind them.

She slid the patio door open and stepped into the kitchen. Puddles toenails clicked across the tile floor as she headed for her water dish next to the stone fireplace dominating the right-hand sidewall.

Placing the application on the table, Courtney moved to the refrigerator. Opening the door, she found several choices. "Sit where you'd like, Zander. Cola, iced tea, or flavored water?" She turned to watch him scan the room with a look of approval.

He sat on a stool and swiveled to face her. "Water will be great." His cell chimed. "Dad." A frown dug into his face as he listened. "That receipt was for house staging furniture." He turned the chair in the opposite direction and dragged his fingers through his hair. "Not a big deal to anyone, but me. I'm giving it my full undivided attention."

As she grabbed two bottles, a bell rang from the living room. She jumped.

"Courtney, is that you?" Mother's voice bellowed.

Handing the water to Zander first, she pointed in the direction of her mother's call. Sliding the application to the center of the table, and nodding in Puddles direction, she whispered,

"She's been known to eat documents—paper of any kind really."

Zander chuckled, and unscrewed the lid to take a drink, as he listened to his father.

Courtney moved through the specially ordered baby gate that matched the kitchen.

Mother cradled her head in her hands—holding the mind that never stopped thinking.

"Could you help me get ready for bed? I'm feeling a bit dizzy right now." Her voice seemed more subdued than her usual attitude.

Was she okay? She didn't look right. "Sure. Let me tell Zander that I'll have to see him another time."

"Zander?" Mother lifted her head from her hands and turned to peer at her.

"You met him in Williamsburg."

Her mother's intense stare and speechlessness signaled she waited for more information. She leaned back into her La-Z-Boy, settling in, before folding her arms in front of her chest. She wouldn't be moved now until her silent questions were answered.

"Zander and I were training Puddles. He brought her back for me just a few minutes ago."

"You were gone a long time tonight. Why didn't you bring Puddles back?"

Courtney folded her arms in front of her. *Please not now, when Zander is in the kitchen.* "Bethany is getting ready to leave early tomorrow morning for job interviews, and I helped her with a few ideas for the wedding. Zander just kept Puddles a little longer, so that we could visit."

Mother's mouth opened to speak, but Zander came through the baby gate. "Mrs. MacDuff, how are you doing tonight?"

Lillian jerked her head in his direction. "Hello, Zander.

Courtney mentioned that you are training the puppy. How is that going?"

Zander grinned as though trying to hold in a laugh. "Pretty well, for their first time." He pulled the backpack off and laid it on the floor next to the television stand.

"Aren't dog classes expensive?"

"Can be." Zander's face sobered under the direct question.

Aiming a glare at him—trying to catch his attention with a shake of Courtney's head—didn't work. He focused on her mother with uninterrupted courtesy.

Mother peered at her, "I thought you were broke—from that escapade with the apartment complex."

Courtney's stomach dropped. A fiery burn crept up her throat and into her face. She couldn't even chance a glance at Zander. And Bethany wondered why she didn't want to spend time with Mother.

"Actually, she's been kind enough to allow me to film the training sessions for my video project." He patted the backpack that he'd placed on the floor. "I'm developing a training technique for dog owners. I consider that sufficient payment."

"I have a DVD player."

Oh, to crawl away and disappear. For a whole couple of hours, Courtney had forgotten that the session was filmed. She narrowed her gaze at Zander. He glanced back. Uncertainty clouded his expression; did he see her plea?

His voice deepened. "I'm heading to a friend's house soon to make the movie. I'll only keep useful examples. Right now, everything I have is in its rough form and not on DVD."

"Oh, bring it on. I'd love to see what they are learning. Maybe I could put in a few pointers." Lillian's hands almost trembled as they slid up and down the armrests on her chair. "I've been watching several shows on television." She looked refreshed and quite recovered from feeling dizzy just moments before.

"That's okay, Mother. You were just asking for help to get to bed a minute ago. The training session is long and not edited. I'm sure Zander will add his own interesting teachings to finish the film. He might not want to show this for free."

Lillian frowned as soon as her *needing help to get to bed* was mentioned. "Nonsense, I'd like to see it *now*." Her eyes redirected their intensity toward him. "You wouldn't withhold simple joy from a cripple, would you Zander?" Her fingers gripped the armrests.

He grinned like firecrackers sizzling to go off. "Wouldn't you want to wait until it's edited?"

"No, I wouldn't, thank you."

Zander sobered. "Well, alright." He bent over and lifted the backpack. He opened it and fished around for Courtney's unedited nightmare.

He glanced at Courtney, and his eyes narrowed as though in thought. Was that apology shading his eyes into a deeper green-brown? "I'll have to leave here no later than ten." He looked at his watch.

Turning on her phone to capture the time—thrilling—thirty-five minutes of torture.

Puddles whined from the kitchen. "I'll take her out." Courtney turned and fled the tastefully decorated living room that smothered her with its ridged calculated lines and anticipated laughter meant to humiliate. She let the dog out and noticed the kitchen light pooling overtop of the job application, which looked better and better every second.

She followed Puddles into the warm night air. The outside heat would provide an excuse for her—no doubt—fire-engine-red appearance. Hopefully, he'd not noticed her flush before. A spray can squirted, and she smelled and tasted the bug spray that her dad used to counter persistent mosquitoes and moths. She moved Puddles to a safer location and coughed. "Hey, Dad." She waved her hands to push the toxic smell away.

"I thought you would be helping your mother right now." He sprayed one more cloud of repellant before he capped the lid and set it on the lawn table situated on the small patio.

She'd need something to get rid of the bad taste in her mouth. The strong urge to cough pressed her throat. "Zander is inside talking to Mother. It was time to take Puddles out."

Her dad moved closer to her. "I can see that." But his eyes stayed with Courtney. "Make an effort, Butterfingers. I believe you can... make a difference."

Heart-felt confidence. Courtney wished she had some. Before she could reply, the patio door rolled open, and Zander stepped outside. "Mr. MacDuff, spraying bugs I see."

"Yes, how are you?"

"Fine. Mrs. MacDuff asked to see the filming of Courtney's and Puddles first training, but maybe we can watch it together another night."

"Maybe." Dad's eyes shot to her, taking measure.

Courtney's temper flared. Not only was he going to humble her in front of her mother, but her dad too. A bug bit her neck. Then the puppy ran toward the man she thought was nice earlier that day. She couldn't even look at him.

Zander brushed Courtney's arm. "I'll be right back." His voice soft as a fleece blanket. The kind she liked or used to.

Lord, what did I ever do to deserve tonight? "See you inside, Dad."

Puddles approached Courtney's dad, but the cloud of insect spray changed her direction.

He nodded from the shadows. Courtney entered the kitchen, and Puddles followed. Inside the puppy lay down by the sliding glass windows and licked the curtains.

She'd use the excuse that she needed to unpack her belongings so that she could hide in her room. Still, Mother would need help to get ready for bed immediately after the humbling viewing. Wonder what fresh, sassy comments she'd have to endure?

Zander entered and grinned at her.

Glaring at the movie camera grasped in his hand, she pointed her feet toward the living room. "I have to puppy proof everything in my bedroom. Have fun with my mother and dad."

"Trust me."

Stopping to study him, her body wanted to melt into the wallpaper and disappear. She was good at that, but something about his expression gripped her. His eyes laughed, but not with mockery. Maybe he realized how embarrassing this was, but the movie camera in his hand teased her and called her naïve.

Every nerve in her body tingled. Puddles stood up and walked to her, sniffed her, and gazed at her face with sleepy-eyed curiosity. Courtney stroked her ear and head. Puddles melted into her hand.

Zander reached out and touched her arm and motioned toward the living room. She hesitated, pressed her lips together, so she wouldn't say anything stupid.

They passed through the baby gate, and the dog stayed in the kitchen, laying down with a grunt on the tile floor. Mother waited, eyes sparkling, posture straight, so alert. Courtney's unease grew. Every movement Zander made seemed delayed. Nausea churned in her stomach.

He turned toward the television, yet dug deeper inside his backpack as though preparing for their evening's entertainment.

Courtney reminded herself to breathe. "Trust me," he'd said.

Lillian sported a smug grin and leaned forward.

Zander's cell rang. He put the movie camera inside the case before standing up.

Courtney shifted in her seat. Every position pinched like a

bed of needles. Earlier that day, she'd focused on the dog and her pedicure until distracted into forgetting about being filmed for the world to see. Didn't the Lord see all of her vulnerable situations that she had no power to cover-up? Every embarrassing failure and thoughtless moment. She cringed.

Lillian twisted in her chair with halting movements and readjusted her broken leg with trembling hands. She waved at him as he continued to listen to his phone. "Excuse me, Zander."

He took a couple steps away. "Yeah, Mike, we can solve that. I have 9:40. He bent his head closer to the phone. Yes, I'll be there in ten minutes. No problem." He turned off his phone. "Sorry about that, but Mike needs me now. Technical problems, I forgot my computer and the SD cards that he needs to transfer the information, so there will be no show tonight. We can plan a date for the future once the editing is finalized."

He turned his back to her mother and tossed Courtney a wink but all she could think of was the train wreck of a reveal—that first lesson in video.

⌖

ZANDER

Half an hour later, Zander sank into Mike's leather couch. He grabbed a bowl of buttery popcorn from the coffee table. Mike inserted the memory card into his computer connected to the smart television and turned it on.

"Don't be telling anyone about this. Courtney was pretty embarrassed when I mentioned this recording to her parents." He started laughing so hard he wiped his eyes, smearing butter on his face.

Mike crinkled leather as he sat on the opposite side of the

couch while cradling his own bowl of popcorn. He shot Zander a sideways glance that seemed to question his buddy's sanity. But, as soon as he saw her all dressed up and scoping out her sandals when Zander told her that he was training *them*, Mike lost it. "You didn't set this up, did you? Hilarious!"

"She looked fabulous, alright." *Just right.* "She thought I'd be training the dog, apparently." Mike couldn't breathe for laughing. "You're the guy who didn't check to see if his television was plugged in a minute ago. Be nice."

"Yeah, yeah, yeah." Mike sucked in a deep breath and then grinned. "The one time I'm off my game. Enjoy it, Zander."

The training proved just as funny now as it had been during real-time. Starting out with a frown, Courtney limped aghast at first. Gradually she appeared relaxed, as though she enjoyed training Puddles—until that last fateful fall. Good thing he'd had his camera on the tripod to catch her charming inability to command the dog, which led to her hitting the dirt at the end. His sides hurt from laughing.

"Well, you couldn't have picked a better person to model how not to do training. Did she do anything right? I don't remember." Mike's eyes continued to tear as he shook his head. "This is unbelievable. Not much editing needed, except the dead-nothing-happening parts."

Zander sobered. "There has to be tons of editing." He tossed the last piece of popcorn into his mouth.

"This is exactly what Mancel wants. You have everything here that irritates a trainer and causes a trainee to fail." He looked down at the list he'd written. "Not listening to the trainer. Not firm with the dog. Owner not alert at all, and when she hit the dirt—how could you not want *that* in here? You're not going soft, are you?"

"I'm not going to humiliate her. Just because there are a few great examples—"

"A few?"

"There's no need to discourage her further." Courtney and Puddles would grow to work together, eventually. Plus, he wanted her around. He laughed again until he saw her haunted expression in his mind's eye—when her mother demanded to see the uncut version, to offer *advice*. Courtney had shrunk before his eyes in a way he didn't think possible for this confident, beautiful woman. Her personality brought humor and challenge into every situation. She intrigued him. Her mother though—there was something off about her. Lillian MacDuff's attitude was one he wouldn't have expected or hoped to find.

Eight

COURTNEY

The blank, white page on Courtney's laptop lit the room like an oversized nightlight. Her fuchsia bathrobe reflected off the polished cherry desk and the clear glass vase at the edge of darkness. Murky chocolate brown walls—her mother's choice—and dark accents blanketed the joy she wished would rise inside her heart. Stretching her neck, she glanced around and then wished she hadn't. The room appeared to shrivel into the size of a prison cell at midnight. Only useful for sleep. Not a haven like her bedroom at her apartments.

Correction—not her apartments anymore. The acid of bitterness tried to take root once again. She pushed back those black thoughts. Time to focus.

Her scratchy eyes defied the limited light as she tried to ignore the haphazard snores from the oversized dog draped over her bed. There'd be no squeezing underneath the sheets even if she'd wanted to, so she may as well be productive.

Writing choices ranged from fantasy, historical, or her genre—contemporary with a touch of mystery and suspense. She drummed fingers against the desktop next to the ebony keys, interrupting the silence and intermittent snores. Waiting for inspiration to stir felt—unnatural. Awkward. She usually enjoyed a trunk-load of ideas.

Finally, one picture-thought, then another began. It always started this way. She pushed her computer toward the back of the desk and grabbed her sketchbook, where notes and images filled the page with ease.

Fantasy this time. This choice surprised her, but she could stretch her wings. No one would ever read these pages anyway, so there was nothing to risk.

Nidella, the main character, seemed most like her mother. Controlling, smart, bossy, and efficient. She named several more characters, then looked on-line for personality traits and logged the details. She almost nodded off in front of the desk. The clock beamed 2:00 a.m. before she closed the lid on her computer.

Turning toward the bed, she frowned. Puddles still stretched across its width. "Don't mistake me for an oversized chew toy." She lifted the covers weighed down by her deep-sleeping fur ball and tugged harder. The blanket almost tore.

A new tactic would have to be employed. Courtney hung her robe on the bedpost and sat high against the bumpy head-board. The AC blew and chilled her as she slid a foot under the covers as far as possible. Puddles pawed at her as though she was running in her sleep.

Courtney sighed. Fingering the silky black nose, she then made a big push to lift the puppy's head. Sleep dulled eyes opened unfocused in her direction. The dog stirred and read-justed, allowing her to slip entirely inside the covers. Courtney closed her eyes before Puddles laid her head on top of her stomach. The canine huffed a long deep sigh.

The weight on her stomach was somehow comforting. Anchoring. She drifted off to sleep in a nanosecond, or so it seemed, because come morning, she really couldn't remember.

A lawnmower buzzed to life too close to her window. They jerked awake at 7:00 a.m. What a fantastic way to wake up after such a late night."

Puddles jumped off the bed and glanced around, appearing confused. Courtney laughed, and grabbed her robe, kissing it for being brilliantly colored. The edge of an application for Leman's Fine Furnishings curled off the side of the desk, where she had worried the edge instead of filling in the blanks. She'd ignored it last night, but in the light of day, hemmed in by brown walls, she knew what she had to do.

⁂

COURTNEY

Patriot-blue paint peeked between the soap suds at WetGo as her PT Cruiser sparkled under the much-needed attention. There wasn't enough time to use the do-it-yourself car wash at Bubble Bear this morning. Water sprayed, and brushes whirled like her thoughts. She didn't want this furniture job, but she couldn't miss the opportunity to have a get-out-of-jail bona fide reason to leave the house. Savings and checking accounts needed replenishing. Oh, the second that Mother became independent of her care. . .

Her finger traced the rivulets of soapy bubbles pouring over the driver's side window. Brushes whirled around the front and sides of her car again.

Maybe Natalie could sit with Mother and Puddles when she had to travel or be at the furniture store—if they hadn't filled the position. So much for hoping that Bethany could give her a break. Bethany's joyful news about job interviews and house searches squelched her plans, tethered her to this commitment while peppering her longing to flee. This morning's botched breakfast with Mother motivated a quick shower and a polished application for Leman's.

Her mind rehearsed Mother's, "I want orange juice. This isn't the right kind. Don't you know any better?" And then the pancakes. No wonder she didn't cook anymore. She'd probably have nightmares tonight. Pans would probably grow legs and chase her. And the *one-minute egg*? Please. Doesn't one cook an egg till it looks done and then serve it? Why time something like that?

Brushes pulled away from the hood of the car. The rinse cycle began. It was vital for her to mentally prepare. Expectations for first impressions made her palms sweat. If only she could interview on the spot and acquire this job today. Then she wouldn't have to worry about finding a job. Had Mr. Whippier mentioned her? He was so critical—would he even be a safe choice for a reference?

She could do this. Switch on the positive and leave the negative in the dust. Didn't Bethany call her *Princess Joy*? Hadn't she practiced deleting unhappiness from her thoughts for years? Yes, and until lately, she'd been an excellent pretender.

First happy thought, what could that be? A glance at the mirror showed shadow smudges under her eyes. She sucked in a harsh breath. Well, that didn't help. She couldn't show up at the furniture store looking like that. Digging through her purse, she found the under-eye concealer and fixed her face. The carwash buzzer rang her cue to drive into the sunshine.

Think happy thoughts. Zander and Puddles working together came to mind. That sparked a smile. He enjoyed training Monster Dog, a definite accomplishment, and she'd tasted success with Puddles and recognized elation. She sputtered a grin. How about that? Zander and Puddles put her on track toward the right perspective. Sunshine sparkled off the hood, cleansed from dust and bugs. Rejuvenation felt great. First impressions—no worries, she got that covered.

Minutes later, she opened the door to Leman's Fine Furnishings. It had been years since she'd seen the inside of this store. Wasn't she only ten when her parents placed that last order? Several front areas were sectioned off, displaying specific styles, lending an exclusive atmosphere. An impressive vintage style furniture section drew her attention toward the rear of the store. That's where she hoped to work.

"Welcome to Leman's. Is there something I can show you?"

Courtney turned toward the pleasant voice to see a darkhaired woman, about thirty, dressed in a black tailored dress and high heels. "I'm here to apply for a position I've heard about." Courtney smiled and turned her attention toward her large purse holding the application. She pulled it out and looked up expectantly.

"Oh," a noticeable chill entered the saleslady's vocal cords as she motioned for Courtney to follow her. "This way." They walked past a beautiful arrangement of traditional furnishings. Then a showcase quality grouping of Victorian-style couches, tables, and eye-catching lamps. Impressive.

They approached the command center, as Mr. Whippier had often referred to it, which stood front and center of the room. A man of about thirty-five years, dressed in an expensive suit, occupied himself with paperwork on the countertop next to the register.

"Mr. Angerton, this is..." She turned her dark eyes toward Courtney, which held a less than friendly light.

"Courtney MacDuff." Courtney shifted her attention to Mr. Angerton.

Sharp black eyes looked back at her as he reached over the counter to shake hands.

"I'm here about the position I've heard you desire to fill." She handed her application to him. A doorbell rang, signaling a potential customer. The dark-haired saleswoman moved toward the front of the store in a flash, flooding Courtney with relief. She felt her shoulders relax.

"Follow me to my office, Courtney. You may call me Bruce."

Leman's offered a variety of inexpensive and quality furnishings. A little something for everyone and Courtney could appreciate that. In a snug corner at the back of the store was the space provided for the genuine antique section. An old-fashioned sign, *The Original Article*, hung from the ceiling.

Several beautiful hutches, dining room tables, and couches, along with period lamps and knick-knacks, filled a good portion of the space. If their marketing expanded, allowing their pieces to ship distances and they allowed Courtney to visit notable antique dealers across America to replenish stock and match pieces—they could do well. Her pulse raced, she felt more alive and connected to this than she ever did with the apartments. He motioned for her to move into the room before him. She sat in the first available chair.

Bruce Angerton's mahogany desk shone like a mirror. The bookcases and scant decorations lent a nicely stated class. He slipped into his chair and then took his time to read her application. "I see you know both Mr. Whippier and Mr. Hayward."

Three raps at the door made her jump.

Mr. Angerton nodded for her to continue.

"Yes, I do. Mr. Whippier has been a family friend for years. Mr. Hayward is a more recent acquaintance. I've bought antiques from him, and now I'm working with him with his video project."

The persistent knocking sounded again.

"Yes, what can I do for you?"

Courtney's eyes traced the stubborn jawline of her potential employer. He was not happy, nor would he pretend patience either.

"Zander Hayward is on the phone. He said this call is urgent, and he's unavailable for the rest of the day."

Angerton picked up the phone. "Zander, Bruce here. I've got Courtney MacDuff in my office interviewing." He listened while tapping his pen on a notepad.

Lowering her gaze, she breathed slowly to keep calm. His eyes had inspected her so intently before that she looked away. He'd probably turned this into a test for how she stood up under pressure.

"Would you hire her if you were interviewing her?" His eyes inspected the ceiling. "I see."

She adjusted her skirt. The "I see" made her insides do a flip flop. What on earth did Zander say? She chose to focus her attention on a small colorful dresser to the left of the room. It imitated a stack of antique books, no doubt a foreign-made item. The lamp, set in the middle on top of the dresser, accentuated its style. She glanced at Mr. Angerton. He watched her with coal-black eyes, as she forced a smooth as silk smile before averting her attention to the bookshelf behind his desk.

The conversation switched into scheduling Zander's next furniture rearrangement. *So, he worked here too.* Soon, the conversation was finished, and the saleswoman rapped lightly and walked into the office.

"I need you to approve credit for this customer." The woman seemed excited until her eyes drifted toward Courtney, where they hardened with contact. Hopefully, Mr. Angerton didn't notice the woman's' attitude and think it could be a potential problem.

Courtney glanced at him, and unfortunately, he seemed to notice the exchange. He stood to his full height. "I'll be there in a minute. We are almost through here." Once the woman left, he asked, "Do you and Daria Barns know one another?"

"I've never met her. Has she lived here long?"

"Lived here long? How did you know that she wasn't from here?"

"Her accent, she sounds like she came from Boston."

He laughed. "Zander did say you are attentive to details. Tell me, what is she wearing?"

A grin tugged Courtney's face, "That's easy, a classic black dress and black leather, closed-toe high heels. A scarf with black, blue, and white swirling designs. Silver jewelry. Her eyes are brown, hair brunette."

He held up his hands, "You have the job. If you pay as much attention to antiques as you do people, you'll do well here."

She planned to do precisely that. "Sir, Zander told me about the antique acquisitions position, I'm very interested in that. I'm willing to travel." *At Leman's expense.*

Mr. Angerton frowned. "We are not ready to move forward yet. Show some success on the floor, and I'll talk about this later."

No problem. She'd have customers eating out of her hand in no time. She smiled as she visualized New York, Atlanta, San Francisco, and her bags packed and ready to go.

⁂

COURTNEY

Hours later, her knuckles paused, ready to rap on Natalie's beautiful antique door, while Courtney rehearsed her requests one more time. She needed Natalie—always a hard sell— to agree to sit with Mother. Several bartering points came to mind as she drove from Leman's Fine Furnishings. *Mother used to run a business with expertise concerning money, and she loves Victorian anything. Natalie could brainstorm event concepts with her.* Those ideas could be vital for acquiring a successful agreement. Complementing Nat's color choices and repairs on the latest interior project would put her in a good mood. Natalie denied that flattery won her over, but everyone who knew her realized the truth. The living and dining room walls were finished at least. Such a tedious, time-consuming activity would have prevented her friend from helping Courtney escape to a day job.

A white van pulled into the driveway and drove behind the house. *What was that about?* She grabbed her tote filled with casual clothes and followed the wraparound porch on the right side of the house. Nat's refurbishing efforts were impressive. Courtney touched the three-tone paint design of the railing spokes and also admired the windows that could now open and close and keep out stray mice. Often, she'd told Natalie that she'd be crazy to buy this fixer-upper-Victorian that her uncle was trying to unload on her. Her best friend's dream wasn't so shallow, after all. Even if Courtney believed it would be a money pit.

Natalie's Uncle Tom's dream-project passed to appreciative hands. Several customers were scheduled to rent the bed and breakfast rooms next month, so she had to finish what she could, quite soon. Nat's breakfasts were legendary. She'd also made a stockpiled of crafts for a store she chose to place in a small room on the first floor. All good reasons for her to have advice from Lillian, as Nat called her. Mother liked to eat and hated to cook so Nat could test her recipes on Lillian. Win, win, win, win, win. Her confidence dug roots into solid arguments. She felt more than ready.

Voices, male and female, gently carried on the wind. Sweet-scented roses perfumed the air making her imagine that she'd tasted Natalie's rose petal dessert again. Oh, to have a piece now.

The voices grew more distinct. "I want four dozen more of

the Peace and six dozen of the Mister Lincoln roses. Can I half-up this package deal for rosebuds at this price? I want three crates of baby's breath and…"

"When do you need these?" The man in blue pants leaned away from his floral transport truck and toward Natalie.

"August twenty-third for a funeral scheduled on Friday."

"Right, sign here please."

"Who died?" The question popped out of Courtney's mouth.

Nat and the man startled. Her friend faced her with a look tightened with agitation.

"I'll go change this outfit. See you in the kitchen." Courtney's imagination revved up. Natalie and funeral flowers? That didn't make sense. But now, she'd slip into something casual before heading home and facing a million questions from Mother.

Natalie gave her the nod and turned back to the man.

Fifteen minutes later, Courtney and Natalie enjoyed the ornate metal table and chairs on the front porch and sipped pink lemonade. "So, you're expanding your business, but you don't want to tell people that you do floral. How do you expect business to thrive if no one can talk about it?"

Natalie blew out a breath and leaned against the flowery cushion behind her. "I want to try it out with one or two orders and see if this is a way I want to expand or not. If it feels right—I'll know to go with it. *Don't* tell anyone."

"Start out small—and you have a funeral planned." Courtney tucked her feet under the chair.

"Remember Sierra from school?" Nat continued before getting a response. "Her relatives are holding a late summer service to remember her uncle with their non-local family. A great-uncle is footing the bill. Frankly, I need to pull in some cash."

"I see. Isn't that expensive to get into, though? That's a whole other business."

"My charge card is straining for sure. Zeta is helping me with some of the tools and arrangement styles. She's sharing her ribbon supplies too." She sneezed.

"Gesundheit! You'd better not be allergic to this new side business." They laughed. "I'm glad Zeta can help you out. So, will you still make it to Bethany's wedding? The twenty-fourth is the big day."

Natalie scrunched her forehead, "Your right, I don't believe I got a card on that yet."

Courtney cringed. "That's what I have to do today." So many details. So little time. "I got a job." She turned in her chair, twisting a little to face Natalie.

Her friend squinted. "And this means what to me? You have *the look*."

Seriously, the look? Courtney broke eye contact and found the lemonade in her glass fascinating for the first time since she sat down. "Sometimes, Mother will need company when I'm at work." Courtney peeked at her friend's expressionless face—no response—whatsoever, "You see, I landed the job at Leman's Fine Furnishings. I'll need money to move out as soon as Mother is on her own."

"Going crazy already?"

"Yep." She pulled out her, *please pity me smile*.

"You just moved in there. Why should I put myself in your spot and make myself crazy?" Natalie's expression teetered on smug.

"Because you love me."

"No, that's not it."

Courtney leaned closer. "Because you could ask Mother anything Victorian-businesslike and she'd be brilliant. You love to cook—she loves to eat. Experiment on her."

A wicked smile braced Natalie's lips. "So, you'd stoop to offering all things Victorian through Lillian's expertise."

"I do."

"I will."

Nine

COURTNEY

Coffee and burnt toast—typical morning aromas—followed Courtney as she rushed around, making time to accomplish Zander's day-to-day assignment of walking Puddles.

She almost heard the warmth of his voice whispering behind them as they left her parents' home. "Walk her early in the morning when it's not too hot." His eyes had found hers as though he could read her mind. "You need to do this, so she'll get used to your commands." He really seemed to want her to succeed. But, one look at the Leonberger fueled her doubt.

Her white Nikes—not so brilliant now because of muddy paw prints—jogged their way down the sidewalk flanked by grass freshly-sprinkled with morning dew. Seven o'clock seemed perfect since Mother still slept, and work didn't start for a couple of hours. Another bonus was that the dog hadn't bounced into her energetic self—yet. Puddles only pulled off course when she'd recognized squirrel bait or rabbit soufflé crossing their pathway or teasing from the bushes. Those were rare occurrences, though. Still, progress increased or vanished according to how much she listened to Zander's advice.

The sun hung low above the hills leaking apricot, grape, and blueberry colors across the sky, making her so hungry she'd pour some of those fruit choices into a bowl of yogurt with granola once they returned home, and a cinnamon roll from Oram's Donut Shop. It was worth waiting in line yesterday for their delicious treats. She'd probably gain back every pound she burnt-up on the pavement. How could such effort be worth all that time and energy?

Twenty minutes later, they entered through the gate in the backyard. Courtney closed the sliding glass door, and Puddles collapsed in a heap on the tile, panting heavily, and leaving a small pool of drool. If only the dog listened to Courtney the same way, she did Zander. His commanding presence could make any dog cower or jump for joy with an expression or a word. *Or any girl.* Except this girl. This girl was immune. Well, honestly, the only female captivated by his charms barked her greeting and wagged her tail.

COURTNEY

Arriving on time for the first day of her job—Courtney almost did a dance in the parking lot. Even after feeding and walking the dog and providing a couple of keep-her-mother-busy projects, in addition to planning dinner and getting ready for work. It seemed incredible that she could stand outside Leman's Fine Furnishings and feel so ready to begin. But this was definitely the last time she'd get up at 4:00 a.m.

She hated to admit that this job provided a new sense of direction and purpose beyond the promise of a definite cash flow. Desperation to own her own home or apartment drove her on. Knocking on Leman's doorway accomplished nothing. Peering through the glass entryway revealed lights shining inside. A shadow moved across the back; someone was already here, but why didn't they answer the door? Enthusiasm dropped several levels since the shadow looked like Daria. Now she'd have to make-believe she enjoyed being here.

Mr. Angerton parked his car and turned off the ignition. He smiled at her as he approached to unlock the entrance. "Just what I like to see, a punctual employee."

As the door released its grip, Daria's soft laughter floated over the quiet morning from the offices in the back. So, she was the first employee to have arrived. Her heels clicked against the linoleum floor as she approached them with a cell phone pressed to her ear. She squinted up and saw them. Dropping her phone, she shirked.

Courtney bit her lip and turned her face as though she were interested in furniture to the left to keep from laughing aloud.

"Daria, it's only us. If you punched in, then you're on the clock."

She bent down to retrieve her phone, then whispered, "Gota go." Then she slipped her cell inside the right front suit jacket pocket. "Sorry, Bruce." She smoothed her hair and turned on the toe of her shoe to retreat toward the back.

"I want Courtney to learn the filing and register protocol. Also, familiarize her with the floor. Teach her how to greet customers after you are sure she knows furnishings and sale info." Mr. Angerton's voice roped Daria's shoes to the floor and prevented her from withdrawing further.

"Absolutely." Her eyes turned on Courtney and pinned her with disdain. "What about the *new* employee paperwork?

"She stayed yesterday to complete those. Zander said she's skilled with customers and knows antique furniture." He turned toward Courtney and nodded before heading in the direction of the command center.

"Zander." Daria's brow puckered at the mention of his

name. "Well, come on then." Not waiting for a reply, she made a beeline for the back of the store.

Another female—interested in Zander. It would be amusing to see if Daria would bat her eyes and turn syrupy sweet once he walked through the door. Did she hide her snooty attitude from him? Under Courtney's breath, she said to no one but herself, "Compared to Mother, you're a walk in the park." She smiled to herself. "I can do this, yes I can. All the way to the bank." A glance toward her feet made her happy that she'd chosen her low-heeled pumps today. A marathon of linoleum miles was about to begin.

COURTNEY

Later that day, Courtney stood in the hallway of her parent's home. Mother reclined in her chair on the other side of the wall. The visit to the Stationary Shop had turned out to be more time consuming then she'd hoped, but that purchase couldn't be postponed again. The shower date approached at break-neck speed, and her nerves screamed and performed flip flops to prove that fact. Bethany had e-mailed the names for the invitation list and told Courtney where she'd hidden the address book—top drawer in the chunky hutch, on the dining room wall—across town in Bethany's empty house.

Enlisting Mother might make her feel included and shorten the completion time. She swallowed unwelcome feelings and commanded ugly thoughts to back down. She could do all things through Christ who strengthens her. Just as Apostle Paul wrote. Slow, determined steps brought her next to Mother's chair in the living room. "What do you think about writing some of Bethany's invitations with me today?"

The television glared back as the recorded soap opera

played. Mother mumbled something then pushed the remote to mute. Now she turned full attention to Courtney. "Fine, do you have them already?"

She smiled, inviting Mother to enjoy the simple yet classic design as she showed the embossed card, decorated with metallic gold letters and edged with a simple, crisp gold border.

"Silver is better. Is it too late to change this order?"

Courtney stiffened, "All done and paid for." *Respond briefly.* It wouldn't help to remind her that Bethany was a gold, not silver girl. Mother ignored such simple facts. "We have very little time to send these out. I wish Bethany were here so we could write these together." She forced an unwilling smile across her face and headed toward the dining room table.

"Bethany is busy. She knows it's time to find the perfect job, now that she's *graduated*." Courtney turned to see Mother beam like a rare splash of sunshine until they locked eyes. "You going to help me with these, or am I on my own?" She shook her crutches with short jabs.

Courtney moved to the dining room table and dropped the boxes of cards and pens before she returned. Mother's musk scent pressed the air stealing her breath while she linked arms to help her up. *Was that a tremble?* Courtney looked straight into her mother's face, who diverted her focus to the television.

Tomorrow she'd mention her new job. Precious Natalie, her savior, agreed to sit for the day with Puddles and Mother as long as Courtney shared the carrot pie recipe that tasted like orange sherbet. She hoped she didn't run out of desirable recipes.

Several minutes later, Mother's perfectly manicured fingernails picked up the gel pen, and she wrote the first address, her penmanship had always been neat and precise. Today her hands quivered slightly. "I'm thirsty."

Courtney stood. Leaving the room would be a great option. Her mother's presence felt heavily equipped with discouragement.

Dad entered. "Passport, Lillian, have you seen it?" His nervous confusion—customary before every trip—made them laugh after he completed packing and stepped on the plane, but not before.

As Courtney padded down the carpeted living room, her mother's soft voice trailed after her, "On your chest of drawers inside your wood box."

The silver tray would be perfect for carrying the iced tea and decaf coffee. While she waited for the pot to percolate, she tossed some extra ice cubes into the pitcher. Puddles slept outside in a contented heap under a Maple tree. Their fenced-in yard proved to be perfect for the dog.

Courtney breathed in the scent of coffee and slid her eyelids closed for a few seconds. Renewal flooded her mind and steadied the nerves that her mother's negativity had deflated moments ago. She couldn't explain why, but she knew the Lord was present. But why, when others were more worthy than her? Wrapping her arms around herself, she waited, not wanting to move and lose the sense of closeness. She was a beloved daughter. At least to the Lord, though doubt nipped at her sneakers and darkened the brightness of the moment.

She shook herself as if she'd been in a dream. What just happened—she didn't know, but she wanted more of the same. Refocusing her attention, she chose two different flavored waters. That would be a nice touch. Her stomach grumbled, alerting her to the fact that Lorna Doone cookies were a present necessity. She moved to fill the tray. The cookies fit snug inside a small cut glass bowl. Anticipating her mother's surprise stretched a genuine king-size smile on her face. This should be fun.

A small pile of completed invitations rested in the center of the dining room table. Mother lifted her head. As soon as she spied the tray, her mouth dropped open. The thrill of canceling the expected criticism fizzled joy inside Courtney's heart.

"Coffee or tea?"

"Water." Mother stated with brows lifted. Watchful.

Courtney set the tray down. She moved both of the waters hidden by the coffee carafe in front of her mother. "Need a glass?"

The astonished woman's shoulders flinched. "No, that will be fine." She tossed a look at Courtney. "Thank you."

Courtney stifled a laugh, grabbed her pen, and began to create her own little pile of envelopes.

LILLIAN

Lillian held back a complaint as Dan shoved her wheelchair away from the push of the crowd before their daughter bent to hug her.

"I'm home. I'm really home, Mom." Bethany's face glowed with welcome, contrasting the anxious, slow-moving crowd at Pittsburgh International Airport headed their way. "An early morning hour shouldn't bother anyone. But look at them, business people in suits, wailing children, and overheated parents, pushing down the hallway in a race to grab their luggage."

"It won't be long before you're married." Lillian basked in her daughter's welcome. Earlier, she'd felt the burn creep up her face when Dan suggested—no insisted—that she use a wheelchair. Her body might seem fragile, but her spirits never dipped into real dependence. And she let them all know that too. Yet, gratitude warmed her heart for sitting and not having to walk so far, but she'd not tell them. She glanced at her watch. They had plenty of time to drop Dan off for his plane—destined overseas. Her eyes watered so much that they could spill over at any moment. The dreaded day for her husband's departure had marked their calendar with a black check off that promised many empty days to follow.

"I forgot my sunglasses." His furrowed brow deepened. "I absolutely need protective eyewear.

"You always forget your sunglasses. That's why we arrive a half-hour earlier than the normal required time." Lillian arranged her face into a grin for him.

His appreciative smile still held such power over her, after all these years. His feet pointed toward the escalators, seemingly eager to go. Lillian's heart pinched. Wasn't he always ready to go? They headed for the Central Core of the Airmall. He'd already checked in for his flight, so now they could shop.

"A cap first, I'll want that type of eye protection too."

"We'll find what you need." She decided to provide the perfect cap or two, which would match his outfits.

As soon as they arrived at the Central Core, they found Lids. She maneuvered back and forth to view the many hat choices. In the corner of her eye, she saw Dan motioned for Courtney to talk privately. She strained her attention in their direction and could barely hear them.

"Your mother doesn't want me to tell you this. But I must." He lowered his head toward Courtney. His voice lowered, becoming gravelly. "The doctors are concerned about the trembling and dizziness she's experiencing. They have run a number of tests, and we are still waiting for the results."

"When did this all start?"

He turned away. The tone of his voice faded. "It's been a while." Grave concern weighted his words.

Heat singed her heart. How dare they talk about her as though she were crippled. She'd show them. Lillian moved the footrests to the up position and then gripped the armrests of her wheelchair. She stood failing to remember to lock the wheels—the chair slipped from behind.

"How long?" Courtney's voice trailed her as she hit the floor.

The last thing she noticed was the puzzled, desperate look on Courtney's usually hard to read face and the hectic cries from Bethany that grew louder as she came near.

Ten

COURTNEY

"How many job interviews did you go to already?" Courtney snapped a picture, with her cell, capturing the wedding colors spilled over the white blanket between them as they sat cross-legged on Bethany's queen size bed. Dangerous laughter bubbled inside her, which would need a cork if she let it loose. Bethany's excitement grew almost tangible, electrifying the air with expectation. Didn't the very room seem brighter?

"Two interviews, but I have three more spread out over this next week. I've looked at several houses too. Otherwise, Brandon and I just hang out and discover the area together." Her voice floated wistful, dreamy on the warm current of air.

Filling colored netting squares with tiny pastel mints became challenging as they swapped stories and shared laughter. Together they tied navy-blue ribbon, securing tags announcing Mr. and Mrs. Strege with gold metallic ink.

She tossed the phone down and scooped up ten of the favors and tossed them into the box beside the bed.

"Twenty more to fill." Courtney stretched and rubbed the back of her neck. "Oh, let me show you what you sent out for invitations." She flopped her legs over the side of the mattress, feeling the stiffness painfully unfold as her feet met carpet. She reached inside her tote to lift the weighty framed invitation. "Your first wedding memorabilia."

"Yuck, couldn't you have picked silver?" They crumbled into laughter. "Well, had I shown Mother the design one day too soon, it would have been silver."

"Thanks." Bethany leaned toward Courtney and gave her a squeeze. "Did you find the dresses yet?" Hope skidded up and held its breath as the quiet air between them begged an answer.

"Well, no, not yet. I have the girls lined up for two Monday evening appointments. One is for Gwendolyn's Wedding & Formal Attire."

"Impressive. More than I imagined."

Courtney sobered. She laid the framed invitation on top of the dresser and turned as though admiring the bookcase.

"I'm saying I left you so much to accomplish by yourself. Plus, you're taking care of Mom and Puddles and working. The frame for the announcement is perfect, by the way."

"Thanks." Courtney turned and pressed a smile toward her sister. Of course, Bethany didn't mean to insult. Life had become so demanding, and sleep at times fleeting. Her nerves wore raw by Mother's presence. She shook her head to banish the negative emotions. There could be no room for sensitive types in the MacDuff family. Especially now that Dad flew away with the secret—

"You didn't tell me about Puddles and Zander."

"Not much to tell." Courtney flopped on the bed to help finish making the favors. She combed her fingers through her hair to fluff and separate stubborn tangles. Her stomach ached. One day his videos would be finished, and her incompetence exposed to the world. Would there be anything outside of blackmail she could threaten to make him destroy that dream?

She had nothing over him, but he held every advantage over her.

"Spill the goods, Courtney. What's that look about?"

"No look." Denial dragged her eyes everywhere else around the room, except to her sister's face.

"Tell me about the training sessions with Puddles and Zander?" Bethany leaned in. Vanilla fragrance, her sister always wore, softened the air between them.

"The first and only training was—a disaster."

Her sister narrowed her eyes and tilted her head as though searching for more details.

"Puddles listened to him, ignored me, and I ate dirt when I fell on my face. He laughed, and then he canceled the second meeting for last night because he had an important meeting with an *important* client."

"Oh." Her sister leaned backward to scoop-up the wedding shower favors pooled at her feet and dropped them in the box. "Did you learn anything?"

"That I'm not any more of a dog person than I ever was." When he called to cancel training film number two, relief had flooded her mind. Yes, Puddles responded to the training and became more manageable, but Courtney's pride couldn't handle the aftermath of the video series. Somehow obtaining the reputation and fame for being the girl who ate dirt and knew nothing about dog communication or discipline didn't excite her. *How shocking.* This was as bad as ending up on Funniest Home Video's for all the world to see. And laugh at.

Laughter was only good when she could call the shots.

"I've got the feeling that Puddles will grow on you. Keep training with Zander. You'll see a good friend and companion come out of this."

Who did she mean? The man or the dog? Well, she wouldn't ask. "Did I say I was going to quit training?" Her voice pitched higher before she could stop it. She had every intention of quitting. But how could she now? Bethany was watching for any of what she called *Courtney's drop-out-tendencies.* What she called—finding a reasonable excuse. Zander could become tired of the no-pay-check arrangement and find other important business meetings to attend. Like he already had. One could only hope.

Bethany smiled, her pastel blue eyes signaled challenge. "I bet you quit the dog classes in—less than two weeks." She straightened out her bedspread and plumped her pillows.

Courtney's mouth dropped open, and she tried unsuccessfully to hide the shock.

Her sister burst out laughing. "I knew it. Does Zander have any idea?"

She tucked her head, "Not yet. I'm just not a dog person. Dogs are—so much work. Who knows when or if Tanya will ever return?" Though any seeing Tanya would be too soon, it would be more convenient for the woman to pick up her abandoned dog. She picked up the snow-white blanket, and the fragrance of mint enveloped her. Straightening the uneven corners, she folded the blanket in half. Why couldn't life be easily arranged? Predictable?

Laying the bedding on the hamper, she felt drained. But she just couldn't quit. There was no escape route in sight. Must be losing her knack.

"Have you heard anything about Tanya?"

"Well, not her, but I did hear that Mr. Mancel, who owns the mansion on Belleview Drive, bought our apartment complex for a song."

"What would he want with your apartments? Doesn't that man own enough around here?"

"Maybe he liked my decorating skills or something. Let's not talk about him." *Or her broken dream.*

"What did Dad say to you at the airport? You seemed upset."

Courtney squared her shoulders. "When do you mean?"

"You know when I mean. At the Airmall, when we were picking out Dad's hats. Before Mom fell. What did he say to you?"

She needed to skirt this conversation. Dad swore her to secrecy as he'd kissed her good-by. Bethany's biggest, maybe only fault, was that she couldn't keep a secret. If her life were at risk, she'd still tell-all. Especially juicy secrets. "I'm thinking."

"You're a Christian. Lie to me, and you'll get a spankin' from the Lord."

Guilt, her sister resorted to guilt. "Well, I—"

A saucy Spanish tune played on her phone. Zander. Excellent interruption. Bethany seemed as intent on digging up Dad's secret as she was hooking her up with Zander. "I need to get this. Hey, Zander."

Bethany's eyes crinkled a smile before she lay down on the bed sideways.

"Such a deal I have for you." His deep voice poured through the phone like sweet cream.

"Does it include filming the movie?"

"Oh, I didn't know you were so eager to get a copy." His deep voice rumbled humor.

"How about not producing the video. Please destroy any copies you have." She gathered empty mint bags and wasted netting then tossed them into a trash can while she listened.

"Never fear, the first couple of lessons are deeply edited. I didn't realize you were this averse to taping. Trust me, you'll be pleased."

"I'm sure the only pleasure I could experience from that video is its total annihilation." His laughter boosted her spirits despite the touchy topic. Maybe, just maybe, he'd hear her concern and agree to make another video attempt—staring someone else?

"What I'm calling about is the contract for your furniture.

I need to rent it for longer than this month. Would you be willing?"

She plopped on the bed, sending Bethany bouncing and falling over. "I'll have to think about this. Once Mother is better, I'm renting my own place. I want my furniture with me, so I can settle in."

"I understand. That's why I'm willing to pay you twice the amount I'm paying now."

"Twice, huh." She sat up straighter. Hours at the furniture store fluctuated, and she would more than likely have to find another job to make ends meet. She could benefit from commissions, but then again, she'd have to acquire sales. And she'd not been allowed on the floor to sell yet. Not to mention that she'd have to wait for full-time employment until Mother didn't need her so much. Sigh. "Do these people like my furniture that much?"

"Not the same place where your furniture is staging now. I'm talking about the important client I canceled our dog training for last night. They have a vintage Victorian house that fits your furniture exactly. They'll move soon and take their belongings with them. They're excited about how your furniture could attract buyers, show off the home's charm—for a quicker sale."

Thoughts and feelings warred in her mind. She liked to move and become settled at once. How would she claim her new space if she didn't have her favorite pieces? How could she afford not to, though?

"I'll have to think about it first, Zander."

"Sure, but I need to know by tomorrow. No pressure though."

"Oh, no pressure felt over here." Her words strained across her larynx.

"Your car was at Leman's today, but I didn't see you. Where

were you hiding? Or did they send you off on your first purchase for their new antique department?"

"I wish. Daria headed me into the office to sort through files and look through inventory books to become familiar with them. She wanted to test me later to see if I could be trusted on the floor." And that never happened. Just as she'd expected.

"She had you there for two hours, at least."

"Oh, she did. She seems to want me to become an expert in filing." Courtney smiled to herself. Daria seemed to be very interested in Zander. Did he know that?

"Don't let her stick you back there all the time. If she does—you'll never sell anything. Gaining commission will be a thrill, I imagine."

"I'm determined to take my commission opportunities seriously."

"Those poor unsuspecting persons who you'll get hold of! They'll not stand a chance."

"Mr. Angerton seems to think that same way about me, especially after whatever you told him. Thank you, I should buy you dinner, but I've not received a paycheck yet."

"What are you doing tonight?" His voice grew serious. "Want me to meet you at your Mother's house? We can play *The Humiliation of Courtney?*"

"I definitely don't want to watch it at my mother's. Tonight, we are packing up Bethany's kitchen and knickknacks."

"If I bring dinner for us, can I show you and Bethany what we have filmed? You could sign the release for me— if you like it."

"Release form?" If only she'd known that bit of information. How much worry would have been averted and sleep regained if she'd thought to ask details about this project? She'd know better next time. "I'll stick it right on top of the pizza box if you let me come over right now."

"Are you—begging?" Courtney drummed her fingers on the floral bedspread. She mouthed to her sister," Is it okay if Zander comes over with dinner?"

"Ahh. You could say that." His voice dipped a few notes.

Bethany sparkled and nodded at Courtney. Then she jumped up, bouncing the bed, knocking Courtney back, before she headed toward the kitchen.

"Bring another movie besides *The Humiliation of Courtney,* and we're on."

Eleven

LILLIAN

One step. Another. Almost in reach. Lillian halted next to the kitchen table. Muscles ached from her recent ungraceful fall. Nasty metal walker, but at least, for now, it worked better than crutches. The beautiful kitchen seemed to close in on her today. She squinted at the oak table, reflecting sharp patches of light bordering the abandoned plans and wedding notes—the lists she needed had to be easy to find.

She craned her neck to see if Courtney could see her from the backyard. There, at the far side of the fence, she repeated commands and motions, trying unsuccessfully to train that rambunctious puppy. Right next to the crabapple inhabited by a squirrel. Squirrels were Puddles downfall, and if Courtney didn't learn that, she couldn't learn anything. No dog would pay attention to her when interesting vermin were around.

All morning she'd listened as Courtney made phone calls for Bethany with that cheerful, phony lilt of hers. Ordering flowers, music, and finding the reception hall. The phone calls she should be making, but was denied.

Once Courtney took off to take care of that hairy dog, Lillian decided it was time to move. Where was that phone list?

Numbers came into focus on a yellow lined tablet flipped open and weighted down by a rock paperweight. All the information she needed seemed to be here. Lillian leaned closer, observing the huge stars next to the chosen businesses. Courtney hadn't cleverly hidden this information.

An acidy taste filled her mouth. This was proof. Courtney wanted to rub her face in the fact that Lillian was left out of planning one of Bethany's most significant events. This list of numbers wouldn't have been exposed unless it was done deliberately. Lately, no one cared about her feelings. Even Dan. She hiccupped. A ball of pain lodged in her throat. Her fingers trembled as she rested them on the tabletop. She swallowed hard.

She knew how to run a business. Look how many years she'd proven her ability with QAK Company. Since she'd retired, did they think they could ignore her? Well, she'd show, Courtney. Bethany wouldn't exclude her without being influenced.

Peering at the list, she blanched. How could Courtney choose Clark's Flowers over her friend's business, Jenson's Favorites & Flowers Boutique? Clark's limited selection offered cheap spiritless flowers of a more modern arrangement. Nothing traditionally Victorian. Lillian skimmed past the price lists beside each of the flower shop's information. The house phone lay so near her fingertips she couldn't resist. She gripped it though her hand trembled. That quiver probably showed her excitement—of being a part of her daughter's wedding—and showing Courtney she was no invalid. Not yet.

Peeking outside, once more. They were still occupied. She'd have time. "She punched in the numbers. Waited. "Hello, this is Lillian MacDuff. I'm calling for Bethany MacDuff's wedding."

"Oh, we are thrilled—"

"Yes, ahh. Well, I'm calling to cancel the order. You see, my daughter changed her mind. Thank you. Good-by."

She dialed again. "Mary."

"Hi, Lillian."

"I want to order flowers for Bethany's wedding."

"I was beginning to think you weren't going to call."

"Yes." Another peek outside—they were headed her way. "It took Courtney long enough to include me in the planning, but here I am. Mary, I'm in a hurry" Laughter and barking moved closer. Her heart pounded. "Color, pink and white. Do you have a package deal?"

"What type of flowers—"

"My—our favorite flowers, Calla Lilies, irises, some exotic flowers with bright pink tips." She pushed the words out as though she were in a fast run. "Yes, and tip the White Dahlia's for the groom and best man with just a touch of pink also."

"How many—"

"Three, bridesmaids and grooms."

Courtney unhooked Puddles from the training leash and yelled a greeting to the neighbor as though they lived in the slums or something. *Hurry Mary!* It wouldn't do to get caught. She slid the list over in its original place on the table.

Her heart knocked like kettledrums. Mary's ordering methods needed tweaking. Especially for customers who experienced time constraints. She leaned over for a better look. A mere four feet from the door. Courtney put her in this position, making her hide when all she wanted to do was help Bethany. "I'll call you back with more details as they arise…"

"Just two more days, and then you can't cancel this order."

"Now, why would I cancel an order?" Her heart pinched. "I've got to run. Bye." She hung up the phone and slipped it onto the table, then gazed off to the left as though admiring her kitchen cabinets for the first time.

The glass door slid open. "Oh, Mother. How did you get in

here?" Lillian turned to face her. Courtney stood smiling from the doorway. Probably laughing at her, just as her sister-in-law did years ago.

COURTNEY

Courtney's eyes shifted toward the yellow tablet on the table. Breath escaped her. Nothing looked altered or crossed out from where she stood. Mother acted as though she was the cat who swallowed the gerbil, but otherwise, she seemed unaware of the information resting at her elbow.

To see her get around again, even if it had to be with the walker bubbled gratitude inside her. How she'd accomplished standing today, by herself with all those bruises, was a mystery. Such a naturally independent woman would hate being hampered from charging into busy committee meetings and volunteering like she always did when Dad worked away.

A week ago, she'd fallen, and dad worried that she'd fall again. How long would it take to heal those bruises and achy muscles? A rush of hurt swept over her heart. Missing her father and the desire to move stung her anew.

Though she loved Mother, well, she was quite difficult. Guilt jabbed her in the ribs for eagerly awaiting her independence. No one could pick their relations after all. She pushed out a smile and scanned Mother's face. Judging from the frown reflecting back—that wish about choosing one's relatives—was mutual.

And it stung. She should be used to it.

Obviously, Bethany saw something she didn't. Her sister had told her that doing her best for this wedding would earn Mother's favor. Unease hovered like a black storm cloud hiding a deluge. Why did these thoughts always inspire her to write?

Nidella's next scene ricocheted inside her mind. A genuine smile forced its way forward. She turned toward the refrigerator, "Mother, would you like something to eat or drink?"

"Yes, some French toast would be good. Coffee too. Can you help me into the living room? I'm tired now."

"Would you like a movie instead of television?" Courtney noticed her mother glance at the wedding list and smile. Her heart warmed and expanded its beats. Mother appeared—proud—of her efforts! She couldn't wait to tell Bethany that she might be right after all.

COURTNEY

"Natalie, can you host the pedicure bachelorette party tonight?"

"Tonight, what's the rush?" Something metallic fell to the ground. "Oh, no."

Courtney rubbed her ear. "Looks like I'm not the only one with butterfingers. Bethany is heading back to Indianapolis tomorrow morning. Is Zeeta Zookey available?"

Sigh. "Zeta Zachek is not a problem. She's here now. I suppose it will be fine. I have everything I need already. I'll run the sweeper and make dessert. Sure, bring the gang over."

"Another favor, I know you saw a lot of Mother the other day when I had to work, but can I bring her?"

"Really, why? Sorry, if you want to. I'll need one more foot soaker. You have one, right?"

"I have one. I'll bring it, and if you don't mind, I'll bring pizza for dinner."

"Papa John's Pizza?" Her voice climbed, ethereal delight. The phone dropped and clanged against metal.

After an immediate wince, Courtney waited for her friend's

sigh. "Absolutely. Hey, let's hang up before you hurt yourself." She finished wiping French toast mess off the kitchen counter. Puddles lay against her ankles, so she dared not step backward, or they'd both get hurt.

She dialed Bethany, "The pedicure bachelorette party is set for tonight at Natalie's."

Bethany squealed. "How did you manage to work that out?" Though she didn't love Victorian, she did love Natalie's friend's pedicures. Cassie and Nicole would luxuriate in the whole experience.

"I twisted Natalie's arm, and I asked her if Mother can come. She said yes."

"Perfect, thank you, Butterfingers." The nickname her dad penned for her made her heart ache for his presence. They still hadn't heard if he arrived safely. Sometimes it took him several days to contact family when settling in for a job out of the country. Mother usually stayed by the phone until she'd gotten to talk with him.

"Wait, how will we get Mother inside her house? Victorian—all those steps?"

"Natalie has a ramp for situations like this at the back of the house. I'll need to park near the garage, so let the girls know not to block us." Mother could walk up the ramp, it wouldn't be easy, just do-able. "We're bringing Papa John's Pizza."

Her sister laughed and said, "My favorite. You've thought of everything."

<hr />

COURTNEY

Zander called Courtney half an hour later. "Can you bring Puddles to class tonight?"

"If you want her you can have her all by yourself. I'm taking Mother to Bethany's bachelorette party."

"A bit early to have that party, isn't it?"

"It's now or never. Bethany has more interviews and house searches to do." Sigh. "There is so much to order and decide yet. Planning a wedding is a full-time job, let me tell you."

"As long as you don't quit Leman's before I collect on that bet with your mother."

Courtney laughed. "Yes, that should be one of my main priorities, though I doubt that Daria will ever let me out of that back room. So, you still won't win Mother's bet." She tapped the breaks and waited for the sports car to pass her at the intersection of 11th Street and 7th Ave. Traffic broke up and flowed smoothly now that rush hour had passed. She took a right turn and followed traffic, making the PT's four cylinders kick to life and pull her forward.

"I'll take Puddles tonight and babysit if you promise to come and train with us tomorrow night."

"I'm working the later shift tomorrow night—no can do." Mr. Whippier had switched his schedule with a co-worker. Her most un-favorite man would be training her. Who would be worse to work with, Whippier or Daria? Tomorrow would nix any guesswork on that question.

"Tomorrow morning, then?"

"My my, are we in a hurry to train her—how come?" She used this filler line as she scanned the excuses she'd been working through. None of them seemed potent enough. If they didn't convince her, they wouldn't sway Zander either.

"I have to wait until all the edits are finished before I can launch this side business. Dog training has always been a passion. I have an investor waiting to see if he wants to risk backing me for national exposure."

Courtney's heart spun and missed beats like a stone skipping along the surface of the lake. The DVD again. She couldn't let herself be humiliated in front of the great USA. National exposure—there would be nowhere to hide after their release. What a hit they'd be, just look under humor… at her expense.

"You still there, Courtney?"

Courtney found herself at the end of her parent's street. How had she passed their house? "Wha… what? Oh, I can't get my thoughts wrapped around it." She jerked the wheel to turn the PT in a tight U-turn before hanging a right into the driveway.

"Excited? This must be a thrill for you. I can't tell you how I appreciate your helping me out here."

She'd start looking for another home for the dog immediately. Her heart stung at the thought. Her original reason for keeping Puddles failed miserably. No way she'd allow herself to become attached. Was that even possible? "Sure Zander."

As soon as Mother handled life on her own—it was apartment hunting time. Oh, to purchase her own house, but with the foreclosure—well, couldn't that take years to clear up? That research would have to wait for when she had a moment to breathe. Did apartment complexes allow dogs like Puddles? She had to consider that in case no one wanted a behemoth for a pet.

What was she thinking…keeping Puddles! Why even think about it? A quick change, that's what she needed before her heart got in the way.

"Courtney, the connection is breaking…can…call you later?"

The words passed through the cell in chunks, but she understood his meaning. "Sure, call me after the pedicure party." She emphasized each word.

"I'm home, drop off Puddles any time. Later." The connection died. Courtney shuddered at the void that filled the car. The emptiness that would increase once she told him she couldn't keep Puddles. Zander would never understand her de-

cision. He counted on her. Didn't everyone lately? It all felt...
overwhelming.

Stepping through the living room archway, she paused to
watch Puddles and her mother. Mother focused on the latest
soap opera, and Puddles stretched her head backward, to be
pet, while she warmed her mother's feet and legs. Her mother's trembling fingers stroked Puddle's neck and ears with what
looked like continuous absentminded repetition.

Courtney tiptoed backward and cleared her throat, making
her footsteps louder to alert Mother of her presence. Just as she
thought, Mother drew back her hand and folded her arms in
front of her chest. "Took you long enough."

Courtney glanced at her watch, early by twenty minutes.
"Where's your friend Samantha Jenson?" The driveway was ab-
sent a car, and from what she could see, there was no sign that
anyone had visited.

"She came, she went. Otherwise, it's just been Puddles and
me." Her mother's eyes turned in the direction of the canine
who had jumped up and spun around to meet Courtney with
the raw raw rawwww rawwww. Then she hopped and tried to
take Courtney's arm in her hand to lead her into the living
room.

"Don't allow her to grab your arm and lead. I read in this
book," Mother's finger pointed to a very thick book on the
table to the right of her chair, "that behavior is a show of dominance. She'll never listen if you do."

"I thought you didn't like to read." Courtney wiggled her
arm out of the puppy's grip. "Sit."

Puddles sat immediately and looked at her with puppy
worship.

Sigh, Courtney's heart beat a treacherous rhythm. She
tugged on her shirt and shifted her shoulders and glanced away.
Soon Puddles would have to relocate.

"Zander would be proud of you right now," Mother said.

A bittersweet smile stole a spot on her face at those words of praise. That would change in a sliver of time.

COURTNEY

Courtney popped the trunk and grabbed three hot pizzas to bring inside Natalie's kitchen door. "I'll be right back, Mother."

A woman Courtney had never met before opened the door wide. Platinum blond and gray hair lead her to believe this woman must be in her mid-fifties. The utter shock on the lady's face struck Courtney as odd.

"Did your mom come?" Natalie asked as she breezed into the kitchen carrying folded towels and washrags.

"She came. And she's eager to find a seat on one of your fancy couches." She glanced at the older woman. "Mother loves Victorian."

"Yes, she does." The woman said as though she knew.

Courtney puzzled her response—

"Papa John's Pizza!" Natalie made an obnoxious sniff in the air. "I can imagine what your mother says about this dinner." Natalie chanced a glance outside. "You'd better bring her inside." She turned toward them. "Have you met Zeta Zachek, my famous Miss Z?"

Courtney glanced at the retreating woman in question as she headed toward the door leading into the dining room. Compassion welled in her heart. The lady seemed so utterly shy. "No, I've only heard about the results of Zeta Zachek's work." She offered her best smile in hopes that she could make her feel welcome—if she'd turn around.

The woman's footfalls quit. She twisted and aimed a smile

at Courtney that seemed familiar somehow before she fumbled with her hands and then burst from the room.

Courtney and Natalie gazed at each other in total silence. The hot pizzas burnt the tips of her fingers and began to grow heavy. She walked to the kitchen counter and laid them down. "Is she always so withdrawn?"

"In all the time I've had her work for me, I've never seen that reaction." Opening a drawer, she laid the towels and wash rags inside. Natalie bumped the drawer closed with her hip.

A car horn blared. Courtney jumped. "Mother, I forgot her."

Nat nodded and grabbed the pizza cutter and plates, while Courtney sped out the door. Minutes later, Mother's impressive moves up the incline were better than she'd dared to hope.

They stepped inside, and Lillian said, "I thought you'd have a fancier kitchen than this."

"Many people think this kitchen should be fancier, but I wanted an authentic Victorian kitchen. Natalie grabbed the dip and crackers and moved toward the door. "Follow me, ladies."

"Mother, you go first." They made their way into an elegant dining room fragrant with pizza. Their shoes clattered against hardwood floors, the noise broken only by the Oriental rug positioned under the large oval table and chairs set. Thick draperies parted, allowing the last rays of the afternoon's sun to peek through the window panes and spill onto an ornate still-life painting hung from a cord attached to the trim near the ceiling. Mother stopped dead when it came into view.

"That's new. You took my advice and purchased an authentic piece, didn't you?" Courtney loved it when she'd influenced Natalie in a positive way. It was as though she'd given something valuable to a very precious friend.

"Miss Z. gave it to me. I had to hang it right away to catch your reaction."

"Exquisite." That was her only word for the grace and elegance captured in the painted snapshot of another time.

Nat squirmed with joy she wrestled to hide, but her eyes glowed with satisfaction. She was surrounded by her dream come true. "We'll feast and visit before we enjoy a pedicure."

Beveled glass squares in the French doors sparkled as they divided the dining elegance from the living room. The doorbell rang. Zeta darted across the hallway to answer the need. Bethany and her bridesmaids, Cassie and Nicole, moved inside to join those at the dining table.

"Mom, I'm so glad you could come tonight." Bethany held out her arms to embrace Lillian.

But Zeta leaned into the room and grabbed her purse off a chair located close to the beveled door. As she did so, her face turned, revealing her profile.

Mother gasped and crumbled into a chair, keeping her glare fixed toward the entryway.

"Mom, are you all right?" Bethany's voice strained with the words.

Zeta hesitated as she grasped the antique doorknob, pulled it open fast, then fled through the open door. Windows shuddered as she pulled the door closed with force.

Natalie and Courtney gave each other a hard stare.

"Everyone, please, take a seat and dig in." This highly un-Victorian announcement served its purpose before Natalie left the room with her cell phone clutched in hand.

Twelve

COURTNEY

Conversation hummed around the flickering candle-light at Natalie's dining room table. Bethany, Cassie, and Nicole traded pizza slices, laughter, and stories. Courtney sensed her Mother's restlessness. Her usual launch into the middle of the conversation and stay there with enthusiasm—vanished with the slamming of the front door.

"Mother, would you like pepperoni or supreme pizza?" The pinched expression Lillian tossed her way gave warning. *This is Bethany's night; I'll not go there. Only precious memories allowed.*

Natalie walked into the dining room, wrapping and unwrapping a piece of yarn around her pointing finger. Never a good sign. Her friend's unique finger quirk revealed that something was bothering her. Deeply.

Courtney's stomach rumbled with hunger. Still, she couldn't touch a bite. Not until they could decide on what to do tonight since the pedicurist left. Was Zeta coming back? Courtney needed everyone's opinion about the nail design and some dress choices she'd seen. Natalie walked toward the Victorian lamp in front of the window. Only a sliver of hazy sunlight filtered past her friend between the velvety drapery folds. The conversations completely extinguished.

Natalie reached toward the tassel hanging from the switch. With a click, lamplight flooded the room. Everyone leaned toward her as though wanting to catch her words. Would they find out what happened to Zeta? Could this night be saved from being a total disaster?

"Zeta had an emergency and needed to leave."

"Is she all right?" *Emergency.* Courtney's heart moved at the explanation. Her mother turned and looked her square in the face.

"She'll be fine—just not tonight. But she's been teaching me the tricks of her trade, so if you don't mind me doing your pedicures, I'm game. What do all of you say?" She gave an energetic twist to folded paper circling her finger, and the paper broke. This was just like Natalie, so talented at solving predicaments. Agreements blended as everyone spoke at once.

"Courtney, can you help me bring soft drinks and tea to the front room?"

Standing, she followed her friend down the short hallway past the staircase on the right-hand side to the kitchen. The fragrant warmth of freshly baked confection quickened her steps, but there were none to be seen. No stealing a taste in Natalie's kitchen tonight.

Her friend reached inside a cabinet and pulled out several pitchers. "Want to put ice in these?"

"Sure." As she wrestled with the ice cube trays, she considered asking about Zeta. Something about her whole manner stoked Courtney's curiosity. "I was wondering—"

"What do I have to do to get some tea around here?" Lillian's voice sounded, drowning out her own.

Both of them turned to glance in Lillian's direction. Natalie wandered next to Courtney and plunked a glass of iced tea in front of her. "Sample this. Does it need anything?" Then she approached Lillian. "I don't have a chair for you in here. How about I take you back to your seat? I'll bring you a glass."

"Just pour it and come with me now."

"I'll be there soon, Lillian. Sugar or..." Natalie took her finger and swirled it in the air.

Lillian laughed and slowly turned her walker to head back to the table. "You know it's two scoops of sugar."

Courtney shook her head before taking a sip. "Delicious. You have a way with her, truly you do." She dumped ice in each pitcher and filled the ice trays with water. "So, who is Zeta? Where did you find her?" She turned to watch Natalie's next kitchen chore.

Her friend hauled some miniature cheesecake desserts from the oven. The vanilla aroma filled the kitchen, making her taste buds tingle with anticipation. Natalie placed them on the trivets and locked her hands on her hips. "You're not trying to get me to gossip, are you?"

"Yes, I want to know all."

"Ha!" Well, Zeta lives behind me. I met her when I was jogging. She has a yard full of roses, and the air is so fragrant."

"You jogging? Roses—Orlando's place? There must be every rose imaginable planted there."

"Yes, and yes again to me jogging. We both know that's just not me. Zeta moved there after you bought your apartment building. She shares rose petals with me for my recipes, and we get together and make crafts." Nodding her head to the left directed Courtney to a beautiful little flower arrangement. "She doesn't spray her roses with pesticides. Do you know how hard it is to find uncontaminated roses?" She grasped the ladle from the large soup pan brimming with freshly brewed tea and filled each of the four pitchers.

"Got Mom's tea ready?" Bethany breezed in to see their progress.

Natalie handed her the tablespoon. "Two sugars, and can you come back to carry some of this?"

"Teaspoons not tablespoons, Nat."

"And you wonder why she likes Natalie's tea better than yours," Courtney said with a laugh as she loaded the ice trays into the freezer.

After a little more visiting, they cleaned up the dining room. Natalie parted the French doors, which opened the way to the front parlor.

"Bare your feet in this room, ladies, and stick a foot in." Natalie tugged her shoes and socks off to lead the way. "Courtney and Nicole, could you help the helpless, please?"

Lillian and Cassie contested for the most intolerable whine.

Nicole grunted when pulling off her socks. "The water is barely warm. I like mine hot."

"Now, now. Let's have some fun." Natalie gave Courtney the pumice stones to handout to everyone. "Use this handy dandy callus remover like this." Nat got her feet wet and began to rub the stone on her foot in a circular motion.

"I can't do this. I thought we were supposed to be served tonight, not put to work." Lillian huffed. "You should fire that woman. She left us here to fend for ourselves."

"Good thing we have separate stones. My calluses are so huge everyone would've waited all night for their turn." Courtney plunked her worse foot into the soothing bubbling water.

"Who said you could go first?" Natalie laughed. She led them step by step before she handed out tangerine scented lotion.

Courtney watched her friend and pride swelled her heart. In high school, Nat had messed up big time, but Courtney stuck with her and never regretted keeping her talented, slightly unusual bestie. Sometimes it was like Natalie could read her mind—yet not judge her. Holding up a lotion sample, Courtney said, "This lotion is sold at Victorian by Natalie, the small gift shop down the hall." Earning a grin from her friend, they both knew a few sales wouldn't hurt.

Natalie whipped out the polish and tried to keep her aim aligned. By the time she finished, air bubbles and painting past the toenail edges—because of shaky attempts at placing decorative squiggly lines—made everyone laugh. Maybe they should have looked at photos instead, but they would have missed the fun. The polish fumes were so overpowering that they had to turn the overhead fan on high.

"Want to pull up some Bridal Shops on your computer? We could pick out dresses." Otherwise, except for the laughter and picture taking, it was a completely fun waste of time. She could live with that, but there would be pressured choices to deal with later.

"Actually, it's time for the games to begin. Our lovely Cassie contributed the questions and prizes," Nat said.

Games—yuck. No help choosing dresses tonight either, but the thought of the competition was enticing.

"I only have a couple of games since Courtney is a poor loser. Pass around the paper and pens."

"Oh!" Several guests replied at once.

"Okay now, everybody take a seat. First question. When was the first time in history that brides wore white dresses?"

Nicole leaned over and whispered loudly, "History major question. Not fair."

Everyone chimed in their complaints about that question.

"Write the answer. Now, the second question. What was the first memory you have of your sister or brother?" The timer was set for three minutes. Everyone wrote their answers on the sheet of paper.

Courtney couldn't wait to hear Bethany's first memory of her. They had never talked about that.

"Third question. How many marbles are in this jar?" Bethany had collected marbles since she was eight years old.

"Who has the answer to the first question? Nicole, put that smartphone away." No one had an answer.

Bethany raised a bashful hand. "The year 1840, when Queen Victoria wore a white gown, while wedding Albert of Saxe." Cassie tossed her a wrapped prize.

"Winner for the second question is the one with the earliest memory of their sibling."

"My sister was nine, and I was eight. She was throwing mud pies at me because I stole her Barbie," Natalie said.

"I've got that beat, I was five, and my brother just turned three when he jumped into the water and couldn't swim."

"How awful, Cassie. Was he okay after that?" Bethany asked.

"He wasn't okay after that." Everyone grew quiet and waited for her to say more. "But, he wasn't okay before that either."

"Oh." Everyone yelled together. Lillian was next, and all eyes turned to her expectantly.

Lillian ducked her head. "I'll pass."

"How about you, Courtney?" Bethany's eyes glowed with curiosity. She leaned back into the Victorian chair.

"My first memory of you. Hmm. It was when you were reading a story about a mouse who didn't care. We sat on the couch, and you were turning the pages too fast. I was probably around four. So, what is your first memory of me?"

"Since you were about two years old, you'd dumped cereal all over yourself and the floor. I thought you quite entertaining. You were crying, 'Mommy,' but when Mom came, you ran from her."

"I bet you thought you would win this game too, but I remember my little sister when my mom was pregnant with her. She kicked my hand through mom's tummy when I was four years old. Mom was on her way to the hospital to have her," Nicole said.

"You won then." Bethany reached for the bag of gifts to have her choose one.

"Wait, you are seven years older than me. What was your first memory of Mother being pregnant with me?" Courtney asked with the spirit of competition.

A puzzled expression overtook Bethany's face. "I really don't remember mom being pregnant." They looked at Lillian as she studied the floor. The trembling in her hand increased.

"Mom, are you okay?"

Lillian brought her hands together, looking like she wanted to hold them still by sheer will power. "I'm fine." When she tried to pick herself up, the effort seemed too great. "Just tired. I want to go home now." Her one hand moved up to rub her jaw. Her voice was soft and quiet. Very unlike her.

"I'll take you home, Mom." Bethany stood. "Thank you so much, Natalie and Courtney, all of you really. This was fun."

"Wait, how many marbles are in the jar?" The answer is I don't know, but if you all wanted to count them with me, we could have done that."

They crumpled up their papers and threw them at her.

Thirteen

ZANDER

Puddles danced around Zander's bay window, all but knocking the plants that his mother had just brought off the window sill. Courtney rang the doorbell.

Mother pinned the dog with a displeasing glare. "Your father and I have evening plans with the Dickens, so I have to run. Don't forget to read those journals. I'm counting on you." She leaned over to offer Zander a peck on the cheek, then she beamed up a hopeful smile.

Puddles move between them.

"Sit." Puddles backed up and sat down before she bounced up again and ran to the window. Zander tapped her backside. She sat.

Opening the door for his mother to leave and Courtney to come inside, set the Leonberger to dancing. Requiring another command. "Puddles stay."

"So, you're Courtney, owner of the big dog. I wish I could stay, but I'm running late, nice meeting you."

"Sorry you have to run, Mrs. Hayward." Courtney's warmth made his mother take a second look and spout a smile of her own.

After stepping inside his living room, her eyes glowed appreciation that wouldn't have needed a word. "Wow, I like how you've decorated." If there was one thing he sensed in Courtney, it was sincerity. She moved toward the Leo.

"If you ignore her for about fifteen minutes, it will establish that you're alpha."

She stopped walking and gazed up at him. An emotion he couldn't identify passed over her face. "How did things go tonight?" She asked in a guarded sort of way.

Fantastic. "Pretty well. It will be smoother when you come with her tomorrow. While you're waiting for your fifteen minutes of ignoring Puddles, do you want something cold to drink?"

"Sure." She glanced at Puddles. She'd have to resist reaching for the puppy.

He glanced down at her feet to check out her pedicure. "Looking good."

She laughed. Curling one foot in toward the other didn't hide her feet one bit. "You're too tall to see the blunders. Zeta couldn't be there, and we were left to Natalie's devices."

"Did your mother have fun?"

"She was… reserved tonight. I don't think she's feeling well."

He leaned toward the bay window and parted the metallic bronze curtain. "Is she in the car still?"

She cringed. Did Zander think she left everyone in the car since that first training day when she'd left Puddles cooking in the heat? "Bethany took her home tonight." She aimed her feet toward the kitchen to their left.

"Juice, water, tea?"

"Raspberry tea, if you have it?"

"It's my own recipe. I grow raspberries in my backyard."

She took a step forward, but Puddles blocked her way. Turn your back to her and follow me." He watched to see how they interacted. She followed his footsteps, and Puddles clawed at her feet and tried to pin her in place.

"Ouch, she scratched my leg." Courtney frowned and turned toward the dog, so like a puppy.

"Do you want a time out?" Zander's commanding voice asked Puddles. The puppy groaned and lay down in front of the couch.

"I think you tricked me, and we are training tonight. Is there a camera somewhere…hidden again?" Her attempt at humor seemed to have a serious note.

He laughed. "Me—film you unawares? That doesn't sound right… does it?"

She slipped a look his way with an expression that seemed to agree that unawares filming wasn't all right. Then she stepped into the kitchen and gasped. His reward. He looked behind her to make sure Puddles behaved. He faced Courtney again and enjoyed how she gazed wide-eyed at his creation.

"I wouldn't have expected such a big kitchen. This is… amazing. Was the kitchen like this when you bought the house?" She turned in a circle and took in every inch of the room.

The spacious cabinetry and counter space made this a cook's wonderland—at least in his opinion. "This was my grandparent's place, and when I inherited the property, I made some changes. The original kitchen," he moved over to the middle of the kitchen, "ended here."

"This is exquisite, Zander."

"If you think this is good, wait until you have some of my tea."

She grinned as she moved over to the table and chairs. Puddles entered the room, following at her heels. "Even this antique table and chairs match the décor so perfectly. How did you manage that?"

"They were my grandparent's original table and chair set. I designed the cabinetry to match."

Courtney's hand smoothed over the table top's surface with an almost reverent slowness. Zander's heart skipped a beat as he watched her. This woman appreciated family, and the sentiment of things passed through generations.

She glanced up at him. He jerked into action. Caught staring, what was he about to do? Oh, tea. He opened the refrigerator and grabbed the fresh-brewed homemade concoction. Gram's favorite glasses stood too long in the cabinet—without being admired. He just bet that Courtney would fall all over these! It was time to pour tea inside a bit of Hayward's history. Deep within him, something clicked. Her reaction mattered.

They bantered back and forth while he added ice cubes and filled glasses. He approached the table. Courtney leaned closer and stared intently at the glass, more than he could have hoped. Even turned it from side to side. He felt his chest swell with pride. He wished she'd met his grandmother. The sweet elderly lady would have liked Courtney's spunk and kindness.

She looked up at him with tension in her eyes before she focused on the tea again. Plopping a finger into the glass, she moved an ice cube over.

"Take a sip, it tastes better that way." *What is she doing?*

With an apology written on her face, she said, "I can't."

"Can't?" *Or won't?*

"There is a bug in my tea. Do you mind..." She picked up the offending glass of his favorite tea and handed it back to him.

The mood flattened. Although, finding the bug before she drank was exactly what Grandma Hayward would have done. He couldn't stop the smile that stretched over the tense muscles of his face. Before he left the table, he chanced a glance at his own tea. Another bug struggled with the backstroke toward one of his ice cubes. Yep, those glasses had stayed too long in the cabinet without attention.

COURTNEY

Courtney stepped into her temporary bedroom and closed the door—the dark hole crater. What was Mother thinking when she picked this color? She leaned against the door and heard the hollow thump of wood hitting the door jam, heartbeat pulsing through her ears.

Were there any stars out tonight? She hadn't even noticed on her drive home. Puddles took over the back seat whining all the way. Grieving leaving Zander? Her own head was full of Zander Hayward. She'd never met anyone like him. Why did life have to be so complicated? Her heart surged forward tonight—reaching out to him. Now that she was back in the real world, her heart took a backward step and turned into a full retreat.

She pushed away from the door and dragged her feet across the deep and hideous chocolate-brown carpet. Soft cushioning was its only redeeming quality. Parting the draperies at the window seat didn't answer the other question humming in her breast. No full moon floated in the heavens wreaking havoc on human moods with its gravitational pull. There had to be a genuine reason for everyone's strange behavior tonight at Natalie's.

Mother seemed off-kilter. Especially in the dining room. Zeta's leaving without explanation? Natalie's nervousness? Bethany? Her sister seemed fine at the party despite everything. She appeared delighted about how the celebration unfolded. It didn't seem to matter that Nat had to pedicure their feet. She couldn't remember anything she or anyone else said that could've tumbled her sister's mood into the dust, which she'd discovered when calling Bethany after the party. What was she missing?

She'd always read people and situations. Unless she'd been more distracted than she realized. She owed Natalie and Zander for all they'd done with no real payback in sight.

Bethany's words came back to her full force. Maybe she did depend on others too much. But how was she to be independent when she didn't even have her own place anymore? The apartments had potential.

Oh, Tanya—that was one mode of thought she needed to back away from—right now. The slight headache brewing and a small twist of her stomach reminded her of how she would end up if she didn't forgive and forget—as far as it was possible. Last Sunday's sermon was timely.

She needed to protect her purpose and plan. Her future. Sigh. She didn't even know her place in the world. Where, oh, where would Courtney Rosemarie MacDuff fit anyway?

The stars winked at her as though they held some superior secret to joy. She dropped the draperies and turned away. She needed to write. When she entered Zander's world, she experienced the illusion of how excellent fiction could be. What inspiration. Yes, the kind she would have to steel her nerves against, so she wasn't heartbroken in the process.

The Land of Knockdowndragout, her latest adventure in Neverland, needed a hero in chapter two. She knew who he would be. It was only fiction after all, and he'd never read this. Courtney leaned toward her computer keys and hugged the space. Loaded with ideas, she was ready to write. Redanz's hazel eyes blazed on the pages. This character was adorned with the ability to see beyond the inky boundaries of bookbinding to confront his archenemy. Any woman craved a man of courage by her side. The scene grew until Courtney could almost picture everything 3D style. As though people and situations lifted off the pages on their own accord.

The digital beamed 2:32 a.m., and she'd have to work with Mr. Whippier tomorrow.

Stifling a yawn proved an impossible attempt. The groan she spent chased all the joy of creation out of her, and she didn't have the energy to chase it down. Tomorrow would hold its own adventures. Any difficulties at Leman's would have to find their way onto these pages. The courage and power of the almighty pen would squelch those memories as she wrote again. She determined the outcome, and no one would despair forever on her pages.

A few minutes later, she slipped between frosty covers while needing warmth to allow sleep. Bethany's face came to mind. She shut her eyes, but concern that her sister hid some secret distress didn't disappear. Bethany had never hidden anything from her before. Secrets were not her forte. If only she could tuck these worries into the back of her mind and sleep.

Like she used to.

If these concerns kept up—she'd have to deal with them. That couldn't possibly be as neatly tied up and controlled as words carefully pounded out on ebony keys.

COURTNEY

Oh, thrilling. A double dose today. Courtney placed an expert smile on her face. One that had diverted many difficulties in the past. But even fabricated confidence challenged motivation today. Mr. Whippier and Daria Barns stood side-by-side in Leman's office, whispering, and snickering together—until she walked into the room. Now they stood quiet as statues, and their eyes were as warm as cold marble surrounded by an overcast winter day.

Mr. Whippier held up his wristwatch. "You're... not late?"

Courtney didn't enjoy the surprised lilt at the end of his *greeting.* "Good morning to you, sir. And Daria."

Mr. Whippier squeegeed out a smile, and Daria chanced wrinkling her forehead with her uplifted brows.

"Morning," Daria whispered as she turned her attention to some paperwork in her right hand.

Courtney punched in with the time clock and then turned to discover four eyes staring back at her. Determined to stay positive and make the best of the situation, she said, "What's on the agenda today?"

"We don't start for another twenty minutes. Don't think you can leave early just because you punched in sooner then you should have." Daria snatched more paperwork off the desk and spun away from her. Then she and Mr. Whippier stalked out of the room.

Left to her own devices, she picked up a rag and window cleaner. Surely, she couldn't get into trouble for cleaning glass top tables. The scripture in her devotion this morning talked about not returning railing for railing because we are called to inherit a blessing. Unfortunately, the bible didn't explain how hard it would be to deliver that kind of grace to Daria Barns.

Mindless duties would allow her to think of ways to be strong and use the weighty knowledge of serving the uncharitable. Considering how important it was, even needed, to be kind without expecting thanks or appreciation from these co-workers would also benefit her. With such excellent thinking, maybe today would be easier than she thought. Courtney looked at the doorway... then again, probably not.

Two hours later, Courtney burned through a pile of files and paperwork stacked beside her at the command center. She scratched the imaginary itch with a pencil and tried to dispel the ache to get out on the floor to begin selling. Her sigh puffed her hair dangling over her forehead. She stretched her taut neck muscles. Several interested buyers were seeking their perfect piece of furniture as Mr. Whippier, and Daria scooped up sales and pushed more expensive pieces. This is why she resisted pushy sales techniques and did her own research instead of relying on a sales person's integrity—

"Excuse me miss." She glanced at an older man. He seemed troubled and quite wrinkled. "I thought this store sold antiques. Could you tell me where I could find the best antique dealer in the area?" He glanced at his watch before his attention bounced up at her.

Courtney looked around. Both Mr. Whippier and Daria were busy pressuring their customers. She stood up and said, "Please follow me, Mr.—"

"Mr. Greenwood. Soon to be the late Mr. Greenwood if I don't find the piece my wife requested for our anniversary." A half-smile lifted the right-hand side of his face.

Smiling back and sucking in the giggle, she said, "We have a few nice pieces located near the rear of the store if you're interested, that is." She hoped they had price tags.

"Quite interested. Lead the way." He pushed his glasses higher on his nose and scanned the back of the store.

She wondered at him, not seeming to notice the huge sign for antiques. She'd make a note and alert Mr. Angerton. The sign needed to be simplified and much larger. The age group Mr. Greenwood represented might escape the store and not find their treasured items if they didn't have proper advertisement pointing to the antiques.

Mr. Angerton had several more pieces delivered recently that she hadn't had the opportunity to check over. Some were partially wrapped in paper and cardboard. She reached into the drawer with the razors and pens and found a cutter with a secure handle.

"Off we go, sir." She weaved their way toward the back of the store and entered the antique corner. It needed to be rearranged—Zander's touch—to have the best effect on the customer and show off the pieces as they deserved. "What does Mrs. Greenwood desire to have?"

"Well now, you don't want the whole list—right? Just the anniversary gift." Faded gray-blue twinkled between the folds of his squinted eyes, making her laugh.

"If it's furniture, her wish is my desire."

"We had a robbery last month. The robbers set fire to our place once they were done. It's time to get our own place again. She wants to replace her cherry-wood bookcase. As close in style to what she had before."

"Hutches and bookcases are over here." Courtney moved to the right toward several sheets covered furnishings." She pulled off the first sheet.

Disappointment shone in his eyes.

She pulled off two more coverings and switched on the lamp before she faced him.

Mr. Greenwood's mouth dropped open as he stared at the third bookcase. "I can't... I just can't believe it. This looks exactly like the one we lost."

Courtney pointed at the cherry and brass mountable bookcase. "I'd say it is an American Aesthetic probably from the mid to late 1870s. What beautiful inlays. Remarkable. I'm so glad that you could find one so quickly. I believe these are rather rare." She studied the windows and the molding. She touched the brass latch that opened a drawer at the top of the bookcase.

"Especially when they have a scratch in the exact place and length of our original piece. I imagine that will discount the price significantly." The warmth in his voice turned frigid.

When she turned toward him, his eyes held a glint of cold steel. She bit her lip and didn't know what to say. Was he really suggesting that this was his piece of furniture?

Fourteen

LILLIAN

Trembling fingers. Oh, how Lillian wished they would stop! She tugged on the blouse button securing the tight-collar trapping the air in her throat, as Natalie carried a rattling tray of tea and snacks into the living room. Was the girl nervous just because she'd told her she'd pay her for her help? *Ridiculous.* A commercial blared noisier than it needed too, drowning any unnecessary attempt at conversation. She must think. Her fingers slipped their hold a time or two. Finally, they tightened their grip and pushed the button through the buttonhole, one jerky motion at a time. Pressure released and allowed her to relax her shoulders and sit back against the cushions.

Natalie's face tensed. Noise bothered her; Lillian observed as they spent time together. She chuckled, drawing Natalie's attention. "Thank you for the tea. Oh, where are my favorite cookies?" She spoke above the television. A smile would reward such thoughtful efforts. She willed her hands to stop shaking and reached for the cup, which Natalie filled halfway. If she were alone, she'd throw the cup. Apparently, Natalie noticed she needed less tea so that she wouldn't spill. The sweet drink turned bitter in her mouth.

Though Natalie left, she'd returned in a blink of time with a small plate loaded with cookies and a napkin tucked underneath. Lillian diverted her hand toward those additional treats. Her favorite. This young woman seemed to anticipate her every need. Unlike Courtney, who needed step by step directions. Always daydreaming and not paying attention to household details—like her friend here. She took a bite. A soft, moist, warm cookie. What a reward. Natalie's talent exceeded that of Bella's Bakery, in her opinion. A perfect blend of warmth and sweetness coated her tongue. She closed her eyes, savoring the moment. Before she opened them again. It was time.

Lillian found the remote and lowered the volume. She shifted her body to partly face Natalie. The young woman paused before eating her cookie and seemed to notice another need floating between them. She nibbled only the edge of her treat before she placed it on the plate and brushed away a crumb that stuck to her lip. Natalie turned to face her. A fresh question, or anticipation, filled her youthful expression. It had been a ton of years since she'd seen her own reflection radiant and wrinkle-free like that. *Oh, well.*

"So, this woman you hired to work at Bethany's party, did you fire her?" She tried to hold back the eagerness but felt sure it revealed itself in the lift of her voice. Uncertainty niggled her mind. Natalie's reaction, or lack of one, didn't help her gage how her statement was received. Lillian heaved a sigh.

"Zeta is a neighbor of mine. We've become fast friends. Originally, she taught me how to do pedicures for fun. I thought I could handle this party, but I chickened out at the last minute and asked her to do it for me. It didn't work out for her to stay."

Lillian narrowed her eyes to focus on the young woman. Natalie's face still didn't show much emotion. Maybe she knew a few things about Zeta. Then again, perhaps not. "She seems irresponsible to me. If I were you—I wouldn't use her in a situation that mattered."

"Zeta is okay. Don't worry, Mrs. MacDuff. But I would like to ask you some questions concerning…"

Just what she wanted to avoid, more business questions. If she had wanted to talk business all day, she would've kept her day job. She considered smiling brightly but thought better of it when Natalie stopped and looked toward her with an expression that screamed *puzzled*.

· ⚜ ·

COURTNEY

Unfortunately, too far away from everyone in the store, Courtney watched as the sweet older man—who'd asked about a bookcase for his wife—turned boiling red. He looked wildly around. What a mistake to move out of everyone's view. What if he became violent? Courtney's pulse picked up in rhythm as her attention darted left and right to gage an escape route. The entrance to this antique display area gapped open too far away. Mr. Greenwood's pacing blocked her exit. The other salesmen were busy, so she couldn't be sure that anyone had noticed her lead him here. Showing the antiques to the man seemed like such a great idea earlier. Now—not so much. Should she scream? Or would that set him off?

"You're a stinking thief. Why don't you get a job and work for things honestly?"

"But—"

"Listen to me, Karen, I'm not tolerating this. Not one bit." His voice climbed in pitch. "No more, I say."

The louder he got, the farther his voice would carry. Courtney resisted the urge to cover her ears. She should say or do—

144

what? She'd never worked with an unstable person before. Think. Just think. First, she glanced at the bookcase, pushing as much admiration her shaky face muscles could carry. She willed herself to calm before approaching the furniture that was as much a piece of artwork as anything Michelangelo had painted. "Where did you get this beautiful piece of furniture, Mr. Greenwood?"

He stopped and glanced with a faraway look at the bookcase and then back to her. His labored breathing slowed, and he walked toward her. She didn't know if she should run or continue to pretend that everything was fine. He was almost close enough to grab her arm, so she decided to portray a calm exterior. "God, help me, please," she quietly pleaded.

"What?" He halted his step and glared at her with perturbed focus.

"Yes, it's beautiful, so pleasant to look at." She stretched her lips wide. Directing her gaze toward the inlay on the bookcase, wanting to draw his attention away from her. Keeping aware of him. *Could he have dementia? Did he have a gun, knife, or know karate? Calm yourself, Courtney, a snail could run away from him.*

"Courtney, I see you've met our Mr. Greenwood. Hello, Mr. Greenwood. How about if we have it delivered to you before the day's end?" Mr. Angerton's voice calmed the remaining hostility from the older man. But Angerton's eyes matched his last name as though lava danced behind the pupils—waiting to erupt.

"That's fine. Right fine." Mr. Greenwood nodded, seeming a tad confused, and he turned around to walk away from the antique department. But he couldn't find his way.

"This way, Mr. Greenwood." Mr. Angerton directed him to the door and pointed the way through the furniture store toward the exit.

Courtney's limbs shook. Watching Mr. Angerton's reaction made her insides sink to the basement of her reserves.

"What were you thinking? Bringing Mr. Greenwood back here is dangerous. I could have lost some fine pieces." Mr. Angerton stocked toward her.

Movement to her far-left caused her to flinch and turn to see if Mr. Greenwood decided to return. Daria glided into the room with Zander at her side. They moved steadily toward them. Zander's eyes fixed on Courtney.

"Daria, Zander." Mr. Angerton nodded.

"Bruce, did you see who just left the store?" Then she turned hardened eyes toward Courtney. "What are you doing back here?"

"Serving Mr. Greenwood for the greater good."

Mr. Angerton gapped at Courtney. "Don't you know about that man?" He turned toward Daria. "Please tell me you've been working with her to steer her in the right direction."

Her co-worker's tan turned notebook white, and her mouth hung open in the most unbecoming way. She stole a glance in Zander's direction but kept her face pointed toward the floor. Her eyes held a plea when she locked eyes with Courtney.

Courtney's heart pinched to see Daria's interest in Zander. She would have to ignore that. Sigh. Maybe this was the answer to prayer she sought this morning. A notch in her co-worker's armor made it easier to be kind.

"They were busy, Mr. Angerton. It looked as though it would be a while before they could peel themselves away from their customers. I met Mr. Greenwood at the desk. He seemed perfectly fine, so I left the desk to show him these antiques. He was okay until he saw this brass and cherry bookcase." Courtney ran her hand down the side of the beautiful piece of furniture. "He remembered the scratch, and that's when he lost it."

"So, he told you that he'd been robbed and that this piece of furniture belonged to his wife?"

"Yes, he did." She tilted her head and looked up at her boss to read his expression.

"Well, the theft and fire happened, but his wife died in the process. He wanders in here from time to time, looking for his furniture. Looking for her sometimes too. We direct him outside and refer him to a fake antique store so that he doesn't get into trouble by flipping out on someone. Like he almost did today."

A shiver coursed through Courtney's limbs. This sweet older gentleman must have mental problems, triggered by his loss? Maybe dementia. She glanced where he'd paced, visualizing him in that less-than-calm state of mind—while blocking her escape to safety.

Zander moved closer. "I'll work on the front right bedroom set first. I only have a couple of hours to spare today. See you later." Zander slanted an alarming deliberate grin to her before he pulled away from Daria's side.

Bruce Angerton nodded.

Her treasonous gratitude followed him, while Daria's confident attitude seemed deflated—which Courtney couldn't help but think that woman deserved.

"Courtney, I've not seen one sale from you yet. Is there a problem?" Mr. Angerton's tone lowered into a soft growl. She studied his face and saw displeasure tucked in every crease.

"I've been—"

"She hasn't shown great aptitude in that area yet. But I'll work harder with her to get her going, Bruce." A sly smile emphasized Daria's classic features as she stepped closer to their boss.

Courtney's mouth dropped open. How could someone look so—beautiful when actively poisoning someone's reputation? And right in front of them.

"I heard such great recommendations about you from Zander Hayward. He's never steered me wrong in the past. I hope he will not also be disappointed."

Focusing her attention on her boss turned Courtney's limbs to rubber. Where was the closest seat? Her mouth dried up like the Mojave Desert, and she couldn't reply though she wanted to explain. Out of the corner of her eye, she noticed Daria lifting her hand, seeming to study her manicure and smiling a smile that made Courtney regret she thought she knew anything about anything anymore.

Her boss gave a clipped sigh and stalked out of the room. Courtney willed her jittery nerves to relax now that she was not under his stern gaze. What did Zander say about her that caused her boss to expect so much? She would think twice before she used him as a reference again.

"Don't you have files to finish?" Her co-worker glanced right toward the heart of the store where customers mingled near an expensive bedroom set. "See me when you're done."

She turned and left Courtney floundering, and oh so vulnerable.

⁕ ⸎ ⁕

COURTNEY

For the next two and a half hours, Courtney updated and categorized file upon file. Too bad Angerton insisted on a hard copy filing system. Neither Mr. Whippier or Daria stopped over to see if she needed direction or correction or offer their pointers about sales strategies. She was on her own since the only one on her side left half an hour ago to work at his father's furniture manufacturing business. *Wonder how work in a factory would be?*

Finished with the files, Courtney straightened the desk area. Every time they lingered near the control center or finalized a sale, she listened to their conversations and methods of educating customers. She needed to know the register—then she'd be equipped, well, at least in her mind— to tackle customers by herself.

The bell rang as another customer entered. Courtney glanced up at the tall suit, who looked intently at a particular dining room set. He circled the table, pulled out a chair, and sat down. The man stood and nodded to himself. He headed toward her with a mannerism that reflected that he wouldn't be one to waste time. His impatient steps toward the desk emphasized it was time to buy.

Shoulders straightened automatically, while Courtney deliberately relaxed her face into a welcoming smile. "Hello, are you in the market for a Dorthnor dining room set?"

The question confused him at first, and then he jerked his head toward the furniture. "Oh, the name on the tag. Do you have extra chairs?"

"Let me look." She'd found the reference books earlier while straightening everything on the desk area. She lifted the catalog and took it to the table he showed interested in so that she could match the number. This style of furniture definitely would fit in with this man's older age group. Her finger glided to a stop on that particular set. "Each chair..." she squinted her eyes. Better relay the right price and not wholesale. Mr. Whippier walked toward them from several feet away. "Mr. Whippier, could you look at this, please?" She moved next to him and showed him the item in question.

He stopped and frowned. "I'm in a hurry. Can it wait."

She glanced over at her customer and smiled as he shifted his body weight to his left side. His jaw set ridged on his face. "Sorry, but it can't wait. I need you for one sweet second."

An appreciative gaze bounced toward her and then rebounded to the table from the customer.

"I wanted to make sure that this is the store price." Her fingernail tapped the box with the largest amount.

"Yes, that's it."

"Also, should I need to ring up a sale how do I find my code, so that I can use the register?"

"I'll have to look it up for you." He smiled at her in a predatory manner. "I'll be right back. Write him up if he is ready to make a purchase. Then if you share half of your commission, I'll help you out." His hairy eyebrow followed his wink.

No wonder she didn't like him. "You're such a kidder." She wrinkled her nose at him for effect before turning toward the customer. "Don't you worry, any commission will be all mine."

The handsome older man's gaze loitered around the room with a dull expression. Definite sign for lack of interest.

"Dorthnor chairs are three hundred and fifty-three dollars each." Heavily upholstered, she found that some fabric choices were more costly than others. "Can I ask what your color scheme is?"

He turned toward her and raised his eyebrows to a peak. "Blue and yellow."

"And your walls and draperies?"

"White walls and red drapes."

She cringed but tried to hide her reaction. She glided her fingertips on the cushions. Orange. He may as well have the whole rainbow in his room. He would need purple and green next.

"You don't like my choices?" His previous wandering glance held fast to her face.

"If you limit your color choices to three, I believe you will really enjoy your dining room and show off this beautiful set in the best way." Her fingers crossed behind her back as she hoped he would not be offended.

His lips slid into a why would I care smirk. "I'm color blind, so it won't bother me at all."

Glancing over his suit and shirt, she noticed that all seemed to match.

"I have someone who helps me coordinate." His hand grabbed the lapel of his suit and gave it a mild yank.

Warmth attacked her face. "That's nice. You look good." Oh, could she mess up any more? She dug her feet into the low pile carpet.

"Thank you. From what I can tell, you do too."

"Well, thank you. Back to what I was saying, you can order fabric that will match your color scheme, which you can't see, but will please others. Would you like me to help you with that?"

He glanced over her. "Courtney, are you expert with colors? Should I trust you?"

She gasped. The Leman name tag—would she ever get used to strangers calling her by her first name? "I do relatively well."

Courtney carried the catalog to the control center. She slipped behind the counter and opened the page with his chair fabric information.

"Did you want to place an order today? The sale price will save you twenty percent if your purchase is over one thousand dollars." She peered at the set arranged several feet away.

"Your set is over that amount, so you'd qualify."

He nodded. "I want to order four extra chairs. Eight chairs in all."

Lifting a pen that worked, she filled out the item numbers for the order form. Next, she added his address and phone number with his help. "That will be great. Do you want this?" She pointed at the page, showing fabrics offered for that dining set. Adjusting the book for him to view the patterns, she asked, "Will plain colors work or any of these patterns for your home?"

"I've never cared so... hmmm."

"Do you have stripes or plaid in the room, or is your room basic and easy to add patterns too?"

He grinned at her. "The pillows and draperies are both plain."

"Excellent. You are free to splurge on patterns then. Are you married, or do you have a woman in the house?"

"No." His eyes narrowed as though he were suspicious of her motives for such a question.

Pointing out a couple of masculine choices, Courtney played like she was unaware of his discomfort to get past that awkward moment and onto the sale. Her insides quaked with excitement that she didn't dare show. Realizing this was one sensitive, even self-absorbed man, she chose the safe all-business approach. While in her mind, she could hear the cha-ching of this commission fluffing up her barely-green bank account. She waited for him to decided.

By the time they finished the paperwork, Mr. Whippier provided her personal code by handing over the sealed envelope from Mr. Angerton's office. Whippier approved of the charge card sale and did a double-take when looking at the man's name.

Her co-worker took a step in the customer's direction and took on an expression she'd seen when Mother served beef with manicottis for dinner. "I've joined Spencer's Golf Club recently. A few friends and I are getting together for dinner this Thursday. I'd be honored if you'd come as my guest."

"No, thanks." The customer's dull voice landed flat with dismissal before he looked away. Mr. Whippier's shoulders hunched down as he stepped backward. His olive-green complexion darkened a shade or two as he turned around to leave.

What happened to Mr. Whippier's statement of belief? *A sale is a sale. Customers are customers and are not your friends. Stay professional.* Apparently, he needed to reread the sign he posted above the employee mailbox.

"You'll have to stop back and let us know how you liked your furniture once it arrives, Mr.—" She couldn't speak when she saw the name on the card.

"Mr. Donald Mancel." His tone chilled when recognition of his name caused a reaction.

Imagining herself picking up a marker and adding to Whippier's sign, *And, customers who are enemies are customers just the same.* Courtney peered up at him, wondering if he knew that he just bought furniture from the woman who had painted the walls of the apartments he practically stole for a song from the bank's foreclosure sale. Of course, he couldn't. He was up there, and she was a furniture store clerk.

Beloved daughter— reverberated inside her heart and lungs, taking her breath away. She placed a steadying hand on the counter. Beloved daughter? It didn't feel that way. Tears burned at the back of her eyes. Suddenly, she couldn't wait for her first Leman's customer to leave.

ZANDER

The phone rang as Zander dragged his razor across his jawline. Shaving cream on his fingers made the smooth surface of the phone slippery. He tightened his grip, and the smartphone ejected from his grasp, landing next to the sink full of soapy water. "Woohoo." He grabbed the towel, hanging on the rack, and wiped his fingers so that he could rescue his phone from taking a dive. Tapping speaker, he said, "Mr. Townsteader, what a surprise."

"Hello, Zander, I hear that you have your hands on a Rococo Rosewood Center Table from the 1850s and you're staging furnishings in Mark Lunge's house that's up for sale. Any interest in selling that furniture?"

Zander's thoughts scrambled. Townsteader must know something of its value, or he wouldn't be calling so early in the morning. "Oh, you like the piece?" Zander stalled.

Both times he'd sold antiques to Townsteader, the man almost took him to the cleaners. If he hadn't discovered the real value before the sale, he'd have been out of a lot of money. Fortunately, this man provided enough real estate connections to compensate for his obvious flaws. Still, Zander had decided not to engage in any more antique deals with this man. And, Courtney's hutch went for what? Somewhere in the neighborhood of five thousand dollars, after all, it was an American Empire hutch by Joseph Meeks. Townstesder had offered him $2,000.00 tops.

"You know that wife of mine loves fancy carving on furniture."

So, he'd lie to get his hands on Courtney's table. Zander knew from Charley Leans that Townsteader had been separated from his wife for over a year now. "What do you think the table is worth?" He'd look for higher bidding on the internet after Tonsteader told him where to start, and he'd share that info with Courtney.

"Well, maybe $2,000.00 or so. What do you want for it?"

Zander tensed his face and dragged the razor bumping across the last of the stubble. He needed a new blade. He rubbed his hand on the not so soft remains. "It doesn't belong to me."

"Oh, who then?" Townsteader's pitch rose higher.

"A friend of mine, who was nice enough to allow me to stage it."

"Generous friend, I'd say."

He cracked open his bathroom door and headed toward the bedroom closet. Tonight, he would try to motivate Courtney to increase the frequency of dog training classes by showing her what he had of the video. He chose a dark blue shirt. Something she'd call sapphire.

"Generous, but not the type to give her furniture away."

"Oh, right. Well, let me know if this person's in the market to sell." His voice roughened from the friction Zander's comment provided.

COURTNEY

"Sit down. Sit down. You're making me nervous." Lillian's mood dashed between irritability and elation. The ice in her drink clanked on the side of the glass, making too much noise.

Courtney tried to relax, but Zander stood in front of her with that despicable DVD in his grip while he made small talk with Mother. Puddles walked over to her and sat on Courtney's feet. The puppy leaned her head back, black and brownish golden ears flopping as she molded her body against her leg.

"Mother, you don't want to watch us. Tell him you don't want to see this, *please*." Courtney reached out and captured one silky ear and rubbed it in a way that made Puddles melt into her palm.

"You'll love this, Courtney." Zander's back was to her, but she sensed his determination to show their lessons to Mother. *So stubborn.* He actually talked as though he were proud of them. Probably, because she'd had such a huge improvement arc and he would be able to sell a lot of videos—making more money than he'd ever dreamed. At her expense. Her fists tightened, just thinking about it. Puddles growl-talked. Courtney released her tightened grip on the dog's ear. How did she get herself into this predicament?

"And so, it begins." Zander slid the DVD inside the player and pushed start. His friend and so-called movie producer had completed the introduction page listing the title and their names, including Puddles, along with a quote by Zander. *Dogs who do it right are rightly prized.*

Courtney's eyelid began a nervous tic. She pressed her hand against her face. Maybe, this would pass. A relaxed expression radiated control, which influenced one's situation—or so she hoped. What excuse could she use to leave the room? Oh, to disappear—any window or back door was all she'd need to remedy this feeling. *What's worse, staying here and taking it?* Her shoulders gave a shiver. *Or hiding in the kitchen, she'd wonder at every laugh.*

Not see her humiliation, would probably be worse. Her imagination activated strangely when others delved out judgment.

Mother leaned forward, eyes focused toward the television—hands grasped tight in her lap. She obviously couldn't wait.

A sick feeling stirred inside Courtney's stomach. Why did she just sit here and tolerate another reminder of her lack of accomplishment? She should stand up. And leave. But she couldn't.

The television screen filled with Zander sitting on his living room couch. Puddles sat against his leg panting. That huge tongue hung extra-long on the left side of her mouth. The peaceful setting did little to quail her sporadic spasms. Zander's friend had taped segments where Zander explained the rules for canine behaviors before each of the examples began. Puddles made a charming star of the show. She'd be the side-kick clown.

Courtney's conscience gave her a hard pinch. Earlier today, she'd placed an advertisement at Pet Supplies Plus, listing her cell phone number for those interested in interviewing for Puddles's ownership. Zander counted on her. Puddles's lovey attention right now—this moment—made her feel doubly treacherous.

Zander glanced at her from a nearby chair. His excitement dimmed when she glanced back at him. Courtney pushed a grin over her features and tried to turn on a welcome light in her eyes, but it probably only shown with the quality and strength of a nightlight. She glanced back at the television.

There she stood with Puddles at her side. The canine's attention was anywhere but on her. She stood staring at her toes.

A poof of dust rose around her feet since she had just positioned herself in the fenced-in area. Ready, but not willing to train was written all over her face and the slump of her shoulders. Her legs and arms tensed as she commanded her lungs to breathe. *Courtney, breathe.*

Zander chuckled, and she wanted to throw a pillow at him. Her fingers twitched with desire, so she moved her hands in front of her knees and massaged Puddles back. The dog leaned heavier against her legs.

More training action appeared with Zander taking Puddles in hand. Courtney realized he'd inserted these training sessions to replace her most embarrassing moments. Gratitude flooded her. Tears of joy clouded her vision.

"There sure isn't much here showing Courtney with Puddles." Mother's crisp voice pointed out. "Courtney, you really should get some pointers before you allow yourself to be on a video like this." Mother leaned back in her chair, her eyes narrowed, and a frown creased her face.

The phone rang, and Lillian jumped. Her eyes lit up when she peered at the caller ID. "Dan, it's about time you called." She glared at Courtney and Zander, communicating that she wanted to be alone.

"Why don't we look for a snack in the kitchen? Courtney didn't offer anything earlier. She didn't want to prolong her agony one second. Zander's kindness, even though he brought the DVD, won her over some. Mother's earlier comment caused her temples to throb.

Zander stood, and she motioned for him to move through the baby gate first along with Puddles. How she wanted to hear what her dad had to say. *How was he? What conditions did he find in such a war-torn country?* She strained her ear to catch the last words her mother spoke into the phone. Mother tossed a sulky look her way before Courtney snapped the gate shut and turned to move further into the kitchen.

Her elbows leaned on cool marble as she positioned herself on a stool next to Zander. His shoulder bumped into hers with the warmth of a gentle nudge.

"Why so tense?"

"Tense." She attempted a laugh. "Me?" Her voice typically sounding like alto mimicked soprano.

"You don't need to play that game with me, Courtney." He waited a few seconds. "Does the video upset you?"

"Actually, I'm grateful you kept some of my more—harrowing experiences—off of your lessons. I think that you showed me great respect because of what you didn't show. I have to ask. You didn't happen to include my grand-finale, did you?"

A chuckle erupted from his chest, deep and comforting. Except, it kept rumbling.

"Okay, it wasn't *that* funny."

Rumbling kept coming.

She fought a smile and lost the battle. "Really, you can stop now." She shoved his arm. "Stop."

He swiveled his stool toward her, so close. Reaching around her, he pulled her close. Kissing her square on the lips with laughter still gushing out of him. Out of them.

They both froze. Zander dropped his arm and released her to back up a couple of inches. They stared at one another for a long golden moment. Did that just really happen?

Her cell phone rang. An unrecognized number showed up, and she took the call. A man with a huge voice boomed from the other side. I'm calling about that Leonberger you have posted at..."

Courtney's glance jerked Zander's way.

He seemed to have heard. Though he'd turned his face forward, she saw the hard glint in his eye. His face colored with deepening shades of red before her eyes.

She stepped off the stool and moved toward the refrigerator. "I'm merely collecting phone numbers at this point for those interested in her. I'll be moving soon, and I'm sure I'll not be able to take her with me." She listened to the man's demand.

"I want the dog now. You can't just post a dog and then play this game. You'll break my kid's hearts. Do you want to get a home for the dog, or not?"

Automatically, she placed him in the *not interested in giving you the dog list.* "Yes, I'll choose a good home for her." She opened the refrigerator and pulled out the ice tea. She waved for Zander's attention, which he grudgingly gave to her. Pointing to the drink, he nodded back at her before yanking his attention away.

Shadowy gloom took over the room. Courtney flipped the light switch, but the bright kitchen did little to dispel the growing discomfort squeezing her heart. Zander seemed paralyzed, as he perched stiff and morose on the edge of his stool. The man on the other side of the cell continued to ramble.

"Excuse me, sir. We have company, and it isn't a good time to talk. I have your number. Thank you."

Zander's head bent down as though he studied the countertop. "Why didn't you tell me?" His tone strained like too tight strings on a guitar.

She poured the tea over ice inside the large glasses, her fingertips so chilled from the cubes that she rubbed her hands together before she approached him and lay both glasses on the stony surface of the marble island.

"I'm sure Mother will be strong enough soon. I need to find my own place, Zander. She and I do…better when I'm not under the same roof."

"I can see that."

She flinched at his reply.

He turned his head toward her. His eyes swept the length of her face. "What I mean to say is I understand your desire to move. You never mentioned *this* concern to me." His eyes found Puddles next to the kitchen gate. "Never asked if I could keep her for you till you have a place where you can have her back again."

"That isn't going to happen in her lifetime, Zander."

"You don't know that."

"Yes, I do. Tanya embezzled my money and failed to pay on our apartment complex. Allowing a Mr. Mancel to purchase it for a song because it foreclosed."

"And?"

"And I didn't pay attention. My credit record is... crushed."

The doggy gate squeaked open. "If Courtney listened to me, this wouldn't have happened. She never listens to me. Just like..." Mother stopped talking and reached a trembling hand out with the phone. "Your turn to talk."

Courtney wanted to talk to her dad, but she hesitated to move away from Zander. Their relationship would be different now. Sadness wound around her heart. This is what she'd expected. Why feel shocked by it?

Her dad's comforting baritone waited to tickle her ear with good wishes. At least he always provided that emotional haven. Never mind that he wouldn't correct Mother. Who could? He was the balm that kept her encouraged and moving somewhat forward. His ability to ease the hurt always provided a glimmer of hope.

"Didn't you offer Zander anything to eat?"

Courtney jumped up. Her stool tipped, but Zander caught it before it smacked on the tile floor. Heat filled her face, and she hoped it didn't show. "Thanks, Zander. Ice cream, cake, crackers?"

He held up his hand. "I'm good."

She nodded, grateful that he remained calm, especially since he probably wanted to choke her right now. She'd disappointed yet again. Apparently, that was who she was for that's who she'd always been. He'd proved to be an exceptional man who wouldn't retaliate, even though she made revenge far too easy.

She kept her eyes on the phone and approached her mother. Reaching a handout, she took it in a firm grasp and said, "Hey dad." How she needed his gentle tones of comfort desperately right about now.

"Dad—why are you calling me—dad? This is Bethany. I've called to find out what you planned for the shower and the date, so I can attend."

Sixteen

COURTNEY

Gwendolyn's Wedding & Formal Attire in Beaver Falls supplied such desirable and varied choices for bridesmaid's gowns that would match Bethany's taste. Courtney snapped photos of Cassie and Nicole as they squabbled over styles and colors. Blue and gold were options, pink, black, fire engine red, and orange were not. She didn't know how they'd receive their dresses in time. Felt like she'd been living on adrenalin. Hard to believe since she'd not had any coffee this morning.

The last photo showed the girls wearing navy blue. Nicole couldn't stand the tight waistline. She couldn't zip it up, and her temper flared when Cassie insisted that this was *the* dress. Courtney chuckled, making sure to take several shots of any action. Each photo had a small caption added before she sent them off over cyberspace.

"No way, no how," texted Bethany about the first three gowns. Her sister couldn't be here, but this was the next best way to gain her input.

The girls were hamming it up and posing in each dress, sharing the moment with their soon-to-be-married friend.

Courtney would find someone who could scare-up a scrapbook. She made a mental note that these photos would definitely make it into a pre-marriage section called *Battling Bridesmaids Dressed to Kill.*

"Positions girls." She eyed them as they posed for a pretend to be oh-so-mad-at-each-other shot. Then again, maybe they could design the scrapbook for Bethany. Her cell phone buzzed as she took the picture, making her almost drop it on the stage. Her quick hand pinned it against her leg.

Zander. "Hello."

"What are you and Puddles doing today?" If she heard right, there was a hitch of excitement zipping through those words. Maybe he thought he'd changed her mind about getting rid of the dog.

Heading toward the dressing room, she put him on speakerphone and sent the group photo to her sister.

She kicked a bag of decorative ribbon beside her on the platform. These rolls would match the exact tones Bethany wanted in the flower arrangements. "I'm with the girls trying on dresses for the wedding, and soon I'll be home with Mother. I have to run her to a couple of doctor appointments. Then we just go home." Sigh. She fingered the next gown to be tried on. She'd sent the picture of this dress to her sister because it impressed her. The periwinkle would complement the bridesmaid's skin tones, and the bodice sported an elegant, not trite lacy look. The simplicity of the gown beamed elegance.

"Would you have time to see me tonight to film a session?"

"I don't have anyone for Mother tonight. I've been running or working a lot and need to spend some time with her."

"Here's what's happening, I have an important meeting with the man wishing to sponsor me for these videos. This is important because I'll meet with him in three days. The more lesson plans we have finished, the better my chances to make a go of this."

"Oh, did you want to borrow Puddles and have someone else walk her through the lessons? Your welcome to her anytime."

Silence on the phone. "I'll consider that. When do you get back from the doctors?"

Cassie threw a clutch purse her way, and she caught it one-handed. "Probably four o'clock. I can talk to you then. Sorry, I can't train with Puddles." Her conscience spit fireworks over that—not even white lie. She would have to find a way out of these lessons. Maybe redirect Zander to someone else with a dog. Having several dogs in a training video would be a great idea.

"There's something else I want to talk over with you. Soon. But not yet."

"Well, doesn't that sound cryptic." She laughed right out loud.

Her phone buzzed. A message from Bethany about the periwinkle wonder text. "*Keepers. Just perfect.*" Courtney sucked in a satisfying breath. Her *I thought so smile* settled over her from head to toe as she sat down in the changing room chair to slip off her sandals.

Ten minutes later, the girls were dressed in the selection Courtney tagged as 'the one.' She handed her cell phone, camera-ready, to the sales lady and trusted her to take a somewhat complimentary photo. Once she'd e-mailed some photos to Bethany, she expected a reply that would undoubtedly applaud their choice. Nicole still fussed about fittings and her need to diet, but didn't she always? Otherwise, color, style, and price proved just right.

COURTNEY

The dust rag picked up way too much dust. Courtney sneezed and continued to rub the coffee table, and at intervals, she folded over the cloth until there were no clean spots left. The sweeper sat in the corner, poised for attention, and an emptying. Tanya created a system for such mundane tasks. If she only had her ex-partner in her back pocket for days like this. Then again—maybe not.

"You'll never get done if you dilly-dally like this."

"Mother." Could she not use a more archaic term? "I'll get it done." Though it was the last thing she wanted to do on the planet. Running Mother around to the doctors earlier and to the drug store was problematic enough. Now her mother's critical eye surveyed her every move.

She pushed her knees up off the carpeting and stood. A slow glance around the room made what little energy she had slide into sluggishness.

The cell phone rang *Lost Dog* by Sleeping at Last ring tone. Zander was calling. She jumped—wishing for the first time she would be free to be filmed.

"Are you home yet?"

"In a manner of speaking, yes." She moved down the hallway and tossed the dirty rag in the laundry closet next to the bathroom. A pile of clean rags waited in the laundry basket begging to be used. She snatched one and turned to pad down the hall in the direction of the living room doorway.

"Great, I'll knock on the door then."

"What?" Courtney fixed her attention on her ripped jeans and stretched out beyond belief stained t-shirt. Looking at the front door, she saw his eyes crinkling with laughter through the front window.

She shook her head. Tried to pin her grin to a minimum.

She should have known. Courtney walked past the door, still holding the phone against her ear while aiming her gaze toward the living room.

"Hey, I'm out here."

"Hey, you must have forgotten to knock."

Three loud, but not obnoxious knocks on the front door made Mother and Puddles jump.

"Who in the world?" Mother said over the news station as she slid an irritated glance in the direction of the entrance hall.

Puddles took off at a run and barked the deepest, most satisfying bark Courtney had heard in a long while. She sprang in place until Courtney arrived to open the door.

Zander walked inside, wearing a white pullover shirt and Khaki shorts. He looked great. He almost forgot his *ignore the puppy for fifteen minutes rule*. Puddles could just about melt anybody's resolve that way.

Courtney glanced at her awful outfit. Self-consciousness was merely the start of a list of feelings merging and fighting for dominance. Her hair wasn't even combed. She covertly tried to slip her hand up to straighten the tangles on the right side of her head.

Zander zeroed in on her with "a look" before bringing a whiff of soap and spicy cologne as he leaned her way. "Trust me." His deep voice teased her. She felt the wisp of breath tickle her neck. And her smile slid on her face before she'd realized she needed to block it.

"Okay." *Why did she say that? When someone said 'trust me,' there was a reason not to.*

"Oh, Zander, you scared the devil out of me," Lillian said.

"I sure hope so, Mrs. MacDuff." He strode into the living room and held out his hand to greet Lillian. He turned toward Courtney and said, "Courtney and Puddles and I would like to invite you to a training session. Right in your own backyard."

Courtney's mouth dropped open.

He gave her a wink, "Why don't you change into training clothes and meet me here in a few minutes?" Then he turned a charming smile on her mother and began making small talk like he knew Courtney would run to do his bidding.

How dare he! Liberation from the mundane versus filmed training tangled into a wrestling match. Thoughts of sunshine and cool breezes and Zander won far too easily. She all but ran down the hallway to change.

Smart clothes and shoes this time around—denim shorts with a classy t-shirt. That way, when Puddles slobbered, then dirt wouldn't show so noticeably. Simple but sweet jewelry draped around her neck and ears. Grass covered the ground in her parent's backyard, not dust like Zander's training pen. She slipped on her sparkling white Nikes—okay, this pick was for pride alone, and she could only hope that the dog would keep her feet to herself. Courtney combed her hair into submission. She was ready in ten minutes and wondered if Zander could brag the same.

Striding down the hallway, Courtney took her time. It was one thing to dress for a training class, but quite another to be in the spotlight—literally. She rounded the corner into the living room. The television news played in the background and Mother pet Puddles, who leaned against her knees. Zander's deep voice explained the focus of this training session.

She stepped inside the room. Puddles rose to greet her by nuzzling her soft muzzle against her hand. Courtney smoothed her fur around her ears and shoulders. Smiling down at her upturned face. "The star of the show needs to be brushed."

"Another suspicious fire took place last night." The broadcaster said, "This time, the Gottwell residence was destroyed. This morning the owner claimed that valuable antique furniture was stolen first before the fire was set. No one was hurt since the family was away on vacation. Anyone with information regarding—"

Lillian turned down the sound. Then she motioned that she wanted help getting to the bathroom.

Zander grabbed the remote and turned up the volume. "—call this number. There is a reward for information regarding this possible theft and the fire."

Mr. Greenwood's face came to mind. She reached for her mother's arm and steadied her trembling limbs. How odd that these two cases were so similar. "That's just what Mr. Greenwood said."

"That man has dementia or something. Pure coincidence, I imagine." Zander nodded.

Courtney lifted her eyebrows to acknowledge him, but something stirred in her belly that didn't bode well. She'd never find out though. Yet, what if Mr. Greenwood told the truth? What if she worked with a murderer—her imagination kicked into the farfetched category Nat accused her of so often. She had to let these concerns go.

Once they were outside, Zander cornered her near her dad's cabinet, built for outdoor yard chemicals and equipment. He covered the flat surface on top with instructions and drawings.

"Before each lesson or skill, I want to go over the directions with you. That way, you will relax and be familiar with what is expected of you and Puddles. The first skill you will practice with Puddles is the sit and stay commands." He paused to see if she followed.

She nodded.

"Sit your dog, put your hand flat in front of her nose. Tell her to stay. In a firm way. Big girl voice."

Courtney laughed. Yes, she spoke in a wimpy way to the dog.

"Next, step forward a leash distance in front of her and wait for one or two minutes. Return on her left side; circle around to her right side. Reward her immediately."

Courtney gazed at the details before her. "Impressive. I particularly like the stick figures." Her manicured finger pointed at the most outrageous crippled drawing.

"Yeah, yeah, yeah. I can't draw." His smile never dimmed when he pinned her with a look that swirled with challenged. "You'll shine out there." He nodded his head toward the grassy area.

Warmth filled his gaze and her face—such open acceptance—was almost too splendid to take in. She could do this. And she would perform despite Mother's attention.

"Thanks for doing this, Courtney. I really appreciate your help. Impressing my investor will move me toward success with one of my most important goals."

"Success, helping your V.I.P. goal—well, if I'd known that—I would have charged you a mint to star in your training class."

"Yeah, right." He chuckled.

"I'll situate Mother while you set up the camera." She hoped that she wouldn't be too distracted. There could be no forgetting the camera was running this time around.

Puddles headed toward her outside food dish, and Zander swooped it out of reach.

"What are you doing?" Courtney hooked her fists on her hips as her elbows winged out to her sides. Puddles sounded off with her raw raw rawwww complaint.

"She'll be more interested in earning her treats if she isn't full during training. You can feed her afterward."

That would be helpful. "How do you come up with all this info?" A soft breeze slipped by, sharing the fragrance of several unidentified bushes edging the yard with purples and yellows. She situated the patio table and chair out of the sunshine, and her fingers tested the cushion. Mother would be comfortable.

Zander opened the sliding glass door. "I'll bring your mother outside. Want to hook Puddles up and stand where I placed the red marker?

"First, I'll pour Mother a drink, and then I can do that. You want something too?"

"Anything cold will do. Thanks." He disappeared inside the house, and she followed him into the kitchen. She heard them talking in the living room as she doused the ice cube loaded glasses with lemon-flavored sweet tea. Snagging a box of crackers, she placed them on the tray also. Once outside, she positioned Mother's drink and crackers in easy reach.

The leash and training collar lay on top of the instructions. Puddles chased a butterfly nearby.

Courtney spied the liver flavor treats, Puddles's favorite. That would amp up the canine's obedience. She rolled one moist ball between two fingers. They were easy to handle too. She placed some in a pouch she'd hung around her neck and called her big girl. Amazing how a little motivation in a pouch quickened Puddles's hearing and listening abilities.

Ears flapping, Puddles bounded across the yard in record time. Then she sat for the tradeoff of collars and to accept a juicy treat. Courtney walked the dog to the spot. Turning, she faced the camera as Zander led Mother out of the house and to her chair.

"Heel Puddles." She sat obediently beside Courtney and waited. Training continued to be successful. Not anything like the painful experience she remembered from their first session. Puddles seemed to enjoy the teamwork and activity as much as she did the treats.

Courtney's muscles relaxed, and giddiness took the lead. She and Puddles moved with practiced rhythm and grace. Walking her each day, Zander's recipe for alpha maintenance must've helped. Eager thrill stirred her like her childhood ballerina days had at one time. Dog training was an art form too. Puddles responded to her commands with that innocent *I'm so glad to be here* look on her face. Just like when working with Zander.

She stole several glances toward her mother. Lillian stared in the direction of their neighbor's roof or yard or at her hands. Watching her mother stirred ugly feelings she wished were long gone.

She tripped over Puddles's paw, and the puppy yelped and danced away from her feet. Courtney gasped and stepped back, holding tight to the leash.

Mother zeroed in on the action and added, "You ought to be more careful. You could hurt the dog that way." The first and last comment she'd made concerning their training. It was just as well.

They'd worked for almost an hour when the sky became streaked with muted reds and purples as the sun rolled behind the trees. Bugs proved their gargantuan appetite as they attacked humans and canine alike.

"That's a rap. You were—exceptional." Zander looked like he could fly.

"Looks like a monkey could train a dog with your instruction, Zander." Lillian's voice clanged hollow as she gathered her crutch in hand and readied to move inside the house.

Courtney's heart sank. Why was Mother so insulting?

Zander turned to Courtney, linking his gaze with hers. The zing knocked away his joy. Apparently, he'd heard it too.

COURTNEY

Chocolate brown walls closed in on Courtney as she sprawled over half of her mattress. She fought the darkness encroaching throughout the room, except where the nightlight's glow highlighted the space under her desk. Exciting thoughts— depressing thoughts—all wrestled her away from sleep. Puddles's dream-jerking shook the bed. She blamed the last few distracting squeaks of the metal bed frame for keeping her from oblivion, though she knew better. It wasn't nice to lie to yourself. You always got caught.

Courtney turned on her side and watched as fuzzy long-haired paws flopped and twitched as though running after rabbits in a wide-open field. Mother tried to talk her into trimming the dog's hairy feet. But the paws, backside, and ears made Puddles, uniquely Puddles. She couldn't bring herself to change that Albert Einstein look that was taking over. She was only two years old, and Courtney had just read that this breed matured at three or four years. At intervals, the puppy clawed her leg and exhaled mini barks.

"Well, at least you can sleep." Puddles didn't respond, still caught up in the false pursuit. Stifling air blanketed the corners of the room. Was the air conditioning on? She could row a boat in this humidity. Her mind played with word descriptions for the heat, exhaustion, and utter discomfort she felt. Surely, she could use this experience in some future novel.

Her earlier moody pacing did nothing to ease the muscle cramps in her legs. Nat would tell her she needed to drink water. Water solved everything. She scanned the four walls and the odd shadows. Rolling over, she faced the clock that glared three in the morning. Another sleepless night practically guaranteed she'd arrive at Leman's looking baggie eyed and dull-minded at 10:00 this morning.

The toilet flushed down the hall. Mother never got up without ringing the bell for assistance. Her heart skipped a beat, and her hand fell to the mattress. Puddles lay sleeping, blissfully unaware that they had an intruder who had the audacity to *flush*. Courtney pulled jogging pants over her pajama bottoms and grabbed the cast iron poker crowded next to the fake fireplace along her outside wall. As she pulled the door open an inch, the hinges squealed, triggering her rapidly beating heart. Dizziness nearly made her stumble. Her free hand grasped the molding around the door frame. Oh, she needed to breathe.

Pulling the door wide open with a quick motion cut the noise in half. This could be used for a haunted house manuscript—except she didn't write that genre. Had the intruder noticed?

Shadows pushing in from the hallway reminded her about the robberies and fires she'd heard about on the news. Her grip tightened around the poker, pinching her hand and fingers. She kicked her neglected slippers away from the doorway. She pushed them out of the way. An intruder could be fought off better with bare feet – not cushioned ones. She padded down the hallway. Pressing her face against the chilly surface of the wall next to the bathroom door, allowed her to hear the hiss of running water. Her limbs seemed paralyzed. The tinny metallic taste of fear trickled down her throat. Breathe, Courtney breathe.

Running water stopped, and the towel rack banged against the wall startling her. She hopped back. Light peeking from under the door switched off. The doorknob turned briskly. She backed up two steps and mentally prepared for battle even as she raised her poker high and stood facing the bathroom's entrance. A shadow stepped out of the bathroom.

Swinging the poker, Courtney stopped when the muted glow from the nightlight inside the bathroom exposed familiar gray-brown hair bound with several pink sponge curlers. Her cane-less mother, seeming to have no problem walking after all. Further proof that she was capable of taking care of herself.

Courtney huffed. "Mother. What are you doing?"

"I'm going to the bathroom, what does it look like?" Mother waddled to her room across the hall.

Blinking hard, Courtney tried to stop the trembling in her arms and legs. She'd almost clobbered her mother. In the dark. In the hallway. She dropped the poker then approached her parent's bedroom.

The door snapped closed, the sound of a lock jerking into place boxed her ears. She placed her fingertips on the cool, jagged, molding of the door frame and leaned close to the oaken barrier blocking her way. Listening.

The creak of the bed, surrendering under the weight of a body and swish of silk sheets, confirmed that her mother met her destination unattended. The light beneath the doorway disappeared with a click, abandoning her in the dark, stifling hallway, further away than ever from sleep.

ZANDER

Huffing and muscling the bookcase to the opposite wall winded Zander and his helper, Ken. This house sale would be an important one. Three separate home-owners almost acquired Zander as their agent because of his house-staging services. But first, they'd watch the outcome for this property he worked on. Would his service shorten the amount of time on the market for this cape house, and increase the price garnered because of being adorned with period furnishings?

"Man, this is heavy." Ken placed his hand against the upper section of the bookcase, his lungs scooping up the oxygen in the room, while sweat trickled and pushed a path down his face.

Zander's recently scuffed knuckles knocked against the wood three times. "Real wood all the way through." He'd advised the owners to paint the living room and office rooms with cream or neutral tones, pumpkin to compliment the dining room woodwork, and off-white to brighten the bathrooms. They hired a friend of his for that purpose, and everything looked as it should. Networking—the key to success in this business. Any business.

Now to add pizzazz and sizzle with furnishings, lamps, and pictures. The owners had crowded this huge bookcase between sliding glass doors leading to the deck outside and the archway for the kitchen. The arrangement caused the woodwork, doors, and furniture to dwarf that side of the room. He chose the longer wall to accent the qualities this larger piece of furniture offered.

He liked a home to breathe. Too frequently, owners packed furniture and hoarded possessions into a room, making it a prison and not a haven it was built to be. This residence would go on the market in half a week, so he needed to finalize the choice rooms for the realtor shots that would find their way onto the internet advertisement.

"Gary and Penny Ross are putting their home up for rent in two weeks."

"That will get snatched up quick. Gorgeous place, nice location."

"Maybe. Maybe not. They want this spread by word of mouth so that they will have more control over picking the occupants. People in their income bracket are usually buying. Course if someone is building, and they need a stop off place that could entice the right people to rent this house."

Hayward backed away to view the whole side of the room. "That's smart. Don't want someone damaging all the work they put into their home. I remember when they first started adding woodwork and drywall. I thought they were crazy."

"I hate to say it, but this bookcase needs to move over a couple inches to the left."

"I hate to agree, but I do." Both men grabbed the sides and grunted as they angled and centered the bookcase.

His busy schedule pushed ample weight against Zander's mind. He needed to finish this dining room and then head out to the next job. Leman's Fine Furnishings.

COURTNEY

Courtney bumped into her car door. "Ouch." She shook her hand, trying to dislodge the pain shooting up her arm. So, walking around while in a daze could be dangerous after all.

She hurried as a car sped past. If she'd been a few seconds slower, she would've been decorating the pavement. Sigh. She rubbed her knuckles as she rehearsed how she almost mortally wounded or killed her mother in the hallway last night.

Mother's deceptions had always disturbed Courtney. This time it would have cost them both dearly had the nightlight been out. Her mother's secret independence stewed her insides, even though this discovery—opportunity—offered her the chance to move to a new home.

Courtney glanced at the rolled-up newspaper gripped under her left arm. The key to her new home might be lodged between these inked pages. During break time, she'd scan apartment listings. Hope welled up inside her, but not with the buoyancy she'd expected. Probably lack of sleep contributed to her lack-luster attitude. She'd have to leave that melancholy mood under her feet on the sidewalk today before she walked into the store.

The door gracing Leman's Fine Furnishings in gold script pushed open. She stepped back and gazed into Zander's *so glad to see you* smile. Her shoulders hitched up. He wasn't laughing. Maybe, he hadn't seen her walk into the car door. *The Beaver County Times* slipped downward a couple of inches, and she pressed her arm to her side to prevent its fall.

"Oh, one of the last of the good guys, huh? Thank you." She released a full-force smile past last night's sleepless memories and the nightmare that repeated itself from time to time. Maybe he'd know that he was appreciated. Then she strode past him and entered Leman's. All the front arrangements were changed. "Wow! Is this some of your work?" The classy balance of staged furnishings, pillows, and accessories embraced Zander's quality and brilliance—in her opinion.

"Thank you, and yes, thank you again." He allowed the door to close behind him.

Hair pulled loose from her clip as she shook her head back and forth. "You are gifted." She took the newspaper in her right hand and tapped his arm. "When I move out of Mother's, you want to help me arrange my apartment? I can pay you in cookies and Chinese?"

Serious eyes surveyed her face. "You have to get an apartment or home where you can keep Puddles. That's my condition. Along with cookies and Chinese." No self-respecting man would turn down an offer of food.

She turned her eyes to scan the living room arrangement to her left. The perfect balance of colors and proportions made her feel wobbly, or was it his request? "Places like that are few and far between." She couldn't push away the sadness that weighed her words. Heat stirred within her. Why did he have to push the reality of what giving Puddles away would cost her? He shouldn't be so concerned. Puddles wasn't his responsibility.

What was this war inside her heart? She was definitely *not* a dog lover, but unexpected emotions surged—grief—possibly pain? What? No, she was not a dog lover—at all. This puppy, she'd called *The Beast* or *Monster Dog* when Tanya first brought her home, was still beast-like. Five more calls from families interested in adopting Puddles waited on her voicemail from the last couple of days. The list of viable homes grew larger, yet she'd just been too busy to check them out—or had she? Zander wouldn't be pleased if he knew. Ugly truth weighed her heart, even though he'd heard that first phone call he hadn't changed toward her like she expected. Like what would happen once she gave Puddles up for good.

Mother's antics last night shifted the move and relocate Puddles idea from possible reality into the nearer-than-ever reality. She stole a guilt-ridden glance at him. His pinched expression revealed how he cared for Puddles, pouring gloomy oppression over her already flailing emotions. No doubt, he'd be the perfect person to adopt her, except for the fact that he was never home. Puddles needed companionship. Not just a heart that was hers, but always out of reach. These other families had...

"You going to stand there all day, blocking customers, or

are you going to punch in?" Mr. Whippier peered at his watch in an exaggerated deliberate motion.

Aiming her attention at their intruder, Mr. Whippier, she noticed his face blotched with red spots, and narrow red-rimmed eyes pointed their glare at her. He sported this shady attitude toward her since she'd witnessed his crash-dive attempt at befriending Mr. Mancel.

"On my way." Her feet moved forward as though weighted with bowling balls. What was wrong with her? She'd longed for freedom even more since she'd become aware of Tanya's embezzlement and mismanagement, which had lost their apartments.

Living with Mother oppressed and challenged her more than anything she'd ever experienced. Her secret hope of breaking down the walls that had accumulated between them over the years—felt lifeless. It seemed impossible to change the mold. Close contact and supporting her mother seemed to only breed contempt and served to strengthen the layers between them.

She chanced a peek at Zander. He jerked away in surprise when their eyes met. This would be a stressful day, indeed.

Several burdened steps later, the scent of roses enveloped her. She stopped. Shut her eyes for stollen moments. *Beloved daughter,* blew over her mind like a whispered breeze, gently lifting the weightiest burdens off of her heart. She breathed deep. Her thirsty spirit drank in comfort.

Hissing from an aerosol spray caught her attention. She glanced toward the sound as dark hair rose above the counter-top.

Daria.

Courtney accepted the blessed lifting of her spirit despite who triggered the release of fragrance. Wouldn't Daria be miffed is she knew how she'd cheered Courtney today? Those whispered words, though, how did their meaning sink so deeply into the crevices of her being? Joy rippled inside, causing her to laugh soft—so soft— that she doubted anyone else heard her. Moving forward, she noticed her heals clicked a cheerful beat against the hard linoleum floor.

Only five minutes late, according to Leman's clock as she continued toward the employee office to punch in. Hopefully, the boss wouldn't dock her a half hour.

A couple of hours later, there were no customers in sight. Since Courtney could log onto the computer, she was given the daily task of checking the logs and entering information. Courtney's mind took advantage of this downtime and began to roam. Her attention stayed tuned with the second hand of the clock, which hung over the service counter, dragging seconds and minutes to a near standstill.

Mr. Angerton shook his head. "Why don't you take a break and Courtney... come back focused." At least his eyes twinkled when he spoke.

Courtney smiled an apologetic grimace. Why she'd felt guilty for no sales when there were no customers, she didn't know. Her mind itched to look over the rent ads. She couldn't imagine even one more week under her mother's roof. There'd be several more weeks before the cast came off Mother's leg, but obviously, she could get around right now without a problem.

That cave of a bedroom would be happily relinquished. She laughed at how Puddles knocked boxes and clothing down when she turned around next to the bed. Her heart squeezed, and she forced her thoughts away from the Leonberger, who stole her affection as easily as she did a bone.

Once she entered the employee office, she sat down behind the only desk. The chair rocked with rickety motion until she forced it to stop. Armed with a bright yellow highlighter, Courtney made a bold zigzag across the interesting house rentals.

Zander made his way inside the office then leaned closer to see what she was up to. He pulled back, standing away from the desk. "Rentals. Anything interesting?"

"Only two." Worry tried to encapsulate her nerves, but she fought the concerns. "I only need one place to live. Just one." She glanced over the ads flat on the desk. One refused pets, and the other didn't mention them.

"Did you call yet?"

She slipped her cell out of her pocket. "I'll do that now." She sought the wall clock. "I have ten more minutes of break time."

As she dialed the first one, he said, "I'll go with you if you're going tonight."

Gratitude flooded her. Tears collected in her eyes, and she blinked them back. If her dad were here, he would have offered also. How she missed him. She nodded her thanks and listened to the answering machine message. After leaving her phone number and time to call, she said, "One down and one to go. And then I call the moving truck."

"See if they are available when you are finished with work, and we'll run straight there. Maybe we could grab a bite to eat and bring some home to your mother also."

"Now, you're talking." She winked at him. "Let's see if this landlord is home."

Eighteen

COURTNEY

Courtney's finger traced the phone number on the wrinkled *The Beaver County Times* advertisement. Lifting her fingers, she noticed black smudges soiling her hand. Zander grinned at her and tossed a box of tissues from the other side of Mr. Angerton's desk.

A man's gruff booming voice made her hold the phone an inch away from her ear. She jotted an appointment on her calendar after a bit of discussion. The tip of her pen drew a mini-map and captured the address and landmarks on a loose-leaf page.

The door swung open, drawing her attention. Mr. Angerton strode into the office. He crossed his arms in front of his chest. "Courtney, do you mind if I send you home early? Let's say 4:30. I have too many workers scheduled. Next time, I'll think about town events."

"No problem at all." Being released early would work out well. Natalie would not expect her home until after 7:00. That would give them time to look at apartments and pick up dinner.

"Thanks, Courtney." Mr. Angerton nodded at Zander before leaving.

"Time for me to get back to work." She stood up and moved toward the door.

"Spare time on your hands! I'll buy dinner if you want to film another lesson." Zander's question flowed velvety soft against the background music filtering in from the store's speakers.

She stopped dead in her tracks—halfway through the doorway. In slow motion, she turned her head toward him. Courtney couldn't say no, especially when he came into view with a smirk that caused her to laugh.

"I suppose. I'll have to since you're feeding me."

ZANDER

The aroma of spicy chicken and baked bread teased his senses as they waited for their order. This would be his first meal of the day. Not smart. His stomach growled in complaint. Had she heard the rumbling? Zander glanced at Courtney, standing at his side.

Her thumb rubbed the corner of the small calendar in her hand. She took a pen and scratched out the two apartments—overpriced in his estimation—on her list. Her shoulders drooped a bit. There were too many dead ends and high prices.

"I know a family who is particular about their house. They want to rent it to the right person. Someone who will take care of it."

"I'm not exactly Suzie homemaker. That is more my mother's style." She paused and looked into his eyes. "And what about Puddles?"

He knew it. Courtney and Puddles were bonding. He could plan more strategies to help them stay together. Hope withered at the thought of Gary and Penny interviewing Puddles. That would be their biggest problem. Would a dog up the rental price?

"I'll call them, and on our way to your mother's, we will do a drive-by." He could see the bounce emerging in her eyes and smile. And her shoulders took their rightful place again too.

***

Courtney

Stirring music, The Passion According to Matthew by Johann Sebastian Bach, whispered in the background. Natalie's favorite music. Citrus-orange fragrance permeated Lillian's kitchen as Courtney and Zander walked into the warm glow of candlelight.

They approached her. One of Nat's original cheesecake recipe cards lay sprinkled with flour, while the remnants of batter fanned out around the counter only a half-inch away. Knowing Natalie, she probably didn't have an extra copy of her precious recipe. Courtney made a mental note to buy her friend some plastic sleeves to protect them against the very dishes she prepared. Bowls and measuring cups and spoons stacked or leaned against one another beside the kitchen sink. Lillian would not approve.

She enjoyed the relief spilling into Natalie's face as her friend lifted her gaze off of her creation toward them. Courtney grinned.

Puddles pawed the door, wagging her tail and every part of her body with excitement. "I'll be back in a moment." Zander strode toward the door, grabbing Puddles's leash on the way.

Courtney snickered. "Rough day?"

Her friend tossed her a scrunched-up expression anchored with a frown. "You could say that." She finished pealing the last slice of orange, releasing another cloud of citrus fragrance.

Courtney sniffed. "Umm. Anything I need to know?" She could almost taste oranges. Fried chicken and gravy smells trailed her inside the kitchen as she plopped the loaded bags onto the other end of the countertop.

"No, and you don't want to either. Any of that for me?" She leaned toward the bags and fanned the fried chicken aroma her way.

"Wait—the owner of Natalie's Victorian Bed & Breakfast wants to eat fast food?"

"We are starving. You haven't properly stocked the fridge." Natalie rounded the counter-top toward her and placed her fists on her hips. "I refuse to shop with her. That's one thing you cannot bribe me to do." She grabbed a wet napkin and rubbed her hands. When she twisted the napkin around her finger, Courtney knew something big happened.

Focusing her eyes on the wrapped finger, she grabbed Natalie's hand. "What's up?"

Natalie hesitated. She pulled her hand away and hid it behind her back. Lowering her voice, "Do you know how well your mother gets around?"

"I found out in the wee hours last night. I suppose you saw her walking around without help today too. I'm planning to move out as soon as I find an apartment."

Nodding, she asked, "When are you starting to look?"

"I already did tonight. Neither place was affordable. Plus, there would be so much to fix and paint." She shook her head, more hair loosened from her clip. She reached up and tucked the strand behind her ear. Pulling the everyday plates out of the dishwasher, she moved to the kitchen table to lay them on placemats. "But Zander knows a couple who want to rent to someone who doesn't throw wild parties. He is looking into it for me."

"Where is it?"

"It's right down the road from you. Actually, it's on the other side of the house with the roses. You know, the house next to the lady who works for you sometimes. Zella?"

"Zeta."

"The house is gorgeous outside. I can't wait to see the interior. Literally, I feel like I'm walking into a dream. We don't know how they would handle Puddles, though. I can't help but allow my hopes to climb high."

"Wouldn't that be cool to be almost neighbors?" Natalie's words tumbled toward her with the warmth of sunshine.

"I'd love being neighbors. I'm so ready for a place of my own again. I'll still take my mother places and shop for her, but I don't feel I have to live here anymore."

"But—"

The sliding glass door scraped open. Zander walked into the room, holding Puddles at his side while looking toward the living room.

She turned in the direction of his gaze. Mother's practiced look of disapproval stared back. Turning again, Courtney faced the table and nearly dropped the plate in her hand, barely catching it in time.

Zander released Puddles, who ran to Courtney, begging for attention. That didn't succeed. The dog used her black muzzle to poke her leg and danced around the table and her feet. Courtney continued to ignore her.

Mother harrumphed. Then the whirl of the walker's metallic wheels caught Courtney's attention. Turning toward the sound, she watched as Mother quickly jerked right, before falling on her broken leg. Mother's shrill scream split the air.

Courtney's breath caught. She dropped a plate on the table, which broke before bouncing to the floor with a loud crash. The room blurred as she ran toward her mother's crumbling form. Zander appeared by their side. Courtney rolled Mother into a tender embrace, lifting her body away from the floor. He pulled the walker out from under Lillian.

Both mother and daughter's eyes teared as Courtney gathered her with trembling arms.

Lillian's wrinkled hand reached up to tap Courtney's face. The cold fingers touched twice, so lightly on her cheek, the motion seemed only to be imagined.

"You would leave me? You would leave me when I need you so?" Lillian's hand dropped to her side as she wept and wept, tears dampening her cheeks.

⁓ ⁕ ⁓

COURTNEY

Natalie carried the last box of craft supplies from her car and laid them at the far end of Lillian's dining room table.

Courtney reached to lift a corner of the cloth draped on the one lidless box and earned a slap on the wrist. She yanked her hand back. "Ouch."

"I have something to show you first." Her friend's eyes sparkled. "Then, you can look in there."

Courtney wanted to yank the cloth off the box. "Oh, girl, you're driving me wild."

Her friend quirked a mischievous smile and slid a cover off the box situated furthest away. Lifting a feather pen inserted into an ink well labeled in gold letters, Mr. and Mrs. Brandon Steele, including the wedding date, she wiggled the plume before placing it on the table. *Adorable.*

Sigh. "I hope Bethany won't think it's too Victorian. Where did you find it?"

"I knew you'd appreciate these. I think your sister will too. Zeta did." Natalie stroked the feather with the tip of her nail bitten finger. "This larger pen goes with the guest book for the wedding."

"You need to hire her full-time. She seems quite talented. Think about it—the nails, ordering unusual gifts, and who knows what else—"

"Roses. Definitely roses."

"What? Oh. Yes, those." Courtney picked the pen off of the table.

"She's a writer, but she writes under a pseudonym. She keeps pretty busy with that. I think she's multi-published." Natalie shifted her feet and relaxed against the table. "I sure do need the help. I wish it could be her. Some days I don't know where to start because there's so much to accomplish. Thank goodness your mother doesn't mind me working on my business calls, designs, and ledger books."

"I wish I could help you with your business. I'd probably get frustrated and ..."

"Quit."

Courtney glanced at her. "Yeah, quit." What Nat said was true, so why did her heart take such a tumble over what people said? Courtney fumbled with the pen from the table and dropped it next to the fake inkwell.

"We love you anyway, Butterfingers." Natalie rubbed her back with a gentle caress.

Warmth bubbled up, almost erasing the pain. "What is Zeta's author's name?"

"Bonnie Greenleaves."

"That name suits roses too."

"I'd never thought about that. You must think alike. Author types and all."

"Hmm, a local author using a fake name and one whom I've never seen mentioned in the Times or book stores. Is she trying to hide?" She stopped and locked full gazes with her friend. Natalie hadn't lost the connection—how Courtney hid her work and yet couldn't stay away from writing. Did she remember that sleepover, years ago, when she'd discovered Courtney's manuscript tucked in a drawer?

Her friend's dark brow lifted; promising what Courtney wouldn't want to hear right now. Not ever. Unless she wrote the great American novel, she'd never risk her words to public scrutiny. Squealing wheels approached from the end of the hallway. Mother's walker. It would never do to have her know about secret writing.

"I love this inkwell, but it flirts with Victorian. You know how Bethany feels about that."

"It is so elegant, and Bethany loves history. So, we're only appealing to that interest. I think we can please her when she realizes we have her true preferences in mind."

Courtney reached for her friend and gave an excited hug. "Okay, maybe that will fly. I want to see the table centerpieces."

Natalie's rough fingers lifted a delicate base decorated with thin blue and gold ribbons and fresh, blue-tipped carnation, which encircled an ornate glass candle holder. Inside the glass rested a periwinkle votive, which perfectly matched the bridesmaid's dresses.

The floral scent stole her breath away. "Bethany will flip when she sees these. So gorgeous." She took the centerpiece in hand and turned it from side to side. Then she put it down and slipped her phone out her pants pocket. Looking around, she said, "Wonder where I should snap the photo?"

"Oh, no, you don't. These are a surprise." Her friend's hand grasped the arrangement and cradled it in her arms.

"But I've made her a part of each choice. She's the one who chose the bridesmaids dresses though she was hundreds of miles away. Also, she agreed on the roses and—"

"Carnations, those are so common. Why don't you get her irises instead? Those flowers are worthy of a wedding. And this—" Lillian's finger poked at the edge of the flower, causing the glitter to fall onto the table. "white flowers? Really now? Even the glitter you have on the tips will not disguise their utter lack of imagination." Mother's raspy voice drilled into their conversation.

Natalie mouthed 'utter lack of imagination' to Courtney when Lillian wasn't watching before placing the centerpiece on the table with far too much force—waking Puddles. Nat crossed her arms in front of her, as a frown dug into her face.

Lillian smiled back at them with the power of an office manager.

Courtney paused. If only she could please her mother once. Just once. "Bethany gave me a list of flowers she wanted for the wedding. Those are her choice of flowers and colors."

"Irises are much better, in my opinion, *if* my opinion mattered."

"Carnations are beautiful flowers too, Mother."

Lillian's chilling unidentifiable look shined back at her.

Courtney sighed. "Too bad Bethany can't stand how irises smell. She wants all the wedding flowers to match the ones she carries and the ones we carry, which are a simpler style. Besides, irises are pretty expensive too."

The flush on Lillian's cheeks was unmistakable. That shade of crimson had announced Mother's volcanic explosive tantrum many times over. "Irises have various fragrances."

"I'll set up a TV table and make your favorite coffee—thanks to Natalie." Her friend curtsied and showed off a fresh bag of beans while Courtney pushed a smile onto her face hoping it detracted from the high pitch of her voice. She snuck a peek at her exasperated friend, who sported an expression that screamed—why are you leaving me here with your angry mother?

Escaping mother's anger was all she could think about. Surely, Nat understood. Only leaving the room would diffuse the tirade her mother could work into if she'd stuck around. The doctor ordered her to keep an eye on Mother for another six weeks since the latest fall. She'd already be gone if he hadn't.

Six weeks. Could she last? A vision of her own funeral flashed before her mind. Many mourners with Mother laughing and sipping her coffee.

"Well, get on with it, then." Mother's frustrated tone broke into her thoughts. Lillian shoved her walker, banged it on hardwood planks, spinning wheels, and pushing the joy of Natalie's accomplishment far out of reach.

· — ·⚜· — ·

LILLIAN

"Hello, Jenson's Favorites & Flowers Boutique, how may I assist you?" Lillian pressed the speaker button off and held the cell phone to her ear.

"Karen, this is Lillian MacDuff. I'm wondering if this is too short notice to order table arrangements for my daughter's bridal shower this Sunday?" Lillian paused and listened as she heard Natalie's car fire up and pull out of the driveway. Courtney showered for work, so she had alone time and a plan.

"Real flowers."

"Yes."

"Sure."

"Wonderful. I knew you would be able to help me." She took a drink of lukewarm coffee. Not enough sugar as usual. Now, if Natalie had made coffee— "In six days, the shower will be held at Fellow's Branch Church here in Beaver Falls." Trembling began in her right hand, and she switched the cell to her left. Must be the excitement of helping Bethany plan something for once. Seemed like no one would consider her without a little encouragement.

"Okay, this Sunday. What kind of flowers?"

"Irises would be the best. Something blue. Can you deliver them at 1:00 this Sunday afternoon at the church's fellowship hall? Add lots of ribbons. Make it fancy." Lillian attempted another sip and almost choked.

"How is your daughter?"

"Bethany is still out-of-town, acquiring a job and searching for a home before the wedding. You wouldn't mind billing her for these flowers…"

Nineteen

COURTNEY

Hot chocolate would taste so good. Courtney had finished dusting and sweeping. Only the mirror and window were left to clean. She wiped the mirror with a paper towel and counted the streaks left behind. Shaking her head, she turned and pulled on her robe. As she padded down the hall, she heard Mother's voice. *Who was she talking to?* She paused and listened.

"Oh, Courtney, well, you know the same old, same old with her. She has a second-rate part-time job after she lost those apartments. The ones I told her not to get involved with."

"Well, who knows what her future plans are. She is living off of us for now. I'm sure she can't afford her own place yet. I doubt she will ever amount to much with no schooling and with her not having the *right* experience."

"Yes, you remember well. She is just like her. Looks and personality as well as ambition. Nothing at all like our Bethany—"

Courtney stifled a cry. Hot chocolate wouldn't be needed after all. The mixture of anger and pain infiltrating her emotions mentally drew her out of the front door and beyond.

Later that afternoon, Daria and Mr. Whippier were like vultures circling under the copper tin ceiling tiles of Leman's Fine Furnishings. Courtney almost made it to the couple that just entered the store, but she hesitated five seconds too long. Mr. Whippier swooped in for the kill. And kill it was. The poor young couple didn't know what hit them. When they saw the bill, the agonizing expressions that overtook their faces made her sick. Mr. Whippier would be strutting and bragging in the office later to anyone equipped with ears. It wouldn't matter if they didn't want to listen.

He always tried to sell as much as he could to each customer. Courtney preferred discovering what pieces customers actually needed and how much they could afford. Since she'd been allowed to start selling, several customers had made return visits. No doubt from her being sensitive to their priorities and goals. Trust. If you didn't have trust, what did that one big sale matter? Those customers would become flaming mad later on and might never return to the store because they'd felt manipulated. Her experience at a furniture store left her unsettled. Though their furnishings were amazing—she'd never returned.

Daria claimed the only other buying customers in the store, right before Courtney made her approach. The zip was gone from her stride after overhearing Mother, but she couldn't think about that now. She didn't want to stampede the customers, but it looked like it might come to that if she wanted to compete.

The door dinged, and she heard Daria groan. Her co-worker turned her back to the door. Mr. Greenwood approached the desk.

"Mr. Greenwood, how are you today?" Courtney put down a pen and offered her full attention.

The most delightful, youthful curiosity dominated his wrinkled face. The twinkle in his blue-gray eyes snagged her heart. If only she had her small notebook and a pen to capture his appearance and how his whimsical expression of anticipation made her feel. Hopefully, she'd remember all the details later. His character would fit nicely into her plot in her current work in progress.

"Fine thank you, Miss.—" Should she tell him her name? Sure, he'd forget in a minute anyway.

"Miss. MacDuff, but you may call me Courtney. Are you looking for anything particular today, sir?" She felt her fist tighten around the pen in her hand, so she deliberately relaxed her grip. Sizing up his baggy pants and suit coat relaxed the concern teasing her mind concerning *what if he gets violent.* He couldn't move too fast in those.

"I want to look at those living room sets." He pointed his chubby finger toward the upscale designs. Courtney looked at Daria and only received a shrug before her co-worker tuned and zeroed in on the next customer who walked inside the door.

Courtney winced, another lost opportunity. She tried not to be too disappointed, but she might be the only one without a single sale tonight. She generously poured out a smile for the lonely man and said, "Right this way."

They laughed as Mr. Greenwood sat down on several deep-seated couches designed for long-legged types. His baggy pants and leather shoes stuck out at amusing angles. He wiggled his feet, making each mismatch fun. His legs were not too short for a couple of the living room couch and chair sets.

"I'll take this couch, love seat, three chairs, and of course, the coffee table and three end tables. Neutral colors and no pattern fabrics. They'll easily match my accessories."

Courtney's mouth dropped open. "Are you sure you have enough room for all those pieces? I can play with the numbers and see if we can get just what you need so that you don't crowd your room."

Mr. Greenwood's sympathetic smile surprised her. "I have

a huge living room, and our sons and daughters will be coming to visit soon. It's time for me to furnish the place." A shadow, resembling sadness passed over his eyes.

Muscles tensed in Courtney's arms and neck.

"I'll need a dining room set with extra chairs. Also, a total of three-bedroom sets." He tilted his head as he glanced her way. "Well, we don't have all night. Let's get a move on." His voice held an urgency that he tempered with a smile that reached into his eyes.

Moodiness seemed to be as much a part of Mr. Greenwood as his friendliness had. Courtney hoped that he didn't sink into his darkest mood, the one she'd seen and hoped to never witness again.

Once they'd chosen all the furnishings, she led him to the service desk, ever keeping aware of his attitude. Courtney distracted him into pleasant tones by discussing varied furnishings. She put her hand in her pocket to retrieve a pen but felt a photograph instead. Oh, yes, the photo of her Rococo Rosewood Center Table, she allowed Zander to stage for a new customer. He'd taken the picture and written a note on the back of the page. A man, Mr. Bernard Townsteader, wanted to know how much she wanted for the piece. Her faithful dog-training friend had cautioned her about dealing with the man. The money did tempt her despite the fact it was one of her favorite pieces. Her customer seemed to fidget with his hands. Courtney laid the photo on the top of the counter. Mr. Greenwood snuck a peek.

He picked up the photo with his short chubby fingers. "This Rosewood Table is in great condition."

She quirked an eye his way. "That's my table, and a gentleman wants to purchase it from me. It's one of my favorites, though. I'm not sure how much it would be worth anyway." She typed the next model number. They waited while the computer configured the order. Courtney felt so grateful that Mr.

Angerton agreed to use the computer for keeping track of sales and making copies. This was a more accurate and speedy way to bill the customer.

"How much is he offering, may I ask?"

"He offered two thousand dollars." She glided a smile in his direction. So appreciative that Mr. Greenwood stayed in his right mind and that he placed such a generous order, she hoped he could afford. Wouldn't Mr. Angerton be pleased? Her cheeks began to hurt from all the grinning.

"Then he is not your acquaintance. Or at least he is no friend."

His bland reply unsettled her mood. "Why do you say that?" She typed more information into the computer.

"This piece would be worth in the neighborhood of two to three times that amount. The man intends to rip you off with such a price. I advise you not to sell. At least not to him."

He placed the photograph carefully on the countertop as though it were a priceless antique worthy of tender touch. His hand lingered over the photo.

Courtney couldn't resist, she reached over to pat his hand. "Mr. Greenwood, I'll take your advice. I didn't want to sell it anyway. Actually, I'm making some money on the piece as we speak by allowing a friend to stage it in a home that's for sale. At least until I find a place to call home." A sigh pushed out between her lips. Pain from Mother's earlier phone comments raked over her heart with a rude intrusion. No, she wasn't ready to give up the table. The home Zander showed her would be the perfect place to show off this table's beauty. If only she could move out right away.

Another five and a half weeks to watch over Mother, then she'd be free. The wedding was to take place in fourteen days, so maybe time would fly since she had more to accomplish than she knew how to get done.

A queasy feeling wrapped around her stomach at the

thought. If she could only bolt and hide until everything blew over. Being the maid of honor wasn't all it was cracked up to be. This wedding situation caused more problems and stress than she'd ever known. So many expectations would rise or fall depending on her decisions. And then there was Mother, dogging her every move, criticizing all along the way.

Mr. Greenwood's clear eyes clouded, and he moved with jerky unsure motions.

"Are you okay, Mr. Greenwood?"

He didn't respond to her, but once his gaze landed on the antique's sign, his face flushed and every movement seemed halted and strained. He gripped a paper promotion and then ripped it into tiny pieces.

Oh, please, Mr. Greenwood, not now. Courtney closed out the sale and focused her attention entirely on the man in front of her. He'd begun to look like he needed an excellent care facility instead of a house full of furnishings.

COURTNEY

She'd survived the workday and now wiggled her middle finger's broken nail. A low break. Lousy timing when she needed to look her best for the shower. She hated fake nails, but that could be her only option now.

Her cell rang. *Cassie.* She took the call. "Hey, how is the food planning coming along?"

"I've got nine people signed up for casseroles and three for fruit or veggie trays. And we don't have to worry none about desserts."

"Yeah, that is what I needed to hear today. I'm grateful for all your help." She rubbed her face and yawned.

"Well, just for that, I'm hanging up." Cassie laughed. "Seriously, I'll see you at the church."

Courtney dragged her foot spa out of the closet and positioned it on the floor in front of Mother's expensive recliner. Once filled with water, she aimed the jets and pressed the heat button—easing herself onto the padded comfort seemed too good to be true. Slipping aching feet into the warm bubbles was the perfect way to pamper herself. Wiggling her toes before they submerged did little to make them appear any less like a disaster. She needed them in tip-top shape for the wedding sandals, which showed every bit of flesh, heel to toes.

The grandfather clock struck 9:00, and the steady rhythmic tick-tocking eased her mind into relaxing patterns of thought. Mother had gone to bed, and Puddles was in the backyard. Quiet reigned, allowing her to rest. No demands.

She scooped excessive amounts of cream from the jar on the end table beside her. She rubbed each finger, thumb, and fronts and backs of her rough hands, massaging each muscle into submission. Vanilla fragrance dominated her senses. Her shoulders relaxed. Her mind slowed.

Ink stained one of her index fingers. For as long as ballpoint remained the memory of tonight and Mr. Greenwood's flip into more-than-a-senior-moment wreaked havoc on her emotions. To see him transform before her eyes and become the frightened, accusing man chilled her. Wasn't he too young for such a disease, maybe in his early seventies, so hard to tell his age? The cares of this world obviously did a number on him. Would her mother ever have to suffer that fate?

Pray.

Prayer was always good, but she needed to think about wedding plans, and the shower, which would be here in a couple of days. Would she get everything done? Her last talk with Bethany deepened her realization that her sister truly was beginning a new life elsewhere.

This town would never be Bethany's home again, and her sister's new beginnings were literally already starting. Emptiness settled in the hollow of her stomach, and loneliness moved in, so close she could sense its breath on the back of her neck. This wouldn't be her home without Bethany. Maybe the absence of her dad and wondering when and for how long he'd be away struck harder than she realized too.

What was here now? Just plugging along in her mother's house—no less and no more—while planning a bridal shower and wedding. But what happens after the wedding? And did Mother notice her efforts? Was Mother happy? Of course not. The real question was, would she ever be pleased with what Courtney achieved? Was she capable of noticing?

Knocking at the front door made her nearly jump out of her skin. She tried wiping vanilla cream off of her hands—not successfully—and a frown settling in where contentment had rested. Continued knocking hammered away her peace. She bent over and turned off the machine. Sloshing her feet out of the water, and onto the Teri towel. She moved toward the front entrance. Zander. She breathed a sigh of relief. He pressed his nose to the glass and winked at her. She laughed then tried to turn the knob on the door, but it slipped. Unable to get a good grip, she motioned for him to come inside.

His dark brown curls poked around the doorway. Once inside, he grabbed the inside knob, but his fingers slipped. An uneven grin stole over his face.

She grabbed a tissue from the hall table and handed it to him while she chided herself for enjoying his presence so much. Her glance swept over him. How could this man make jeans and a t-shirt look so good? When he turned his hazel eyes on her again, they were watchful. Her hand needed somewhere to roost, so she grabbed her elbow and squeezed.

With a nervous step backward, she turned and said over her shoulder. "Come on into the living room. I'd offer a drink to you, but it would end up on the floor." She waved her hands at him.

He snatched them in his, causing her to stop and lean closer. He rubbed his thumbs along the back of her hands and wrists. Tears bit the back of her eyes. No, she couldn't go there.

She felt her grip respond to his in kind before slipping away. Courtney motioned for him to follow her out of the hall and into the living room.

Grabbing more tissue, she began to rub the cream away.

"So, I heard about Mr. Greenwood. Are you okay?"

"I feel s—sad, concerned... confused. He's so normal one moment, and then something triggers him, and he... changes. I wanted to cancel the orders he placed, but when Mr. Angerton arrived at the store, he called Mr. Greenwood's son. Apparently, they know each other. The son said the family would be visiting soon at his father's new home and not to cancel the order. There was a true need for furniture."

"Your co-workers are jealous. They hate that your numbers are climbing so close to their sales totals."

She snorted. "They were grabbing up customers left and right, literally seconds before I can. They ignored Mr. Greenwood as though he weren't important. And if they'd bothered to see that he wanted to make a purchase, they would have tried to sell him more expensive items, and more then he'd ever need."

Zander reached out his hand and brushed her cheek. "You are so very kind." His eyes glowed with warmth and something very much like appreciation.

Squirming under his scrutiny, Courtney asked, "So, what's on your mind?" The determined set of his jaw made her think that something besides Mr. Greenwood zigzagged across Zander's gray matter. She plopped on the recliner and then curled up. Waiting.

He flinched when she'd asked him. But his immediate response held nothing but pleasure. "I talked to those people I know with the house for rent. I told them about you and Puddles."

"And?" She leaned forward in her chair. Every nerve ending tingling. What if he told her they didn't want her... or Puddles? This day had been littered with hurt and sadness. She didn't wish to stomach more. Her heartbeat quickened, and the fragrance of his aftershave edged its way to her side of the room.

"Of course, they aren't happy about the dog."

"Oh." I understand." Disappointment draped over her enthusiasm. She slunk back into the cushions of her chair.

"They're thrilled about you. It took a bit of convincing and a promise that you'd continue lessons with Puddles for them to allow you to rent their home."

Almost speechless. Almost. Courtney dragged her feet from underneath her and leaned forward again. Looking at him full in the face, swallowing hard, she pinned her arms against her sides to avoid wrapping him in a hug. Did her teeth just chatter? She felt positive they did. "What rent are they asking?" Her mouth dried up and tasted like week old cotton. Water, where was her water? She spied the glass beside her and grabbed it carefully to drink deep.

"Well, that's the thing. They want someone responsible to take care of their home, and they don't care what the rent is. They figured whatever you could afford will be fine. But, no more wild parties."

She grinned back. "But wild parties are so much a part of my life."

"No roommates unless otherwise preapproved."

"What about my circus friends down the road? They need a stop-over spot in-between gigs or whatever they are called." She placed her glass on the end table.

"Puddles can't have boyfriends or other friends moving in or visiting either."

"They will let—" Her voice cracked. She blinked to stem the trickle of tears pushing for release. Her hands covered her eyes to block their blatant reveal of her vulnerable heart.

Zander stood and approached her chair. She sensed him kneeling down in front of her and leaning closer. "Yes, they will allow you to have Puddles."

Courtney risked a peek and saw him reach around her. His embrace pulled her toward him. She relaxed into his hug and fought to control the tears, which insisted that her heart be exposed for his eyes to see.

Twenty

LILLIAN

nd when are you planning to finish those centerpieces for the shower? I doubt that you'll get them done." Light streamed in from the sliding glass doors. Garlic and burnt butter fragrance collided with her senses. Lillian's hand tapped the tabletop as she waited for her breakfast. She glanced outside and watched two birds fight over a nesting area in the bushes. Why couldn't Courtney give up already and do things her way? If this rebellious daughter didn't agree quickly, she would have to call Jean at Jenson's Favorites and Flowers Boutique and tell her to deliver the centerpieces before Courtney would have the chance to show up with hers. That is if she did show up. Courtney's track record proved to be extremely erratic.

Therefore, Bethany wouldn't consider her help as meddling after all. She would be a hero when those centerpieces she ordered from Jean arrived at the church on time. Like the Mom should be.

The aroma of garlic-seasoned eggs and coffee mingled together, making her stomach growl. Courtney set the plate and coffee—minus sugar—on the placemat before her. She grunted. This girl brought out the worst in her. Always had. Why couldn't she be more…well, more like Bethany? But then she couldn't, could she? Her hand began to tremble.

"Would you turn on the TV for me?" She picked up her fork and stabbed her rubbery eggs.

Slowly Courtney looked at her watch and then glancing out the window. Puddles danced like she needed a trip outside ten minutes ago with her nails clicking on the tile floor. "Can you wait until I put the dog out?"

"If I'd wanted to wait, I wouldn't have asked."

"One minute. Come Puddles." Courtney dragged her fingers through her hair. The sliding glass door scrapped open, and the dog plunged onto the back porch then beyond.

Lillian polished off her plate as Courtney sped past her toward the living room. As she took another steamy sip of bitter coffee, she heard the television channels switch until settling on her favorite nine o'clock show.

She returned. Hesitation seemed to be her attitude lately. There was something about the way those dark blue eyes glanced over at her and then pulled away quickly. That nervous fumbling of the hands. She had seen those tale-tale signs with former co-workers when she led meetings at QAK Company. Later, she'd always discovered that someone wasn't doing their job. Something was up. Better get to the bottom of it.

"What are your plans today? Do you have to work?"

Courtney looked at Mother and held eye contact. "The girls and I are getting together here to work on the photo collage for Bethany's wedding shower. I found family photos when looking for cleaning supplies in the hall closet." There seemed to be no organization of previous times or events for the MacDuff family. The box of photos was a daunting task—inspiring exhaustion just to think about it.

Lillian flinched when she spotted the stack of family memorabilia already on the table. She dragged her attention from the albums. "That's not all, is it?" Leaning forward, she studied Courtney for a reaction.

Biting her lip, Courtney held quiet for some moments. "Puddles and I have a place to move into as soon as you are steady on your feet. I'll still come and take you to your appointments and… shopping."

Well, didn't she just have to drag out the word shopping? Like it was pure torture. Her heart pounded. *How dare she?* "So that's it. You're going to take the first opportunity to desert me." She pressed her lips together so hard they hurt.

"Mother, we both know that we get along better when we don't live together."

The sun shone through the window, making Courtney's hair glow, accenting her sickening sweet expression, which soured her own stomach, bringing a swirl of memories better left forgotten.

"After all I've done for you. You'd turn on me when I need you the most?" She pulled her gaze away and stared at the far wall. Anywhere away from her.

"We can't live together forever. I'm sure you want your home back for just you and Dad."

"I've been good to you, provided for you, always acted in your best interest—in spite of your—"

The house phone rang from her pocket, where she had placed it an hour ago. She hoped upon hope that Dan would call her soon. How she missed him. If he were only home to depend on now. Then she wouldn't have to put up with Courtney and her irresponsible, flighty ways. She pulled the phone up and smiled.

"Dan."

Courtney appeared as though she would speak, so she held up her hand to stop her.

"When are you coming home? Here. Well, Courtney told me today that she will be moving out as soon as possible in spite of the fact the doctor told her I needed someone to help me for the next five weeks."

His voice raised on the other side of the phone, and she could see Courtney wince out of the corner of her eye. She relaxed comfortably into the curve of the chair. Dan's sympathetic words were like a balm to her troubled heart. Maybe he would come home sooner now, knowing that she needed him. Knowing that his Courtney wouldn't be there—even for a crisis.

"Can I talk to Dad? Mother, please?" She stood tall, her face turning red and her arms crossed in front of her.

Irritation tightened her temples, starting a headache. She held up her hand to demand quiet so that she could hear this most important phone call. If only Courtney weren't so selfish.

"What's that—I couldn't hear you just now?" She leveled a glare toward Courtney. "Oh, you have to go. Okay, I love you too." She pressed end and gazed out the window at the birds, diving at one another for their place in the evergreens, next to the kitchen window.

COURTNEY

The Grandfather clock struck one o'clock. Cassie and Nicole leaned over the box of yellowed photos sitting on Courtney's parent's family room table. Those discolored images made her feel older. Discovering them in the hall closet today seemed meant-to-be. When opening the door, heat pushed against her face. Something else to raise her temper after her mother's conversation with dad. *Why did she have to be so complicated?* Courtney grabbed a handful of slick photos and spread them on the table before them.

"You have to use this one." Nicole tapped the selection with her burgundy fingernail. "Bethany's spaghetti legs stretched out on a Barbie beach towel with you sprawled on the blanket beside her." The waves were choppy behind them, but they were calm sun-burnt little clams.

Courtney's giggle slipped out. "We were planning our *dream date* that day."

"Well, we know *who* Bethany's dream date is, so anywhere with him is perfect, but where would your dream date take you?"

"The Gateway Clipper for a late-night dinner and dancing. What perfection. Any man who came up with that on his own is worth my time and attention."

"I'd prefer winter sports, the crispy sparkling snow falling all around and a fireplace later." Nicole's dreamy tone caused them to sigh together.

"Hiking the mountain tops with a hunk of a man who would carry my backpack for me would be just about right."

"Just about, right? What would make it perfect?"

"Marshmallows cooked over a fire and a talented cook for a date." They laughed.

"Start a pile of keepers here." Courtney's smile dipped back to a time of carefree summers and beach house vacations where sandcastles and swimming like mermaids were their highest priorities.

The doorbell rang. "I'll get it, Mother." She pulled the door open. Shock registered when Jean from her mother's favorite florist shop, stood in the doorway. "Oh, how can I help you?"

"I'm here to visit Lillian." Jean's squinty eyes gave her the once over, making Courtney uneasy.

"Sure, follow me." She led Jean toward the kitchen, where Mother sat playing Solitaire. "Here, she is. Will either of you need anything?"

"A glass of something cold and sweet would be fine." Jean plopped heavily in the seat despite the fact that she was quite thin. She and her mother grinned and made small talk, while Courtney dropped ice into two glasses. She may as well pour one for both of them. If not, Mother would call her back as soon as she settled into making the album.

"Coffee for us, Courtney." Mother held up her, *I'm the BOSS,* mug waiting for her to fill it.

First, she brought over the glasses, then she retrieved the mug. There seemed to be a secret between these two—the way they glanced at one another. Funny, she never thought they got along. Placing the refreshments and some cookies on the table, she left without a word.

As she approached her friends, giggles and someone hitting the palm of their hand on the tabletop met her ears. "Okay, what now?" She found herself giggling along with them. "You'd better not make me sorry about whatever you're laughing at. You're only allowed to make fun of Bethany."

"Look at these." Courtney at the beach with a bucket of sand poured over her head and shoulders while she wore a huge grin. Bethany standing behind her, laughing. Every Santa photo with both of them sitting on his knees were lined up side by side. Cassie continued to sort pictures, placing them in rows representing each year.

Their childish expressions grinning back from the pictures made her laugh some more. "Hey, childhood shots are limited. We can't stick to one season or subject girls." Looking over the years, spread on the table before her, stirred a renewed sense of appreciation that Bethany was her big sister. Her protective arm draped around Courtney in a photo, after photo. Another grouping showed their secret hideout. She could almost hear her big sister's laughter encouraging her to step out and try something new.

"Here's your photo. You must have been two or three."

"Probably, I was two there." Come to think of it, she never had seen her actual baby photo. Courtney leaned closer and

dug deeper into the pile. She heard her mother's walker—
which had developed a louder squeak—maneuvering through
the living room toward them.

"Thank you for stopping by to see me, Jean. We need to
visit more often."

Jean's crisp, choppy laugh sounded forced. "I'll come by
next week then. How about that?"

Courtney shoved aside more photos and some repeated photos. Then her hand paused on one that looked to be
another Christmas-time snapshot. Bethany must have been
around seven years old when comparing her hair length and
overall size. Other people were in the photo. Something tugged
at Courtney's heart. What was it about the photo that stirred
qualms in her heart? It looked ordinary enough—

"See you next week, Jean." Mother slammed the door and
pushed her walker in their direction.

The broad smile adorning Mother's face faded. Her eyes
grew bug-eye-big as she stared at the mess on her tabletop.

"I'll get it all picked up, Mother. We only need a few of
these old pictures for the Wedding presentation and then Bethany's shower photo album." She waved the photo in her hand
toward her mother. "Cute, right?"

Tension stole over Mother's face. Her brow wrinkled as her
eyes tried to follow the photo moving with Courtney's swinging movement.

"Would you..." Lillian wiggled the cup in her hand. "I
need another pot of coffee and take my freshened cup to the
living room." Her eyes fixed on the photo in Courtney's hand.
Lillian's right hand snatched the picture away. "I'd like to pe-
ruse the memorabilia myself."

Courtney flinched and stepped back. "Sure, why don't you
take your seat in the living room. I'll be right in." Courtney
turned around to face the table and dragged her hand over

more photos, spreading them across the table. Exposing the ones hidden at the bottom of the pile.

"Let's pick about ten pictures, ladies." She turned her head to see what Mother was doing and found her standing in the same spot. "I'll be right back," escaped her lips before she realized what she was saying. Courtney turned to do her mother's bidding.

On her way back from the kitchen, the doorbell rang again. She carefully placed Mother's fresh coffee down and the ice water. She moved toward the door. Mother stood in the entryway, reaching for the doorknob.

"Mother." I can get that.

"I'll be on my own soon enough. I think I'd better be able to answer my own door."

Courtney shrugged and approached Cassie and Nicole. "No, no, no, no, no. What are you cleaning up for? We've only begun to gather photos for Bethany's shower." She glanced at the clock. "Zander's friend Mike will be here in an hour to pick up pictures for the slideshow he will put together." She felt pin-pricking signs of panic building in her stomach. The shower was tomorrow-they couldn't put things off.

Cassie's attention darted toward Courtney's mother.

"Back so soon, Jean." Her mother's not pleased voice cranked into action.

"Lillian, I forget to leave this with you." Her arm moved as though handing something to her mother.

Nicole moved, blocking Courtney's view of the ladies at the door. Leaned her head to the side only allowed Court to see Mother shoving her hand deep inside her pocket.

"Thanks. I'll see you next week."

"Bye, Lillian."

She'd be visiting again next week too. Oh, joy. She turned her attention back to the bridesmaids. "Seriously, we can't stop. Mike is pulling the slideshow together tonight."

"Your mother allows these photos." Nicole pointed to a small pile next to the gold placemat.

"The others need put away—*now*," Cassie said, imitating Mother's voice as she closed the box newly labeled for Bethany.

It figured. Mother never could handle their messes as children. Why should she react differently today—even if it was for Bethany's shower and wedding? *But it's for Bethany's wedding, not for her.*

Cassie padded down the hall with the photo box tucked underneath her arm.

"Where are you going with those?" Courtney picked up the pile of allowed photos then turned to watch the box buckle under the weight of the pictures she'd hardly been able to investigate.

"Your mom wants them in her bedroom. On her desk."

"I didn't get to look through half of them." Her blood boiled. This picture project was a good idea—no, a great idea. How could Mother interfere with something so significant?

Behind her, the walker squeaked its way toward the La-Z-Boy chair. Mother's coffee and the channel changer at the ready on the side table. Another perfect example of how Lillian Kerner MacDuff ruled—by pressing buttons or snapping her tongue. Yet, her mother was changing, becoming more difficult right before her eyes.

Why?

Twenty-One

COURTNEY

Courtney dropped her car keys on Natalie's kitchen counter; the hard-metallic tap dance shattered the quiet of the otherwise silent room. Nat's red-faced glared in her direction as though expecting Court to understand the message—*possibly you could have called*. All the troubles of the morning melted in the heat of that expression.

Natalie rushed to dump glasses and measuring cups scattered through her perfectly messy kitchen before fussing with dough sticking to the counter. Courtney knew it would be forever before the kitchen could be found in such disarray again. She'd better savor it—remember this chaos tonight when she found herself buried in dishes or paperwork. She pretended to pound on the kitchen counter with a light hand, "Come on, come on, what's the hold up here? We have centerpieces to finish tonight, you know." She tried to still the gushing glee from pushing across her face.

Air escaped Natalie's lips, sounding like fizz. "Zeta and I were just about to work on them. Don't you have something else to do tonight? Isn't Bethany home yet?" She looked toward the door as though expecting the bride-to-be to discover the surprises any minute.

"No—double no." Courtney plopped on one of her friend's tall stools and dropped her purse at her feet. She placed her elbows on the counter and leaned in before resting her head in her hands. "Bethany called, and she had a late start for driving home. Mother hid the family photos from my sight for who knows why? Mike stopped in—"

"Mike, who?" Natalie's forehead puckered into amplified confusion. Her fist punched the unidentifiable dough into a pan before she covered the top with a linen towel.

"Zander's friend, Mike, is working on the dog training videos. Puddles and..." she pointed toward herself, "ta-da, yours truly are starring in all those episodes. He's also making Bethany's slideshow presentation for tomorrow—*tonight?*"

"Yep, and Zeta and I are making the centerpieces with that same deadline."

"That will make everything fresh and full of surprises, won't it?" Courtney hated the minuscule edge to her words. Natalie's kitchen wall clock ran fifteen minutes fast. Her friend always seemed to struggle with being on time. But then again, so did she. Who was she to judge?

Behind her, the kitchen's back door opened. Footsteps approached, and Courtney turned. Zeta moved closer, her hands full of roses, ribbon and craft supplies. They'd certainly collected enough materials to make centerpieces and then some. Oh, the fragrance—exquisite. Maybe Nat and Zeta did have everything under control. It wasn't like she excelled at making crafts. Perhaps she should leave this to the experts.

A sinking feeling settled in her stomach.

How dare she feel like a third wheel when this was her sister's wedding, and she was responsible. *Responsible.* Now that was a word no one ever made the mistake of attaching to her reputation. Except recently it just seemed...

But there was Natalie. If Courtney left now, wouldn't her friend think she'd once again chosen irresponsibility? This issue had been deemed their fighting topic too many times. One she'd never been able to explain to her overly responsible friend.

"Oh, ah, I didn't know you had company." Zeta's voice sounded gentle, timid, even a tad familiar. Courtney turned her attention to the lady.

Zeta's step faltered as they faced each other. She looked—scared—as though she didn't want to take a step closer to the counter though her arms were burdened with supplies. Was this woman just Natalie's friend or secret business partner? Secret. Yes, *secret* seemed to fit here.

Sliding off the stool, Courtney closed the distance between her and this overly shy lady. "Let me help you with that." She took hold of several items, lightening the load. The woman's dark blue eyes deepened in color. Courtney turned and led Zeta toward Nat as her friend finished wiping the counter.

Natalie threw her hands up in front of them before they had the chance to lay their load down. "Nope, don't you dare. Move to the dining room table with all this. Scoot."

Courtney trained her eye on Zeta. "Isn't she the bossy one tonight? How will we tolerate her?"

The woman's smile warmed her heart. Courtney glanced at Natalie, noticing how her friend glowed under Zeta's presence—even with the deadline looming. It seemed as though this woman fit into Natalie's life like a mother figure in every good sense of the word.

Her precious friend had grown up without one because her mother had deserted Nat and her father when she was maybe three years old. How difficult and overbearing her father had become, or perhaps he'd always been that way. Still, he'd never fully recover. Natalie proved to be the emotionally strong one, depending on herself, or her friends alone. But now, it appeared, she enjoyed support from this delicate and seemingly genuine lady.

A stab of envy jabbed Courtney's heart. Shame on her for feeling sorry for herself. Maybe her mother's deepening coldness toward her was the reason for her selfish outlook tonight. Her own mother's approval would be difficult to win, but once won, their relationship could improve. Maybe Dad would stay home more if a positive shift in their relationship developed. If only he were back now. It felt like forever since she talked to him last.

The sting of her mother's last conversation with her father burrowed into her heart. How receptive would Dad be toward her since her mother's manipulative words? Would he actually take Mother's side in this situation, sight unseen, despite knowing Lillian's controlling nature? Their history? Dad never really defended Courtney against Mother's attitudes and judgments. Was she so unworthy that she didn't deserve his protection? She shook her head and continued on toward the dining room table.

"You okay, Courtney?" The warmth of her friend's hand pressed against her arm.

She dredged up a smile and nodded. "Fine, just thinking of all we have to accomplish for the shower and the wedding and stuff."

"And stuff." Natalie nodded her head.

How did she know? She almost always seemed to know what stirred her moods.

"Oh, your carnations and vases await us in the dining room."

Zeta's face appeared pinched. Her attention moved away from them. "Well, I don't know that I should stay. I have a few deadlines to accomplish for some magazines. I can leave these centerpieces."

"Nonsense." Natalie's voice interrupted. "We need your expertise. Courtney isn't into crafts, and I sure don't want to be working on these till the wee hours of the night. Please stay and help a while."

Peeking at Courtney, Zeta nodded. "For a little while. Then I have to go."

Once everything was arranged in order and placed in reach, Zeta demonstrated how to make bows and attach them.

Decorating the flowers with blue dye and glitter before fastening them to the base seemed quick and easy. Courtney watched Zeta's graceful movements, similar to a seasoned dancer. Laughter and humor bubbled from this lady, turning even Natalie's grumblings into smooth as cream antidotes. This woman was exactly who she desired to be like. If only her own mother weren't so crabby, demanding, and—Courtney sucked in a laugh. *Bet Zeta wouldn't have a thought like that one.*

"What was that?" Natalie's quick eye didn't miss a thing.

Zeta stilled and looked puzzled.

"Nothing. Maybe a gnat tickled my nose or something." She ducked her head and tried to tighten the floral tape around the stem, forgetting to add the wire. The stem separated and made a gooey mess.

"A gnat?" Nat lowered her hands.

"Or something." Laughter tried to bubble inside her throat, but she stemmed those thoughts.

With precision, Zeta spread the glue needed to secure a dusting of glitter on the bows and flower edges. Her small fingers slipped flower after flower into the right location. "Place the bigger flower on the bottom, near the base. Reserve this space for the smallest flower." She paused and pointed so that they both saw what she meant. "Now, see this gap?"

Natalie's eyes shone with interest, while Courtney felt her eyes widen. They nodded together and burst with laughter. When had Natalie ever been so engrossed? Or quiet? How about—never.

"This is the tricky part of the arrangement. You get this right and..." Her fingers slipped the bow and latched it with a twist of her wrist and tuck of her fingers. "You'll get this result."

"Aww." They chimed in together.

"Remember to fluff the bow to cover all open areas." The satisfaction beaming off Zeta's face proved catchy.

As though they were in a race, Courtney and Natalie grabbed flowers, ribbon, holders, and wire along with floral wrap.

Former childhood art classes came to mind. They'd offered Courtney opportunities to sneak away, hiding until Mother fumed. She used to be proud of those antics. Her skill—infamous. Now, her shoulders dipped. Why should she dwell on past failures and defeats? Bethany's joy would prove to be her reward. She took a breath and straightened her spine and admired the beauty before her. She placed her first flower. . . the next one... another. And finally, the bow.

"Well, looks like you girls can take it from here." Zeta's area swept clean of crafts, and debris appeared as neat as before she'd begun.

"You must stay for Natalie's famous cappuccino." Courtney bit her lip. Hopeful.

"I can't. Caffeine." Zeta's soft answer floated toward her.

Moodiness stole Courtney's joy, anchoring her determination to find a way to make Zeta stay. "Yes, it's late." Courtney turned to face her friend as Zeta grabbed her purse to leave. "How's your decaf, Nat? And Zeta, let's go show her how to brew properly. I won't take no for an answer." She slipped her arm through Zeta's and moved them toward the kitchen.

COURTNEY

A half-hour later, Zeta had her way as she padded toward the kitchen doorway with a long strap purse slung over her shoulder. She turned with a glimpse so full of longing that it tugged Courtney's heart.

Courtney almost yelled out, "You can stay. Really—you can."

The door swept closed behind Zeta with a whoosh. A sense of emptiness spilled into the kitchen in the wake of her absence, crowding the air between them. They turned toward each other.

"Better finish those centerpieces," Natalie said.

"Yeah, let's." They stood, almost bumping into each other as they turned to leave.

"After you." Courtney stepped back and waited for her friend to move.

They dug their hands into the flowers and ribbon. Zeta's influence stilled their hearts and conversation. Unusual. "That's one special lady," Courtney whispered.

"Yes, you can believe that." Natalie remained still until she bounced in the direction of the CD player, resembling an old gramophone. "How about some music." Before Courtney could reply, Nat turned on 70s rock and roll.

Courtney straightened. Natalie preferred classical. Humm. Her hand pushed the flowers into the wrong angle crushing the stems.

Natalie bit her lip and looked at their lack of progress. Then with unusual, wordless patience, she pointed out the step-by-step directions Zeta had explained so efficiently.

After several attempts, Courtney picked up a new pack of ribbon and rolled it back and forth between her hands. She'd allowed irritation to claw its way into her thoughts. After pinning the bows, she grabbed flowers in her left hand and drummed fingers on the table with her right, itching to throw the carnations down and call it a night. But instead of giving up, she paused and took a breath. Moving slow and steady, she followed Natalie's lead. Fear of bungling the centerpieces subsided. She took each piece and carefully slid them in place until she found herself wallowing in the rush of creation.

It wasn't long before several finished arrangements decorated the far side of the table. The beauty and fragrance of the pieces stimulated excitement for the party. melting the powerful thoughts of dread and anxiety that had built throughout the day.

"Five more to go." Natalie cheered at her. "I can't believe you're doing this." Her hand swooped past the line of centerpieces and pushed Courtney's arm. "I'm proud of you."

Courtney grinned back with an 'I told you so' smile. Then she reached for the next clump of flowers and ribbon as the clock struck 9:00. There would be no problem with her arriving at Mother's around 10:30 for sure, a time that was not too late to check on mother. A long slow grin swept her face as her fingers sped through the creation of centerpiece number six.

"Your mother really helped me this past week."

"Oh, how?"

"She really knows what to do with a fledgling business. I showed her the order for the flowers and my recordkeeping. She simplified my ideas and added some categories I needed on my list to keep track of expenditures and order records."

Courtney nodded. "I'm glad she could help you out."

"She actually saved me a bundle. A conversation with her about business is like attending Community College of Beaver County."

"Does she break out the old ruler to crack your fingers?"

"Be nice." Natalie pressed her lips together and straightened in her chair.

Mother and Zeta, Courtney, shook her head. "Mother and Zeta are polar-opposites."

"Got that right."

A wispy breeze carried a mixture of floral scents her way. "Sniff the air." Courtney lifted her face and closed her eyes to enjoy the spicy fragrance.

Natalie laughed.

Courtney tried to pull her hand away from the ribbon and ended up in a wrestling match. *The flowers...how long before they'd wilt?* She didn't know anything about plants, and Natalie was new to the whole flower delivery business. "Do you have anywhere to put these to keep them fresh all these hours? We don't want the flowers to—"

"Have a little faith, I bought a floral cooler to be used just for my flower orders. It's empty and waiting for these beauties." She tilted her head, and her crooked grin teased Courtney. "No worries Court."

"Umm." Impatience fumbled her fingers and stiffened her back. She noticed Nat's progress. How could anyone handle ribbon and glitter with such precision? She felt a frown anchor itself on her face. Sigh, she looked with longing at the door.

"We need to take a photo of these all bunched together on a colorful cloth when they're done. Don't you think?"

When Natalie lifted her trophy smile, she froze. "Uh, uh. No Courtney, I see your attention fixed on my door. You're sticking with this till the end—no argument."

"I'm not running— and—leaving you with these." She held up her hand twisted with ribbon. "I'd be naughty to do such a thing."

Natalie burst into laughter and picked up her phone, choosing the camera function. "This is too good to pass up."

Twenty-Two

COURTNEY

"My place might not look like much to anyone else, but to me, this bed and breakfast feels like home. The perfect fit." Natalie's words hung wearily on the shallow breeze threading the air between them. After the bridal table arrangements were finished, photographed, and secured in Natalie's pink flower-power cooler, she and Courtney relaxed on the plumped-up, too-soft cushions hidden in the spare bedroom—not Victorianized as of yet. This room would be the next project once the budget allowed.

"You've definitely worked hard on the place. When do you think you'll schedule the open house?" Nat's hopes for her Victorian business still hadn't materialized. Was she spreading her energy and finances too thin by taking on the floral business? Would she end up neglecting the bed and breakfast, submarining its success? Yet, since the first business wasn't established or making money, it made sense that she'd have to generate income another way.

Courtney rolled her shoulder. A bit of Icy Hot and an aspirin brought some relief to her achy muscles. But, smelling the ointment rubbed onto her neck and upper back caused her eyes to sting and tear.

Broken dreams. She hoped Nat didn't have to suffer that. If there was anything Courtney excelled at, it was running or recovering from derailed or crushed dreams. Well, maybe not so successful concerning recovering from. Still, it was a subject she knew intimately.

Too intimately.

As if she'd sensed Courtney's thoughts, Natalie said, "I've taken all this to prayer. I don't want to waste energy on point-less pursuits." Her friend slouched further into the pillow cush-ioned chair. Her broken fingernails and paint-splattered shoes were evidence of how hard she'd worked.

The former cracked, plaster walls were freshly painted with salmon eggshell paint, emitting a warm, relaxing atmosphere. She couldn't wait to see the trim and flooring finished. Not to mention the decorations and furnishings for this room. So, Natalie had prayed. Now, it was time to wait on God. Time to consider things that were not as though they were. Waiting certainly grated against her own nerves, which began to tingle at the very thought. A quiver ran through her.

"Most of my finances come from selling baked goods and house-sitting your mother. I'm just so ready for the time when I'll run the bed and breakfast consistently in the green."

"I don't think you'd want my business savvy. Some say it didn't really work out."

Natalie grinned. "I think 'not-so-business-savvy' fits Tanya. Not so much, you."

"I let it happen. I didn't pay attention." *Didn't want to.* How peculiar that Natalie's, Mother's, and her own dreams lin-gered just out of reach. Sort of on permanent hold.

Courtney

Every time Courtney struggled for independence, the noose tightened. Zander's friends wouldn't wait forever to rent to her. Hopefully, she'd move before the wedding. But, every time she mentioned her plans, Mother's condition worsened, and her demanding nature flourished. Dad wouldn't be in the picture until who knew when.

Her mood darkened, blending into the chocolate walls of her temporary bedroom. Stretching her fingers, she decided to write. Courtney leaned toward her computer screen. Her fingers pounded the keys with a vengeance. Eventually, the words blurred, and she rubbed her eyes. Tiredness stole over her, but not enough for her to sleep.

Her evildoer, Nidella, leaped onto the heroine's porch and slipped behind a column for cover. This darkly-motivated character perfectly interfered with her heroine, Elena. The wicked woman's deception and intrigues brainwashed her captive, Elena's sister. A detailed rescue was to commence, but would it be successful? It was imperative that the heroine's faith take a hit. Could that happen because of the potion glistening in the ornate bottle Nidella held in her hand? The woman's cruelty knew no bounds, and she was committed to fulfilling an awful promise. A promise no one should ever consider...

Puddles's soft snores distracted Courtney for the tenth time tonight. She turned and laughed as her furry companion's sleeping form filled the bed. Her bed.

She faced the computer screen and read further down the page. Something's missing, but what?

Lighting a candle on the top of her bookcase, she breathed in the heady scent, deliciously cranberry, not chocolate her former favorite. She turned back to the words. Something missing, what could it be... Oh, yes. Elena did everything in her own strength, never asking the King of Kings to direct her choices. Her character needed to be less strong-willed and more heavenly minded. How many times that situation had played out in her own life? Her heart pricked at the thought. Swallowing, she forced her attention back to the story.

How would she add intimacy between Elena and the powerful Father God near the final victory? This would have to be motivated by a sincere surrender to His will. Her fingers tapped the desktop over and over. *How to make this happen?* She supposed she'd have to experience a bit of that before she could write such a scene. Cranberry scent tickled her senses and eased away the disturbing thoughts and burdens from the day, except for one lingering concern. Elena didn't know how to please God, because she couldn't even imagine it. Surrender her future? *What did that look like? Did she even want to?* Courtney closed her eyes and waited. Yes, Elena wanted to, and so did she.

Peace like a comforting fog permeated the room. She stilled under the awareness that she wasn't alone. Something warm caressed her cheek. Reaching up, she brushed her fingertips against the flow of tears. His presence warmed her from the inside out. This depth of His presence she'd never experienced before. Renewing strength filled her. She would move forward. It didn't matter how or when. Courtney's fingers dropped away from the keys as she sat there for an unmeasured amount of time soaking up the peace she could never generate with plans, control, or running.

COURTNEY

An alarm rang, erasing the fuzzy edges of a dream. Courtney smacked the snooze for the second time that morning. Unplugging her phone, she dialed her sister. No answer.

Bethany must have arrived home especially late last night. Ordinarily, she'd have called or text back. She pulled herself up from the covers and pushed Puddles off of her legs. Today was a new day. And she didn't face it alone. Knowing that she'd finished what needed to be accomplished for the bridal shower felt—satisfying, even though Mother's ire would rise today. Considering that made her heart skip a beat. Anxiety still pursued even in the presence of accomplishment and last night's assurances.

But now, Puddles-time awaited.

Mother hadn't called for her yet. No music played, and no light shined from under her bedroom door. Surely, she still slept. Courtney snapped the chain onto the dog's choke collar, and they headed toward the door. She tightened her jogging shoes and whispered, "Stay close, girl." Opening the sliding glass door to the muggy air and taking in a sky hung with an indigo curtain dotted with full clouds that blocked the sun, didn't deter them. She breathed out a sigh. Everything needed to run like clockwork today.

Itchy fingers of panic assailed her mind like a familiar foe who knew its target well. *Would she ever be free?* The scripture she couldn't stop thinking about this morning was *God has not given me a spirit of fear, but of power, love, and a sound mind.* She needed this to be true, believed that it was, and held on tight, repeating that scripture as they traveled several blocks for their walk. Threatening clouds sank lower over their heads with heavy burdens.

Despite the expectations and responsibilities she'd face today, their footfalls were buoyant as they climbed the front steps to her parents' home. Once inside, Puddles settled easily, and Mother still didn't stir.

Courtney gathered her belongings and headed to the bathroom as thunder crashed terribly close. After she'd dressed, Puddles suddenly stood and ran out of Courtney's bedroom, turning down the hallway toward Mother's room. Courtney's heartbeat grew wild as she buttoned her pants and followed.

Sobs sounded behind the door. Courtney turned the knob. Unlocked.

She ran into Mother's room toward rounded shoulders, head bent over a pile of damp tissues. Her nearly hidden face—purpling from emotion. Puddles paced back and forth, turning toward the bed. Whining. Nudging close to the source of those tears.

"Down," Mother's firm voice kept Puddles at bay.

Smart dog. No one messed with Mother in the middle of any emotional episode.

Lillian picked up an empty glass and threw it at the pile of broken knickknacks, which used to be displayed on her bed-side table. Shattered glass flew in every direction. Courtney pulled Puddles away.

"Mother, stop!" When had her temper ever been this bad?

Puddles cringed, looked toward Mother, and then pulled toward the broken glass.

"Puddles, come." The whining continued, as the dog ignored the command. "Puddles here." Courtney forced the words out with what Zander called, her big girl voice. The canine paused before heading in the direction of the glass shards.

"God help," escaped her lips. *Please, save Puddles from the glass and Mother's temper while you're at it.* She yanked hard at the collar and dragged all one hundred and twenty-five pounds of determined curiosity away from danger.

"I'll be back."

Mother's hiccup was her only reply.

Guiding her charge down the hall, through the house, and out the sliding glass door seemed to be Courtney's best option and would keep Puddles safe. What was at the bottom of Mother's grief? The canine banged on the door with hairy paws. Barked several times.

"Knock it off." Courtney grabbed supplies to clean up the mess. She turned and ran toward her parent's bedroom.

Pausing outside the bedroom door, soft sobs escaped through the sliver of an opening. *A soft answer turns away wrath.* Maybe that would work with Mother too. Sucking in a deep breath, she pushed the door open. "Mother, what's wrong? What can I do to help you?"

Lillian lifted her head; nose pointed toward the ceiling and pulled her hunched shoulders back to a formidable poise. "Nothing at all. *You* can't do anything. We need to be ready for church in an hour." Her mother turned her head away and sniffed.

Courtney grabbed a box of tissues and laid it next to the quivering hand lying on the bedspread before she reached for the shattered memories cast upon the floor.

COURTNEY

Stained glass filtered light streamed its brilliance onto one-hundred and fifty faithful at Fellow's Branch Church. Various perfumes and aftershaves mingled on the air-conditioned breeze. Crinkling Bible pages, coughing, and here and there a whisper, were interrupted by Pastor Thomas Dean's commanding opening prayer. After a couple of worshipful tunes, Deacon Peterson announced the message, Strength to Cling to One's God-given Purpose. Another power-house message was about to begin.

Courtney's spirit rose invigorated until she realized this sermon revealed that she'd never identified her purpose if she had one at all. Surely, if God wanted to use His disciples, He'd at least cause them to discover this essential focus. How long before he'd allow her to discover hers? She shifted on the cushioned pew and tried to focus. Mother's still form drew her attention time and time again. Questions and condemning thoughts of incompleteness befuddled her thoughts, pulling her away from receiving any further direction. Mother's display of emotion—without a hint of what bothered her—plagued Courtney's conscience. Was this a mere grievance again? If so, she hoped she or Puddles were not the offenders. Would her mother, could she ever accept a comforting hug from Courtney? Like she did from Bethany? Yet, Mother never accepted that type of comfort from her, only physical service seemed acceptable.

In the middle of the benediction, she jerked to attention. Disappointment slackened her shoulders. *She'd missed it.*

"Now, may God be gracious to us and bless us and make his face shine upon us…" Courtney glanced down the pew as her mother flipped a page on her calendar and marked a comment in purple pen.

Pastor Thomas Dean continued, "Let us stand and sing together 'Blest Be the Tie That Binds.'"

Everyone rose to sing one of John Fawcett's old-time favorites. Mother dropped her calendar and pen inside her open purse and allowed Bethany to loop arms with her as they stood in unison.

Courtney lifted her voice, hoping it would reach His throne and bless Him.

The song finished, Bethany gave her the nod, and they hurried to the basement stairs, greeting church members along the way.

"Did you bring the favors?" Bethany's heels rang on the steps in their race to beat the guests to the fellowship room.

"Yes, they're inside a huge box on the serving table." Chilly basement air tingled her arm and face when they reached the next to the last step.

"Oh, Court, this fellowship hall is the best." The congregation, blessed with talented craftsmen and decorators, provided classy, traditional moldings and unique woodwork. Tables and flower arrangements along the walls were exquisite, none of those cheap plastic throwaways here. The congregation loved on one another in this unique way.

"Even Zander would approve," Courtney said without thinking.

"Zander, is it?" Bethany grin grew impish in the moderate light.

Courtney aimed a grin back at her and then flipped the light switch. The cheerful room shone bright with welcome. "Come on, let's spread the table cloths. We have a bunch of to-dos to accomplish yet."

"Where are Cassie and Nicole?" Bethany's voice climbed to a higher pitch.

"Well, Cassie couldn't come. Prior engagement or something like that." She snuck her sister a withered smile.

"She'd better make it to the wedding…"

"Settle down sister, she'll be there."

Courtney had wiped off each rectangular table before church. They moved toward the box holding the table items. Bethany reached in and pulled out a lovely blue table cloth, which complimented the neutral tones in the room. Bethany hugged it to herself.

Classy-traditional—Bethany style—and Courtney's joy over doing something right settled like rich cream over a fruit cup.

Bethany beamed, "Well, it won't be long until we say our vow's and—"

"Are imprisoned together forever in the bonds of matrimony." Courtney grabbed another table cloth and flicked it, watching it settle over the table.

"Hey, now, I don't mind being imprisoned by Brandon…

at all." Sunlight filtered in behind her sister, adding to the glow already radiating from within. Bethany was beautiful—especially when she was in love.

Courtney's heart tapped a staccato rhythm creating the beginnings—of what? Maybe a desire to share that kind of love someday. Zander's face came to mind. Her rebellious lips grinned.

"Okay. Alright, already." Courtney needed to focus on something other than the warmth of Zander's eyes, the soft-roughness of his voice. Maybe she could attack some poor daisy with *he loves me—he loves me not*—later.

They moved as a team to cover the tables. Placing white strings of Christmas lights around the food table elevated the elegance of the room. Courtney had hidden the flower centerpieces inside the kitchen earlier this morning. With her first pay, she'd sprung for the supplies and flowers, all ordered through Natalie. Joy surged inside her. Surprisingly her sister and planning this shower turned into the highlight of her day. *Not the disaster she'd expected.* Discomfort tried to invade her thoughts concerning Mother's attitude this morning. She pushed them away, choosing to ignore them like she'd done for years.

Helping the newest branch of her friend's business grow, significantly increased her pleasure. She'd tell everyone where they could order their next batch of flowers—well maybe after Nat's funeral project. Procrastination—always her curse—yet she'd beat its consequences last night with Nat and Zeta. Plus, the flowers and crafts weren't destroyed by her lack of talent and patience despite the fact that she wasn't all that skilled—not at all. They landed the last cloth on top of the gift table and smoothed wrinkles over the edges.

"I'll be right back. Stay here." Courtney ran for the kitchen. She uncovered the closest box of centerpieces and lifted the first-round vase decorated with Bethany's favorite flowers sparkling with gold glitter.

She danced the rumba around the centered kitchen island. *Bethany will love these.*

A burst of exuberant voices sounded from the fellowship hall. She could hear footsteps, well wishes, and someone dropping a package as guests filed in. Courtney took a deep breath. The scent of carnations, roses, and cinnamon brought a rush of memories from her childhood with Bethany. Her throat choked; a sense of loss intruded. Bethany wasn't just a sister, but a best friend, next to Nat. *Not now, no, not now.*

She moved past the kitchen doorway and past the fellowship hall entrance, watching the tile floor pass underneath her sandals. She made it through without incident. Anticipating Bethany's praise drew her like an elixir. She would not be able to keep her hands off these.

"Where did you get those centerpieces, Bethany?" An excited voice fawned.

Courtney laughed softly and moved the centerpiece over to peer around. Bethany stood with her back toward her holding the most obnoxious Victorian flower arrangement she'd ever seen. She braked and waited.

Mother rounded the corner with several ladies from the congregation and beamed a smile when Bethany held the centerpiece up between them.

"That nice girl, Kate, from Jenson's Flowers, came by and taught me how to make those. I adore irises, don't you?" Mother's mood had altered significantly since this morning.

Courtney could see the side of Bethany's face wither. Her mother had not been this animated since—she couldn't remember.

Courtney stepped back again and again. Bethany would understand, wouldn't she? Her heart ached. Too bad. Natalie had hoped people would eventually acknowledge the new extension of her business. Courtney had counted on these arrangements to do that.

More backward steps until she drew utterly out of sight. In slow motion, she laid the centerpiece safely inside the tissue paper wrap. She tucked more around the top for protection. Maybe they could use centerpieces for the shower in another capacity. Possibly decorate Bethany's table or the food table with them? Or they could give them away for prizes today.

Leaning her head against the kitchen cabinets, Courtney's neck muscles tightened their cords. She actually followed through for once. Did something right. But if she showed these off, she'd wound her mother, who was very fragile right now.

On the other hand, if she didn't, she'd offend Bethany. It was Bethany's wedding reception. She straightened up. Paused for several long seconds before pulling the towel over the top of the box, completely covering the treasures that lay inside.

Then she slapped on a smile and turned to leave for the fellowship hall. Bethany almost ran her over as she skidded into the kitchen. The scalding expression on her sister's face caused Courtney to back up a step, and suck in a breath as her fabricated smile dissolved.

Bethany's joy had obviously departed. "I thought you were going to protect me from Mom's Victorianism." She slammed down an extra towel they'd used for wiping off the tables onto the towel covering the centerpiece boxes revealing its contents. She peered inside.

"What's this? More frou-frou?" Gasping, Bethany turned a sharp eye her way. "Smell that?" She reached inside the box carefully. Lifting one of the centerpieces, "Don't suppose you know anything about these?"

"It would crush Mother. Didn't you see her reaction when you held her creation? Besides, she was distraught this morning and wouldn't tell me why."

"Dad extended his construction job obligations. He will be gone a few months past my wedding." Bethany's eyes glided over the centerpieces tucked tight inside their boxes. "Did she know about these?"

"I never told her they were finished. Natalie brought them straight to the church from her house. So probably, no." *She needed to start talking details with Mother, so this kind of thing wouldn't happen.* Dread at the thought of opening herself up to more of Mother's criticism lessened her resolve.

"You need to start standing up to her, Court. She doesn't respect you because she thinks she can walk all over you." Her finger traced the glittery edge of the pure white carnation. A few of the shards of glitter fell to the tabletop. "So perfect. Just what I like." Bethany set it back into the box. Her smile revealed an emotion Courtney feared—that determined look mirrored their mother's stubborn grit.

"We are taking these out there, and that is that." Bethany's arms wrapped around the first box of centerpieces and lifted. "Take this box, please, and follow me." Bethany nodded to the next box of hidden centerpieces on the counter.

"But Mother—what about her—feelings?" Courtney's muscles tensed as though she were in a sprint race.

"She should have thought of that before she went to all the trouble. This is my wedding shower. I *hate* Victorian." She blew out a breath, fluffing her bangs. "She knows what she's doing." A puff of floral fragrance wrapped around their conversation. "Go ahead, grab the next box." She turned and marched out of the room, leaving Courtney surrounded by a bubble of confusion. Loneliness scrunched her heart.

Courtney hugged the box, lifting it high to summon the bracing scent for courage. She placed the box back on the counter. Moving toward the door, she caught the outside EXIT sign in her side vision. Her feet itched to chase that path. She closed her eyes, searching for self-control when every previous experience told her to run.

"Wow," Several people said in unison.

"Giving those away, I do hope? I want one. Can I fix a win to get it?"

"Courtney planned these for the shower. They are perfect, aren't they?" Bethany's words were tinged with a smile, making each word sparkle."

"Courtney opened her eyes and turned toward the fellowship hall. She took a step closer, hearing praise from the ladies, which definitely would heighten the disapproval waiting for her like a brick wall.

Mother stood across the room. Her profile revealed a countenance falling from the pillar of praise into the distress of being all but forgotten. Courtney's thoughts centered on her mother's criticism, which would point blame at her when they left the church that day.

She froze as she watched Mother shrink into a cushioned chair. Not knowing she was being observed, Lillian ceased talking and cast her attention over the small crowd of females gathering around Bethany with festive squeals of joy. Lillian's shoulders hunched as though defeated.

Courtney couldn't stand the sight. How could she wound her mother, even though she'd been sneaky and assumed that she could waltz in here and take over? She was what she was, and that wouldn't be changing anytime soon—if ever.

Her heart ached, desiring that bond and connect with the woman who gave birth to her. To luxuriate in the relationship that never had been. The most honorable idea she could come up with was to turn around and run right outside into the blinding light of day and past the blur of red from the EXIT sign.

As her foot hit the step going up, she heard a voice yell behind her, "There she goes. Bet she'll take two steps at a time. Any takers?"

Twenty-Three

COURTNEY

couple of hours later, earth pounded outside her window under the weight of Puddles's massive paws. A reminder for Courtney to check what her Leaping Leo chased or for any poor squirrel or stray cat that needed rescuing. A puppy stampede would not be a fun way to perish. She uncurled from her cocooned position and padded her way toward the kitchen.

A trip around the world looked pretty good right now. If only Courtney had a bank account with numbers in the black. Sigh. Would Bethany ever forgive her for deserting her post? Allowing Mother to dominate with those hideous Victorian centerpieces might be unforgivable.

Certainly unforgettable.

Imagining her sister's angry face increased the anxious beat of her heart. At the end of the week, they would celebrate Bethany's and Brandon's nuptials. Would her sister ever talk to her again? Later, when nieces and nephews came along, would she be denied visitation and be placed on the forbidden aunt list? *Don't hang out with Aunt Courtney—the coward!*

The beginning of a headache speared the front side of her

head and pushed a finger of pain deep in her brain with a twist. Her hand went to her forehead, and she tripped on the throw rug. She would have to look for an ibuprofen as soon as she checked on her girl.

She grabbed the handle of the sliding glass door and pulled. Heat rushed in on the tail of a breeze, pushing the air conditioning backward. She wanted to curl up, hide, disappear, but instead, she tipped her head into the high temperature blanketing the backyard.

Puddles stopped short and tilted her black, inquisitive face toward the scrape of the door before digging her feet into the ground and dashing toward the house. She blazed through the open glass door. Golden brown legs slid askew on the tile floor. Courtney's cell phone chirped for attention. *Zander.*

The dog pulled herself upright and then danced close, demanding attention before tromping on her master's feet.

"Ouch!" Courtney stepped away from the hairy paws. Her heart skipped a beat before she answered the call. "Hey." The dog poked her nose into her leg. She turned her back to communicate that this was not time to play.

"If you have time tonight, I really need to film a new lesson I designed. What would you say if I invited you to enjoy the best pizza in the world? The perk is a night out with the boys?"

"Puddles is a girl. So, it would be a boy and Puddles."

"Pure technicality. What do you say?"

As her lips positioned themselves for the big decline, she heard the front door open. Her feet found a chilly spot on the tile floor when sidestepping the dog.

"Courtney, you there?"

Bethany's nondescript voice yelled her name. Was her sister furious or just plain angry? Next, her mother's voice griped about something. Oh, no, *the* tone…

"Yes, I'll come later." She tossed that comment at her cell before she knew what she was doing. At least she could hide with him since he didn't know what she'd done. "I've got to go *now*." Zander didn't need to know that she'd abandoned Bethany, and if she stayed on the phone, he'd catch an earful. She couldn't take one more person looking down their nose at her and wondering—why?

Why was she this way? Why did she do what she did—when she did it? She'd asked herself those questions a few hundred times. Well, thousands. Answers never seemed to materialize.

"Great. I'll expect you around 6:00 tonight."

Glancing at the time—*or sooner*—came to mind. Courtney slipped the cell into her pocket before Bethany's distinctive ring tone chimed. Her nervous fingers coaxed the phone out of her pocket. She took a shallow breath and then answered the call. "Hey, Bethany."

"Forgiven."

"Wh…what." Courtney gripped the phone. The volley of words clambering for release collected in her throat, bunched inside her esophagus, and collided as though there was no exit.

"Forgiven. Forgiven. Forgiven." Soft like rose petals after rain.

Puddles leaned her weight against Courtney's legs of putty, pushing her back to stumble against the granite countertop. She held on tight and righted herself.

Puddles turned her attention toward the living room and stood.

They were coming. Heart pulsating against her ribcage, she anchored her feet to the kitchen floor.

Moments later, Bethany strolled around the corner and into view, wearing a huge smile and holding one of Natalie's centerpieces in her hand. She tipped her head slowly, with exaggerated movements, and sniffed. "I kept one of them. The others were used as prizes." Her smile spilled out from her eyes before she winked.

Joy leaped into her heart, and Courtney could have cried happy tears until Mother sided up beside her sister with that critical, arching brow lifting high on her forehead, aimed like an arrow at her heart.

***

COURTNEY

"Come, Puddles." Courtney twisted inside the car parked in Zander's driveway, twenty-five minutes late. As she attached the prong collar, Puddles dipped her head to dodge the restraint. But Puddles pulled her like a rag doll through the quiet streets of her parent's neighborhood, whenever she used a regular collar or choke chain. Courtney wouldn't take a chance tonight. Not with the camera rolling.

Disappointment and regret still wrung her heart. Mother hadn't understood how hard she'd tried to spare her feelings at Bethany's shower. Why did Mother only believe the worst about her intentions? Always the worse.

She opened the car door, and stepped aside, before slamming it shut. At least Bethany forgave her. Forgave her for what everyone else expected from her. Did her sister understand why she needed to escape today? They'd not had a chance to talk, but the liquid warmth in Bethany's eyes allowed her to relax and let go of any defensiveness that rose up at the mention of the shower.

Tweeting from a nearby evergreen attracted Courtney's attention. The rustic setting of Zander's front yard energized her. Birdsong filled the air, raising her spirits, as curiosity hit her full throttle. *What did Zander have in mind for them to tonight?*

She opened the door and grabbed the leash. Puddles dove at a butterfly, reminding her to stay alert. Courtney yanked her close to even out their strides, while they approached the training area. The excitement she'd heard in Zander's voice about the new *try it-out* lesson caused her stomach to churn. "Let's hope we're up to this, Puddles."

The canine kept her nose to the ground, possibly sniffing for game as though Courtney hadn't said a word.

Once they reached the gate, she rang the bell and waited.

Zander slipped out the back door wearing jeans and a casual cotton, button-up shirt. That wasn't all he wore. His dangerous smile produced a gleam in his eyes that eradicated her power to ignore. He opened the gated fence. "Let's get started. Daylight offers the best lighting. I'll try filming different angles tonight."

"Wrong angles can be a beast. Can't have that."

"Nope, can't have that." His voice sounded as smooth as tanned leather. Zander reached for her face and trailed her cheek, feather-soft, with his finger. Treacherous breeze coaxed his aftershave into her space.

Scolding herself, she reversed the lean she didn't realize she'd moved into. She stepped back as heat scorched her neck and face. When had he become far too interesting for her own good? She didn't need the complication of a relationship now, not when her life held no bearing. She didn't need a broken heart, nor did she want to cause one. They were only here to train Puddles. This was strictly business.

Just concentrate. She could do that.

Inside the fence, several colorful displays were lined up along the walls of the training pen. Two round cloth tunnels were interrupted by triangular ramps, and collections of large orange cones spaced in patterns at opposite ends of the training area drew her attention.

"Today, we are going to have some fun." Zander's excitement nearly sparkled.

"Hey there." A male voice sounded behind her.

She turned. *Mike.* The first time she'd met him, he'd looked familiar, but she still couldn't place why. Even his deep baritone stirred a surreal memory. When he'd talked about being involved with Zander's project, and when he'd retrieved Bethany's photos at Mother's, that familiar connection stayed elusive. Zander hadn't mentioned Mike would share their pizza. Somehow that possibility disappointed.

Mike shifted a weighty photo bag with a tripod strapped to the side.

"What you got there, buddy?" Zander's slight frown dimmed his enthusiasm. Maybe he didn't know his friend would show up today.

Courtney crossed her arms, but still held tension on the leash. Puddles tried to pull toward the man as he approached them.

Mike stopped in his tracks and kept his distance as he eyed the canine. "Mr. Mancel wants me to do more close-up shots."

"Mancel, you mean *the* Mr. Mancel." Her words turned high pitch, scraped the upper side of her throat on the way out. When had he become a part of this project?

"My silent partner." Zander's voice spoke low.

Had Zander hidden the name of his financier—this invisible partner—on purpose? Didn't he remember that Mancel foreclosed on her dream apartments, forcing her into her current situation? She squeezed the leash.

"The one and only, I'd say." Mike's full attention riveted around the fenced area. He pointed toward the shelter crafted with electric plugs for Zander's personal equipment. "Can I?" Then he pulled out an additional microphone.

Zander nodded none too enthusiastically. He slipped a toothpick in his mouth and clamped down. The grim look on his face made her neck muscles tighten.

If they were alone right now, she'd tell Zander just what she thought. No holding back. Since Mike was here, she decided to hold her angst in until he left. Something about the man didn't sit well with her. Maybe that feeling was unfounded. He'd never done anything to her. Still, the uneasy feeling lingered, fogging her concentration.

Zander turned to her. "I've got something different to show you tonight."

Courtney made a point of focusing on the props, anywhere but at him. "This week's lesson isn't hard to miss." *How on earth would Puddles do with those tunnels?* She'd always jumped over everything in her life before this. And the ladder-like contraption, could she climb it? If only she could have practiced with her girl before Mike was here. Zander wanted fresh, unrehearsed reactions. Or maybe his *silent partner* called the shots. She jabbed a look at Zander.

"Actually, there is more." He smiled in a disarming way.

Gravel and dry grass crunched from behind. Mike moved closer. So, distracting.

"I'll be back in a moment." Zander turned toward the house before she could stutter a reply.

Dropping her gaze on Puddles, Courtney smiled. The brushing session had really paid off. "Looking mighty fine little lady." Puddles looked up at her. Did Courtney just imagine a smile on that black mask?

The door pushed open, and Zander emerged with another Leonberger. Puddles barked and leaped toward them. Courtney gripped the leash and held tight, bracing her feet against one hundred and twenty-five pounds, interested in meeting an even bigger Leo.

Mike snapped photos, and Courtney gritted her teeth. She'd like to—

"For training purposes, we'll not allow Maximillian and Puddles to play right now. He belongs to a friend of a friend, and I asked to borrow him. We'll order pizza later." Zander's smooth as silk voice drew her attention.

She glanced his way. His smile, a smile that could conquer

Queen Elizabeth, glossed over her foul mood. Zander kept his charge in place. Eagerness and zest for life radiated from this massive canine and transformed his trainer. Noticing this made Courtney just a tad mad.

"Does this mean that you don't have the pizza here already?" She pointed a dramatic frown in his direction. That would cover the real reason for her angst.

Perfect white teeth slid into a broad grin, as though he *knew*. Then he began his outline of what they'd accomplish. *If all went well.*

Mike stood just out of reach of the dogs.

"Courtney, fall in line behind Maximilian and myself and do exactly what we do." He positioned Maximilian by his side and approached the first prop. He faced the camera and explained the lesson. Then he took a treat and threw it inside the cloth tunnel. Maximillian dove inside, and Zander called him through to the other side.

After about four tries, Puddles decided to follow along. "Can we do it again to reinforce her success?" Courtney's hand pinched for holding the leash so tight. She loosened her grip.

Zander nodded.

"She can't ask questions. Mancel won't like it," Mike sputtered.

Before Zander could reply or she could focus her anger, Puddles scooted through the tube and ran out of reach. Five minutes later, she approached Maximilian like a moth to the flame. Zander caught her leash and handed it to Courtney.

Mike's huge smile dominated his face. He'd kept the camera rolling the whole time Puddles avoided Courtney. If only the training pen were smaller. Nervousness dried her mouth and made it taste like cotton—she'd kill for a drink of ice water.

They continued to mimic the teacher and his dog until they reached the next cloth tunnel. Zander and Max were excellent, but she implored him with a look that she hoped spelled *help*.

"Mike. Come spot the end of the tunnel."

"No way, Bud. Besides I'm filming this. Remember."

Zander tied his Leo to the fence and jogged toward his friend. He grabbed the camera strap. "I'll take that."

Courtney relished the sight before her. Mike squirmed but didn't move. Zander swung the camera off his friend's neck. With slow, plodding steps, *Mr. Cameraman* made his way to the other end of the tunnel. "Just go already."

She bit her lip, tried to behave. Where was Mike's smirk now? Puddles leaped to the left, trying to run around the tunnel from the outside. Courtney pulled her toward the opening, so grateful for the training collar. Once Puddles looked through the tunnel, she sniffed and then ducked her head inside.

For a few brief seconds, the dog stood at the neck of the cloth tunnel and kept her head lowered. Courtney let go of the leash then tossed a particularly succulent treat inside. Once the leash dropped to the ground, Puddles scooted through the tunnel fast. She headed toward Mike with predatory speed.

Mike watched the end of the tunnel and saw the dog coming. He bolted while a smear of red, gold, and black hair pursued. Puddle tripped his foot and fell on top of him. He lay pinned as Puddles licked his face and neck.

"Get her off...me *now!*"

Courtney ran as much as being hunched over in laughter would allow. She grabbed the leash and commanded Puddles to release him. Her sides ached. "Sorry, Mike. Can't... help—myself!"

"You laugh now, but we'll see who laughs in the end."

Courtney sobered. She glanced at Zander, but the dog trainer stared at Mike with a puzzled expression. If he knew, he'd hidden it well.

Perspiration collected on her forehead and dripped toward

her eyes, and she wiped it away with the back of her hand before noticing her hand was smeared with mud. Where had that come from? She glimpsed up at Zander with a quick turn of her face. He clicked the camera, pointed at her, and didn't only just grin. He laughed right out loud.

Twenty-Four

LILLIAN

In spite of weariness tugging and weighing her eyelids shut, Lillian woke early from her evening nap. Scraping sounded on the hallway tile. Something heavy was being moved. Usually, her bedroom muted sounds from other parts of the house. *Was Courtney home already? What was she doing?* A glance at the clock proved she could be wrong. The digital shined 10:30 and, Courtney had left for Zander's home at 6:10, claiming to be late as she bolted out the back door. She wouldn't be thoughtful about her mother being home alone, in need, and feeling lonely. The older Courtney got, the more unlike her upbringing she became. But that was to be expected, wasn't it?

A slight tremor shook her hand, and she gripped the side of the mattress to steady her movements. Parkinson's Disease. Who would have ever thought that Lillian Kerner MacDuff would suffer such a malady? She didn't believe it. She couldn't. Wasn't she stronger than that?

Something crashed to the floor. Porcelain?

Puddles barked ferociously. Lillian jerked upright, and her hand moved swiftly to press against her chest. Was the dog in the kitchen? Somewhere closer, Courtney's room? She really couldn't tell. Her heart beat wild. Sitting up this way proved how unsteady her limbs had become. The walker, a foot away, slid easily toward her when she tugged the light metal frame. Courtney would catch a piece of her mind. That better not have been Grandma's vase.

A minute later, Lillian swung the bedroom door open and followed the walker into the hallway lit by a nightlight. She'd not moved this fast in... well, she didn't know when.

The vicious snarling and barking continued. How odd. It sounded as though she was on the steps leading to the garage, and the barking didn't travel any closer toward the commotion. Had the animal gone daft and attacked Courtney? If so, what could she do? Stupid walker—

Banging sounded in between Courtney yelling from that stairway. *Was she calling Lillian?*

She heard a loud scuffle from the living room. A crash, like the sound of a roof falling in, caused her to tremble. A deep male voice yelled. "Move it—grab what you can. The door is giving way. Go—no, out the front!"

Snarling and Courtney yelling, "Get them, girl!"

Her heart froze in her chest. If that dog bit a visitor, she could be sued for everything she owned. What had the girl thought when she'd brought that ferocious dog here to live?

Someone fumbled with the front door locks. Lillian could only see his form by the weak glow of the living room lamp, the one she'd turned off.

The maple door swung wide, banging against the wall.

What kind of visitors would slam the door so hard the glass could possibly break?

Two men in dark clothing carrying stuff darted outside. A man cursed. His high pitch shouted, "Shut the door! Look out—the dog!" He disappeared outside.

The next man stopped at the doorway and turned. Puddles

massive paws pounded toward the front hall. Lillian saw the whites of the man's eyes grow round inside the holes of his dark ski mask. He and Lillian gasped in unison.

Puddles snarled viciously as she leaped at him, knocking him down with a grunt. Then she grabbed his arm in her mouth and shook him.

The free gloved hand dropped a box before he grabbed the doorknob.

Her Grandmother's box? "Get him Puddles, get him good," Lillian yelled.

Pulling himself up, dragging Puddles with him, he then turned and punched the dog.

She yelped and fell back.

Stumbling outside, he slammed the door shut before Puddles could follow. She leaped high and banged the maple panels with her heavy paws. Sharp barks bounced down the hall.

Lillian fumed. "Thieves!" No one better mess with her. She'd take them to court. And they thought they were afraid of the dog.

Courtney flew around the corner from the living room. "Yes, send an officer. Oh, there are gas cans and rags here too." Fear coated those words causing terror to shrink Lillian's heart. Trembling, she nearly stumbled, though her grip tightened on the walker. Anger fueled her strength.

"How dare those men come here!" Her unsteady steps moved forward.

Courtney flinched with each of Puddles's excruciating, loud barks, which seemed to bounce between the windows and walls. She parted the curtains and pressed her face against the window. "We won't touch the cans. Yes, we'll wait before we look things over. Oh, there's the car—the color? It's too dark. They drove away in a midsized, two-door" Sigh. "They're gone. Someone was parked in a large van with the back doors open on our side of the avenue. He pulled away when I turned into our driveway."

Puddles stopped barking and turned away from the window. Heading toward Lillian, the dog continued past the walker and down the hall with heavy steps. She circled around sniffing then returned to the door.

Courtney grabbed her collar and snapped on the leash when she got into reach.

"Mother, are you okay?" Courtney ran down the hall toward her, tears spilling from her eyes. She reached out, offering a hug.

With a well-timed push to her walker, Lillian turned away. Courtney drew back. No one needed to give her a pity hug. Courtney hovered and hesitated. How irritating.

She headed toward her front door hating the contraption she, unfortunately, needed in a time like this. Now, to move through the living room and kitchen to see to the damage. Blood pulsed through her veins. Anger was her strength, had been for years.

It would serve her still.

⁂

COURTNEY

Movers were emptying the back room at Leman's that had gradually filled with antiques the last couple of weeks. Courtney cringed to see their rough handling of the furnishings while they headed through the front door as they lifted them into the truck.

"Mr. Whippier, where are they taking those pieces?"

His eyes pierced her with a *how dare you interrupt me* look, then smacked the stapler with more power than it needed.

She pressed a breath through pinched lips. She'd have to

wait until Mr. Angerton arrived in about an hour or so. He'd never mentioned this change. Imagine getting rid of the antique department. Would she still have her job? *Sweet Lord, help me, please.* Calm lightly touched her heart until her mind took off on its own accord. This was supposed to be her opportunity for advancement, the reason she'd applied. She'd hope to start traveling and connecting with antique dealers all over the eastern states as soon as she'd worked exclusively with the antiques.

"Hurry it up already." Mr. Angerton's voice cracked over the movers as he pushed through the door like a raging bull threatening an intruder.

Courtney dropped the tape dispenser. Her head snapped up to see what was going on. Mr. Angerton's attention aimed in their direction.

She felt like he looked at her for an apology. Why would she even feel that way? She ducked her head and waited. Keep eyes off the angry man. That had always worked in the past.

Mr. Whippier laid the stapler down with a clatter. His jerky movements followed him outside the control booth, and he practically ran toward the movers. "Hurry up, you heard him. Watch that post."

Those poor movers better have a lot of patience to put up with two angry men. She shook her head as Mr. Whippier scurried in front of Mr. Angerton, stepping into the mover's path. Oh, how that man took advantage of this opportunity to yell at someone. When the boss wasn't around, he was so lazy. Courtney sighed and focused on the desk work. There were some files to put away—

"In my office, Courtney. Now." Her limbs stiffened, mimicking Mr. Whippier's awkward walk. She chanced a look at her boss.

Mr. Angerton's face, still red, tilted down, and his shoulders were taut and fists clenched. His shirt was rumpled and suit coat… missing. Acid burned her stomach, and she glanced toward the front door pinned open for the movers. Too bad, her purse was locked away in the office with her car keys.

Her pulse accelerated as she followed him. What could he possibly think she'd done or not done? Nothing had happened that could get her into trouble. Unless Daria fabricated—something. Courtney, wouldn't put it past her.

Opening the office door, he flipped the light switch on. The harsh glow spilled on the desk littered with plates, coffee mugs, and several files open and almost merging into each other. *Did he think she left this mess?*

He must've seen her focus. "Ignore my desk. I worked late last night and didn't clean up."

She nodded then risked a glance at his face. His angry look had a softer edge. She released a breath and forced her shoulders to relax.

His hand gestured toward the walnut chair in front of his desk. "Please, sit."

Gratitude filled her. How much longer would her legs hold out if she continued to stand? Slipping onto the expensive chair, her fingers wrapped around the edge of the seat, locking onto its support. She lifted her face to receive—what? Displeasure, direction? *Did she still have her job?*

"We've had a few adjustments to make concerning Leman's. I'm sure you are wondering about the antique department since the movers are here."

She nodded as her fingers clenched tighter.

"We discontinued the antique department for now. I'm not sure if we'll reinstate it in the future or not." His eyes bored into her. "There have been more… complications than I anticipated. That's all."

He turned his attention to the desktop. Should she leave or stay? The quiet grew annoying.

"Yes?" He snapped. "Is there a question?" His tone suggested that questions weren't welcome.

She had to risk it… "I still have my job then?"

A grim smile played on his lips. "Of course, you have your job—if you get back to work in the next ten seconds." She popped out of the chair, almost tipping it over. Grabbing the back, she set it upright then fled the room. "Lord, I don't deserve your help, but thanks." Relief warmed her insides and began to settle her shaky limbs into familiar grace once again.

Now that her mind was not so focused on her own concerns, she sensed negativity, or was dread obscuring the usual pleasantness of Leman's. She looked around at the well-positioned furnishings, a sprinkling of knick-knacks, lamps, and floor coverings. What was different?

Mr. Whippier kept his beady eyes on the movers, when not busy with customers for the next hour. He groaned when the bell to the front door rung again.

Courtney watched Mr. Greenwood and a police officer enter and head straight for her. "Mr. Greenwood, how are you today? And you, sir?" She knew how difficult Mr. Greenwood could be when his mind drifted, but there was just something about him that intrigued her inner child. He must've been a brilliant man before dementia intruded upon his life.

"Ms. MacDuff, good to see you."

Courtney brightened at his greeting. "What can I do for you today, sir?" She heard the bounce in her own voice, a pleasant departure from late last night's and this morning's mood.

Mr. Greenwood nodded toward the back, where the antiques had been arranged. "Where, I wonder, are the antiques and the sign advertising them, which you displayed." He pointed his pudgy finger in the direction of the last antiques emerging from the space, "over there."

He must be having a really good day. "We are discontinuing the antique department for now, but we may reconsider an antique section later, I've been told."

"What a shame."

"I agree. The department is barely gone and, I'm missing it already."

"No—what a shame that your boss would hide evidence."

Courtney gaped at him in shock. Mr. Whippier turned and sped toward the rear of the building, toward the office.

"Did you hear that the thieves who have been stealing and burning homes were caught last night?" Mr. Greenwood asked, his eyes narrowed.

She leaned toward him. "Yes, I called the police when they broke into my mother's house. I'd returned home, and our dog gave them a good chase."

A flash of what looked like admiration passed over his eyes. "Good for you. Wish I could've made that call."

"Wish I didn't have to. They smashed Mother's favorite vase and moved some heavy furniture that they obviously planned to steal. Had the dog and I not come home when we did—they planned to burn the house down while my mother was home, asleep." Courtney shivered involuntarily.

"Officer, I want this man out of my store now. He has…" Mr. Angerton paused and looked around as though checking to see who'd hear him. "Well, he has accused me of things best left unsaid right now." His voice seemed strained beyond his earlier emotional display.

The officer turned toward Mr. Angerton. "I'm Officer Gregory. I'm here to inspect your antique section. Here is the search warrant."

Two movers grunted and groaned as they waddled close to them, hauling the last piece of furniture out of the antique area.

"Put that down, please. Right where you are," the officer said.

Mr. Angerton stomped toward Courtney. "Did you encourage this man? Did you?"

Courtney didn't flinch as Mr. Angerton's eyes bored into hers. She sucked in a breath. "No, sir, what do you mean?"

Twenty-Five

COURTNEY

Courtney scooped her cell off the desktop and called her sister. In less than three rings, the hands of cyberspace joined and linked all the way across town.

"How about we leave early for the fitting appointment?" Pushing the vanilla sheers open to coax daylight inside did nothing to brighten the darkness of the room, which swallowed up every color except brown. Brown walls, brown carpet more than tightened the bedroom into a chokehold. She longed for freedom. No, she *needed* freedom. More than ever. But where could she escape? The walls seemed to concave a bit at the thought.

Bethany was home—her rescuer. It was easy to call her today like she'd done a thousand times before.

"Mom needs a dress also. Maybe afterward we could all visit Athens Restaurant for lunch." Her sister's voice flowed lacey with joy.

The wind screeched like a train whistle, buffeting the windows, causing her to drop the sheers and cover the chilled glass. She bent over and shoved a box stacked with books and odds and ends under her writer's desk before kicking the corner of the metal file box. Pain shot through her big toe and up the side of her foot. "Ouch, oww oww…" She hopped until she fell on the bed. Her fingers moved firmly over her foot, easing the pain away.

"What are you doing over there?"

"Rubbing my big old calluses." She'd have to do something about them before the wedding. When had her feet ever been so bad? Probably developed these babies while walking Puddles in the morning. Her heart danced an extra beat. Some mornings the sun rose with a spectacular display of color complementing the gentlest breeze that played with their hair as they walked side by side down the aging sidewalk.

"How long will it take you and Mom to get ready? The appointment is at 11:00." Water ran from her sister's sink, meaning Bethany was getting things done, and Courtney hadn't made it out of her bedroom yet.

Where was that elusive sense of escape? The feeling had up and abandoned her. Courtney's eyes trailed the room and landed on the box of books once more. The next time inspiration or frustration drove her, she'd push them out of the way and allow her fingers to transport her into another world. A place where she could regulate the disasters and situations, she—no her characters fell into. Her own divine plan, which was fitted with a perfectly designed escape, to lure the reader—if she had any—to the next chapter… or two. Not a thing like the real-life situation she faced at work. Or with Mother.

Yanking her mind back to the conversation, she said, "How about an hour or an hour and a half?" That might be realistic. She hoped Bethany hadn't heard the strain she felt.

"You sure you can motivate Mom that quickly?"

Courtney measured the time slipping along the hands of the clock. "Do you think you could call her? Demand Mother to hurry like only you could." Every wayward muscle in her back needed stretched and rearranged. She stood up and arched her back to even out the bend. An analytical glance around her room should've inspired the need to gather extra packing boxes. But no, not yet. Most of her possessions already waited for a place to call home. Boxes huddled against more storage boxes, braced against furnishings, and the wall in the basement of her parent's home. Sigh. Oh, to have her own place.

"I've got a lot to finish over here. Can't you do it?" Bethany's distracted voice was nearly smothered by running water. The shower this time. She probably used the spray cleaner her sister had found that smelled like lilacs.

Bands of urgency pressured her tired, achy neck muscles. Her exhaustion had equipped Mother's barbs with strength, which never lessened despite any attempts to serve her fickle nature. Courtney needed to fight her own lack-luster desire to smooth Mother's moods today. "It would be better coming from you."

Ignoring Mother's put-downs and criticisms wilted Courtney's spirit and seemed to count for nothing. Each new *Courtney blunder* took the limelight, minimizing any accomplishments. What was the use? Her hopes were nearly crushed by the days and hours they'd spent together. Would there ever be plain, raw acceptance from her mother? Her willing heart pinched sore as any hope of a positive-connection diminished like a vaguely remembered dream.

"Well, you don't have to sound so *happy* about it." The slight bite to Bethany's words spoke of how transparent she'd become since the stress of pulling everything together weighed on her shoulders. She'd been such a talented chameleon, manipulating emotions, and gauging her reactions *convincingly*. But that was before this wedding planning and living with Mother and coping with responsibilities that weighed too much. Air dragged through her lungs as though she'd breathed every breath through cotton.

"Athens, I want to eat there. Plus, Mother loves the menu

so we can do lunch afterward." She made sure she pumped the last ounce of *Courtney charm* into those words. Her energy dipped with their telling.

"Okay, sorry. I'm tired of everything. The excitement of getting married, relocating, and getting a new job, though good, is scary too."

"I know." Courtney needed to just get up and get moving to shake off these doldrums. She turned the doorknob. After slipping outside into the hall, she pushed the door closed with a click. "I bet you could get Mother moving with a phone call while I get ready." They both knew that was true even though she was a measly few steps away from Mother's bedroom, and Bethany called from across town.

"I'll call if you drive."

"You're on."

⁂

COURTNEY

Heavy breezes shifted east then west all along their drive toward Beaver Falls. Large trees bowed and submitted to the force pushing their branches from one jumbled angle to another. Courtney's fingers tightened on the wheel, steering against each blast of wind and around a downed tree branch, which blocked part of their side of the road. Their appointment with the seamstress wouldn't wait for an enthusiastic breeze to die down.

"Maybe this is a tornado. Did anyone think to look at the weather channel?" Mother's voice grew shrill and thready. Her hand gripped the handle of the car door, while the other braced against the dashboard.

"It will be fine, Mom." Bethany's voice harbored a faraway ring to it. Something about her felt different, but Courtney couldn't place when or where the shift had begun. She glanced at her sister in the rearview mirror. Calm planes shaped her profile. Not the usual wrinkled brow when Bethany tensed over being late or upset. Maybe her imagination ran wild today, but it was as if a sad surrender dulled her sister's eyes.

"Look out!" Mother's scream tore her attention back to the road. A squirrel disappeared in front of the car. Courtney swerved. Heart beating wildly, she tightened her grip on the steering wheel. Pushed out a breath of frustration. She glanced into the mirror at her sister to see the smug *better you than me* smile beaming back at her.

She'd watch Bethany carefully, even though she appreciated the sparkle stirring in her sister's attitude. But, then again, her sister couldn't hold secrets from her. She'd spill this burden soon if there was one. Bethany was Bethany, after all.

A parking spot opened up across the street from the midnight blue awnings with Gwendolyn's in rich gold script. She put the turn signal on and angled her car backward into the space. She hated this change in parking, well, just about everyone complained about it. Though it was easier to pull away from the curb and into traffic, she imagined that more than a few fender benders happened when backing into a spot. Once they stepped out of the car, an unusually strong gust of wind almost stripped their breath away. Courtney put quarters in the parking meter and retrieved Mother's walker. Lillian stood and grabbed the walker firmly while Bethany braced her against the fickle wind. They matched their steps with her, linking elbows offering stability, all the way down the sidewalk and across the street.

The swirling gust packed a punch, forcing Gwendolyn's Wedding & Formal Attire door out of Courtney's hand. Her next attempt to open the door allowed them to successfully enter the shop.

Bethany pointed to the time. Courtney's bangs skimming

her face as she nodded. Ten minutes to spare. Time was so important to some people.

A grunt of pleasure sounded from behind one of the clothing racks. Courtney turned toward Mother, who pinched a bright pink dress between her fingers. Bethany shook her head in the negative. Her sister chose a mother of the bride dress with a golden sheen. The silk rustled when she pressed this gown next to Mother's face and hair. Courtney winced. No wonder Mother hated gold. Silver complimented her complexion and hair.

Mother's face soured into a well-rounded sulk.

Mother frowned then shoved a glittery, silver dress forward. Silk collided with silk as neither of them yielded in the middle of the aisle. Bethany huffed and then turned toward the blue selections that matched the bridesmaid's dresses.

What was going on? They'd never acted like this before. Courtney's eyes scanned the racks hoping to find something that would appeal to them both before this escalated. Or was that even possible?

"Bethany MacDuff." A booming voice sounded from a slight woman.

"We're here." Bethany brightened and grabbed Courtney's arm. "Let's go."

Bethany's dress needed very little altering. The form-fitting pleated bodice complimented her sister's athletic build. Ivory satin flowed toward the floor in three large graceful ruffles.

Bonnie Evans, a seamstress at Gwendolyn's , stepped out from the back room. She approached them, eyeing the wedding gown. She tugged the strap. "I can have this fixed before you leave today." Accepting the nod, she turned back toward the Employee Only doorway.

"Thanks, Bonnie," Bethany fingered the one and only strap on the gown before she turned her attention to Courtney's dress. "Do a spin for me."

Courtney obliged.

"Perfect. No altering needed here."

"Actually, she fixed this dress a couple of times—"

"I've received no help with picking my dress. I hope the two of you are proud of yourselves." Mother's face flushed red though the sales girl's haggard expression proved the opposite to be true. Multiple pink and silver dresses weighed down the salesgirl's arms.

The sisters rolled eyes at each other. Courtney turned toward Mother. "Let's see what we can do about that. I'll go change and then I'll be right with you." Courtney touched the satin flowers beautifully adorned with glass beadwork nestled on the waistline of her sister's wedding dress. "Exquisite." The train ruffle lay gracefully behind her sister, obediently, following wherever she led.

"Do you even like this?" The bride-to-be touched the strap, which added more silk flowers sprinkled with glass beadwork. Her expression begged for a true answer.

"I wouldn't change a thing about this dress. If you weren't getting it, I would be. This strap adds nothing but beauty."

Bethany grinned, and her hands shot out to squeeze Courtney's. A forever moment. Grabbing her camera, she snapped a selfie while Bethany gave her the most marvelous smile.

To *do life* without her sister down the street would be so difficult. Just a phone call away didn't seem comforting, since they were several states apart. Her cell chirped. She squinted and turned her phone to confirm what she didn't believe. Tanya's face and number showed up on her screen, blotting out the new photo of Puddles she'd placed as her cell's wallpaper.

Courtney

Licking her lips, Courtney's inward voice spoke, "Down girl, eyes refocus. This is the Athens Family Restaurant menu. Your favorite." Grape leaves—her mouth watered as she anticipated the flavor. She moved her shoulder muscles and tried to relax in the comfortable booth. Mother's indecision at Gwendolyn's Wedding & Formal Attire led them from light pink to dark and one style to another, challenging Bethany's increasing disapproval and tightening tension like a vice grip in Courtney's back.

The Greek cuisine re-activated the hunger she'd lost when nothing pleased Mother or her sister. If Bethany didn't think a gown complemented her periwinkle bridesmaids' dresses and creamy roses, well, there was no room for compromise. And then the call from Tanya… but that she should save for another day.

Since their mother's decision to make those ugly Victorian centerpieces for the shower backfired, life had been less comfortable, a bit edgier. Mother's insistence and frustration grew with each shake of her sister's head. The shop ladies exchanged glances after the heat of Mother's wilting stare, and no doubt, their eardrums stung at some of her choice words. She'd certainly gotten bolder as she grew older.

Usually, she and Mother argued. One glance at their faces shoved aside every trace of her angst. Scrunching behind the menu, one thing she knew, she was tired, giddy, and could laugh right out loud. And that would not be good.

"Why are you slouching? Sit up."

Courtney bent the menu to peek at her criticizer across the table. Then allowed the flap of the menu to snap into place again as she scooted her angle away to the right. Wonder if the next booth over thought Mother was talking to a ten-year-old? She'd not turn around to see.

"Are you getting stuffed grape leaves, like always?"

Not surprised by the question, Courtney glanced at Bethany. The smile had returned to Bethany's eyes, reminding her of the beach and her sister's protective embrace. She'd always made Courtney feel wanted.

Nodding her head, she said, "A gyro salad as always." Courtney's cell buzzed in her pocket. A sinking feeling landed in the pit of her stomach. Reluctantly, she slipped it out of her pocket. "Whew." *Only Natalie, not Tanya.* "Make it snappy little lady, we're about to eat," Courtney said in her country-western voice.

"It won't kill you to miss a meal—I need *your* help." Panic wasn't something that Natalie did well or ever. *Were those tears in her voice?*

Leaning her elbow on the table, Courtney focused on the floor. "What's up?" The tension, which had started to ease away, claimed territory with more vigor. She rolled her shoulders, but it did nothing to deter the pain, now clutching her neck muscles.

"I'm paralyzed."

"What?"

"Not actually paralyzed. Just get here *pronto.*"

"This isn't like you to beg."

"You've got that right. Hurry up and get here." Dead silence.

Panic flared inside her as though it were her own. She blinked at her family. "Natalie needs me. Let's place a to-go order, and I can drive us home before I head over to rescue her." She tilted her head back against the tall booth and groaned. "I almost forgot. I need to call and check all the wedding orders this afternoon."

Mother's voice purred. "I would like to contribute to this wedding. Give me the list, and I'll make the calls."

Leveling her gaze with Mother's—there wasn't enough time for her to make any changes. Besides, she would appreciate being included. Maybe allowing her to help would soothe emotions on so many levels. A glance at Bethany seemed to confirm that her sister agreed.

"Alright. Thanks." Courtney relaxed against the back of the booth. Things just might turn around yet. A smile eased onto her face.

Bethany winked approval at Courtney, before turning her attention toward the menu again.

And Mother, her eyes sparkled like in days gone by. The way they'd looked for so many friends and family through the years, but usually when she was up to something. Courtney grinned as memories tracked across her mind. Her mother proved to be a real character over and over again. Full of imagination, surprises, and strength. She could really get a job done. Despite their differences, Courtney couldn't help but admire her. Joy bubbled inside as she observed Mother. A genuine smile softened the tension she'd seen build over her mother the past few weeks.

The waitress approached them. "Are you ready to order?"

Courtney leaned over the table with the enthusiasm of a bloodhound in pursuit. "Two orders of grape leaves and two gyro salads to go, as fast as you can make them."

Twenty-Six

COURTNEY

Y ou just ignored Tanya's call?" Natalie fussed over a rose and baby's breath before tying them together with a bow. She had the most irritating habit of pursuing the most uncomfortable topics in the most inopportune times. Courtney shouldn't tell her everything. But her best friend would know. They couldn't hide anything from one another. It could be worse. Nat could've continued this topic in front of others.

The flower arrangements for the funeral were due tomorrow evening, making her friend's quick hands fly while Athens' grape leaves lingered next to her fork. Courtney's worry was that Natalie's huge floral refrigerator couldn't hold all of these flowers. Thank goodness she had an air-conditioned basement to keep these beauties fresh once they were assembled. *Would that be enough to keep them fresh?* She watched Nat's attention skip to the Greek food, slowing her work a microsecond per glance.

Every kitchen counter space overflowed with flowers, ribbon, or containers waiting to be filled. Courtney pulled satin ribbon open, measured, and cut several pieces. Then she grabbed a batch of flowers for the next arrangement. Rose scent permeated the room, mingling with cinnamon from the warm cup of chai tea resting at her elbow. "Why don't you just eat that? You know you want to."

Fingers stopped motion, as Nat gave her the *get back to the topic* look.

Courtney withered slightly. *Oh, the question.* "I'm sure Tanya didn't call on purpose. Honestly, I thought she'd discontinued that number." She lowered her head and voice then continued, "I tried calling her several times right after she'd deserted me and nothing. No answer. No call your favorite business-partner back. Not even to tell me what to do with Puddles, except for the note. I'm suspicious, why would she bother to call me now?"

"Aren't you going to find out? She does owe you a lot of money and explanations."

"I'd rather not have to deal with her. Not with the wedding coming up. And I don't need another round of excuses."

"Ouch." Natalie stabbed her finger with a thorn. Blood puddled quickly. She stuck the tip of her index finger into her mouth, then dug around in a junk drawer with her other hand until she pulled out a plastic baggie holding bandages.

Courtney cleared her throat, and then picked up her phone. "I have one more hour to help you before I need to go take care of some preparations for the wedding." She slapped her hands together, knocking off the leaves and glitter stuck to her fingers. Shimmering sparkles caught the light and played tag on the way to the floor.

Natalie quirked an eye toward the mess. "Well, you're not leaving that for me to clean."

"Hint taken." She looked for the broom and dustpan, then dragged the broom across the otherwise spotless floor sweeping up every bit of glitter. "Your starting to sound like my…"

Her friend stopped and stared at her. "What is going on with you and your mother?"

Courtney sputtered, "Wha-what isn't going on with Mother and me is more like it."

"That helps a lot. Could you share an in-depth revelation?" She wrapped her finger with a tail of ribbon. She seemed to realize what she was doing and grabbed her cappuccino with both hands.

"I just... I... I'm tired of her mean..." Courtney pressed her eyes shut, trying to drive out the pain from a headache beginning to form. "I just want to have a good relationship with Mother, and God hasn't moved her heart toward me—at all. If anything, my own mother is further away from me than ever."

Natalie choked on her drink. She set the mug down and waved her hand, motioning her that she would be fine.

Courtney's phone's Spanish tune played. Mother. "Well, here she is. She never calls, and I'm talking about her, and here she is." Leaning the broom against the edge of the kitchen counter, she then fumbled with her phone to answer. "Hello."

"You need to get home."

Courtney shook her head and blocked an exasperated sigh. "I'll be home in an hour. That'll give us enough time to get ready for tonight."

"Tanya's here, and she will not be here for long. I suggest you come now." The irritation in Mother's voice was unmistakable.

Tanya.

Shouldn't she be hiding from the MacDuffs and not winding up on her parents' doorstep? A groan escaped from her lips. "I'm coming."

An expression resembling betrayal crossed Natalie's face as she looked Courtney in the eye. "You're going?" She broke eye contact and swung her attention from side to side, encompassing the countertops filled with unmade orders for tomorrow.

"Looks like I get to talk to Tanya, whether I want to or not." The broom fell. It's handle slapping the floor, making them jump.

· —❦— ·

COURTNEY

With chest tightening anxiety, Courtney walked past the maroon sports car, taking up her space on her parent's driveway. Tanya was definitely in town. Inside her parent's house no less. This had to be the last person on the earth she wanted to see right now. She glanced at the sky as the sun tucked itself behind the moisture-ladened purple cloud. Exact color as a bruise she'd gotten while moving from the apartment complex in such a hurry.

The sliding glass door slid open. "Sit, Puddles. I'll see you later. Thanks, Lillian." Tanya's voice as smooth as water bubbling in a creek, grated against her ears. A zipper scratched the air as her arm moved to seal her luggage-size purse. Then she turned but took a step backward, and her hand clutched at her throat. "Oh, Courtney. I didn't hear you drive up."

"My space was taken. I had to park along the avenue." Her eyes narrowed. Tanya was always about Tanya. What purpose could she have to stop here? "Are you returning my money you emptied from our account?" That should at least get Tanya moving onto why she came. Payback would be sweet, but not likely.

"Court, I had to leave. You understand."

Courtney's temple's throbbed as her blood sped through her veins at an accelerated rate. "Oh, I understand. Embezzlement is against the law. Your here to turn yourself in, possibly?"

Tanya's eyes pinched almost shut. She appeared uncertain before she turned her head to the side. "It's not embezzlement when the second party agreeably deposits their money into the same account. You were so willing to let me handle the business end." She spoke in smooth mesmerizing tones. Returning her attention, and looking as though her determination were refocused, she said, "I see Puddles is doing well. I wasn't sure you would keep her. And I do want to congratulate you on your new film debut." Her voice lifted with an artificial enthusiastic ring.

She flinched. *Tanya couldn't know...* "What—"

A mocking laugh poured from Tanya. "Are you getting paid for tromping around the dusty field with *my* dog? I believe I would be entitled to all monetary profits from Puddles film time."

Stepping back, Courtney bumped her elbow into Tanya's rental. *How could she know?* She ignored the sting buzzing her funny bone and straightened her arm to lessen the discomfort.

"Mike and I laughed our heads off last night as we watched the finale."

Mike. Mike—oh, no, Mike Bevy. Weren't the embarrassing parts removed? Sure, Zander showed her some of the finished episodes. Honestly, Tanya could be so petty. Something she never did appreciate about her underhanded ex-friend.

Tanya opened the gate and shut it behind her as she approached Courtney with confidant grace. Her manicured hand glided down the railing as she took the steps toward the driveway. "I snagged a couple of copies." She focused intently on Courtney's face before her triumphant smirk. She placed a designer shoe on the driveway.

Courtney tensed. Zander had taken care of all those embarrassing shots. But was there a copy he'd not shown her—one approved by Mancel? The wind tugged her bangs into her face, and she pushed them back, then noticed her nails. Even while remodeling the apartments, she'd taken better care of herself. She tucked her hands out of sight.

270

Glaring at Tanya as the sun reappeared pierced her eyes with pain. The woman pulled open her oversized purse and grasped a DVD case. She flipped that hand in Courtney's direction and waited half a second before shoveling it at Courtney. "Take it." Impatience steamed her words.

Snatching the DVD, Courtney leaned toward Tanya, scooting her back a couple of steps onto uneven territory for the stilettos Tanya wore. She jabbed the DVD at her and said, "Leave, I don't want to see your face around here *ever* again. Unless you pay me what you owe me, I don't want to hear from you. I've not gone to court... yet. But I'm not saying that I won't."

Tanya recovered her shaken expression, rigidly spinning it into a smug, arrogant one. "I want my dog back. I'll finish moving in a couple of days. You can bring her to me then, that would be more convenient for *me*. Oh, and she'll be an outside dog from now on since Mike doesn't like her at all. I believe that's your fault." She tossed over the *you know precisely why* kind of look that Courtney had grown a massive distaste for.

"You abandoned her. She's mine now, and that's final."

Tanya's eyes sparkled as she glanced at her newly manicured nails adorned with dazzling rhinestones. "Well, a dog is considered property, and *I* still own her. You didn't get her fixed, did you? I would hope you didn't damage her value in that way." She aimed a hardened, cold as steel glare. "I'd hate to sue you for any loss that could be incurred."

"If you tangle with me over Puddles, you'll have the fight of your life." The words poured out in a venomous whisper Courtney didn't know she possessed.

Tanya blanched and took three steps backward, allowing Courtney to climb the cement steps and leave her behind.

Twenty-Seven

COURTNEY

Bethany and Brandon were the last to leave her parent's home after a long meeting of sorting out those last-minute wedding details. Mother became upset toward the end of their visit and very put out when Bethany and Brandon refused several of her suggestions. Once her mother's door closed, the house seemed bathed in sweet quiet.

Finally.

If only the stillness would seep into her soul. But she had something to investigate tonight. Something she didn't want her mother's prying eyes on. It couldn't wait until after the wedding. She grabbed her purse from her bedroom and headed toward the living room. Inhaling a shaky breath, Courtney took one more glance down the hallway.

All quiet. All still.

Puddles wanted to hang-out in the backyard, so she'd opened the door and gave her a bone to chew on. "Here you go, girl." Puddles stepped onto the porch wagging her tail with vigor.

"Enjoy." *Would this be one of the last times she could say this to her?* No, she had to quit thinking negatively. She was just tired. The law was there to protect the innocent.

Courtney tip-toed to the living room, the deeply piled carpeting hushed her footfalls all the way past the recliner. When she reached the doorway, she peeked down the hall. Mother's light was still off.

A nagging question tortured her all night long. Just like Tanya had intended, she was sure, for Courtney knew this woman's tactics. How dare she literally shove this DVD at her? Curiosity grew too huge to ignore. Hiding the DVD case inside her purse so that she could watch it without Mother's knowledge had seemed like a good idea. But its constant presence reminded her that she couldn't relax until she knew.

Why hadn't Zander bothered to tell her about this troublesome version of his training video? It had been all she could do to not ask him about it tonight at the rehearsal dinner.

She lowered herself onto the recliner, brushing her legs against the soft velvety cushion. Reaching to turn off the lamp beside her, she noticed that her fingers shook, with anticipation? No, more like fear. The circular holder in the case refused to release the DVD. Pulling again, she almost cracked the disc before angling it free.

Turning on the television blasted the speakers. She fell off the chair and onto the floor, dropping the channel changer. Skimming the carpeting with her hand, she found the controller, then pushed the down arrow to lower the sound into reasonable levels. The type of volume that wouldn't entice the inquisitiveness of her mother. But was it too late?

Fear of discovery moved her to the hall again to peek down its length. Thank goodness her mother couldn't hear well. Mother's light stayed off. Still, her heart pounded with rhythm that would not slow easily.

Dropping the case into her purse, she crawled over to the player and slipped the DVD inside before pushing it shut.

The introduction was impressive. Mike showed real ability. The title and still-shots zoomed in and out, showing the various stages of the training video that were to come. Zander's verbal invitation relayed information—quick and to the point. She hated how eager she was to see him on the screen. Especially since he might not be trustworthy. Soon she'd know.

Snuggled into the cushions, Courtney watched the introduction to the first lesson. Zander gave his philosophy on dog training. She smiled at his confident delivery and his calm demeanor. The man definitely had a touch of class. So easy to listen to. Convincing voice. He'd certainly taught her. And she'd have believed him after this intro immediately—if his honesty wasn't called into question. What would she say when she talked to him next time? *If* she did.

Tapping the end table with her nails, the restless got-to-get-up and pour a drink stole over her. Hot chocolate would be perfect—with tons of marshmallows.

Pausing the video, she moved to the kitchen with an easy stride. Tanya was just jealous. Courtney had always felt inferior to her so-called friend's business savvy and her classy exterior. All that changed when she discovered how deceptive that woman could be. Yep, the tables had turned. Flipped really.

Pulling the small pan from the dishwasher, she set it on the burner. Then she poured in the milk, the cocoa, and other ingredients that added a special touch. And to think she'd worried when Tanya mentioned the dusty field. "Ha."

Well, of course, some dust had flown up during each filming of the training sessions. Really, they should have rented one of those large training rooms with the doggy mats that Zander had discussed before. That would've been the only clean method and weather-proof too. He wanted to build one to support an at-home business. She would have to encourage him to pursue that dream. Snazzy idea. Snazzy man.

So far, so good. Courtney's heart warmed at the thought of

spending time with him at the wedding. He'd be matched up with Nicole, one of the bridesmaids.

Chocolate scent lifted her spirit as she breathed it in. She poured the hot chocolate into her cup and then filled it to the top with marshmallows. On her stroll back to the living room, she noticed the light turned on in the living room. The one she turned off—on purpose. Her heart beat a snare drum rhythm.

Mother was just settling into the recliner when Courtney entered the living room. Her throat throbbed when Mother looked at the television and blew out a breath. Her shaky hand picked up the DVD player controller.

Courtney held her breath.

"If you're not going to finish watching the movie, then turn it off." Mother shut off the power.

Lowering herself into her chair, Courtney spied a corner of the DVD case sticking out of her open purse. She relaxed a little as Mother busied herself with changing channels and raising the volume. Courtney reached down and tugged the zipper until the purse was fully closed.

Summoning her most concerned expression, she turned. "Weren't you tired? Don't you think you need to stay in bed?"

"Can't sleep." Mother squinted in her direction. "When I heard you blasting my television, I knew I needed to get in here. Don't blow up my only pleasure now that I'm dealing with a walker and no way to get out of the house."

"Ah." Courtney's anger flared. Mother had just turned up the sound significantly—but there would be no acknowledging that fact. Courtney settled against cushions that suddenly felt uncomfortable. It didn't matter that Natalie came over each time that she worked so that Mother wouldn't be alone, and she was taxied about town for needs and wants. Mother's arguments made her blood boil. Taking a sip of her hot chocolate stuck marshmallow to her upper lip, and she reached for a tissue at the same time that her mother did. Both of them paused.

Fingers hovering over the tissue box. Courtney snatched one and handed it to her mother.

A grunt that could be interpreted as *thanks* was the only reply.

Taking another long drink, Courtney worked hard to focus on the smooth perfection of her personally crafted hot chocolate recipe.

"So, what were you watching."

Courtney choked as the drink stopped halfway down her throat and traveled in the wrong direction. She plopped a tissue over her mouth. Cough, cough, and a few more later, she held her hand for Mother to wait.

"Nothing important." She squeaked. Her voice, as unnatural as the lie she delivered.

Scanning the end table beside her, Mother grabbed the DVD controller and pushed PLAY before Courtney could run interference. A pinched expression asking *what are you up to* crossed Mother's face.

They watched the beginning of the first lesson. Some training scenes had been excluded from the main film. But, before their eyes, Courtney appeared uncomfortable and angry. The dust flew around her feet, ruining her manicure. Panic and heart-sickness grappled inside Courtney. These were the shots Zander told her *not* to worry about. Her breath came in shaky, and her heart sank. Tanya hadn't lied.

Zander had.

"You really weren't professional during this lesson. Do you want to know what I think?" Mother situated herself in the chair to deliver her dialogue.

Hot chocolate soured on Courtney's taste buds. She put her cup down and moved toward the player. Pushing the open/close button, she retrieved the DVD. She croaked out, "I'm going to my room. Goodnight."

"Fine. I'll retire soon. Will you still be awake... in case I

need you?" Mother's *you're such a disappointment* tainted her words.

Courtney's ticklish throat allowed her to merely nodded.

Once in her room, she slipped the DVD into her disc player and connected it to her computer while keeping the sound low. Why hadn't she thought of this earlier? Watching this extended version with embarrassing scenes seemed a fitting way to mourn the death of what she'd considered a wonderful friendship with the man called Zander. She pushed down the hiccup of grief that nearly closed off her throat. Realizing he would allow this—knowing how she felt—magnified the humiliation.

He'd tricked her.

She rolled over on her bed and leaned into the pillow. First Tanya. Now Zander? Who next?

The doorbell rang. Not now. Who'd come to visit at this hour? *Please, not Zander.* Puddles barked at the kitchen door, wanting in. Dread slowed her footfalls down the hallway toward the front door. A hasty glance at the living room revealed Mother hadn't budged. No surprise there.

Fully expecting to tell Zander to leave, she shut her eyes to gain the upper hand over the tears pushing to spill out onto her cheeks. Swinging the door open, the words almost tumbled off her tongue, but she looked up and took in the exhausted frame of the man standing before her.

"Courtney, come here, dear."

Dad stood there with his bags piled on the stoop—flinging his arms wide open. Tears of gratitude and grief collided in the crush of his hug. Dad was home.

Finally, home.

Twenty-Eight

COURTNEY

A streak of red flashed from the left, catching Courtney's attention at the stoplight on 7th Ave. She slammed on the breaks. Traffic continued to zip past in the opposite lane—like no one noticed the near-miss by a fire breathing sports car racing through the red light—not its turn. Courtney failed to quale her thundering heartbeat. Close calls on the road. Close calls with her heart. Nothing seemed to be going well. Nothing felt safe.

Zander had left her several messages, but she didn't answer his calls. He'd never mentioned the finalized DVD. The enthusiasm and joy in his voice magnified her anger. If she only didn't have to deal with this wedding.

It was surprising she'd come this far without the customary bailing from responsibility. Love for Bethany had pulled her along so far and would have to pull her through the wedding itself. If not for Zander's trickery and Tanya demanding Puddles back, she could be so happy right now. Dad was home. She'd make herself think of him.

She backed into a parking space in front of Gwendolyn's Wedding & Formal Attire and turned off the ignition. She slowed her breath, calming down enough to go inside. Her cell rang.

Bethany.

"Hey, little sister, what's left on the list of to-dos'?"

"Well, I called Olde Stonewall Golf Course and talked to Nicole Catalano, the Event's Coordinator, and all is ready to go. They need a check. Their contact information is on my desk. I'm picking up Mother's and my dyed shoes and clutches and my gown. Do I need to pick up your shoes?"

"Yes, please. Pick up my clutch too."

"Bethany, I didn't think you choose one from here."

"I didn't, can you ask them to bill me. I trust your choice."

"Okay, your mighty trusting. *Good thing Bethany couldn't read her thoughts.* That's what I got done on my list so far today." *Not to mention the wedding gift she would shop for next.* If Bethany knew, she'd tell her not to spend a dime. Hopefully, when she stopped at Leman's, today, it would not be to pick up her final check. "Mother snagged the list of phone numbers for the flowers and reservations and photographer yesterday. That list was nowhere to be seen this morning." Courtney added.

"You know mom, she either has called or will today. She never leaves anything undone."

"Right. Can you think of anything else?" Courtney scribbled a note on her pocket calendar. *Mother, did you call?* Mother wasn't always herself anymore. Thank goodness all those phone numbers were already copied into her calendar, and she could double-check any worrisome details between stops today. No need to upset, Bethany.

"Does Dan Kimball have the chairs and tables set-up scheduled for the reception area? And are we absolutely sure Pastor knows the time? Remember when he missed the date for Cindy's wedding?"

Courtney laughed. "I can make those calls when I'm done shopping—"

"Oh, no, you don't. No shopping for you—just in case…
in case you need a new job."

*With barely a slip of her tongue, she'd told on herself—or
had someone else done so?* Courtney stepped out of the car and
locked the door. "Were you talking to Dad?" Last night he'd
insisted she tell him about those tears in her eyes. She'd shared
one of her lesser disappointments, but she couldn't talk to him
about Zander.

Drama at Leman's saved her from telling her heart-wrench-
ing struggles with Tanya and Puddles as well. She couldn't bear
Mother's *I told you so* since she'd warned Courtney to be ready
for the dog lessons. Plus, Mother had always taught the philosophy—*never trust others*—

"Mother told me she'd talked to Barney Whippier."

"Oh?"

"He told her that there are plenty of other jobs for someone
with your skills." The unusual drag to her words told Courtney
more.

Bethany, always the encourager, never meant to hurt her.
Courtney's imagination ran wild, thinking about that man's
tone as he spoke about Mother. Skills—well—if she'd finished
college or maintained a grown-up job, she could have hope.
But now—

"When will you know about your job?"

Rearranging her purse on her shoulder, Courtney said,
"Possibly today. Maybe I'll stop on my way home and try to
talk with Mr. Angerton."

"I'll pray for God's will, Court. Nothing less than that."

She cringed. *Why did this bother her?* Maybe because she
was only one of the billions of millions of people the Lord
could pay attention to? And who was Courtney MacDuff anyway? "Thanks, Bethany." Her response sounded brittle to her
own ears. She'd better perk up, or Pastor Dean would zero in
and give her a pep talk tonight at the rehearsal dinner. Zander,

author of her humiliation, didn't need to hear any of that. Especially since he was the last person she needed to see.

"You'll be home by 2:30, right?"

"Maybe, why?"

"We have an exclusive nail appointment at Natalie's with Zeta at 3:00, and I'm coming to pick you up. It's all very hush, hush. So, don't tell Mom or the girls."

"All these secrets—sounds like fun. So, how do you plan to break me out of the house? Mother has plans for me."

"Who says?

"She says. She told me so when I was leaving this morning. I think she wants me to vacuum and clean the house."

"Your favorite activities. Are you sure you want your nails done?"

"Quite sure."

"You'll owe me big-time when I break you out of there."

Courtney laughed. "We'll see if your charm still works with Mother this afternoon."

COURTNEY

Leaning toward the afternoon light streaming through the large living room window, Courtney surveyed Mother's nit-picky to-do list. Such details. Had Mother resurrected an old spring-cleaning campaign: dishes, mop floor, walls near the stove, clean appliances, and wash windows? Also, the living room needed attention: dust woodwork, vacuum both floor, and furnishings. She pulled her attention away from the note and gazed out the window—wishing. Would her sister arrive in time to rescue her from an afternoon of absolute drudgery?

Nope, no car. A cloudy sky muted the colors of the world outside the MacDuff window.

Some people made you giddy to be around them. Bethany was one of those. Then there were others made you wonder why you were born. Unless your purpose was to be sandpaper in their lives, for rounding off their edges. Dad was in his *daddy cave* already, and Mother was feeling like Queen Cleopatra. Courtney felt like Cinderella.

She dragged her rag over the middle of the end table, leaving a stripe on the surface as she made her way to the closet to retrieve the vacuum and revved it up. Mother would be upset to know that the dusting didn't take place first, but with a wedding tomorrow, she didn't feel like she had time for any of this today.

Puddles barked and pounced at the vacuum. She detested loud noises, hairdryers, and blenders too. It didn't matter. Courtney played like she was going to suck Puddles up, and the canine hopped and jumped away. Then her dad walked past her and called the dog to go outside.

Someone touched Courtney's arm from behind, making her jump. Bethany. "Whew." Turning the vacuum off, she said, "You really wanted to scare me, didn't you?"

"Get your purse, let's fly," her sister whispered.

"Aren't you going to talk to her?"

"Not on your life, we're sneaking out."

"What about her mood, what about—she's so difficult?"

"Leave that to me. I'll talk to her later. You're the Maid of Honor, now act like it—grab your purse. Let's go."

Courtney loved the impish grin on Bethany's face. This adventure had the taste and thrill of her not-too-distant past, but she wasn't sure about dealing with Mother later. The key was to avoid contact with those she'd disappeared on or disappointed. That minimized the chances of consequences. Oh, how she wanted to run, "We'd better not, for your sake."

Her sister shared a crooked grin.

That temptation proved to be too much. Courtney's heart beat a staccato rhythm as she whispered back, "Fine, let's go."

She ran tip-toed down the hallway—missing the squeaky floorboards—until she arrived at her bedroom, all the while her lungs ached to burst with laughter. Snatching her purse, she retraced her steps. Bethany waited in the living room. Mother stirred inside her bedroom, which caused Courtney to quickened her steps.

Grabbing a marker and notepad, she jotted, *Be back soon. Nail appointment. Courtney.* Faint sounds of their mother's voice called her.

"Oh, no, she's coming. Run." Courtney and Bethany sprinted through the kitchen and out of the sliding glass door.

"Are you girls going somewhere?" Dad was cleaning the windows of his car.

"We're off for a nail appointment. See you later." Laughter bounded from them as they went.

"So, this is what it's like," Bethany's breathless words spilled out between laughing and trying to find her fob to unlock the car door.

"What?" Courtney panted as she waved to Puddles, who barked at them for closing the gate and leaving her behind.

"Escape. Well, get it out of your system. You had better be at my wedding." Bethany's grin dissolved them into laughter again.

Courtney grabbed the handle on her sister's car and opened the door. "And why aren't we taking Mother to get her nails done?"

Sobering Bethany slammed the door and turned the key. "Zeta is sensitive and only wished to take care of you and me. Plus, she has some kind of writing deadline, so her time is limited." She turned her head to look at Courtney. "Maybe you should talk to her about writing as a career."

"One has to write well for that career."

"You already do."

"How would you know?" Courtney narrowed her eyes and watched her sister.

Bethany squirmed then pushed on the gas. "I just know." She glanced back wide-eyed, "Call it a sister's intuition."

Turning her attention to the opposite window, Courtney reversed the smile playing on her lips. It had been far too long since she wrote pages for her latest fiction. She longed to dive into the story again. Nidella was in the middle of some wicked moves, and the hero made her heart ache. Her hand moved up and pressed against the pain. Well, Rednaz The Great, didn't feel like a hero just now.

Minutes later, Natalie welcomed them into her parlor to greet Zeta. The petite woman glanced up at them, grace in her posture, beauty in her eyes. The cream-colored window sheers behind her bellowed in the soft breeze making its way into the room.

Vanilla fragrance filled her senses as Courtney approached Natalie.

"Yep, the vanilla cappuccino is yours, that's your spot next to the window. And Bethany, your Toasted Marshmallow cappuccino is over there. Next to Zeta. You're first in line."

"But we're early." The cappuccinos would have been cold had they arrived on time. She took her place on the smooth cushioned wing back chair next to the open window. Courtney's brow wrinkled.

"If you were to get out of the house at all—you would have to do it before 2:30."

"Why's that?"

"Lillian's weekday programs start then."

Courtney wrinkled her nose. *How did Natalie ever notice that?* She turned toward Bethany, "Did you realize that too?"

"Oh, yes. Mom is… let's call it predictable."

Who would have thought? Well, apparently everyone but

she did. They burst out laughing as they watched Courtney. She shook her puzzled head and sipped her hot cappuccino relishing the flavor, warmth, and company.

Curiosity got the best of Courtney. "How is that huge order coming?"

Natalie frowned. "She made her selections, so I think everything is okay. But I've called Sierra several times lately and couldn't get hold of her. I'll try again later."

"Why do you need to call her?" Bethany sat down and smiled at Zeta. Wrapping her fingers around her warm drink, she took an appreciative sip.

"I need to know where to deliver the order and who to send the bill to."

"Two extremely important reasons." Zeta's warm and silky voice slipped Courtney into a grin.

After finishing their drinks and a lavish Victorian tea cake, Zeta opened up a case loaded with the nail polish colors she offered. Courtney leaned back in her chair, relieved that she didn't have to make those choices.

Bethany bent her head over the case and surfed through all the close-to-white choices. "I want pearl white for the base, and this one for the spattering of blue. It will match the bridesmaids' dresses, I think." Then she held up some pictures of nail design choices. "You offer all these?"

Zeta nodded and continued to organize her workspace.

"You are quite the artist." As Courtney skimmed through the designs. Her attention snagged upon a similar choice—reminiscent of the pedicure which had been ruined in Zander's dog training field.

Pointing at that one, in particular, Bethany said. "Look at this. Do you think this works?"

Courtney hoped her imitation smile still worked. That choice brought back memories of her face in the dust and a handsome man with curly hair that she didn't want to think about.

⁘

COURTNEY

While receiving their pedicures from Zeta, they talked and laughed—a lot. This woman wasn't shy, as Courtney had believed. There was something winsome and contagious in her smile. With gentleness, she held their hands as she worked. Was there anything this woman couldn't do?

Only a month ago, Courtney had ridden past Zeta's house breathing in rose fragrance. Even turning the car around to catch scent off the capricious breeze. Wasn't she just grasping for peace to lessen the stress tangling her inside? Roses for as long as she could remember had the power to soothe her, anchoring her against uncertainties in a way she couldn't identify. She looked at Natalie and Zeta, exchanging smiles and a bit of wit. Her curiosity about them was finally satisfied. This afternoon proved there was no mystery about why her best friend became close to this woman in the space of a few months. She felt the tug of appreciation and admiration too.

⁘

ZANDER

Checking his watch, Zander approached Cassie and Nicole, who talked at the far corner of the Windsor Room. A quick scan of the room didn't satisfy. "Has Courtney arrived?"

"I don't know, but lateness and leaving early are second nature to Courtney. I've known her a long, long time." Nicole glanced at her friend, who nodded eager agreement.

Zander offered a smile and tried hard to pay attention to Nicole as she said, "You'd like my dog, Waldo."

He glimpsed at the door, and there she was. Courtney wore a long skirt and carried a huge bag twice the size of her purse. That was saying something. She could ruin her back, hauling that purse alone. He'd picked it up once, so he knew this first hand. He turned sideways to get a better view, and his foot slid in the direction of the door.

"Zander, like I was saying about Waldo..." Nicole continued. He waited for her to break off the conversation, or at least take a breath. Pastor Thomas Dean's lively discussion snagged Courtney's attention before she got to lay down her bag. She smiled and laughed at his jokes. Was it his imagination, she seemed to sense where he was and avoided eye contact? Nothing like playing up the *nothing is wrong* act and being forcefully joyful. She carried on her part of the conversation with enthusiasm.

What reason did she have to avoid him? He'd never known Courtney to play games with people. He nodded at Nicole, still waiting to break the conversation. Turning back toward Courtney, he'd caught her eye. She jerked her head in the opposite direction pretending she hadn't seen him. He might've been fooled except for the red hue creeping up her throat and spreading on her face.

He'd get to the bottom of this tonight. He was sure he'd not offended Courtney. No disagreement lately, and she seemed to like the dog training video, and from what he could tell at their last training—she enjoyed his presence. A lot. Why did it seem as though their relationship had jumped the track?

Sweet chords of the dulcimer, fiddle, and flute blended together and grew louder, encouraging the sense of mystery throughout the crowd.

Bethany and Brandon entered the room, stepping in time to the melody while greeting their parents first then flocking together next to the dessert table. He admired them as they openly enjoyed the ambiance and the people surrounding them with a canopy of love. Bethany wasn't the only one who enjoyed history, Brandon indulged himself with historical books, furnishings, and events. Zander had to agree that the Windsor Room with its sage, sand, and gold tones set the perfect tone for the rehearsal dinner. Tomorrow it would host the reception.

Courtney laughed a little too loud and excused herself before she walked toward the banquet table. She pulled—what looked to be—name cards out of the bag and strategically assigned one at each place setting.

Nicole raised her voice, "Waldo's bone flew into the air..." for the third time.

"Excuse me, Nicole, I need to talk to Courtney. You sound like you have an interesting dog there." He smiled and turned as she opened her mouth to reply. But he spoke first, "See you at the table." Her strained expression and arms folding in front of her chest were her only reply.

Zander approached Courtney from behind. He wanted to see how she'd react if she were surprised by him. Would she bolt or finally give him a smile? He hoped for the latter. "Hey, Court. Can I help you with these?" He reached his hand out, expecting her to place half of the cards into his palm.

She flinched and stepped away from him. "Nope, I've got this." She turned her back and worked on the opposite side of the table.

Twenty-Nine

COURTNEY

Cobalt skies inked with an occasional faded white stripe shown through the windows of Fellow's Branch Church on the morning of the wedding. Last night's practice kept her nerves wound as over-tight violin strings—without any plucking room. Courtney twisted her page of to-do's in her hands as she watched the traffic pass. Zander had nipped at her heals throughout the long night. Exhausting—she had to stay aware of him yet pretend to not notice his watchful eyes, his hopeful mannerisms to connect with her. It took her long-acquired avoidance skills to dodge his persistent efforts.

What good would it do to hash out their differences in front of everyone? Thankfully, her mother seemed distracted, somewhat elated. Maybe Dad being home made all the difference. Yet something felt off about that.

Glancing toward the sanctuary lit only with dimmers and candlelight caused her to taste the metallic tang of confrontation that had hovered one step behind her during the rehearsal. Sigh. How would she make it through the day? The reception would be the worst.

Jenson's Favorites and Flowers Boutique delivery van pulled up to the curb between the birch and maple trees next to the sidewalk trailing to the front door. Leaves fluttered in the chaotic burst of summer breeze as the driver stepped out of the van.

The wrong flower van.

She pressed her phone on to check the time. "Bethany's wedding takes place in four hours." Her voice carried louder than she intended. She could've been a Bingo announcer with that amplification. Maybe she missed her calling? She turned to see if anyone heard her. Nicole approached. "Where is Clark's Flowers? And why is this van blocking the parking spot in front of our sidewalk?"

"Maybe another business across the street ordered something?" Nicole's voice echoed into the entryway as she drew near the front door from the small study off the lobby. Her arms spilled over with smatterings of decorations, blue, cream, and gold entwined.

A woman driver had stepped toward the rear of the van to open the doors. Reaching inside, she pulled out two huge obnoxious flower arrangements.

"Check it out. Talk about ugly."

"Court, are you talking about the lady or the flowers?"

"Flowers."

Impatience stirred a dark mood within Courtney. "Where is that to-do list?" It had gone missing again. It traveled so many places with her, directing her every step, especially when it dropped to the floor and stuck to the bottom of her shoe half an hour ago. Now she didn't know where to begin looking. She approached the entryway table and searched. Even if she wanted to forget the many not-done-yet items, all she had to do was look around. The most difficult and obvious tasks were embossed forever in her mind. If she didn't watch out, she would be dreaming about those. In reality, she didn't need a list, especially one that remained rebelliously uncrossed. Too much to finish before the wedding. At least, it seemed that way. Who on earth could accomplish so much?

Mother. She'd always accomplished the impossible—

"It's in your hand." Nicole grinned.

"What…" Courtney looked down and found the list. Then she moved toward the sanctuary doors.

"Those flowers are headed this way," Nicole's deep voice landed like a rock on Courtney's thoughts.

She stopped dead in her tracks then turned as Nicole left the window to carry the ribbon and decorative grapes toward the pews in the center aisle of the sanctuary. The flowers for those arrangements hadn't arrived, so they would only hang the partially made decorations.

The sliver of window next to the door revealed their new guest. Mary Thrund bobbed up and down with each step, as she hauled two matching arrangements down the sidewalk toward the front door.

Correction, she carried a couple of the tackiest flower arrangement Courtney had ever laid her eyes on.

"Isn't that *Victorian?*" Cassie's dry tone kicked in as she moved toward the door's window blocking Courtney's view of the woman's fight against the fresh breeze whistling against the church windows, rattling them in passing. Cassie leaned back again as Mary tugged the weight of the arrangements with wind-tossed hair giving a wild appearance to both the woman and flowers.

Heaviness settled inside Courtney's chest. "That's exactly what Mother *getting-her-way* looks like. How did she… I mean how could she…"

"What are you babbling about?" Natalie asked as she joined Cassie at the door and placed her hand on the glass to pushed it open for Mary.

"Mother took over the reminder calls, and I'd never double-checked. Bethany had nodded the okay during lunch at Athens Restaurant." Courtney's stomach spun and twisted. But that couldn't have been enough time to change such a large order. Could it?"

A long slow whistle slipped through Cassie's lips. "Your mother is amazing."

"What else has she manipulated?" If she'd even thought that Mother could change anything, she would've done the calls herself or gotten Cassie or Nicole—so much for trusting Mother. Courtney felt herself wilt under the shock. Why had she said yes to so much responsibility? Served her right.

Knowing the side exit door waited down the long hall tempted her. Following through, now that thought grew more appealing by the minute. Maybe walking out was somehow part of her DNA. Heat filled her chest and climbed toward her neck. How could she face Bethany? She couldn't. It would be better—

"What are you going to do about it?" Cassie placed her hands on her hips and tossed her a how could you allow this to happen look.

The first of many disappointments to follow if Courtney judged this situation right. Yeah, just what was she going to do about it? She squared her shoulders as the woman grew larger, crowding of the window close to the door.

Bethany would flip. Her big day was about to be ruined. Unless—

"Looks like you'll have to go with these, Courtney. No one else could prepare so many flower arrangements in such a short amount of time." Nicole pulled the door open.

Storming her way inside, Mary looked past Courtney into the sanctuary. "Where do you want these?" Her voice scratched as though she didn't want to be there any more than Courtney wanted her here. Not waiting for a reply, Mary leaned forward and stepped on the edge of the decorations lying on the floor. The ones which clashed with the hot pink and silver tones in the hands of the unwanted florist.

"Not in there, please." Courtney stood with her fists on her hips. "These are not our flowers. You must've mixed up the address." She could only hope she sounded convincing, but she feared the quiver in her voice was noticeable to everyone in the room.

Mary dropped her gaze to the crumbled list hanging half-way outside of her tan pants pocket. "Yes, they are." She put one flower arrangement down with a grunt and yanked the paper into the open.

Courtney folded her arms in front of her stomach. "Oh, just when did you receive the call for these flowers?"

Yanking the sales slip open, Mary said, "June first."

Shock hit her like a two by four. "What? No. I ordered from Clark's that day."

"Here's the slip if you want to see." She wiggled the sheet pinched between two cherry-stained fingers on her nail bitten hand.

She turned her head to peer out the window, hoping Clark's florist van would materialize. "They should arrive any minute. This order couldn't have been placed on that date."

"You trying to cancel the order?" Mary's face darkened. "It's too late now. Jenson's has a one-week canceling policy."

"And who ordered it?" *Bethany's day, not Mother's Day.*

Quirking a smile, the woman said, "Lillian MacDuff. She told me she canceled the Clark's Flowers order because of lack of customer satisfaction."

Courtney's mouth dropped open. Her eyes longingly sought the side door exit.

Mary chuckled. Satisfaction slid over her expression like a

shadow. It seemed like Mother and this woman operated with a stacked deck.

Gripping her own arms so hard she almost yelped, she reversed her hold and let go. Her fingers trembled and sought something to grab onto. The metallic taste of fear, seasoned with acute failure, coated her tongue. Just when she thought she'd finally not be a disappointment to Bethany. She'd pressed past every decision as though doing something wonderful for her sister. But no, today she would be letting Bethany down in the worst way.

Again.

Bethany's pristine joy from the night before flittered across her mind. She sighed. That fleeting emotion would sink into the murkiest disappointment—all because she'd not watched over her responsibilities. Why had her sister trusted her and put her in this position? One did not acquire a reputation—famous for irresponsibility—without effort. It took years to hone such skill. Not that she was proud. *God, can you handle impossible? I could use some direction here.*

Exotic flowers tipped in tacky hot-pink dye twisted like crippled fingers pointing the blame at her. Courtney sank into the chair near the sanctuary door. Her mother's betrayal would shatter the Mother-Bethany relationship she'd envied for as long as she could remember. Her sister wouldn't be prepared for this? So much for demanding no Victorian or pink at her wedding. Oh, the disrespect.

Decorations splayed across the floor, the ones which Bethany agreed on, and they'd spent hours creating. Side-by-side, the floral arrangements and decorations clashed, causing another sickening flip of her stomach.

Something has to be done. But what solution could there be? She stood up and approached Cassie. She whispered, "When Mary is done and out of here, please move those arrangements to the spare office."

"But—Whoa, you're not leaving, are you? You can't just—"

Stepping to the desk, Courtney grabbed her purse on the way out the door.

Thirty

COURTNEY

The runaway maid of honor stood on the back porch of her favorite Victorian dwelling. The leaves shimmered in the breeze, and the scent of lilacs filled the air.

She couldn't go back. Fear grew talons and grabbed hold of the unprotected, vulnerable place in her heart. She imagined the ripping, felt the tension, and pain of destruction. How could Mother do this to Bethany? Didn't she realize she'd destroy her relationship with her favorite daughter on so many levels?

Courtney considered her relationship with Mother. They'd probably never be close, but she didn't wish that on her sister.

She pressed the newly installed doorbell and waited for the chimes to do their work.

Zeta opened the door and did a double-take. Her hand holding large creamy colored roses tipped with a blush of salmon flew to her chest. "Courtney, I thought you would be getting ready for the wedding." Her eyes strayed in the direction of Natalie's kitchen clock. "Don't you have a wedding to run?"

"It's an emergency, I need Natalie right away."

Her friend emerged from the hallway, eyes red from tears, and a tissue in her hand. She blew her nose, and it honked.

"Nat, I need you to rescue me like never before."

Natalie looked down at her worn-out flannel robe. She looked up. "I can't rescue me, how am I to rescue you?"

"I left the wedding. I can't go back."

"Can't be that bad. Look at my disaster, Courtney. You have no idea." Sniff.

"But Jenson's Favorites and Flowers showed up on the church doorstep."

"These horrible people canceled on me this morning, and they refused to even pay me. I up to here…" Natalie's hand drew an imaginary line in the air above her head. "in catastrophic debt."

"You have flowers?"

Seconds felt like hours as Natalie sat on the stool in front of the counter, gripping her coffee cup. "What?" Natalie sipped her coffee as she probed Courtney as though she could figure out where this conversation was heading if she just had enough time.

Nat didn't seem to get it. "Of course, I've got flowers, just look around."

Zeta motioned for her to come inside. "Coffee?"

Courtney smiled. "Thanks, maybe later. Please tell me you didn't toss any of the funeral flowers." Courtney bit her lip and held her breath as she resisted pressing her eyes shut.

"I'm about to. My first order became my last. So much for my dream." Natalie leaned her forehead onto her hands and slid to the counter in front of her.

Laughter slipped out of Courtney. "Yes, so much for your dream. After you stop boohooing, can you load up and get those flowers to Fellow's Branch Church? We'll need you to set up before 4:00 this afternoon. And hurry. I do have a wedding to run."

"What happened to Clark's?" Nat's friend looked up from pouring coffee.

"Mother happened."

Zeta cringed.

"She didn't." Natalie's inappropriate laugh escaped. She covered her lips with her fingers. "Sorry."

"Dear Zeta, I didn't mean to drag you in on this. And yes, Nat, she did."

Natalie sat up more alert. "Lillian changed the colors, didn't she? Will my flowers clash with those flowers?"

"Big time. I'll explain later. That's another story for Bethany's album. Trust me. Move these flowers as soon as possible. Start believing, my friend."

Natalie's eyes gleamed with something in her expression that Courtney couldn't identify. "Are you really sure? This could land you in so much trouble." The lilt of hope played out in her voice.

"Make sure you get rid of all the funeral ribbon and anything remotely sympathetic. It's not like Bethany isn't happy to get married. We may even pay you something."

"I'm there in spirit already, and I'll be there in body as soon as I can. She giggled and jumped off the stool.

"Looks like everything might come together for a change." Thanks again to her precious friend, who was as close as any sister. It was time to ditch the Victorian flowers and make room for these lovely replacements. Wouldn't Bethany be proud of her bold standing-her-ground actions?

Courtney paused and looked at the ceiling. Hope displaced discouragement. Exhilaration flooded her parched heart. "Thanks, Lord. You heard my cry."

COURTNEY

An hour later, Courtney's hand paused on the cool silver doorknob of Fellow's Branch Church's side door. Would she and Mother ever be able to connect after today? There would be a price to pay. Always a price to pay when opposing Mother's will. Fledgling hope lingered, desiring respect for her courage because sometimes that was the only way her mother could admire others. Or would she despise Courtney even more? Yes, *even more,* punched the inside of her heart with power that withered.

Entering the church, she heard angry voices biting back and forth and growing louder as she neared the sanctuary. Natalie and Zeta followed her into the front hall. Mother and Cassie argued over the top of the largest Victorian arrangement in the room, a splash of hot pink, white, and silver.

"See me. I'm the mother-of-the-bride, this arrangement goes in the front. Exactly dead center."

"Over my wimpy frame, it does." Cassie leaned toward Lillian—nose to nose. Courtney had never seen such steel in this bridesmaid before. Her face flamed, competing with the hot pink reach of the flowers.

"Arrangements can be made." Lillian's face turned a light purple.

"Mother!" Courtney gasped.

She dropped the arrangement in front of her walker. Turning her eyes on Courtney, "And you," her words seethed. "Well, you may not have run away like you've *always* done before, but you sure did ruin this wedding. You destroy everything you touch."

Reeling inside, Courtney's arms folded in front of her. *Was that true?*

Bethany rounded the corner, her eyes wet with tears.

She sniffed and then lifted her head in Courtney's direction. "Courtney, oh, I'm so grateful." Her sister's voice cracked as she stopped moving into the entryway.

"I'm so sorry, Bethany. So very sorry." Courtney's eyes watered, and her sister blurred into a blue jean smudge. She blinked to clear the tears, but one escaped, squeezing out of the side of her eye and trailed south along her cheekbone. She could hear Natalie and Zeta moving up the hallway, burdened with flowers.

"What's the meaning of this?" Mother's arm swiped a wide arc.

Sucking in her breath, Courtney focused on Cassie. Calling on all her will power, she gave an order that wouldn't be acceptable to her mother. "Please, clear those arrangements out of the hall."

"You can't do that. You can't move Bethany's wedding flowers," her mother's voice shrieked.

"And you shouldn't have done what you did. Mother, how deceitful of you." Courtney motioned for Cassie to take the flowers away.

"Deceitful. You would know all about that, wouldn't you? Your just like…" Mother's face plunged into a deeper shade of red. A shocked expression sped over her features, and then she turned her face away.

"Like who mother? You've tried to tell me who I'm like, all my life, but you've never quite figured that out, have you?"

Someone stumbled behind her and dropped a box of flowers. Golden yellow Peace Roses with the slightest pink edging spilled and rolled on the brown carpet at her feet. Zeta bent to retrieve the precious flowers, their fragrance filled the space— fortifying Courtney with strength.

Mother raised her hand and pointed a violently shaking finger. "You told her, didn't you? You agreed to never interfere. Deceitful, like you always were."

Thirty-One

COURTNEY

Did Mother lose it? Courtney took a step backward. But her mother wasn't looking at her. Not anymore. Everyone in the church vestibule stared. Their wide eyes reflecting her own surprise. She turned to find Zeta standing perfectly still by her side, strength and concern mingled together over her expression before settling on tranquility.

None of this made any sense, but Courtney knew something significant had transpired.

Zander stepped inside the door and glanced around the room. Everyone remained quiet and still. It all seemed surreal. The tension stretching across the room felt almost tangible.

"You had to ruin my only daughter's wedding."

Everyone gasped, swinging their attention first toward Lillian and then at Courtney.

Zander's compassionate eyes met hers.

Courtney's glance shifted toward her mother. "You're disowning me? Because of flowers?" Her heart seared with pain that bled into her words. Yet, something more than these flowers would cause her mother to say such an awful public rejection.

"Ask your real mother who disowned you." Lillian turned her walker and moved away. Complaining and muttering, she headed toward the sanctuary.

"What?" The room felt like it was shrinking. Courtney had to remind herself to take a breath.

Guilt tainted Bethany's pained expression. She knew what Mother meant. Courtney closed her eyes. So, her sister could keep secrets from her, after all. The jab of pain tumbled to numbness in mere seconds, before she turned and gazed into unusually dark blue orbs that resembled her own. Pools of love, acceptance, and warmth from her—real mother?

Something shifted inside her and fit. A strange sort of comfort soothed her wounded heart. Somewhere along the way, the tears had stopped running down her cheeks.

Natalie dropped boxes of flowers behind her to wrap her in a hug. They clung to one another, standing together so that they would not fall. Another set of arms surrounded them with the gentle fragrance of rosebuds. They were like the tethered cords that couldn't be broken.

Not anymore.

COURTNEY

An hour later, Courtney ceased pacing the classroom carpet, reached for her Maid of Honor dress, and she changed her outfit along with her mind. The humiliation of standing up in front of everyone after such a scene was the hardest situation she'd ever had to face. This time she wouldn't run. She'd have to be pushed to leave this wedding and not by... Lillian. How long would it take her to get used to calling her Lillian instead of Mother? No wonder they had never known real bonding. Lillian had resented her presence.

Today she'd stop dwelling on questioning the many hurts and rejections zigzagging over and over her mind, causing the blood to thunder through her veins. There would be time for that later. And time to find out how Dad fit in with all of this.

A rap on the door made her jump. "Bethany wants to talk with you," Cassie's voice pressed softly toward her.

"Very well, then." she sighed. Turning the doorknob, she peeked right and left down the hallway to make sure that she avoided Lillian as she picked her way toward her sister. What should she expect from Bethany? Her stomach flipped like a fish out of water. She pressed her hand against her stomach.

Did Bethany plan to ask her to step down from the wedding party? De-escalate the strife that way? She paused. Sucked in a quivering breath, she rapped on the door that concealed her sister within. Sister, hmm, or was she a mere friend now? Acquaintance? How could she bear that? Erase years of closeness and memories? And Lillian, instead of Mother? Yet Lillian fit.

Their relationship always felt unnatural. Strange.

The door whooshed open, and Bethany sprang to her, rustling her satin, embracing her with a veil of tears. Courtney hugged back, trying not to wrinkle exquisite satin ruffles of the wedding gown pressing against her leg. Bethany leaned back to look into her face. They locked arms and moved toward the windows along the far wall.

"How long did you know?" If only her words didn't sound so hollow. Unfamiliar.

Bethany's hand dropped away, she looked to the side and cringed. "Since the first pedicure party at Natalie's."

"That long, and you didn't tell me? Bethany, you can't keep a secret. Not from me."

Bethany hung her head and swiped away tears with one hand.

"Why did you keep this from me?"

"I'm the worse coward. I didn't want to believe it." She lifted her face and looked her in the eye. "I didn't want to lose you." Bethany's skin paled in the sunshine filtering through the window. Looking transparent. Vulnerable.

"You still want to be my sister?" Courtney's heart relaxed.

"Always, forever, and always…" Her whisper crackled with emotion.

Courtney nodded her head. "Always, forever, and always." They leaned their heads together and felt their heartbeats forehead to forehead.

"Besides, I'll need someone for clean-up duty." Bethany snickered and grabbed her in a loving embrace.

"Oh, that's so me. I'll send the troops home, so I can do it all by myself."

COURTNEY

Pastor Thomas Dean stood tall behind the podium in front of the sanctuary. Waiting. The room buzzed with conversation, possibly about today's juicy gossip, but Courtney found she didn't care as much as she thought she would.

Her sister's wedding pressed around her like a living thing. Though some of the joy had been dashed by the revelation of long-kept secrets, nothing could interfere with the rightness of this day. The bridesmaids and groomsmen stood side by side in line, waiting for the music to signal it was time to stroll down the center aisle strewn with fragrant Peace Rose petals.

Feathery music stirred the air. Most of the crowd hushed except for a few stragglers who insisted on finishing their conversation. Courtney kept her focus forward, concentrated on the aisle ahead, resisting the urge to run past the crowd of nodding, smiling faces. Or to search for his face.

Zander. She observed him from the corner of her eye each time she'd turned her head. He shouldered his tuxedo well. The form-fitted tan coat, topped with a ribbon white-collar, was secured with a periwinkle bow-tie, which perfectly matched the bridesmaid's dresses. His features, as usual, were handsome and serene.

It took a great deal of effort to not turn and look him in the eye and drink in his presence. She missed the generous rumble of Zander's laughter, the husky tone of his voice, and the warmth of his breath, whispering past her shoulder when he bent toward her to share a secret.

Amazing how she remained conscious of his presence without offering him a glance or speaking with him.

"Meet me after the ceremony." Peppermint. The warmth of the words caressed her shoulder, made her jump. Zander's serious expressing was met with the best man's frown. Courtney's breath caught in her throat. She couldn't think of a reply.

A late wedding guest pushed past them and moved inside the sanctuary, stirring a breeze, which carried Zander's scent: soap and spicy cologne in her direction. She'd missed that too—

Gary Thorton tugged her arm. Pulling her attention back to their task at hand. When had the music signaled that their march was to begin? Not the time to daydream in front of hundreds of watchful eyes.

She swallowed. Her mouth became as dry as a desert. Her fingers tightened their grip on Gary's arm, so much so that he turned a stunned gaze her way. Fumbling with her bouquet she almost dropped her flowers halfway to their destination.

A few more steps. Breathe. She pressed her eyes shut as they passed Lillian's pew. Still, she'd noticed Lillian glaring at the white carpet runner, frowning at the only pink allowed in the wedding except for the heat in her face.

Thornton tapped her hand, reminding her to let go of his arm, and she stiffly complied.

Groomsmen split to the right and bridesmaids to the left as they found their places to stand and wait for the grand entrance of the bride. Courtney was on her own. Completely. No one to cling to. Not physically. Not in the sense of family. Her breathing increased. Her insides quivered. Was Mother, no Lillian, staring at her? It almost seemed as though her disapproval thicken the air. But Courtney couldn't look. She stared instead at a rose petal lying on the crimson rug.

Everything in the room began closing in on her. She strained to breathe, and her eyes watered. What if she couldn't do this? How bad would it be if she ran?

She pressed her eyelids shut. Stop. She needed to stop this pity party! *Remember me*— breezed through her spirit, filling her with warmth. The nervous jitters melted slightly. Yes, Lord, you're here. You love me still. Her quiet times with Him had drifted to a standstill since her offense with Zander. That was it, no more wasting time. She needed to stop ignoring Him. A vigorous appreciation for the Almighty swept into her spirit as she opened her eyes to the ceremony in front of her.

The music fell silent, and a breath of rose scent traveled on the air conditioning threading the air into the crowd. Anticipation quieted the guests, and they shifted in their seats, turning their heads toward the back of the room. Watching for the bride.

The Wedding March thundered, filling those in the room with powerful anticipation as the rest of the guests smiled, stood, and turned toward the doorway. Bethany, graceful and shining with joy, clung to her father's arm and smiled toward her soon-to-be husband.

Her dad, the one she'd always know, was probably not her

real father. Courtney's eyes burn. She blinked back the unwelcome tears and willed a smile, which came more easily then she'd expected. Not the conjured-up smile of a day ago—for appearance sake. Or to hide. This one was heartfelt. Sincere.

Bethany deserved this honor with her father. Warm expressions and nods celebrated the bride moving up the aisle ever closer to her future, her new life as Brandon Strege's wife. She glanced from side to side. Regal and honored.

Her father looked straight ahead, ever forward.

Disappointment gripped Courtney's heart. She thought he would notice her too. He would always matter to her. His acceptance brought her through so many trials. Ugly homework sessions, disappointments with friends, and mother—Lillian. She studied him more closely. Had love only really been one-sided?

As though he sensed her struggle, he turned and looked her in the eye. His warm glance filled with daughter-love. Then he winked his special only-for-her wink. Time froze the moment in place. Joy bubbled inside her and threatened to spill out with a laugh. She knew, felt the certainty of, what she'd always thirsted for—there would always be space for Courtney in her father's heart.

While their eyes locked, they nodded to each other. A flood of relief spilled through her stretching her smile ever wider. It almost hurt to feel this good after the shock she received today. Her nervous heart eased its beat against her ribs.

She breathed out a contented sigh as Bethany came alongside her and handed over the wedding bouquet with a smile. Courtney eased into an unfamiliar comfort, as though weights and burdens flew off her shoulders and freedom instead became the order of the day. Pure elation, though her future was as uncertain as she had ever feared to imagine.

"We come together today to celebrate the holy bonds of

matrimony," Pastor Dean smiled at the couple before him. "As Jesus commanded, "Love one another as I have loved you…""

ZANDER

After the photo session, everyone mingled with guests before they drove to Olde Stonewall Golf Course. The reception in the Windsor Room didn't provide him with the best of memories. More like visions of Courtney turning away, always turning away. Weighing him down. For Brandon's day, he had to put on a good face. Zander popped a mint into his mouth, loving the peppermint explosion. He forced his welcoming smile as a wedding guest approaching him in the hallway facing the church lobby.

"So which side of the family are you most connected with? I have known Bethany for a while, but Brandon forever," The elderly lady said.

"Brandon, but I know Bethany and Courtney pretty well also." Her perfume over-compensated any desire to impress those around her. It spoiled his mint, which tasted like it had been dunked in musk. He tossed it into the nearby waste can.

Courtney approached the door. Was she planning to leave already? Could he blame her if she did? Courtney turned toward him as she searched the crowd, and yes, her purse hung over her left shoulder. After giving a waist-high wave to Cassie, she turned and stole a glance behind her aimed toward Bethany and her circle of friends. She paused, watching until a wispy smile played on her lips. Opening the front door, Courtney passed through and disappeared from sight. The door eased shut behind her, leaving an empty place where she'd just stood.

"Excuse me. There is someone I have to talk to." He placed his hand on the woman's elbow, desiring not to offend her.

The older lady smiled a knowing smile and slid her glance toward the empty space that had held Courtney just moments ago.

He'd better move on this before he lost his nerve. She probably wouldn't want to speak to him, but he needed to make an effort. Before he knew what to say, he was on the sidewalk behind her and catching up fast. "Courtney."

She stopped and turned her head toward him, her blond hair swept over her shoulders, blowing soft in the breeze. Her dark blue eyes deepened as they took hold of his.

He eased a smile onto his face and stepped toward her in slow motion. What to say? Think quick. He moved alongside her, breathing in her perfume, and appreciating the smooth contour of her face, and the gentle expression softening her eyes. She'd had so much to be bitter about. But none of it seemed to alter or diminish who she was. Certainly, she was a woman to admire. A nagging feeling suggested that he more than admired her. He needed to ignore that.

Help me fix this offense, Lord.

Courtney's expression folded into what he identified as pain mingled with confusion before she looked away to the right. Thankfully she didn't move away from him.

"I canceled my dog training project with Mr. Mancel. I can't sign a release for this production. Looks like you already know about it."

Her mouth dropped open for a second, and she turned to face him. "Tanya shared one with me. Zander, that man holds the connections you needed for both of your businesses. This is your dream. Why would you do that—for me?" Her expression pierced him as though she probed him—maybe testing his sincerity?

A smile forced its way onto his face. "I'd never do that. I want you to know that DVD wasn't approved by me. I care about you." He touched her soft cheek with his finger.

Her eyes glistened with fresh tears warmed by something looking like gratitude, which stirred his heart to beat strong and quick.

He wanted to ask how she was doing since her mother's emotional display, but he didn't dare talk about that now. Why bring more attention to that ugly scene. "See you at the reception." He took a step down the sidewalk.

Zander turned and looked in her face. Winking at her, he moved down the sidewalk. He appreciated the clear blue sky and that the air had cooled off several degrees. Sticking his finger at his collar, he gave a tug. The sun dipped behind the treetops. Its brilliance poking through the leaves as though providing a last fête before dipping out of sight. Mike will call him crazy for what he'd done with this so-called opportunity. It hadn't felt right from the first when he'd talked to Mancel. He should have known better.

Mike did a lot of work and would have to be paid out-of-pocket to cover the time and expenses incurred for the editing—even though he hadn't produced the DVD as requested. Adding the truly embarrassing sections cheapened the experience and embarrassed Courtney. He'd want nothing to do with that. Mr. Mancel hung up on him when told that the most humiliating training scenes could not be included. The ones Mr. Mancel was most excited about.

Maybe he'd continue to manage his dad's furniture manufacturing business. Expanding the family legacy first before working on his own passions. After reading the family history journals his mother had asked him to edit, he realized his father hadn't instantaneously developed his business either. Did it really matter how long it took him to launch those dreams? Next time, he'd do it right, without agreeing to anything that would compromise his ideals. He'd grow his dreams like his father had pursued his.

Yes, Mike would call him crazy.

Thirty-Two

COURTNEY

Fuzzy large paws clicked against the wood floors of Natalie's parlor.

"I sure hope those nails don't gouge my hardwoods. It took my blood, sweat, and tons of tears to finish these."

"What are you talking about? Your father did them with five of his friends. You didn't even slurp on the sealant after they were stained."

Natalie grinned and then tossed a nervous glance in Puddle's direction.

Courtney drank deeply from the sweaty glass filled halfway with lemonade and tea. Enough sour flavor to make her pucker. Just the way she liked it. Her bare feet rested on top of a fabric covered stool. Puddles wagged her tail and moved over to lick her toes. "Oh, no, you don't." She curled her feet to the floor, pulling away before the wet tongue made contact. Touching her heel to the oak floor, she groaned.

Laughing, Natalie sported her—*I know all about that* grin—which, when used often, worked magic for loosening

Courtney's tongue. "So, did you and Zander makeup? You sure spent enough time on the dance floor last night."

Her small smile betrayed her faux-casual response. "We chatted." She cringed. Her pitch was too high. She kept her head down and rubbed her tender feet.

Natalie leaned forward, "About?"

"A bunch of topics—"

The kitchen doorbell rang, and Courtney released a breath.

"Be right back." Her friend turned and glanced back at her on the way to the kitchen. "You're not off the hook, you know. This is a tell-all kinda day."

Puddles stood on her hind legs—resting her front paw on the armchair of the seat and stared down at Courtney, tongue hanging out, dripping, to let her know it was time to go outside. Courtney reached for the leash, hooked Puddles up, and moved toward the kitchen. Voices soft as warm creamy custard met her ears. Then a burst of laughter.

Zeta headed toward Courtney. Her silhouette framed by the tall kitchen doorway. Her steps were bouncy and purposeful.

Yanking Puddle's leash until her nose stood even against her knee, Courtney moved back with a jerky motion. "Sit Puddles." The dog wiggled and whined with her obvious interest in Zeta.

"I hoped that you'd be here, Courtney." Zeta's voice rang cheerful and welcoming. Her tone such a stark contrast to Mother's—no Lillian's attitude. How long would it take to adjust to this change in the family? She should be happy to know the source of Lillian's discontent and rejection, but her heart bowed a little lower.

Questions circled her thoughts, screaming for attention like untamed children.

Courtney smiled and glanced from side to side. She didn't know what to think, say, or where to look. Was she even ready to talk to Zeta, or who she now knew as her real mom? What would this sweet woman expect to be called? And what was she to do about Bethany, Lillian, and Dad? Everything was so shrouded in mystery. Would her heart, which quivered with each step this kind woman took in her direction, be able to take the strain? This seemed like a nightmare and a happy-ever-after dream come true, all wrapped up into one experience. Was Zeta really the Mom she'd secretly wished for?

This might be the hour she would finally understand why she'd felt different growing up. Feeling like an outsider, and not good enough to be Lillian's daughter. Maybe she'd even be able to make sense of all the rejections and conflicts that had led to this day. Hopefully, she'd be strong enough to hear about these secrets buried under the layers of so many years. Fragile emotions stepped in rapidly to batter her hopes.

Her lungs drew in full breaths. She needed some air. "I have to tie our girl outside. Be right back." When she pushed the kitchen screen door open, she gulped the air. Filling her lungs. She tipped her face toward the sunshine. Warmth caressed her cheeks. She lowered herself on the porch steps and hooked Puddles to the metal chain.

A songbird chattered in the tree above her, the glorious, periwinkle sky and presence of peace began to melt the tension in her limbs and slow her breathing.

Puddles found a log and plopped down to chew it apart.

The screen door creaked behind her. She wanted to turn, but she hesitated. Held her breath.

"You must have a thousand questions." Zeta paused behind her for a mere second before releasing the door. She stepped alongside Courtney and sat down.

Finding the rough, spiral porch railing, Courtney gripped tight. "Why did you give me up?" Fresh hurt, she didn't know the depth of heated her face.

Zeta's head hung down. She sighed. "My husband, your

father, passed away in a car wreck. I wasn't myself. He was…
my everything. My family was everything." Her voice cracked.
She lifted her head and offered a slight smile.

Why didn't it feel like she'd been part or even a portion of
Zeta's *everything*? Frowning, she said, "So, how did you know
Lillian and my dad?" So many emotions vied for her attention.

"Lillian was my sister-in-law."

Courtney gasped. Not the answer she'd expected—more
like an adoption agency set this arrangement up, or a friend of
a friend, of a friend's… "Why didn't my moth—"

An awkward pause between them grew weary.

"Your mother didn't approve of me." Zeta lifted her face to
the sky. Breathed out, before she turned her intense dark blue
eyes upon her. "I was a free spirit in those days. And she was
angry with her brother for breaking away from his family to
marry me."

Free spirit. Courtney raised one eyebrow. Those were the
exact choice of words she would've used for Zeta today, but
not with the negative weights hanging on the syllables. No,
Zeta seemed well put together except for the shyness. Which
Courtney didn't see a trace of now.

"I've never seen a photo of him." An empty hole opened in
her heart—thirsting to know.

"This is my favorite," Zeta pulled one out of her pocket. She
reached for Courtney's hand, turning it palm up; she placed the
photo there. "You have some qualities like he did, but mostly,
you're a lot like me."

Courtney leaned into the photo. Though it was feath-
er-light and faded in coloring, the family resemblance was unmistakable. She reached up to touch her hair.

"Yes, you have his hair and my eyes."

Examining Zeta's features, Courtney said, "I have your face
also." She offered a smile. No wonder she'd never looked like

her father, and she didn't really resemble Mother—Lillian either.

"Why did Lillian accept me as a baby, when she's hated me all these years?"

"She didn't hate you. She didn't want you to be like me. She wanted you to be more like her."

"Why did she hate you?"

Zeta stood on the lower porch step and folded her arms in front of her chest. She turned, and the tears shining in her eyes caused Courtney to sit up straighter.

"I want you to know something else first. Something good."

The screen door creaked behind her, and Courtney glanced up. Natalie stared at Zeta from the half-opened door.

"You can come out now." Zeta smiled at Natalie with such warmth. Their intimacy in a glance stirred Courtney's heart with longing. Maybe she could become close to her mom like her friend had.

Natalie slid in beside her and plopped on the porch step, bouncing the board before settling.

Waiting seemed appropriate. That felt somewhat familiar. The birds tweeted, and a mild breeze stirred the Lilac bush, its fragrance spilled into the air. Inside she churned. Why didn't Zeta just say it? What was the "something good? She couldn't stand it any longer. "What else did you want to tell me?"

"You have a sister."

"Another—I mean—a sister?" She shook her head, a smile sneaking out without permission. "Do you have a photo of her too?" Courtney held out her hand to take it.

Zeta's focus shifted to Natalie.

Courtney followed that gaze. Natalie's eyes brimmed with emotion, bordering on anxious hope. "What? You mean, Natalie's my sister?"

"Twin sister, Court. We are twins!"

Mouth dropping open, Courtney gripped Nat's arm tight.

Natalie covered her fingers with her other hand. "We always wanted to be sisters. Funny thing is, we really were."

COURTNEY

"Sisters and twins," Courtney's mind whirled. And they shared the most amazing Mom. How mysterious that Zeta cautioned them not to tell anyone that they were sisters. That request was already too late because Courtney had already text Bethany. She immediately re-text her sister-friend to not tell anyone! *Why would having a twin and wonderful Mom need to be kept secret?* Yet another question to be answered, later, when they were together again, and Mom returned from this latest publishing responsibility.

In this way, Courtney was similar to Zeta—this was how she'd made everyone feel when she'd ditched childhood responsibilities when she'd hide-out until the coast was clear. Chuckling to herself, she set her brush down on the dresser and then corrected her makeup while using the reproduction antique mirror. Natalie really should find some authentic pieces for this bed and breakfast. It could make all the difference with customers.

Her glance slid to the boxes in the corner of her borrowed bedroom at Natalie's Victorian. Thank goodness she'd finished packing before the wedding. All she had left was to fill several garbage bags full of clothing, shoes, and everything for Puddles. Dad kept a peaceful distance between Courtney and Lillian as she loaded her car.

Now she stayed with her real sister and best friend—who'd always felt like a sister—for a short while when searching for a home of her own. Her new bedroom flanked the backyard. She parted the draperies with freshly manicured fingernails and studied the crooked path leading through the tree line. Incredible how their mom lived within walking distance to Natalie. Their backyards linked by a small patch of woods, woven with a trail that connected more than their homes.

Knock, knock.

Courtney moved to open the door. Natalie held two tall glasses of cherry-topped, old-fashioned Hot Fudge Sundaes in her hands.

"Thought you might want to cool off." She sped past her and paused, looking for an open spot on the small roundtable positioned between two wingback chairs.

Courtney nodded and scrunched the decorator's magazines together before she whisked them off the table, slipping them out of sight deep inside a drawer. Natalie couldn't abide mess, and that was probably the reason they were here, and not in the kitchen, which was occupied by baking bowls, ingredients, and dirty dishes. Bakery orders from a local restaurant were helping to pay the bills plaguing Natalie's dream Victorian bed and breakfast home.

Natalie set the ice cream glasses down, before placing long stem decorative silver spoons into the softened ice cream.

"When did you find these?" Courtney took hold of the slender ornate spoon. Definitely authentic. "Now, this is more like it. Ambiance."

"Mom gave them to me. Imagine us sharing our mom. I was so surprised!" She leaned over the small table catching Courtney's shoulders in a quick hug.

"I'm thinking this is too good to be true. If I wake up from this, I'll be so disappointed." Courtney pinched herself.

"So, you're really not mad? I know you've never liked secrets between friends."

"I refuse to ask you how long you've known. That will prevent my 'mad' from emerging. I'm just enjoying this reality, while the rest of my life settles."

Natalie nodded and took a bite.

Courtney scooped a spoonful doused with hot chocolate. Then she looked across the table. She was glad that her sister's back was turned toward the bed she'd forgotten to make and the clothes still crumpled in a heap on the floor. She'd taken advantage, allowing herself to be messy since Puddles refused to take the steps. She smiled at the untouched, unchewed socks on the floor.

When the hot chocolate and cold ice cream hit her tongue, she closed her eyes to savor the moment. Cold and hot, salty and sweet, were her favorite combinations. Natalie had hidden some peanuts under the hot chocolate. How could she not feel special when her sister and friend went overboard to provide her with her favorite secret joys?

The accumulating mess symbolizing freedom and independence—didn't really please her like she thought it would. That satisfaction had been wrapped up in the rebellion of not doing things Mother's way—Lillian's way. Piles and rumpled sheets distracted from the peace Natalie intended for her. She anchored herself inside the arms of the wingback and tried to ignore the unkemptness that she wanted to jump up and fix.

"So, when is everyone getting together to do Bethany's Memory Album?" Natalie's gaze drifted behind her in the direction of the closest pile of clothes.

"I have to call and see when Cassie and Nicole are available. I'm also waiting for Dad to snatch some photos from our early days. He has his hands full with Mother. I mean, Lillian."

"This must be hard for you. Thinking one family was yours and now to find that your mother is actually our aunt."

"Yes, we share her equally, don't we?"

"We sure do."

"Finding out that Lillian's dislike for me really wasn't personal, helps. I'm shocked that these secrets didn't devastate me. Actually, I'm relieved."

"You're not bitter; are you, toward Mom? Plus, twins share this special connection—"

"You know, I'm not bitter. Special connection, well, we've always shared that haven't we?

Natalie slipped her an *I'm comfortable with you always* smile as she fished inside her pocket to pull out napkins. She offered Courtney two.

Courtney grabbed them quick with sticky fingers. "Thanks." Hot chocolate dribbled down her lip, but she caught it right on time.

They locked eyes and laughed.

A sassy ring tone hit the air. Courtney stood up and retrieved her cell.

"Everything is arranged. I'll be there in twenty minutes. Bring Puddles along." Zander's husky voice warmed up the phone.

"Are you sure about this? She still acts like a puppy—obnoxiously friendly and all that."

"They'll love her. Trust me on this." His voice was as smooth as the whipped cream missing from their Hot Fudge Sundaes.

"I'll be ready."

Thirty-Three

COURTNEY

Blacktop bearing its share of potholes and collapsed edges wound a ribbon that climbed a steep hillside. Woods flanked both sides for most of the way, broken only by homes dotted along its length. These would be some slippery roads during winter. The numerous trees with hardly any houses in sight gave Courtney the creeps. She dug inside her purse to find something to distract her vein of thought. Hand cream. Courtney squirted some of Nat's tangerine lotion into her palm. Distraction bolstered her courage, and this fragrance did nicely.

This was the opportunity that she and Puddles looked-for. Natalie needed to rent the bedroom she'd provided for Courtney. Having available rooms for potential customers was paramount.

As long as she stayed with Nat, she would offer her time and talents to redecorate the unfinished bedroom across the hall. If Nat had drop cloths aplenty—Courtney was more than willing to assist. She'd learned so many skills while working on her dream apartments, and maybe now she could give back to her generous best friend.

Zander followed the wide arc of the road to the left with his SUV before her potential rental house rose into view. A cream-colored BMW sat in the drive, which circled around a perfectly manicured yard. Pristine windows mirroring periwinkle blue sky and shards of sunshine glared above the wide porch steps. Courtney glanced around at Puddles. Dog hair rode the wind whirling in front of the open window before landing on the seat behind the puppy.

Out of reach.

Good thing Zander liked canines.

"They won't want payment. Just someone who will keep the place up." Zander's comforting words produce the opposite effect.

Smiling tortured Courtney's face, while she silently counted six, floor-to-ceiling windows, facing the front porch alone. Had she ever washed a window that was left in better condition than before she'd begun? A quick scan over her window washing lifetime produced one answer.

No.

She stepped out of the car. "This is a beautiful spot. I didn't realize it was so…rich." Courtney scanned the area. Neighboring houses were quite a distance away. Lots of privacy.

Too much so.

Front porch furnishings before them looked both comfortable and expensive to replace. If Puddles got into a chewing mood… but, of course, she wouldn't be allowed there alone. So, no worries, really.

A butterfly stumbled in the air in front of her as the breeze switched direction. Funny, that's the dance her stomach did at that very moment. She opened Puddle's door. They'd talked about her taking the dog out of the car before. The family would need to see that she could control her big girl. She'd insisted. Though right now, she was having second thoughts.

Puddles tried to move past her, but she pulled her tight to her side.

The porch door creaked open, and a warm voice greeted them. "Welcome to our home."

Puddles tensed and then leapt past her, slipping from Courtney's grip. Running at full looping speed up the front porch steps, Puddles scooted to a stop in front of the man, bumping into his legs.

His mouth hung aghast before he recovered himself.

Courtney ran breathlessly up the steps, Zander closing the space behind them. Then Puddles shook her head. Rare slobber splattered the door's window, dowsing a drip that threatened to drag its course to the bottom of the door.

Pulling a paper towel out of her pocket, Courtney wiped the blob of drool, smearing tangerine hand cream onto the window.

Making it worse.

Someone approached from behind the man, and Puddles wagged her tail and danced—stepping back and forth, wanting to greet the next person. Courtney tightened her grip on the leash as her limbs trembled.

They needed to move here so that they could have a place to call home. Courtney glanced at Zander before turning to the couple in front of her. She couldn't read his expression. Would they see how nervous she felt?

Mrs. Jackman's smile melted into a grimace, blending shock, disbelief, and something unidentifiable. A wad of dog hair floated in the air and landed on the side of Mr. Jackman's black suit pants right where Mrs. Jackman could see it. Their elegant dress clothes spoke of their plans for an expensive dinner and maybe an event.

Puddles licked Mr. Jackman's pant leg.

Yanking her back out of his reach proved too late.

"Oh, no. No, I just can't allow that… dog in my house,"

Mrs. Jackman said. "It would be impossible to sell the place if it lived here. Now I remember what I'd read about this breed—something about them not being for people who want to be neat! Look at what it's done before walking through the door." She'd pinched the dog hair stuck to her husband's pants between manicured fingernails. Her expression warped with disgust.

Thirty-four

COURTNEY

Unrest simmered in the pit of her stomach. Another disappointment. Even if she'd not lost her grip on Puddles, they wouldn't have wanted a hairy dog in their home. She smoothed Puddles's silky ears. The dog leaned against her leg, moist hot breath heated Courtney's knee. It was better to know right away that this home wasn't a great fit. Wasn't it? Why did the weight of this blow feel so heavy?

There would maybe be an hour or less to relax or write before they left for mom's house. Her laptop hummed to life as she sat at Natalie's dining room table. Puddles leaned her head back, hinting for some kind words or a hug. Courtney massaged the dog's neck and shoulders. "How could anyone resist your charms?" The dog's tail thumped against her chair.

She curved her fingers over the keys and began to write. *The Land of Knockdown Dragout* had to have a new name. She'd pick that later. And the adversary, Nadella, took on an even stronger resemblance to Lillian. She ripened with secrets and manipulations. Courtney's fingers slowed to a stop. Half a page latter, the character's description—emulating Lillian's strengths and weaknesses—tasted bitter on her tongue. Questions robbed her flow and concentration.

Why hadn't her parents told her about the adoption? Why did Lillian reject her? She was an innocent child when they took her in. What kind of person could do that? Puddles grunted and moved across the room.

Reaching for a pen, Courtney knocked the holder over. Not paying attention had downfalls. Missing while tossing some crumpled notes to the wastebasket, Courtney gripped the side of the chair as anger built a formidable lump in her throat. She reached for a cup of tea. Then halted. Swallowing would probably cause her to choke anyway. Courtney placed her fingers on the keys and began to write again. Ugliness grew in her heart. Plain and simple, she'd been robbed—all her life—from enjoying a healthy and happy relationship with her real mom.

"Stop it!" She yelled out loud.

Puddles scrambled to get up from her lying position and ran out the door.

A hot breath of frustration escaped her. This story couldn't be finished for all the right reasons. She clicked *Select All* and deleted her pages. Stillness stole over her spirit, allowing peace to wrap around her like a hug. She would miss Rednaz, her hero. But she didn't need to revisit the loss which had manipulated her life until her heart struggled to forgive.

Today was a new page, a new day. She blew out a sigh. To think she'd almost given over to bitterness and unforgiveness despite her victories. She never thought she'd harbored those ugly feelings. Pretending everything was okay never dealt with problems. In her heart, she now knew that *Knockout Dragout* began with hidden resentment feeding the ink. If she were to write again, she didn't want a story burdened with oppression, offenses, and bitterness.

"It's about time to leave. Do you need to change?" Natalie's voice called down the stairs. The clock showed 5:45.

"Don't worry about me, Natalie. You could say that I've already changed."

⁕ ─ ⚜ ─ ⁕

COURTNEY

At 6:15 that night, a thick buzz of conversations surrounded Courtney as her excited gaze moved from room to room inside the miniature stone cottage. The cottage, whose yard was elaborately adorned with roses. She'd dreamed about how this place could look inside. Oh, what Mom accomplished was so much better than anything she could dream up. Elegance and buoyancy born from delight carried the themes Zeta had chosen throughout the rooms.

"This way ladies." Her mom's prior shyness all but disappeared as she gave a tour of her beautiful home.

Stepping on the stone floor of the cozy dining room made her hold her breath. Her appreciative glance swept the terracotta walls. The exquisite paintings, furnishings, and rugs—their tones perfectly blended. Even the light fixtures complemented the décor, stirring ambiance, and serving practical needs. The more she discovered about this precious woman—the more grateful she became.

"I've gotta leave early tonight. Let's get started, please," Cassie's voice rose above the chatter.

"Put the photo albums down in the middle of the dining room table. Everyone take a seat." Zeta moved into the kitchen.

They all sat down. Scissors, a glue stick, and a small ruler were situated at each place setting. Stickers and colorful, acid-free paper were organized in several trays located in the middle of the table. Zeta entered the room with frosted tumblers filled with raspberry lemonade and tea on a silver tray and passed a glass to each one.

Courtney stood and lifted the first album high, as though doing a game show impersonation, "This photo album is for Bethany's childhood and pre-wedding related photos. Organize her photos by years as much as you can. Then place them in the slots." Courtney wiggled her finger inside the photo sleeve.

"Someone who is artistic places the stickers on the pages." She lifted the next photo album. "This one is strictly for the wedding shower." She pointed to another album, "this one is for wedding photos and reception, and I'll be sticking the stickers on this baby."

"Booooo," they yelled collectively before they gave into laughter. Everyone dived into the photos, talking and snickering together.

"I heard that Natalie made one of her cheesecakes for tonight. Is that true?"

"You'll have to wait and see." Zeta laughed as she passed-by, heading toward the kitchen again.

The sound of scissors slicing the air drew Courtney's attention to the other end of the table. She crossed then uncrossed her legs, bumping her knee on the underside of the table. She rubbed away the pain with her empty hand.

Natalie raised her hand to fuss with her hair and almost elbowed Courtney's face. The photos that didn't fit the plastic sleeves continued to be clipped to size. The two sisters craned their necks to see if any of the pictures were ruined.

Zeta caught Courtney's attention when she walked into the room carrying crackers and cheese. She nodded her head toward Cassie holding the scissors and then paused to stand above the photo album. She was on her way again after aiming a reassuring wink Courtney's way.

In an hour, three-quarters of the pages in each book were done, which inspired Bethany's bridal party ladies to keep digging for the right photo to place in the next slot.

"Did you find a place to rent yet, Court?" Nicole held two

photos a foot in front of her face, before pinning her gaze to demand an answer. The conversations around the table hushed, and most of their faces turned in their direction. Everyone knew that she'd refused to live with Lillian now that her dad came home.

Flinching, Courtney bowed her head.

"I don't want her to leave yet." Natalie picked up three photos. "I really like these in this order. How about you?" She winked at Courtney, who nodded and slipped her a thank you grin.

"I'm still looking for a place. So, do you know of one?" She pulled her attention back on Nicole.

Nicole's eyes grew wide. Averting her gaze, she shook her head in the negative.

"Courtney." Mom stood leaning on the doorframe leading into the kitchen. "Could you come here, please? And bring your purse."

She frowned and tossed a peek at her sister, who appeared to be as puzzled as she. Obediently, she picked up her purse and then stood to follow Zeta into the kitchen. This was the only room she hadn't seen yet, but that wasn't the reason Mom had asked her to step out of the dining room. What was up?

Everyone watched as she moved toward the Country-Victorian kitchen. Though less elaborate than the rest of the house, this room sported charming cabinets and a surprising amount of counter space. A bay window bumped out of the left wall filled with successfully growing herbs of every description. Her greatest surprise was Zander standing next to the door leading to the porch.

"Hey," spoken simultaneously by both Zander and Courtney, drew out their smiles.

Stealing a glance toward her mom, she waited.

"I'll take care of this crew. You and Puddles have a date."

Courtney leaned in for a hug, breathing in the fragrance

of roses and cinnamon. "Thanks, Mom." She hadn't yet spoken that endearment in this precious woman's presence. This seemed to be a fitting time. Puddles barked from Zander's car, demanding attention, forcing her to release her hold.

As she stepped toward the door, Zeta said, "One more thing."

Curiosity arched her brows. She turned around to face a radiant but curious expression she couldn't read. A sliding sound pulled her attention to Zeta's hand, pushing an old-fashioned key toward her on the kitchen counter.

Lifting her gaze, Courtney tried to understand.

"I'll be away for a year or two, and I'd love it if you could take care of my place. Would you do that for me, Courtney?"

Hands flew to her face. Courtney bounced in place and then lowered her arms to shake them. "I... You." She attempted to clear her throat. "Where are you going?" Her eyes watered, making it harder to see.

Mom turned her glance away. "I have some important business to take care of. No need to bother talking of it now." Her gaze returned to claim an answer.

Courtney's hand touched her throat. "Oh, Mom, you're an answer to prayer. Though I'm not sure how your roses will hold up with Puddles around."

Zeta slipped the cool metal key into her palm. "Puddles can stay, but I'll hire a gardener. No need to try to fertilize anything while I'm away." They all laughed.

"So, my reputation precedes me. Does Natalie know?" Something inside her wanted to be the first to hear this news. So many secrets made her new life a bit unsettling.

"You're the first, Court." Mom reached out and brushed her cheek with her feather-soft touch. As though she somehow understood.

The push to let the tears spill over and yet cry out for joy crushed her at the same time. Desperate, Courtney looked around and found Natalie's cheesecake. "Can you save us each a piece of that?"

Natalie walked in and followed Courtney's stare. She snorted. "You don't have to cry to get a piece. I'll give you one. Plus, there's more at home."

Thirty-Five

COURTNEY

"This looks suspiciously like a training session." Courtney did her best imitation of a scowl.

Zander's hand rose to his collar, and he tugged on it as though he needed air.

The late afternoon sun gave the training field a soft, welcoming appearance. Birdsong blended with the crunch of gravel under each footfall, and the swish of long grass brushed against their legs as they moved toward his backyard.

"Well, I… You see I—"

She placed her hand over his arm. "It's fine. I'm just playing." They stopped at the gate. She reached inside her purse. "There's something I want to change for you."

Confusion played on his face, and she loved that. She showed him the DVD that Tanya had given her. "I can't stop you from publishing this."

His puzzled expression didn't relax. "Mike didn't do that per my direction. I can't use this. Ever."

She huffed a sigh. "This belongs to you, and I'm not going to stand in your way—stopping your dream for successful businesses. Puddles agrees." Puddles looked up at them and made noise sounding like wah wha wah wah wah.

He bent down and rubbed the dog's shoulders with brisk motion. But his eyes tilted toward Courtney.

"You have too much at stake with Mr. Mancel. This isn't only going to affect the video. I know he could expand your reach to high-end property sales. You could become a highly requested realtor."

A mixture of emotions warred on Zander's face. It was clear to her that he appreciated what she was offering and maybe knew what it cost for her to say it. Courtney looked down at Puddles. "Plus, I'll need the money since Lehman's is closing. You were going to give me a cut, weren't you?" She winked at him. After the investigators began to dig into Mr. Angerton's files, the man decided to close the store indefinitely. Her meager savings would not last long, and though she knew she'd not make much from the DVDs, it wouldn't hurt to have a little extra pocket change. If he could even afford to pay her.

His expression relaxed, and something like extreme gratitude lit his face. He nodded affirmation, and his hand took firm hold of the DVD. He laughed. "But we still need to remove some of the most embarrassing scenes. I can't tolerate those."

She nodded. Relief made her giddy.

Puddles barked and turned toward gravel crunching on the path leading toward them.

Tanya.

Courtney's heart thumped in alarm. What's she doing here? The wind gracefully lifted and laid Tanya's hair behind her shoulders. She looked dressed to kill as she picked her steps carefully toward them. Outwardly she embodied femininity and grace. But inside…

Sneaking a peek at Zander, Courtney gathered that he didn't look pleased. Had she ever seen him frown? Well, just once, when Courtney left Puddles inside the car on a hot day.

She turned again to watch Tanya's steps grow bolder as her feet found the cleaner path.

"You were not expected." His rebuke shocked Courtney.

Only Tanya's clip nod acknowledged Zander, but her piercing eyes drilled into Courtney's. When she stood in front of them, she reached out her hand. "I'll take that leash. She's my property." Puddles woofed and stepped back to sit behind Courtney's legs.

"I'm not giving her up. You haven't cared for her. You deserted her."

"The law is on my side. Call a lawyer if you want to. She's all mine. I demand to have her back." Tanya's unusual bristling puzzled Courtney.

"Not possible. You don't have a home for her."

Tanya hesitated, "I'll have an apartment ready tonight."

"An apartment." Courtney nodded the yeah-right nod. "Well, apartments around here will not allow large dogs." Several of Courtney's attempts to find one flashed through her mind. "You can't keep her, it's not like when we had our apartments', is it?"

Something unpleasantly familiar simmered on Tanya's face and looked ready to blow. "Funny thing is that the apartment I'm using right now is exactly the apartment we were in. I happen to know Mr. Mancel, and he's allowing me to stay there until my house purchase is finalized." Her voice climbed loud and arrogant. "I'm his new Advertisement Manager for his Arts-A-Rama Gallery." She'd tilted her head upward to look down her nose at them, before jutting her hand, possessively toward the leash.

"That's strange." Zander's voice seemed far away. Reflective.

They glanced toward him.

"I'm in business with Mr. Mancel. He just sent me your name, asking for a reference. Does he know how little you communicated with Courtney about both the apartment situation and Puddles before he purchased it?"

She pulled her lip up to close her mouth and dropped her hand as she stepped backward.

Stashing the grin that began taking over his face, he continued, "I understand that you and several others are being considered for this job. No one has been hired yet, Tanya. Maybe you ought to talk to him in a few days after all the references are turned in.

Wrinkling her brow, Tanya dropped her gaze. Courtney recognized her previous friend's frantic attempt to think of a way to manipulate the situation. "Well," she pushed her hair off of her shoulder. "I suppose I really won't have time for a dog anyway. I'll be rather busy with my new position." She glared at Zander. "Once it's official and all."

Tanya turned to leave them.

"Hold up, Tanya. I believe I have some paperwork on the table over there. You can sign Puddles over to Courtney, right now." He held the DVD behind his back for Courtney to grab before he stepped away.

Grateful she'd brought her larger purse; Courtney dropped the case inside.

A much less confident Tanya stopped, turned, and glared in Zander's direction.

He moved to the table on the back porch and opened a briefcase to access a file and pull out a contract. Then he grabbed a black pen and wiggled it in the air. "Why wait?"

"I believe I may be late for an appointment." She dramatically lifted her watch.

Turning to Courtney, Zander said, "Did I tell you about my friend's friend who is also applying for that job? I think she could be an incredible fit for that position."

"Alright, already." She stomped her stilettos in his direction and snatched the pen from his hand. After a quick scribble on the document, she sped down the pathway with much less grace and a bit more speed then when she'd approached.

Zander put his hand out for the DVD once again.

"You're working for Mr. Mancel?"

He stashed the DVD inside his briefcase and locked it. "Mancel is an amazing man, once you get to know him. He told me he liked my grit and then hired me for several high-end jobs."

Brows climbing high on her forehead made him chuckle. He took her hand and gave an affectionate squeeze. They turned together to face the orange and purple sky. Soon the muted light would head over the horizon for the night, but for now, their hearts celebrated a huge victory.

Thirty-Six

COURTNEY

Two weeks had sped past swiftly. Courtney splayed manicured fingers over the faux marble desk located in the very room her mom had written several popular children's books. Would her future shine with success once she discovered a way to make a living? The cool smooth surface glowed under the slatted sunshine angling through the shuttered window, until a shadow fluttered over the desktop. She stood and peeked outside. Bethany raced up the sidewalk.

She swung the door wide open for her sister-friend. "I didn't know you'd be in town."

Sunglasses pinned auburn hair away from her face. Bethany's eyes twinkled with mischief.

Courtney dipped her glance, checking to see if she sported any cappuccinos. Not today. Maybe it wasn't big news.

"Oh, give me a hug." They embraced and held on for extra seconds before moving to the living room.

"So, this is your place to settle for the next couple of years. Don't be mad; I never liked the apartment complex." Bethany's breathless words settled, and she glimpsed around.

"This was my real dream, anyway. Tanya talked me into

the apartments. At least I got Puddles out of the deal as well as some skills."

"Some skills?"

"I can plaster and paint walls." They laughed.

"Show me every nook and cranny." Eagerness adorned Bethany's request.

Early American furnishings—Courtney's treasures—mingled just fine with her mom's spattering of antiques, in her opinion. She spotted a clash of a bold yellow and green polka-dotted pillow against her mom's classy berry and black pinstriped wingback chair. She tossed a coverlet overtop it before Bethany could notice.

Dog hair floated past her. Yes, everything looked perfectly natural.

"Make me a cappuccino?"

"Follow me."

Bethany oohed and aahed, ever her cheerleader, as Courtney led the way through the dining room. She picked up the cardboard box holding the photo albums designated to be sent through the mail that day. "Open this." She plopped the box on the table. "What flavor?" She nodded to the considerable assortment next to the cappuccino machine.

"Vanilla."

The hum of the machine sounded as Bethany ripped the package open and pulled out two photo albums. "You didn't…" she looked up at Courtney, "do these?" Her eyebrow arched in an exaggerated angle.

"Yes, I did. Well, we all did. Their creation, but it was my idea." She placed the cappuccino on the table for Bethany and another for herself while the vanilla fragrance filled the space between them.

Bethany flipped the wedding album open. "This is great and…finished!" Her eyes darted toward Courtney. "Sorry."

Her expression moved from confusion to awe. She slurped a sip.

"I did most of the wedding one." Courtney quirked a smile. "We made a party of it." The warm glow of satisfaction heated her face and limbs. She glanced at Bethany. "Does that count as me finishing something?"

Bethany nodded. "Even getting that group together to accomplish anything rates Superwoman status." Bethany shared a crooked grin before she took turns sipping and turning pages. "You did an amazing job." She dragged her hand reverently over the last pages. Tears pooled in her eyes, shining out something resembling pride. "Take me to your favorite room before I start bawling."

When they entered Zeta's *Room of Distilled Writing* as her mom affectionately called it, the rightness of sharing floor to ceiling walnut bookcases, faux marble furnishings, and the ginormous desk supporting her broken computer, warmed Courtney's stomach.

"Wow. This is it." Awe cuddled those words. Bethany scanned the room with an expression that competed with her love for Williamsburg, Virginia.

"This *is* it."

"Couldn't be more appropriate." She opened her purse. "Take a seat."

Courtney slipped into the computer chair and eyed Bethany. Then she glanced into the mirror to make sure her makeup wasn't smeared. Her sister-friend would certainly take a photo and add it to social media. Courtney dragged her fingers over her rebellious hair.

Pulling an envelope out of her purse, Bethany handed it over.

Butterflies took wing in her throat. Courtney hesitated. Anxious eyes stared back, triggering that familiar desire—to run—like when they were children. Or maybe not that long ago. She anchored her feet around the chilly steel legs of the computer chair. "What's—"

"Just open it." Bethany bit her bottom lip.

What on earth? Courtney glanced at the envelope. Break-Nods Publishing House was written in bold print in the return address. Though her name was there, the address belonged to Lillian. She turned it over. *Opened already.* She pulled out the letter.

> *To Ms. Courtney MacDuff,*
>
> *We are proud to announce that you are this year's winner for the unpublished contemporary category—*

The letter fluttered to the ground. "How—"

"You were meant to write, and they want your completed story immediately."

Courtney closed her eyes. "I don't have it anymore." She sagged into the chair then placed her hand on the smooth ebony keys of her damaged computer. "I'd deleted the story, and besides that, Puddles broke this during the move."

Heavy paws approached Bethany, whose face was too close not to investigate.

Clearing her throat, Bethany moved Puddles aside and pulled a portable drive out her purse. "It's here. I knew you 'd delete the story. You can always get another computer."

"If only I had the money." Courtney crossed her arms in front of her chest. "How did you get my story?"

Without apology, she slipped the drive into Courtney's palm. "Before you moved from the apartments—the day I asked you to be my Maid of Honor. There's more. A check for the author's winnings." Bethany snagged and waved another envelope between two fingers.

Courtney grabbed it as the back door banged, making her jump.

Bethany jumped, "What's that?"

Puddles ran toward the sound, barking a deep warning.

"It's just Natalie. I told her the back door would be open. Reaching inside the envelope, she pulled out a check. "Wow, did you know the amount for the first-place winner?"

"Yes—"

"Hey, Bethany," Nat strolled into the room with Puddles hopping around her, trying to nab attention.

"Did you know my sister…" Courtney stopped, then glanced back and forth between Natalie and Bethany.

Natalie didn't miss a beat. "Since you are and have always been Courtney's sister, what does that make us?" She gave the dog a cursory petting and winked at Courtney.

"Technically speaking?" Bethany scrunched her face with consideration.

"Yes. And by the way Court," Natalie's attention glided toward the envelope in her sister's hand and the letter on the floor. "Congratulations," she said with a smile that held no bounds.

Courtney sputtered, "Am I the only one who didn't know?"

Nodding, Natalie continued. "Now Bethany, back to what I was wondering. Are we sisters too? I would love to be sisters. Or are we just cousins? Do you consider me, your friend?" She sniffed the air. "I want a cappuccino too. Come, make one for me, Bethany."

Nat and Bethany locked arms and left The Room of Distilled Writing, jawing back and forth, while Courtney slipped onto her computer chair and gawked at the check. A third voice spoke from the dining room. Four people in the house now? Wasn't this becoming Grand Central Station at Courtney's? Mom entered the room. The scent of roses permeated.

"You've interrupted your trip?" Awe at her mom's sudden

appearance made her giddy. Surveying the room, she breathed a sigh of relief. Good thing she'd cleaned that morning.

"I can't stay away from my roses or my girls for too long."

Sniffing the air, Courtney stood. "I love that fragrance."

"You did as a baby too." Zeta gave Courtney a hug, before glancing around. "I like your stuff here. It fits perfectly." She slipped gracefully onto a wingback chair and removed the polka-dotted pillow hidden under a throw. "Many ideas were birthed in this very spot."

"Like the idea to meet with Natalie and me?"

"That idea was birthed someplace else, but it hatched here. When this house became available, directly behind Natalie's place—I had to snatch it up."

"I'm thrilled you did. But didn't you buy this place a year before Nat bought her Victorian?" She slipped into the computer chair beside her mom.

"I'd talked to her adopted father." Mom looked away.

Something in how she'd cloaked her reply fired a desire to ask more, practically burning Courtney's tongue, but if she dared, would Mom run away or worse, shut down? She'd discover the answers later—for now, she'd not risk the closeness they'd begun to share by asking about a painful time in her mom's past. Courtney's curiosity revved inside. A lifetime of memories needed to be known. Everything really.

"Now, let's talk about the future. You're welcome to stay here as long as you like."

Puddles came in and plopped beside Zeta. She shifted sideways when the dog leaned toward her face, but laughed and rubbed her mussel.

"Have your plans changed in any way?"

"Not yet, though nothing is certain for this necessary trip." She slipped an old Bible off the shelf behind her chair and laid it in her lap.

"Will you share an address with me—us—after you arrive?" The faintest stirrings of tension passed over Zeta's expression, like a shadow that came and went. She dipped her face toward the floor, and Courtney's disappointment and concern heightened. Where was she going? Why?

Zeta faced her with a direct, deep-blue gaze. "I'll probably come and go, stopping here from time to time. You make yourself and Puddles comfortable and keep an eye on the house for me. By the way, I hear that congratulations are the order for the day. It pleases me that you are following in my footsteps, somewhat."

"I never really knew that Bethany could hold secrets from me. I can't believe you knew too. I suppose they both knew that you were coming home?"

Mom arched both eyebrows—they shared a laugh. Looking to the Bible in her lap, she sighed. Tucking some loose paper sticking out from the back of the Bible neatly inside, she handed it over to Courtney. "This has more answers than you can imagine."

"Yes, I'm sure." She placed the Bible on the desktop. Was it possible that her mom's countenance dimmed yet again?

She felt her own brow wrinkle, so she swooped the letter up, chasing the gratitude palatable only moments before. "Apparently, I was the *only* person clueless about this. One thing I know, God has blessed nearly every area of my life." She glanced at her broken computer. Dragged her finger across the smooth keys causing them to click.

Shadow and light danced on the table, catching her attention. She peeked out of the window and saw the back of Zander's head as he rounded the corner of the house while carrying something large.

Courtney turned right into the knowing smile that offered more mystery from her mom's lips.

COURTNEY

Weeks later, a mulberry candle perfumed the room as it penetrated the dark shadows and accented the antique walnut table where Courtney worked. Her fingers moved over the keys of the tower computer her mom had purchased for the house—so she'd said. Zander's arrival with this top-of-the-line marvel had reduced her to tears on several occasions. Such perfect timing for BreakNods Publishing House and Mom's generous gift kept her in a state of awe. Each tug of discouragement motivated her to savor that day three weeks ago when everyone showed up to celebrate her publishing offer. Purpose engaged her curiosity and ignited her drive to write.

Beloved, melted into her being like a whisper and stilled her fingers. Warmth, similar to an embrace filled with acceptance overflowed. She basked in the moment too precious to ignore until the sensation lifted, and she remained sitting. Full and expectant. "Thank you, Lord."

She sighed, snuggled deeper into her comfortable chair, and glanced over the computer screen. Chapter twenty-five began to pour out of her. Rednaz smoothed his hand over the gasping sides of his prized stallion, Métier. Nostrils flared, clouding the dampened air hanging like a weighted cloak separating him from Nidella and her evil hordes.

"I will not," Princess Elena's weak voice sounded as though it were rife with pain.

The only way to save her was to give up his most prized possession. One last smack on Métier's withers and he released his war companion of many years into the hands of his gravest enemy. Nidella's laughter tore up the night as Rednaz slipped his knife clear of its sheaf. It was time to free Princess Elena of Zon.

Puddles pushed past her chair and somehow managed to

sprawl under the writing desk. She let loose a deep-throated groan.

Tears snuck down Courtney's cheek, and she tucked her toes inside the warm layers of dog hair. She leaned over the edge of the desk and scratched Puddles's ears. "I could never give you up, baby. Don't worry, you are not Métier."

After many revisions, she'd rung the bitter ink from her pages. With a clear conscience, she could say that any revenge within this story lie purely between the characters. Her spirit took flight, dislodging the negativity, which had nipped at her heels and drove her to escape situations and people she feared. How could it be that she'd allowed unnecessary anxiety to control her for so many years? But now, God willing, she'd move full-speed ahead to embrace her dreams.

The doorbell chimed an old-fashioned tune. *Oh, they're here.*

"Enter at your own risk." Courtney bellowed as she ran to the living room with Puddles close behind. She turned on a light before grabbing a tissue to dab away tears.

Natalie and Bethany spilled into the room, carrying Courtney's birthday presents.

"Getting old isn't that bad." Natalie swooped in for a tight hug.

Mom stepped out of her bedroom all smiles with twin presents in her grip. As ever, the fragrance of roses followed her but never overpowered the room.

Bethany stepped around Puddles, who demanded a greeting. She smoothed the dog's ear and reached over her back to place cards and gifts on the coffee table next to a stack of manuscript pages. She smiled. "What you working on?"

"*The Princess of Zon.* Deadline in one month."

Natalie plopped in the chair by the fireplace. "What's your next project?"

"Us."

"What—" They all leaned forward, expressions revealed they were poised to argue.

Courtney held up her hand to stop the flow of words. "Not exactly us. This is about sisters and friends, just like us. I'm calling it *Sisters & Friends*."

"Of course, you would." Nat slanted a *that-was-predictable* grin Courtney's way.

Someone knocked on the front door, and Puddles growled and ran behind the couch.

"You brave dog, you." Bethany shook her head.

"She's just smart and has a surprise attack planned for anyone dangerous."

"If you say so." Nat seemed to use considerable effort to tether her smile.

As she approached the door, Courtney shook her head; Zander's nose pressed the front window that she had washed that day. Once he came inside, Puddles began to hop.

"Down girl," Zander lowered his voice deeper than Courtney had ever witnessed before. Everyone laughed. The night proved festive and memorable for their birthday celebration—knowing they are twins—with their real mom present.

Mom brought in a tray filled with sweet tea. I'll be back with dessert." She shut the light out on the way to the kitchen, allowing the glow of candlelight to set the mood. Zeta returned with a two-layered cake, lit with two elaborate candles. Everyone crowded around.

Zander's eyes were the color of molten green-brown, matching Rednaz's in hue and intensity. Courtney broke into a smile under his scrutiny and could feel the heat she hoped didn't show under the dimmed lighting.

As Zeta placed the cake in the center of the coffee table, she knocked something to the floor causing Courtney to move her foot out of the way.

Natalie and Courtney leaned over and blew out the candles together. Laughter glided on the waves of their celebration.

Thinking of everything, Zeta pulled a large bone out of a bag. Puddles took her present with gentleness and strutted past their chairs, showing off her prize with regal elegance. Every few steps, she'd stop to tilt the bone in order to pass through again and again. She turned around each time in an open area of the room, and her tail wagged with abandon.

Several presents were opened by the twins before Zander slipped an envelope out of his pocket and handed it to Court-ney. Though his stance appeared relaxed, she could feel the en-ergized tension as he waited for her response.

She took the offered card and admired the envelope's color and the handwriting—taking her sweet time to open it. The room had hushed. Another secret—everyone else knew but her? As she opened the humorous card, she found confirmation for a Gateway Clipper Dinner Cruise! She gasped.

Leaping into his arms, she hugged him tight. Eyeing Na-talie and Bethany, she mouthed, "Did you tell him?"

Shaking their heads in unison, they broke into laughter. "Mr. Perfect." Natalie mouthed back as she wrinkled her nose at Courtney.

"By the way, it's tonight. You have ten minutes till we leave." Zander seemed ready to burst from excitement.

"I'm a...a..."

He placed his finger against her lips. His smile smoldered with satisfaction and a bit more confidence. "Soon, it will be you, me, and the Monongahela."

Someone turned on the lights. Yellowed newspaper arti-cles and a couple of photos had slipped halfway out of the old Bible that had fallen off of the table. The very one that Mom had handed to Courtney on the day they'd celebrated her win-ning the writing contest. Courtney and Natalie bent down, and each one retrieved an article. Caroline Z. Freedman had witnessed a crime involving the Mafia. The article in Natalie's hand revealed Caroline's full name. "Look, Zeta is this woman's middle name. How unusual." They turned toward Zeta.

Their mom stood-statue still for several agonizing seconds. Her serious expression sprouted a small grin that widened, larger, and larger again.

And then—she winked.

Acknowledgments

Father God, thank you. This entertaining writing journey allows for observing life through different lenses. The situations I tread are filtered through the "how can I share this to equip others undergoing trials." Your daily encouragement provides strength to smile where I once cried and laughter at challenges because I know You command the impossible. You are worthy and good, always.

When my husband traveled for work, he wrote sweet poems to me, and the desire to craft one for him bloomed in my heart. From that pivotal moment, the Author of More Than Enough set everything in motion. Those who encouraged laugher, prayer, and edits every time I sent them a changed sentence or word—my precious sister, Pat Vincenti, and kindred spirit—cherished friend (Becky) Rebecca McLafferty. I'm ever so grateful to you both! Pat, you've been with me from the beginning, strengthening me with your love and listening ears. I couldn't have weathered the tempests half so well without your wisdom. He knew I needed you. Becky, you are—as I always tell you—my best cheerleader ever! Emphasis on cheer. I love our laughter and travels and sharing everything from ideas to how great our God is! I'm excited about your debut novel,

INTENTIONAL HEIRS. You two inspire me to glimpse into delicious possibilities for life and stories. Pens of Praise Christian Writers and Lighthouse Christian Writers you have shared such encouragement, information, and skill—I do so love you. Kate Jungwirth, a co-author of the youth series, MYSTERY AT POINT BEACH, was my beta reader extraordinaire! You are so talented and kind—a wonderful combination and example of the Lord's servant. Kathy Curtis, you gave me my first book about writing and have encouraged me ever since.

A friend and best-selling author, Laura Frantz, I appreciate your genuine and sweet spirit. Your ever-willing-helpfulness when I've asked you questions on navigating this writer's journey. I've appreciated your prayers, well-wishing, and humor through it all! You share so much of yourself in your novels, which gives me the courage to delve deeper and share with abandon too.

Best-selling author, DiAnn Mills, your teaching and down to earth friendship and dedication to your writing journey has powerfully encouraged me. Also, best-selling author Beth Ann Ziarnik, your example to pray through life and the writing process, has touched my life—forever.

A special thanks to those who have prayed and encouraged me for years—you know who you are! Rayma Husk Rutledge, the owner of Bates Flower Shop, Aliquippa, Pennsylvania, was a tremendous source of information about the flower business.

Three businesses allowed me to place a fictional scene that included their names or service. Athens Family Restaurant, Olde Stonewall Golf Course, and Oram's Donut Shop, your businesses are favorites of mine, and I don't get to Beaver Falls and Ellwood City Pennsylvania enough to sample your wares! Nicole Catalano, you took my sister, Pat, and daughter, Jackie, on the research tour of the Windsor Room—quite helpful!

Jenah Shank, you generously shared your song *NEW*

ROAD, which was inspiring to me and Courtney MacDuff, this novel's main character! Much appreciated!

You all have aided the creative journey of this debut novel, and my appreciation holds no bounds.

Note from the Author

Dear Reader,

Though *Sisters & Friends* isn't anyone's particular story, my debut novel was birthed in my heart because I've realized that far too many people sabotage their success. There are so many negative situations and people. I believe that we all have purpose and worth—though some individuals may try to dislodge us from such an idea, this truth is no less real.

I hope that you enjoyed Courtney, Zander, Natalie, and Bethany's story. If their situations and dialogue win a smile from you, I'll be overjoyed. If you've realized your exquisite value and a path to move forward with encouragement and determination, then I've already applauded you in my heart!

Last but not least, dear reader, I've prayed for you during the writing of Sisters & Friends. You are my motivation for exacting story upon the page. My hope is that you found this novel to be uplifting and encouraging so that you can resist negativity or use it as a stepping stone to climb higher. Like Psalm 18:33, *He makes my feet like the feet of deer, and sets me on my high places.* I wish you sweet success in finding your purpose, and that you enjoy the view from the heights!

In Him,
Susan Marlene

P.S. I covet your prayers for social media across the globe as they present God's truth, love, and encouragement. (Please also pray for novelists, movie directors, musicians—well the list goes on!) Thank you—ahead of time—for all that you accomplished through those prayers.